Chilli, Chicks & Heart-Attacks
The misadventures of an intern

by Dr. Manjula Mendis

MEDICAL BOOKS BY THE SAME AUTHOR

Pocket Guide to Internship: *Common Clinical Cases*
Clinical Cases in Infectious Diseases: *A Public Health Approach*

Chilli, Chicks & Heart-Attacks
the misadventures of an intern

by Dr. Manjula Mendis

Sanjaya Senanayake

Published by the Bay Owl Press, 2010
an imprint of the Perera Hussein Publishing House
www.ph-books.com

ISBN: 978-955-1723-11-8

First Edition

All rights reserved

© Sanjaya Senanayake

Chilli, Chicks & Heart-Attacks – the misadventures of an intern by Dr. Manjula Mendis is a work of fiction. All characters and situations are fictitious or are used fictitiously. The right of Sanjaya Senanayake to be identified as the author of this work has been asserted by him in accordance with the Copyright, Designs & Patents Act.

This book is sold subject to the condition that it shall not, by way of trade or otherwise, be lent, re-sold, hired out, copied, extensively quoted or otherwise circulated, in any form of binding or cover other than that in which it is published, without the express written permission of the publisher.

Typeset by Deshan Tennekoon
Printed at Repro Ltd

To offset the environmental pollution caused by printing books,
the Perera Hussein Publishing House grows trees in Puttalam-
Sri Lanka's semi-arid zone.

My wife Dilukshi: thanks for your patience, support and continued good advice without which this book wouldn't have been written.

Our children Saesha and Reshmi: thanks for bringing so much joy and happiness to our lives (we expect this to continue into your teenage years by the way).

Our parents Sarath and Malini Senanayake,
Sunil and Manthri Mendis:
thanks for being there.

Sam and Ameena: thanks
for giving my first novel a chance.

We sincerely thank the grandchildren of Professor Sir Manjula Mendis for releasing the contents of this diary. By doing so, they have provided the public with a unique perspective into the early adult life of one of this country's greatest physicians and dignitaries

– Editors, 11 March 2101.

"You were amazing," said Salma Cruze, the famous Hollywood actress, as we lay in bed together in the afterglow of some fairly outstanding lovemaking.

Even the judges agreed, with the Russian and Polish officials holding up scores of '10'. Not surprisingly, the French official only gave a miserly '7', as usual being reluctant to concede that anyone other than the French was capable of the perfect shag. Naturally, there would be the routine urinary drug tests but the results were unlikely to interfere with this gold medal performance.

"No Salma – it is YOU who were amazing," I replied.

"Don't be silly", she purred in her sensuous exotic accent.

Salma's modesty is one of her many endearing qualities. It is well known that being a Hollywood movie star is one of the busiest jobs around with little time for sex. What with all the travelling from film set to film set, the endless interviews and publicity shots, not to mention those countless hours devoted to learning lines, it is no wonder that Hollywood stars are sex-starved. Therefore, her performance today was quite extraordinary.

The blissful afterglow was abruptly disrupted as my mother materialized out of nowhere brandishing a hand-held video camera.

"Manjula, don't let this woman take the credit. *You* did all the hard work with all that pumping and humping. She just lay there saying 'Oooo, Oooo, Oooo.' Typical lazy Western woman – I bet she can't cook either."

"Ammi, please don't tell me that you watched us!" I said in horror.

"Oh yes, and I've got it all on camcorder," she said gesturing towards the video camera with a flourish that would have made a 'Price is Right' model proud. "After all, your aunts in Sri Lanka will want to see what a great job you did."

"You're sick," Salma shouted at my mother, getting out of bed, draped in the silken white sheets as she backed away from her.

"Why," my mother said enthusiastically as she pulled an object from the folds of her sari, "I've got those nifty glasses for watching it in 3-D! Do you want to watch, Salma?" she asked as she offered the plastic glasses to the Mexican superstar.

This last remark was too much for Salma. Her hand brushed her brow as she swooned onto the floor in an Oscar-winning performance. Salma was unconscious...or worse.

"She's having a heart attack, Manju!" my mother cried. "Save her!" Almost simultaneously, the audience started chanting, "You're a doctor. Save her!"

They were right. I was an intern armed with a degree to cure. But she needed CPR. Sure, I'd practised on a dummy but that wasn't the same as a real human being. It wasn't the same as Salma Cruze. I hesitantly knelt down to start CPR. I looked at the heaving breasts that were no longer heaving and was immediately plagued by doubts. Were they real or were they silicone? Furiously chastising myself for going off on a tangent, I returned to the matter of saving Salma's life. Was it two breaths and ten chest compressions or ten breaths and two chest compressions? No, neither of those sounded right. Should I start chest compressions in the middle of the sternum or just below the diaphragm? I didn't know...

"Hurry up!" my mother shouted. "Save her. I can get this on camera too," she announced excitedly.

I stood up and shouted, "I'm sorry. I've forgotten what to do. I'm only an intern."

My mother started shouting something and shaking her head. The audience united in their booing and started hurling objects at me. The judges looked quite unimpressed and were holding up scores of zero. The French judge was taunting me, laughing at my indecision.

"Save me," shouted Salma from the floor.

"I'm sorry... I'm sorry... I'm so sorry...," I apologized.

The crowd's angry screams increased. My mother, the judges, the crowd and even Salma surrounded me and started pushing me back and forth, back and forth, yelling abuse, shouting for my blood...

    I woke up covered in a bath of sweat. It took me a few moments to realize that I was in the comfort of my own bed. It had all been a dream, and an extremely bizarre one at that. But one part of it rang true: today is my first day as a doctor at the prestigious St. Ivanhoe Hospital. I'm Dr. Manjula Mendis and this will be a diary of my internship.

PART ONE
Emergency Medicine

January 14

As far as special mornings go, today ranks right up there with the best. For my parents however, my first day as a doctor bordered on a religious experience. My mother's pilgrimage to my bedroom this morning involved an offering of incense sticks which she briefly touched to my forehead before heading towards the shrine room.

"Where's Thaththa?" I asked as I stretched my shoulders and shook my head, trying to discard any remnants of somnolence.

"He's still sleeping. You know that he was up till four in the morning saying prayers for you?"

Clearly my father is as worried about my competency as I! Although we are all Buddhists (except for my sister who follows Oprah), I'm not very religious. I firmly believe that a man has to rely on his intelligence, common sense and resourcefulness to survive in the world – that is why I am so worried.

My mother put on a Buddhist CD and very soon the sound of monks chanting resonated around the house. Breakfast was a traditional affair. Ammi had woken up early to make kiri bath – a delicious preparation of rice cooked in coconut milk that she makes on special occasions.

My parents encouraged me to eat a lot this morning because "it takes a lot of energy to run around saving lives." My observation that the first three days of the week were only orientation lectures with no chance of any patient contact fell on deaf ears. Clearly, they were proud of me. My father was a public servant who moved here from Sri Lanka twenty-five years ago. He came from a well-respected family, but like all migrants coming to this country, he began his career as a nobody.

He had done really well for himself and retired with the comfortable pension of a very high-ranking public servant. He still maintained the Eastern belief that doctors were something special. For example, despite being a figure worthy of much respect within our community, he would never call a doctor by his or her first name unless the medic was a very close friend. It didn't matter whether it was a casual occasion or whether the doctor was barely older than me – he still called them 'Doctor' e.g. "Doctor, would you like more cake? Doctor, have you met my daughter? Doctor, did I mention that my daughter is single and that she made the cake?" So it's not hard to imagine how he felt when I got accepted into medical school. And now, having sweated, studied and occasionally cheated my way to graduate with first class honours, his pride reached its pinnacle on my first day of work.

Thanks to the first-class honours, I miraculously qualified for an internship at St. Ivanhoe Hospital. Despite being modest in size, with only a hundred beds, it is recognized as the country's premier hospital with some of the best surgeons and physicians walking its hallowed halls. Only the best interns got to work here and time spent at St. Ivanhoe is valuable for any curriculum vitae.

Even Saesha, Ravi and Kumar dropped by this morning *(Dr. Mendis' sister, her husband and child respectively)*. They lived close by and were off to drop Kumar at childcare.

Akki wished me well. "I can't believe that my little brother is a doctor," she said fondly. "It's a big responsibility – don't fuck up!"

"I'll try not to," I replied.

Kumar, my three-year-old nephew, listened to this exchange, smiled at me and said quite distinctly, "Doctor, fuck up," followed by a bout of giggling.

This, not surprisingly, led to my mother and sister arguing about the impact of my sister's vocabulary on Kumar at such an impressionable age. Although my mother could make a fuss about minor issues, she did have a point this time. My sister had a truly foul mouth and clearly little Kumar was lapping it up.

As the fighting escalated towards DEFCON 1, I snuck off to change for work. Splashing generous amounts of aftershave on my face and placing my stethoscope around my neck, I headed downstairs. My parents' reactions were predictable. Seeing me dressed for work, my mother started crying, mumbling something about how God would have had to create ten ugly people to balance out all the beauty he used for me. It was a sweet thing to say although she spoilt it somewhat by proceeding to note that my cousin Lal was one of the ten ugly people (My mother has sibling rivalry issues with Lal's mother). Thaththa hugged me and said how proud he was. Akki, who had calmed down after her fight with Ammi, gave me a hug and again wished me luck. My brother-in-law said I looked 'real smooth' and that the nurses would be all over me. I hope he is right – doctors are meant to get a lot of sex, an aspect of my life that has been sadly lacking to this point. I picked up my little nephew and kissed him. He smiled and told me to 'Fuck off'. This immediately reignited the fight between my mother and sister. I fled.

As I closed the door behind me, the ongoing family tensions within the house immediately vanished. It was a beautiful January day. Unlike the humid, uncomfortable mornings that normally characterized this part of summer, today was cool with a languid breeze blowing the leaves in a gentle rhythmic dance, reminding me of spring. With an arrogance born of egoism, I imagined that Mother Nature wanted to welcome my first day as an intern with a spring day, itself symbolizing a new beginning to the year.

The orientation program was due to begin at 8:30. Although the hospital was nearby, I left home at 7:30, knowing fully well that due to the morning peak-hour traffic, I couldn't rely on its proximity whatsoever. It was a good thing too. Due to a couple of breakdowns on the road, I only reached the hospital at 8:10. As I approached the bluish structure that would become my workplace for the next year, an almost rabid anticipation developed. This climaxed on reaching the arched entrance to St. Ivanhoe as I took a deep breath and a single step forward into my destiny. My first impression of St. Ivanhoe was shiny busyness. The walls were sparkling white as if a filling of dentists had been vigorously working on them with toothpaste and a toothbrush. People were hurrying everywhere – nurses in their traditional Florence Nightingale garb, orderlies pushing patients in wheelchairs and a variety of others whose vocation wasn't immediately obvious. And of course, there were the specialists in their power suits. Ah the specialists – I felt my loins quiver with nervous delight as I watched them with their power-walking strides, their furrowed brows in deep thought and their stern expressions, occasionally interrupted by a benign smile as they acknowledged the greeting of us lesser mortals. To dare to dream that I might one day be a specialist was almost too much to hope for, but it was something that I deeply desired.

There were signs marked New Interns with arrows directing us to the Orientation Hall. Even though I had arrived early, my other colleagues were already there. Like me, they didn't want to make a poor first impression by turning up late. Other major teaching hospitals would employ up to forty interns annually; however, since St. Ivanhoe is smaller than the other hospitals, there were only seven of us. We were privileged indeed.

The Orientation Hall is a large room, with shiny brown wooden floorboards. Several large chandeliers hang strategically from the ceiling. The walls are covered in grand oil paintings of various dignitaries from the hospital's relatively short but distinguished history, each holding a rigid pose with stern facial expressions, as if they were carrying the weight of the world on their shoulders. I gazed at them with fearful fascination before a benign looking lady approached me, breaking me out of my reverie.

Her name was Susan Stoker and she is the chief administrator of the Doctors' Training Unit (DTU). It turned out that the DTU is responsible for the interns. Susan would look after term allocations, rosters and approving annual leave applications. It would definitely be important to remain in her good books!

I looked around at the other interns. I only recognized one of them, a slim, brown-haired girl who was munching on some fruit. Delilah Convex and I went through medical school together. Due to being in different hospitals as students, I really didn't know her that well. She had, however, the distinction of topping our year and doing it so well that the Vice-Chancellor awarded her the University Medal. Without a doubt, Delilah was one bright cookie. In a corner, two interns were chatting. The black girl wearing red paisley pants, a fluorescent floral blouse, gigantic cuboid earrings and a blue eyebrow piercing would have looked more at home at a Woodstock festival than at a prestigious hospital. Only the stethoscope around her neck betrayed her medical background. Mind you, once you looked beyond the geometry of her jewellery, she was quite attractive. Talking intently with her was a tall, beefy, bearded fellow with red hair who looked like a lumberjack. Close to them was another couple, also absorbed in intense conversation – a short South Asian girl and a slim blond-haired guy. In the opposite corner of the room was a slickly-dressed Eurasian guy engaged in a mobile phone conversation.

I was about to wander over and chat to Delilah when Susan called for our attention and asked us to sit down. Next to her was a distinguished elderly man with tidy white hair in a pin-stripe suit. He reminded me of a bloodhound with his mournful eyes and the generous layer of skin hanging from his cheeks. Susan formally welcomed us to the hospital and indicated that we had a full orientation program ahead of us. She introduced the man as Professor Colonel Sir Ninian Tietas, the Director of Medicine and General Manager of the hospital. He proceeded to give a most unusual speech *(The transcript of the speech was preserved by the DTU and has been kindly lent to us by the St. Ivanhoe Memorial Trust – Editors)*.

> Welcome young colleagues. I have been fighting disease for 60 years. When I was your age, the odds were stacked against us. There were no CAT scans, chemotherapy agents, cardiac bypass surgery or even antibiotics. Legions of patients perished at the hands of ruthless disease agents. We, the physicians, were at the front line and suffered terrible losses with nothing to help us but our stethoscopes and clinical skills. We were on the back foot to be sure, but when defeat seemed inevitable, our laboratory boffins threw us a lifeline. Along came penicillin. Let me tell you that the bacteria were caught unaware and we plastered the bastards. Since then, as technology has advanced, they and the other diseases have been beating a hasty retreat. Today, there is no disease that can hide from us. We have the technology to find them in any nook, cranny, cleft, breast, brain, prostate or arsehole in which they reside. I urge you young friends, look well for them. When you find diseases, kill them! Kill them all. And then great songs will be sung about you as you will truly be a doctor.

I wasn't quite sure whether Sir Ninian had just asked us to practise medicine or invade a Middle Eastern nation. I suspected that the only song that I would be singing about him was "You're nuts Sir Ninian, totally off your brain, somewhere along the line you completely went insane..." Somehow, his speech had made me feel less secure and more uncertain about what I was doing here. I looked around at my colleagues, who were similarly bemused.

The remainder of the day was fairly unremarkable. We had our photos taken so our ID badges could be processed. The only bad news was that we had to find parking on the street since parking spots in the hospital car park were at a premium. The most interesting part of the day was learning about my fellow interns. We sat around in a circle and gave summaries about ourselves.

I was most impressed by Delilah's speech. It was a succinct talk where not one word was wasted. While she had the opportunity to list her extraordinary achievements, including the University Medal, she chose not to do so. Instead she expressed her trepidation at the huge responsibility that was to be thrust upon us and hoped that the support of her fellow interns would see her through. If she'd been running for President, she would have had my vote.

The fearsome red-bearded fellow with a thick East European accent gave his name as Peter Ivanov. "I come from Moscow. It is cold there in winter...very cold. One year, I got trapped in the snow for three days. Conditions were harsh and my finger became gangrenous. My only companion was an uncle who was a surgeon. In the middle of the snow, he amputated the finger with a breadknife. It was then that I knew that surgery was my destiny. After graduating from my local university, I came to St. Ivanhoe because of the excellent surgical program here. But every night before I go to bed, I look at that severed finger to remind myself why I am here."

The slim blond-haired guy made a barely-stifled laugh that everyone heard. "You look at your severed finger every night before you go to bed? Are you sure the frostbite didn't affect your brain cells as well?"

"Do not mock me!" yelled Peter Ivanov as he jumped out of his chair, his face wearing an expression so fearsome it would have stopped a tiger in its tracks and rendered it incontinent. He unknotted his tie and ripped open his shirt, buttons spilling everywhere. He grabbed a chain from around his neck and held it up for all to see. It took a moment to discern the object hanging at the bottom of the chain. It appeared to be a gangrenous finger encased in a thick block of material. We all gasped.

"This is my finger, preserved in a block of wax for the last twenty years! Every night before I go to bed, I look upon it!"

At the sight of the severed digit, Susan Stoker, the chief administrator of DTU, fell off her chair in a most undignified manner. To her credit, she recovered her composure quickly, took her seat once more before politely asking Peter to put his finger away so we could proceed to the next intern. Peter gave the blond intern another venomous look before muttering to himself and sitting down.

Looking somewhat alarmed at the proceedings, Lucky King introduced herself. I had initially picked her to be South Asian, most likely Indian but I may have been mistaken. The sharp nose, high cheekbones and wide hips were all typical of a North Indian woman. However, she had bright blue eyes, strawberry blonde hair, a strong local accent with no hint of curry, and of course, the name 'Lucky King'. She was from an interstate university and said that she would miss the sun and surf but looked forward to her time at St. Ivanhoe.

The Eurasian boy is Copper Tang. He had attended the other university in town and admitted that he was surprised that he did well enough to get employed at this hospital. He also confessed to being really nervous. Now here was a colleague after my own heart.

The black girl with the schizophrenic dress sense is Alternaria Molde. She has a very cheerful demeanour and emphasized the importance of collegiality amongst us interns, irrespective of differences in sex, colour, religion or gender. I think she must be some kind of hippie.

The blond fellow was the last to introduce himself. Like Delilah, Marcus W. Smegman is clearly very bright. Unlike her, however, he had no trouble whatsoever in listing his achievements one by one. By the end of his introduction, we had all decided that the W in Marcus W. Smegman stood for 'Wanker' as he ended by magnanimously agreeing to pass some of his extensive knowledge on to us.

Susan distributed a handout to each of us. Expecting some important medical document for surviving internship, we were rather surprised at what we had just been given. Copper Tang spoke up first, voicing the question that was on all our lips. "Excuse me Susan, why have you given us the lyrics to 'Don't Look Back in Anger' by Oasis?"

Looking slightly embarrassed, Susan mysteriously said, "Sir Ninian likes all the interns to learn the lyrics. It'll become apparent why later in the year. So please just learn them."

"But why?" asked Alternaria.

"Sorry, we must move on. We have to discuss the issue of payslips," said Susan politely but firmly.

Like an old pro, Susan knew that the subject of money would successfully divert our attention away from Sir Ninian's odd request.

If Susan Stoker was concerned about the current crop of interns about to be let loose upon the wards of her hospital, she didn't show it. Ever the consummate professional, she spoke to us throughout the day, back erect, legs crossed and repeatedly pulling down her dress in an unconscious effort to preserve modesty despite the garment falling well below her knees. I think that she'd have made a very good schoolteacher.

January 15

Today was another full day. We were introduced to the Staff Immunisation and Infection Control units. Then, we were given our term allocations for the year. My internship would begin with Emergency followed by Surgery, and finally Medicine. Peter Ivanov has been paired with me for Emergency. The thought of working with the fiery Russian fills me with trepidation but he seems like a nice enough bloke as long as one didn't joke about his severed finger.

The afternoon ended up being the most interesting part of the day. Susan Stoker ushered in an instantly recognizable dark-haired man who was dressed in an expensive Italian suit. It was Dr. Spyder Croquet, a General Physician who is known throughout the country as 'Doctor to the Stars.' We had all, previously, seen him on TV. He is quite a legend. Apparently many years ago, when Spyder was a young intern covering the wards on an overtime shift, he was asked to take blood from a sick woman who had been wasting away with a mysterious illness for some weeks. Various senior specialists had been stumped by her condition. The story goes that during those few minutes, while taking her blood, Spyder noticed a bluish discolouration of the patient's gums. He recognized them as Burton's Lines, a sign of lead poisoning. The diagnosis was subsequently confirmed by a grateful treating team.

Their gratitude however, was far outweighed by that of the patient herself, who turned out to be a senior Hollywood executive in the midst of a messy divorce. Due to well-documented indiscretions with a number of younger men, she had been looking at a most unsatisfactory financial settlement with her husband. However, when she had learnt that her jealous spouse had been trying to poison her, her joy knew no bounds. He was promptly imprisoned and she was left with everything. She never forgot the brilliance of the young Australian doctor who had saved her life and his name spread in Hollywood circles. By the time he qualified as a physician, Spyder Croquet had built up quite a reputation. It was not uncommon for celebrities to fly from overseas to Australia to get an opinion. It is fair to say that the Doctor to the Stars had himself become a celebrity.

Why is this relevant for us mere mortal interns? In order to cater to his celebrity patients, Spyder decided that a standard private hospital bed wasn't large enough. So he made a deal with the Board of St. Ivanhoe to rent the top floor of our hospital for his celebrity patients. This meant that at various times throughout the year, we interns might get to look after celebrity patients. How exciting! Mind you, it must cost him an arm and a leg to rent the whole top floor of the hospital *(In fact, recently opened hospital records reveal that Dr. Croquet was only charged a paltry $50,000 annually for rent. This was because the hospital board realized that such a deal could benefit both parties. In 2004 and 2006, it appears that their decision paid dividends as two new wings were built from the generous donations of two such celebrity patients. There are also rumours that another celebrity patient donated a large amount of marijuana to the Cancer Centre for chemotherapy patients. The Cancer Centre denied ever receiving any of the marijuana but suspicions were raised at the press conference when its Director kept ending his answers with "Yeah Baby" and "Peace, man", while his deputy said nothing but was noisily stuffing herself with kebabs – Editors).* Anyway, Dr. Croquet personally came in today to discuss the issue of confidentiality, which is particularly important when it comes to his celebrity patients. Apparently, it was not uncommon for unscrupulous journalists to try and get juicy details of a celebrity's illness for their TV show, newspaper or magazine.

The next visitor was the Chief of Surgery, Professor Monty Bonkzalot. While similarly dressed and of a similar age to Sir Ninian, his stockier build and broad shoulders betrayed his life of breaking open abdomens and ripping out guts. His other role is Chairman of the Hospital's Welcoming Committee. I wonder if this is someone's idea of a joke since Professor Bonkzalot's stern visage and grim manner is anything but welcoming. His one and only attempt at a smile gave the distinct impression of a lack of practise. Anyway, he announced that St. Ivanhoe has a tradition of a formal dinner for all the specialists and junior doctors on the Friday night of Orientation Week. No expense is spared. In fact, the Hilton Hotel will cater the three-course extravaganza. This is good. He then added that each new intern is expected to perform a solo act demonstrating a singular talent. This is bad.

Being a typical example of the South Asian male born overseas, all I had done for most of my life was study. I can't sing, dance or paint. My sporting skills are modest and I even suck at origami. The only activity that I excel in is masturbation. Even then, I don't know if I am any good at it – I just do it a lot, particularly when I am nervous – like now. Anyway, it is hardly something I can use for the talent night unless my talent is for getting deregistered. I looked around at my six colleagues who expressed similar dismay at this unexpected request.

Professor Bonkzalot's departure heralded the return of Professor Colonel Sir Ninian Tietas. This time he was accompanied by a man straining under the weight of a large trophy. As he entered the room, Susan Stoker rushed to the audio-visual console, located discretely in a dark corner and flicked a number of switches, the result of which was Vangelis' Chariots of Fire pervading the room and accompanying the passage of the golden trophy to the table at the front – on which it was reverentially placed.

"This," boomed Tietas as he gestured grandly at the trophy, "is the Sir Nigel Steelbone Memorial Trophy. It is named after the illustrious founder of our institution. As well as being an extraordinary administrator, he was also an accomplished academic, having published over two hundred papers. He lived by the adage 'Publish or perish' and passed that work ethic onto the many juniors with whom he worked during his long career. To honour his academic achievements, this award was created twenty-five years ago. The rewards of winning this award are immense. There is a cash prize of twenty thousand dollars but even more important is the prestige associated with victory.

Amongst the winners for the past twenty-four years, we have had two Nobel laureates, three University Deans, four Health Ministers and six Presidents of the medical Colleges. The trophy will be awarded at the dinner that Professor Bonkzalot just announced."

He had us spellbound at this point.

"The winner," he continued, "will be the intern who publishes the best article in a journal by the end of this year or has an article accepted for publication by the end of the year. You are allowed to have other authors for your paper. The judging panel will base their decision on the scientific impact of the article, the publicity the article generates and the quality of the journal in which the article is published. I wish you good luck and have no doubt that you will maintain the standards of your intern predecessors."

He left the room and left me deflated. Academic publication was the realm of specialists and occasionally registrars. I was an intern – how could they expect me to publish something by the end of the year?

My colleagues and I sat around eating the afternoon tea provided to us. Naturally, the Steelbone Memorial trophy was the topic of conversation.

Marcus Smegman was excited. "I'm already a published author," he boasted. "It was a fascinating study on cell physiology which I conducted during second year med school. Professor Tompkins was so impressed with my efforts that he made me first author. Hmmm, there's a lot I can do with that twenty thousand dollars." The smug prat was already revelling in his imagined victory! Unfortunately, I couldn't think of anyone who could stop him.

"That's impressive Marcus," chirped a deceptively relaxed female voice. "I only made first author for my first publication. I was second author for the other two." It was Delilah Convex, and I could have kissed her.

Marcus went pale. "You have published *three* papers?" he demanded of her with disbelief.

"Yes I have."

If looks could kill, Delilah would have died instantly, been reborn and died again, such was the venom in Marcus' eyes. Peter Ivanov laughed out loud.

Our discussion revealed that the rest of us had never published anything in our lives. Clearly, Delilah and Smegman had the short odds on winning the trophy. Good luck to them. Academia isn't my thing... although twenty thousand dollars could come in very handy indeed.

I went home that evening to work out what on earth I was going to do for the talent night, which was only three days away.

January 16

Last night, I had the strangest dream. I was a guest on The Morning Show, *(a popular breakfast news and talkback show of the period – Editors)* being interviewed by the gorgeous presenter, Fabulus Hipz.

"It is well-known that the world of medical publishing is a slippery slope to climb. But today I have the pleasure of interviewing a doctor who has not only published an article in the prestigious medical journal, *The Lancet*, but has done so as an intern at the tender age of twenty-five. Please welcome Dr. Manju Mendis."

Applause throughout the studio.

"So Dr. Mendis, how did you manage to get published in *The Lancet* at such a young age?" purred Fabulus.

"Fabulus, I can't take all the credit. Well, actually I can. It was my idea and I did all the writing myself."

"Your paper was titled 'People who live in glasshouses shouldn't throw dwarves'. What made you think of such an unusual topic?"

"Look Fab, and I do mean it – you look fab! (Both Fabulus and I burst into fits of laughter) But seriously, Dwarf Throwing or 'Tossing', as it is known to the purists among us, is a dangerous sport. When confined to pubs or circus arenas, the risk of damage is minimal. Unfortunately, people in glasshouses have taken up the sport with terrible consequences. The amount of shattered glass has been driving up housing insurance premiums, not to mention glass injuries to bare feet. I am proud to say that my paper in *The Lancet* confirms that there is a statistically significant saving in expenses and in foot injuries if people living in glasshouses don't throw dwarves."

"Gosh, that's just so clever Dr. Mendis," said Fab. "I hear that you won the prestigious Steelbone Memorial Trophy for your article and the $20,000 reward that comes with it. What are you going to do with the money?"

"Well, I haven't really thought about it Fab. But I'd probably do something philanthropic in the hope that it would get me into your pants."

"Don't worry, Doctor, you're already there," Fab purred seductively.

Just then my reverie was rudely interrupted by the relentless whining of my alarm clock, with the result that my first words of the day were a scathing polemic directed at the technology that had awoken me; however, this is perhaps a sign that I should try and win the Sir Nigel Steelbone Memorial Trophy – clearly it is on my mind.

For the first time today, the interns were separated as we were taken around to the units in which we will be working. Peter Ivanov and I were sent to the Emergency Department. As medical students, ED terms were always useful because one got to do a number of procedures and see some interesting acute medicine, all with the absence of any sense of responsibility. Peter and I were shown around by the Director of the ED, Dr. Hans Tiberius, a slim man with a thick bushy beard. We were introduced to the Emergency Registrars and nursing staff. One of the nurses, a podgy brunette in her forties asked me my name. I told her that I am Dr. Mendis. She and her nursing colleague laughed.

"Oh, it's 'DOCTOR' Mendis," she laughed. "I think I'll call him 'Mendy'".

After this exchange, Dr. Tiberius stopped in an empty corridor to talk to us. He told us that twenty years ago, the interaction between doctors and nurses was more formal than now. Back then in the 'good old days', doctors were addressed as 'Doctor' and their orders were never challenged by nurses. Unfortunately current times were more relaxed, particularly the ED. An intern had no hope in hell of being called 'Doctor' and we'd better get used to it if we wanted to survive. He regretfully conceded that even he was called Hans by the nurses. Peter (rather bravely in my opinion) put his arm around his shoulders and said, "Don't worry about it, Hans." Dr. Tiberius pushed Peter's arm away and said, "Both of you, however, will address me as Dr. Tiberius. Got it?"

"Yes, Dr. Tiberius," we both said at once.

The rest of the day went quickly. We practised advanced life support on dummies using a cocktail of drugs and electrical defibrillation.

One of the ED registrars gave us a refresher course on suturing, after which we got to practise on legs of lamb. I thought that this was fairly extravagant since lamb is such an expensive commodity. However, Dr. Tiberius said, "Only the best for the interns of St. Ivanhoe". As I clumsily but adequately sutured the leg of lamb together, I held on to my long-held belief that I would never be a surgeon. At the end of the suturing session, the registrar said that we could take the leg of lamb home for dinner. I assumed he was joking since it didn't look particularly fresh and had the antiseptic reek of formalin. Peter Ivanov, however, took the offer quite seriously and walked away with the leg of lamb. He lived near the hospital so he took the opportunity of a fifteen-minute break to amble home with the big chunk of meat in his hands. A stream of brown fluid dripping from the leg of lamb followed him, not unlike the trail of breadcrumbs used by Hansel and Gretel. I expressed to him my concerns about the meat smelling of formalin but Peter shrugged it off, saying that the formalin probably killed all the bacteria and rendered the lamb safe to consume. I must remember never to eat anything cooked by Peter Ivanov!

The last part of the day went through a variety of procedures and protocols in the ED. Afterwards, Peter and I caught up with the others for afternoon tea. Lucky and Marcus had been getting to know their surgical rotation while Delilah, Copper and Alternaria had been on the medical wards. Lucky was highly critical of Professor Bonkzalot, the Director of Surgery, whom we had met during orientation.

"He's a misogynistic dinosaur," complained Lucky. "Even when he was talking to me, he just kept staring at my breasts. Just like those sleazy guys in Indian nightclubs. He then had the nerve to say that the operating theatre is a man's domain. I told him to his face that I found that remark quite offensive. He muttered something under his breath and ignored me completely for the rest of the day. And YOU," she said accusingly to Smegman, "didn't say a word! How could you?"

Smegman became indignant. "First of all, he is a distinguished Professor of Surgery, for heaven's sake, and you are just an intern. What right do you have to talk back to him? Secondly, I only met you a couple of days ago and barely know you. So please excuse me if I don't take up your silly, bolshy cause at the expense of my career!"

Although Smegman was the protagonist, I crossed my legs protectively, ensuring that my manhood wouldn't mistakenly be torn away by the three enraged women sitting around me. For a remarkably intelligent individual, Smegman had the discretion of a mentally-challenged gerbil. Thankfully, one skill that I had learnt over the years of fighting between my mother and sister was to defuse a heated situation. So I quickly asked Copper, Alternaria and Delilah about their experience on the medical wards.

The distraction appeared to work. It seems that they had a great time and were shown around by the Senior Medical Registrar, Dr. Precious Thyme. She told them that the physicians here were superb and they would learn a lot from them. Most of them are quite pleasant too, apart from Servilia Gorgas. Professor Gorgas is the Director of Microbiology and Infectious Diseases. She has a foul temper but didn't generally pick on doctors who kept a low profile and kept their mouth shut unless spoken to. Luckily, Professor Gorgas has a Resident *(2nd or 3rd year doctor – Editors)* assigned to her team rather than an intern so we won't have much to do with her. Mind you, I am kind of interested in Infectious Diseases so it is a little disappointing.

My evening was spent contemplating what to do for this wretched talent night on Friday. In addition, I kept learning the lyrics to Don't Look Back in Anger, which still puzzles me no end. Just as I was about to give up on the talent night completely, I remembered the comedy routine that I'd prepared last year. I have always fancied myself as a comedian. I love listening to comedians and personally enjoy telling jokes to large groups of people. In fact, last year I plucked up the courage to write my own comedy routine, I was planning to perform at a comedy club in the city. Every Wednesday, they have a freestyle night where amateur comedians can perform and more importantly, be 'discovered'. One night, having written the routine and finally plucked up the courage to do it, I decided to head out to the club. But fate intervened. Just as I was about to leave, the phone rang.

My grandaunt Padma died and we had to urgently gather at her home. She was a demented old lady and her demise was not unexpected. Padma had been a spinster all her life and it was well-known that she was a notorious flirt in her youth, particularly when it came to other women's husbands. On a personal level, Padma was the sole reason that I would never specialize in Geriatrics. I'd visited her one evening, in hospital, when she had been admitted with pneumonia. I sat beside her and held her hand as dementia and delirium took her back to happier times. Presumably thinking I was a boyfriend from her youth, she removed her hand from mine and, much to my alarm, started vigourously rubbing my groin, yelling, "Has it got stiff yet? Has it got stiff?" The answer to her question was strongly in the negative and I bolted from the room, the ward and the hospital. It was many weeks before I could even be in the same room with an elderly female patient again. Anyway, the upshot of Padma's death was that I never performed that night at the comedy club. But the material was still fresh and unused. Perhaps I could use it on Friday.

As I lay in bed, my final thoughts were not about the lyrics to Don't Look Back in Anger or the talent night. Instead, I remembered what Lucky had said when describing the perverted ways of Professor Bonkzalot. She said that he kept staring at her breasts just like "those sleazy guys in Indian nightclubs." What an odd thing for a white person to say. In fact, it was a very 'Indian' thing to say. I recalled my initial suspicion that Lucky King was South Asian. Perhaps I am on to something. I will have to consider this further.

January 17

It is 11:00 in the evening and I am both exhausted and invigorated after my first day working as an intern. I managed to see seven patients in my eight-hour shift. My confidence grew as the shift went on but I had a nervous start to the day. I remember my hands trembling as I picked up the top file from the in-tray of patients waiting to be seen. It was no different to the nervousness that engulfed me before opening up exam results at university: the racing heart, the sweaty palms, the loud rumbling of my stomach. My first ever patient was a 60-year-old woman, Mrs. Evershed, who presented with a textbook case of pulmonary embolism *(Clot to the lungs also known as "PE" – Editors)*. Three weeks earlier, she'd undergone a total hip replacement. Then three days ago, she became short of breath with some right-sided chest pain. She was tachycardic with an arterial blood gas confirming marked hypoxia. The CT pulmonary angiogram identified bilateral pulmonary emboli.

I informed Mrs. Evershed of the diagnosis, commenced IV heparin, contacted the Respiratory team and then breathed a massive sigh of relief. Sure, it wasn't going to be easy, but I now felt as if I did have the ability to be a competent doctor.

Mind you, Peter had a very good day too. His fiery personality brings with it an air of confidence that gives one the impression of an old pro at work rather than a spring chicken. We worked well together, complementing each other's limited knowledge and skills to solve problems between us. To celebrate our first shift as interns without killing or disabling anyone, Peter and I invited Pantene, the ED Registrar, for a feed after work. Pantene as a registrar is an intern's dream– he is always approachable and will never put you down, no matter what foolish things you ask of him. The Prince William Pub is just up the road from the hospital and a popular venue for hospital staff seeking to unwind after a long day at work. We ordered a large bowl of potato wedges with a generous side of sweet chilli sauce and quite a few beers. It was a lovely way to relax and reflect upon the day that we had just completed. Afterwards, I went home to practise my comedy routine for the medical dinner tomorrow night.

January 19

The medical dinner was held at the function hall of the hospital – a classy venue and clear indicator of the money behind St. Ivanhoe. Being used to the drab halls and cafeterias of my own teaching hospital, this was truly a surprise. She might be a government-funded public institution but there was no doubt that St. Ivanhoe received generous financial support from outside sources. Perhaps Dr. Spyder Croquet's celebrities helped pay for this place.

There were about a hundred people present. Everyone looked smart in their formal kit. As usual, Alternaria stood out when it came to clothing, wearing something completely exotic. But unlike the confused way in which she dresses for work, tonight she looked great. A number of people complemented her on what she wore. Alternaria told me that it was an African Buba dress. It consisted of a lace skirt and blouse gorgeously embroidered in black and gold. There was a fold of cloth tastefully draped over her left shoulder similar to a sari. The dress was literally capped off with an elaborate headdress. Although partners, spouses and significant others had been invited, it turned out that all seven of us interns were still single; however, most of the senior staff came with someone.

Susan Stoker led the seven of us to the front of the hall next to a lectern. Bedecked in a tux and tails of yesteryear and looking quite grand, Sir Ninian Tietas formally welcomed us as we nervously stood next to him. He spoke briefly, emphasizing the proud tradition of interns at St. Ivanhoe in whose footsteps we are following and the certainty that we wouldn't let the venerable institution down. This startlingly profound benediction was followed by another tradition where all the specialists, registrars and residents lined up and walked past us shaking our hands and wishing us well for the year ahead. I must say that the solemnity of these proceedings had all of us poleaxed. The formality continued as Sir Ninian announced the winner of the Steelbone Trophy from last year's batch of interns. An attractive blond, Dr. Patricia Cubical, triumphed over her colleagues. She received the trophy and twenty thousand dollar cheque with a beaming smile and a standing ovation from the guests. At our table, I suspect that each of us was imagining ourselves as the happy recipient of the award at next year's dinner. Alas, for me it will probably remain in the realms of fantasy.

Things became a bit more relaxed as we sat down to dinner. I was a bit surprised that all seven interns were seated together. I thought this would have been a prime opportunity to seat us with other doctors, to get to know them. However, it appeared that even in a social setting, the class barrier between junior and senior doctors was not ready to be breached. Having said that, I didn't mind sitting with the other interns and felt at ease with them. The dinner was absolutely gorgeous. As an entrée, I had lobster covered in ricotta cheese sitting on a base of beetroot pasta. The main course was an African lamb preparation accompanied by couscous where the deliciously spiced cubes of meat seemed to melt in my mouth. The dessert was simple but no less appetizing as a plateful of fruity sorbets refreshed my tastebuds at the end of the meal. During those brief intervals where we weren't masticating on large mouthfuls of delicious food, we were discussing our last two days as interns. Delilah, Copper and Alternaria loved their medical term but Lucky and Smegman were having a rough time in surgery. Professor Bonkzalot continued to ignore Lucky on ward rounds unless he was openly ogling her. Even Smegman, despite his obsequiousness towards Bonkzalot and extensive surgical knowledge, was being pulled up by Bonkzalot in a most humiliating fashion on ward rounds. Both he and Lucky looked unhappy. I was not looking forward to my surgical rotation.

Then came the part of the evening that I had been dreading – talent night. I was first up and I must say that my comedy routine went down well. Although nervous to begin with, I eased into a steady rhythm once the act had started and never looked back. Delilah followed me and played a violin concerto with the composure and skill of a professional. Copper Tang performed some magic tricks. He is quite the illusionist and the end of his act was met with rapturous applause. Lucky performed an amazing hand shadow show, creating all sorts of shapes on the wall. Smegman, despite being a git, is a talented artist. He asked Susan Stoker to come on stage and pose as his subject. Within minutes, he had sketched an extraordinary likeness of the head of the DTU, which she was more than happy to accept. The finale was Alternaria's performance, and boy was it memorable. People will be talking about her act for a long time, although probably not necessarily in the way she wished. She brought out a guitar and stepped up to the microphone. "Good evening everyone. My name is Alternaria Molde and I am a lesbian."

The background chatter abruptly ceased.

She continued, "I used to hate men. They were nothing more than obstacles in the fight for women's liberation. To my shame, I must admit that I used to protest, argue and even fight with random men out of sheer frustration and anger. But more recently, I realized that the problem was with me and not with everyone else. I don't hate men anymore and I now know that together we can make this world a better place for men and lesbians alike. I wrote this song as a gesture of reconciliation. I hope you enjoy it."

She strummed her guitar and proceeded to sing her song. The title was 'My Vagina is your Friend.' I wish I had recorded the lyrics *(Fortunately, this song was included in the record-breaking album "Alternaria's*

Greatest Hits" in 2030; we have included its lyrics below. The inclusion of the song in this 2030 compilation had been a surprise at the time as Alternaria had never recorded it in her previous albums – Editors).

> I always preferred women's company
> Men were never ever the go
> The only kiss I would give a man
> Was the one they call Glasgow
> When it came to steamy romance
> Or hot and wild sex
> The only partner I'd take to bed
> Would be those who were XX
>
> I was an angry woman
> Who hated every guy
> It didn't matter if they were kind or caring
> If their chromosomes were XY
> But now I've seen a better way
> My anger's on the mend
> And I can say with confidence
> That my vagina is your friend
>
> It's a new and pleasing trend
> My vagina is your friend
> No more hitting unarmed men
> My vagina is your friend
>
> Now the world is more than lesbians
> And our fight for equal rights
> With terrorists killing innocent people
> And destroying building sites
> There's global warming, climate change
> And illicit drug sales
> Of course don't forget the activists
> Who are trying to save the whales
>
> I have fought for equal treatment
> And have achieved equality
> Many men whom I used to hate
> Have also fought for me

There's Peter, Paul, Wayne and Walter
And my good friend Mike
Their exertions on my behalf
Have made me one real happy dyke

It's a new and pleasing trend
My vagina is your friend
No more hitting unarmed men
My vagina is your friend

Now the raging fog has lifted
I only hope and dream
That there will be a future time
When we all live in peace supreme
Whether gay man or lesbian,
Heterosexual, black or white
To tolerate and respect each other
Will be the greatest human right

It's a new and pleasing trend
My vagina is your friend
No more hitting unarmed men
My vagina is your friend

It's a new and pleasing trend
My vagina is your friend
Your manhood you need not defend
Because my vagina is your friend.

Alternaria was sensational – she has a voice like Gloria Gaynor and plays the guitar so well and with such consummate ease that I barely realized she was playing it at all. She could be a really great musician one day *(And she will be –Editors)*. Unfortunately, due to the less than conservative lyrics, there was a stunned silence throughout the audience rather than the rapturous applause it deserved. I was about to start the applause myself when I heard Monty Bonkzalot sitting at the table behind us. He hurriedly whispered to those at his table, "For God's sake, give the dyke a standing ovation. Otherwise she'll sue the lot of us for discrimination!" Thus, the talent show ended with a thunderous standing ovation for Alternaria, led by the politically-correct, misogynistic homophobe, Professor Monty Bonkzalot.

Alternaria sat down smiling shyly as we congratulated her. She asked, "Do you think anyone minded me mentioning terrorism in my song? After all, it's quite a controversial topic."

We assured her that terrorism would have been the last thing on people's minds when listening to her song. The clueless but delightful Alternaria took this remark at face value and seemed satisfied.

There was dancing and more casual mingling after this. We met some of the first year Residents who had been interns here the year before. We had seen them around the hospital in our first two days on the job but never had a chance to talk with them at any depth. This was an important meeting for me that I had contemplated with some trepidation. They say your wife will look like your mother-in-law in twenty-five years. Similarly, I examined the Residents closely to see what our future held. In one year's time, would we be stressed, balding, overworked and overweight zombies, our personalities and our spirits sucked out of us by Monty Bonkzalot and his buddies at St. Ivanhoe? Thankfully the answer seemed to be no. In fact, the Residents are normal and happy-go-lucky individuals who still look young. Patricia Cubical, the winner of the Steelbone Memorial Trophy tonight, told us about her victory.

"Don't worry about the Trophy. Despite what old Sir Ninian says, they don't really expect every intern to have published an article by the end of the year. Only Carlisle Divine and I ended up publishing an article. Mine was a pure fluke. When I was doing the medical rotation, I saw a case of AMPPE – Acute Multifocal Placoid Pigment Epitheliopathy. It took me about six weeks to learn the full name. Anyway, this patient had proptosis, which had never been described in association with AMPPE. Professor Carver made the diagnosis and got me to help her write it up. It got published in the journal 'Primary Ophthalmology' a couple of weeks ago. I can't pretend it isn't great to win the trophy but I was just in the right place at the right time."

"How is Professor Carver?" asked a greedy voice. "I want to be an ophthalmologist and I've heard she's one of the best in her field." Naturally, it was Smegman.

Patricia nodded. "Professor Carver is great. The only thing to remember is that she is President of the League of Women, a really powerful pro-feminist group. Don't make any crass sexist remarks around her otherwise you'll be in her bad books. But if she likes you... well then, your career in ophthalmology is assured. Like most of the specialists here, she has enormous influence in her own field."

Smegman hung onto Patricia's every word as if it were gospel. If his mouth had hung open any longer, he would have drooled but thankfully he had to breathe so it closed for a few moments.

I asked Patricia if they had been given the lyrics to Don't Look Back in Anger last year during their orientation. She looked at one of the other Residents and smiled.

"We were," she said. "But I'm not going to spoil it for you. Which of you are doing Emergency first?"

Peter and I put our hands up.

"Well then, you'll be the first to find out," she said mysteriously, barely suppressing her mirth.

Why couldn't anyone be straight with us on this issue? First Susan Stoker and now these Residents. I didn't like surprises, especially when it came to work.

Casual chat ended as we turned to dancing. On the dance floor I realized that I hadn't done any Elevator Grooving for ages. So I said bye to my fellow interns and made my way to the elevators. Elevator Grooving is when I get into an empty elevator and stand quietly looking straight ahead until the doors close. Then I let loose and dance like crazy as the elevator moves to its destination. I keep dancing even when the elevator stops. At the moment the doors start to open, I quickly return to the neutral position, hands by my sides and face expressionless. I never know if anyone entering the lift has detected that I am breathing too fast, the only sign betraying my altitudinal exertions, and wonder what on earth I have being doing. I guess other people must elevator groove but I have never discussed this with anyone and nobody has ever mentioned it to me. It can be good exercise and I get a thrill out of doing something so unconventional. I'm sure someone could think of a better name for it, but I'm not going to reveal my deepest secret to anyone.

It was almost 1 am when I entered the elevator. Not surprisingly, I was the only passenger. I was on the Ground floor and pushed the top button – Level 10. Deciding to be topical, I hummed the languid melody of Alternaria's 'My Vagina is your Friend' to a slow waltz as the elevator began its ascent. My eyes closed as I moved around the elevator imagining I was in the arms of a beautiful woman who wanted to make her vagina my friend. The trip to the top was uninterrupted – not surprising at this late hour. As the door opened, I considered just going straight back to the Ground floor. But at the last minute, I fortuitously changed my mind. I stepped out and gasped. It was absolutely beautiful, like something that you would expect to find in the Presidential suite of a hotel. The beautiful large white mosaic tiles, the polished wooden floor, a luxurious marble reception desk which was currently unoccupied, beyond which a grand oak door heralded the entrance to the room. I was momentarily puzzled at the existence of this oasis in the midst of our public hospital system. Then I realized that this was the level reserved for Spyder Croquet's celebrity patients – the so-called Celebrity Ward. Wow – he really made sure that his patients felt at home! I was unsure if the floor was currently occupied.

I wandered around. The oak door opened into what appeared to be a patient's room. It was massive. I suspect that the builders had taken three adjacent four-bedded rooms and knocked down the walls, thereby creating this enormous space for the patient. There was a sitting area with leather sofas and a full-wall plasma TV, a kitchen area and adjacent dining space complete with table and chairs. Even the bathroom was huge with a jacuzzi. Instead of the standard narrow single bed, there was a king-size four-poster bed above which was another TV. Next to this was a small study. I was mightily impressed. I left the patient's area and walked to the other end of the ward. There was a nurse's station, the only object on this floor that reminded me that we were in a hospital. Even so, it was so far from the patient's room that the patient would have complete privacy unless they buzzed the nurse for assistance. While privacy is nice, this was probably not a good idea if the patient was really sick and needed to be closely observed.

I made my way to the elevator contemplating how healthcare was oh so different for the rich. My thoughts were so engrossed with the Celebrity Ward that I forgot to Elevator Groove on the way down. I am really looking forward to treating patients up there. I bet you that none of the other interns around the country will ever get to experience anything like this.

January 24

I now realize that work is going to be too hectic to make a daily entry in this diary as I had originally planned. It has been five days and I have been dreadfully busy. I am enjoying the Emergency Department and the variety of cases that get thrown my way. More importantly, I haven't made any serious mistakes as yet!

Today, we celebrated the engagement of two of the ED staff, a nurse called Teri and a registrar called Hadrian. They will get married and go off on a six-week honeymoon. The tearoom was packed with cakes, savouries and a variety of drinks, saving me from buying lunch in the cafeteria. Hadrian gave a brief speech, noting how it had been 'love at first sight' when he first set eyes on Teri. I'm fairly cynical about love at first sight. I have spoken to various couples, including my sister and brother-in-law, who claim that they knew that their partner was 'the one' when they first laid eyes on them. In my view, what really happens is 'lust at first sight' based purely on physical appearance. Then, if the relationship works out, the couple have the luxury of looking back and claiming that it was predestined love at first sight. I think that the epidemiological term for this is 'recall bias.' As a Buddhist however, I believe in rebirth and that people keep meeting each other in life after life. So I guess if two people have been an item in many previous lives, it is possible that a karmic spark could trigger love at first sight when they meet in a new life. But one thing is certain: I'm not going to be foolish enough to let it happen to me.

February 2

I have three days off and am enjoying my first free weekend since starting the Emergency term. To date, I have only been rostered on, during the day and in the evenings. Next week begins my first set of nightshifts. I am quite nervous about the graveyard shift for two reasons. First and most importantly, there are fewer senior staff around to supervise us. Also, being someone who needs his eight hours of sleep, I don't know how I will function at night. I just hope that I have the stamina to stay awake for the whole shift. I have been having nightmares about falling asleep while performing CPR or some other vital task.

Talking about nightmares, we had a family dinner tonight. Naturally, Akki, Ravi and Kumar were there. In addition, my aunt Mallika, uncle Sarath and cousin Lal attended. As usual, Mallika Punchi and my mother wore sari. In fact, I can't recall seeing them in anything other than a sari since migrating here. They have stubbornly resisted the push to wear a dress, slacks, or perish the thought, jeans. Furthermore, they only wore the sari in the Kandyan style of draping. This, in addition to their sharp, fair, facial features and similar age, meant that they were often mistaken for twins. Like twins, they certainly had a single and rather terrifying purpose tonight – introducing me to single Sri Lankan girls.

"I'm too young Ammi," I protested. "I'm only twenty-five."

"Perhaps you are too young to *get married*. But there is no harm in getting to know a young girl. Spend some time together, and in a few years, then think of wedding bells. What, men! Your sister and Ravi started courting when they were in their mid-twenties and they got married after four years. Anyway, it's much better than going out with all those *hora* white girls."

At this point I should mention that racism is not exclusive to the 'White Man'. The bigotry gene is found in all human beings, irrespective of sex, creed or colour. It doesn't matter if their chromosomes are XX, XY or KKK. For example, my mother and her sister are appalling racists. The thought of their precious sons marrying a 'white girl' was a constant source of anxiety. This is why we were indoctrinated with Sri Lankan culture from a very young age and went back to Sri Lanka for holidays every one or two years. For them, white girls were promiscuous, disrespectful and incapable of cooking rice and curry. This propaganda was fed to us like vitamins from our teenage years. Conversely, we were told that Sri Lankan girls, particularly those living in Sri Lanka, were angelic maidens who would make perfect wives and daughters-in-law. The problem here was that my mother and aunt were describing the type of woman who had lived in Sri Lanka thirty years ago when they were growing up. These members of the second major diaspora from Sri Lanka didn't realize that the resplendent isle of their youth no longer existed. Both Lal and I knew better. After a number of outings to various nightspots in the absence of 'adults', we had quickly seen how things truly worked in modern Colombo, a city with a burgeoning nouveau riche subclass with too much money and time on their hands.

Whenever these rich parents gave birth, much in the manner of the party game 'Pass the Parcel', the baby was quickly handed from the obstetrician to the mother to the full-time nanny, who was declared the lucky winner. The nanny kept the baby for most of the day while Mummy continued her pre-pregnant lifestyle of lingerie parties, sleeping around with her friends' husbands and quick shopping sprees to Singapore and Hong Kong (only flying First Class, of course). They also made up for their parenting deficiencies in the way that rich people do: by giving the children loads of money and leaving them to their own devices. So it wasn't really surprising to see groups of teenagers hiring penthouse suites in five-star hotels and ordering bottle after bottle of champagne before ending the night in drug-induced stupors or group-sex orgies. Believe me, the last thing that these 'angelic maidens' had on their minds was cooking rice and curry! Yet my mother and aunt were blissfully unaware of such goings-on, or perhaps, chose to be unaware of them. Certainly my sister, Lal and I all knew that many of the 'evil white women' here were a million times more decent, kind and selfless than these Sri Lankan girls whom our mothers placed on pedestals. Naturally, there are still many wonderful girls in Sri Lanka but I fear that they make up a minority, particularly in Colombo. For these reasons, I'm not that keen on being introduced to anyone. To be fair, the Sri Lankan girls who had lived here all their lives were often quite nice due to the sobering influence of their Western upbringing and the absence of other spoiling influences. Regardless, I still considered myself too young to be getting set up. Lal would have been dreading these arranged meetings too, but for a different reason – Lal is gay. Well, he hasn't 'come out' yet but the evidence is fairly compelling. He has never shown any interest in girls, porno magazines or movies. He loves Abba, has posters of The Village People all over his room and always visits the aircraft carriers when American sailors come to town. He claims that this is due to an interest in naval vessels but many conversations have revealed that he wouldn't know a bow from a stern if it hit him in the hull. He probably thinks that 'submarine' means that

the marine is on top. Anyway, it doesn't bother me one way or the other since he is a top cousin and a good friend. His mother on the other hand would have to be committed if she ever found out. Being a conservative Sri Lankan woman, she firmly believed that:
- Gay men are primarily an issue for Western societies only,
- Gay men in Sri Lanka possibly existed but they would do nothing more than kiss on the cheek and hold hands.

Anyway, Lal seemed to be spared tonight's ambush set by my mother and aunt – probably because he was still at university. No such luck for me though, the 'working boy'.

Mallika Punchi continued, "Now Manju, there's a sweet girl who's twenty-three. She's from a good family. A very good catch. Her father is an accountant who was a few years senior to Sarath at boarding school. He played cricket in the Royal-Thomian and captained the hockey team. Her mother was a Wickramaratne before she got married and topped the island in her A' levels, carrying away all the prizes."

My mother gasped. "From the Wickramaratnes in Jeffrey Lane?"

"Yes."

My mother clasped her hands together with joy. "Oh, how wonderful! What good people! Her grandfather was the Inspector General of Police and her mother's brother was the Deputy Chief Justice. You've done well Nangi," my mother congratulated her sister.

In addition to being racists, my mother and aunt are snobs. Marrying a Sri Lankan girl isn't enough. No – she has to belong to some well-connected and respectable family. In fact, it would be better to marry a promiscuous white girl than a Sri Lankan girl from a dodgy family.

"What's the girl like?" I asked, feeling that this most important factor was being overlooked because of her supposedly impressive ancestry.

"Ah, she must be nice," said my mother dismissively, "if she comes from such a good family."

"Akki, I need to tell you that she had a boyfriend for a while," my aunt confessed.

My mother said, "That's okay. She's twenty-three after all."

My aunt wriggled uncomfortably in her chair. "It was a... white boy."

"Aiyooow no!" wailed my mother. "She must have slept with him then. Those white boys aren't happy to hold hands. They want to poke with their little white *poppas*! I can't introduce Manju to this girl. That boy must have poked her!" Her visage bordered on hysterical.

"He may have had a big white *poppa* for all you know, Lokuamma," my cousin Lal added most unhelpfully.

"Chickayaa, Lal! Shut up, men! So crude, I tell you. If my father had been alive to hear such language, you'd have got well and truly hammered. Anyway Nangi," my mother said turning to my aunt, "a good boy like Manju can't be introduced to a girl like this."

"Wait, men," pleaded my aunt. "I've spoken to the mother and she assures me that the girl and the boy are well and truly finished. And she'd be a great catch being from such a good family. What a shame to let this one go."

My mother wrung her hands with a pained expression on her face before turning to my father. "What do you think?"

After a moment's contemplation, Thaththa said, "I think that if she is single now, what harm in introducing them?"

"Okay then, I'll speak to the mother and arrange a meeting," said my aunt, looking quite pleased with herself.

"Excuse me, do I have a say in this matter?" I piped up sarcastically.

"Not really," laughed my sister and brother-in-law, immensely enjoying my discomfiture. "We've been through this before, Malli," said my sister. "Just go with the flow."

"Resistance is futile," my brother-in-law said, quoting the unrelenting Borg aliens in Star Trek who would turn you into one of them by sticking metal bits into various parts of your body.

I hadn't played my trump card yet, but desperate times called for desperate measures so I asked, "Have the horoscopes been matched?"

People in Western countries would be surprised at the central role of horoscopes and astrology in Eastern culture, particularly in India and Sri Lanka. For Westerners, astrology means a daily paragraph in the back pages of the newspaper full of vague messages about friendship, finances, romance and work. For us, it is something completely different. An astrological chart is drawn based on the position of the planets at the time of birth. The chart varies according to longitude and latitude. This means that two people born at exactly the same time but in different countries will have completely different horoscopes.

Even at birth, the horoscope plays a pivotal role in the newborn's life since it determines the baby's name. Western couples are lucky enough to have the whole pregnancy period to choose the baby's name. South Asian couples on the other hand, have to wait till the child is born for the astrologer to give the auspicious letters. Only then can the parents choose a name for the baby. This precipitates a mad rush to go through books or internet sites to find a suitable name. Another role for horoscopes is in arranged marriage. Even before the couple meets, the astrologer will examine both horoscopes to determine compatibility. If the horoscopes aren't compatible, the couple will never even be introduced since the marriage is destined for doom. Therefore, I was counting on my mother and aunt not having the foresight to compare horoscopes at this stage thereby delaying the meeting indefinitely or that the horoscopes wouldn't match so we wouldn't have to meet. Once again, I had underestimated the deviousness of these two ladies.

"Yes, Manju. We've matched the horoscopes and the astrologer is happy."

"Wonderful," I mumbled with little enthusiasm, marvelling at how quickly my trump card had been negated.

"Face it, Malli," my sister said with a smile, "you're fucked."

As my mother started yelling at my sister for swearing, I contemplated how right Akki was.

Thankfully, dinner arrived and our famished family's attention was rapidly diverted from matters of the heart to those of the stomach. This was further facilitated by the superb quality of my mother's and aunt's cooking. Tonight they had whipped up a glorious combination of string hoppers with a spicy crab curry, pol sambol and kiri hothi that left you wanting more.

"You guys are real magicians in the kitchen. This food's just lovely," I said to my aunt and mother.

My mother laughed. "Yes, we just wave our magic wands and say 'Abba and Debra'."

"Abba and Debra?" we all asked.

"Yes, what magicians say," she said impatiently.

"Oh, you mean Abracadabra," my cousin said.

"Yes, that's what I said – Abba and Debra."

"You're such a dag, Ammi," I said laughing.

After greedily devouring a couple of enormous servings, my brother-in-law, cousin and I withdrew to the TV room. Out of earshot of my parents, sister, aunt and uncle, Ravi immediately asked, "So has our new doctor been getting any action in hospital?"

With a certain degree of despondency, I had to answer no. Over the holidays, just prior to beginning work, I had tried to prepare myself for internship. This involved reading 'The House of God' and watching every episode of 'Grey's Anatomy'. All those doctors seemed to have romance galore, somehow managing to see patients in between lovemaking sessions. Though these were clearly works of fiction, I had hoped that at least some of this would come to pass. Alas, it had not. This is not to say that I disliked the work environment. All the female doctors and nurses have been a pleasure to work with to this point. It's just that there were no sparks (or condoms) flying about.

I asked Lal if he had anyone special in his life. "No, too busy with studies. Anyway, I haven't found the right girl yet."

Given that the 'right girl' for my cousin would need a penis, I knew that he would be waiting for a very long time.

Anyway, I am now off to bed feeling full of anxiety. On top of concerns over upcoming night shifts, I'll now have to meet this 'astrologically-compatible' girl. This does not bode well. Just out of curiosity, I took today's newspaper to read in bed and found the horoscope section. Under Libra it read, "Beware. You may be pushed into an unwanted relationship." Perhaps there is something to this astrology stuff after all.

February 10

The curtains are drawn. I am not sure whether it is night or day. I don't even know whether it is Saturday or Sunday. This disorientation has resulted from four straight night shifts. I'm sleepy and short-tempered. No wonder vampires are so nasty – they are sleep-deprived. I bet you if vampires slept at night and were awake through the day, they'd be absolutely delightful. They'd probably still suck your blood at the first opportunity, but I'm sure they'd be pleasant about it.

I just can't sleep through the day no matter how hard I try. Part of it is due to sounds that you'd never hear at night such as the renovations from the house next door, traffic from the busy road and even my mother roaming around the house doing all sorts of odd jobs. So after barely getting any sleep following my first nightshift and stumbling around like a zombie the following night, one of the senior ED doctors told me to use temazepam. This drug is commonly used to help people sleep and treat anxiety. Apparently, many night staff are in the same boat as me and use temazepam with great success. A week ago, if I had been asked to take sedatives to help me sleep, I would have taken the moral high ground and self-righteously refused. But by the end of my second nightshift, I was so desperate that I didn't care anymore. My father used temazepam to help him sleep in hospital after a prostate operation two months ago. He was given a month's supply on discharge from hospital that he hardly used. I was certain that he hadn't thrown the bottle away and that it was with his other medications. As soon as I got home, I wandered up to the medicine cupboard in my parents' bathroom. Like a junkie desperate for a hit, I furtively looked over my back to ensure that nobody was watching before rifling through the bottles to find my panacea. I clumsily opened the temazepam, knocking over some other bottles in the process and gulped down a tablet with a glass of water. Quickly rearranging the cupboard to some semblance of its previous state, I stealthily and silently moved to my bedroom and collapsed into bed. It worked. Although it felt nothing like a 'good night's sleep', the temazepam knocked me out for almost six hours, giving me the energy to function on my next nightshift. I did the same thing the following morning on returning home, this time taking two temazepam tablets with even better effect. After my fourth night, however, things didn't quite go to plan. I went to the drug cupboard as usual. Perhaps because I was so tired, I had forgotten to check on my mother's whereabouts. When I opened the cupboard door, I heard footsteps approaching and my mother calling out for me. She would have killed me had she found me taking Thaththa's sedatives. As she reached the entrance to the bedroom, I grabbed the bottle, opened it and swallowed a couple of tablets. I hurriedly closed the cupboard just as my mother entered the bathroom.

"What are you doing here, Manju?" she asked.

"Oh, just looking for some toothpaste," I replied without hesitation, my relaxed demeanour not betraying my nervous excitement at almost being discovered.

She accepted my explanation without a second thought. I had been stealing drugs like a junkie, now I could lie like one. Ammi wanted to make sure that I'd eaten breakfast before she went out to meet her friends in the city. She told me that she wouldn't be home till late afternoon. I replied that I had eaten and said goodbye. I retired to bed and quietly waited for the sedative-induced stupor to envelop me. As I started to fall asleep, I was only peripherally aware of the fact that I had an erection, which was weird because my thoughts were only on sleep and far from matters erotic. I fell asleep before suddenly waking up. I looked at the clock – it was only 10:30. I had been asleep for barely two hours. It only took a few seconds to work out what had awoken me. It was the erection. But it wasn't a normal erection. My penis was really painful. I got out of bed and strolled around the room waiting for it to return to its flaccid state – but it wouldn't. I then concentrated heavily on a couple of un-erotic images: Albert Einstein pole dancing in a bikini and the Mona Lisa rubbing herself in butter. However, despite these grotesque thoughts, I was alarmed to find that the erection only seemed to get harder. I had an epiphany, realizing what must have happened. I painfully waddled to my parents' bathroom and grabbed the bottle from which I had hurriedly taken tablets this morning. I read the label and my worst fears were confirmed. In the rush to avoid my mother catching me taking the pills, I had erroneously taken tablets from the wrong bottle. It was an antidepressant my mother had been using after a close friend passed away some months ago. I booted up the computer and looked up its side effects. There it was – 'priapism'. This is the medical term for a painful prolonged erection. I hurriedly looked up one of my textbooks and found what I had suspected, namely that untreated priapism can lead to permanent erectile dysfunction and even impotence. The effect of the drug would wear off eventually, but by then would the damage be irreparable? Even with the increasing pain in my penis, panic was rapidly overtaking me as I contemplated a life of impotence from such a tender age. It was ironic that despite having overdosed on antidepressants, I had never been more miserable. I quickly read through the two treatments for priapism that would be relevant to me: intra-cavernosal injection of alpha agonists or aspiration of blood. Both involved inserting large needles into the distended blood vessels of the penis to reduce the swelling. A prick in my prick? How ghastly! But I also accepted that I would have to go to hospital now or risk permanent damage. Yet could I really go to St. Ivanhoe? Imagine the humiliation as my colleagues laughed behind my back about me. Even if I went to another hospital, I would almost certainly encounter a familiar face from my university days who would happily betray my anonymity. There was only one other option. I picked up the phone and called Peter Ivanov. I knew that he was on days off so was surprised when someone else answered the phone.

"Oh, it's Manju here. Is Peter around?" I anxiously asked the stranger.

"Hi Manju, it's Copper here. I'm Peter's new flatmate. How are you doing?"

"Miserably," I replied and asked for their help. Copper Tang asked if I minded going onto speakerphone so both he and Peter could hear and take part in the conversation at the same time. I said that it wasn't a problem. Once on speakerphone, I demanded that they wouldn't laugh at me once I told them what had happened.

"Wouldn't dream of having a laugh at your expense," said Copper.

"Certainly not. We are interns and colleagues. I would die for you," said Peter. I was touched by his passionate devotion.

I explained the whole situation to them. There was a prolonged pause.

"Remember that this isn't a laughing matter," I warned them.

"Of course not, Manju. We wouldn't want to *jerk you around*," said Peter.

"Have a *stiff* drink – it'll do you a world of good," said Copper.

"This must be really *hard on* you," said Peter.

"Stop teasing Manju," Copper said to Peter. "After all, he's in one hell of a pre*dick*ament."

They both burst into fits of laughter at the other end of the phone.

"Very funny," I said. "If you've finished with the comedy routine, is there anything constructive you can offer before my gangrenous dick falls off?"

Peter then spoke seriously. "I have treated this condition as a medical student in Moscow. I aspirated blood using ultrasound guidance to find the blood vessels of the penis. I could come over to your home and try, but without an ultrasound machine, I'd be 'stabbing in the dark'. Also you wouldn't be anaesthetized so it could get painful."

We all briefly contemplated Peter blindly jabbing a large needle and syringe into my penis several times without any anaesthetic whatsoever. I shuddered involuntarily.

Copper said, "Clearly, that isn't an option for Manju. Perhaps you will have to get this treated in hospital."

Copper was right. Oh the shame! The humiliation! I was about to get ready to go to hospital when Peter shouted out.

"Wait Manju! I have an idea. One treatment for priapism is injecting alpha agonist drugs into the blood vessels of the penis to reduce the swelling. Why don't you swallow some alpha agonist tablets? It should have the same effect."

"That's not a bad idea, Peter," commented Copper. "Clonidine, phenylephrine or methyldopa. Check the medicine cupboards at your place. We can bring some from hospital if your parents don't have any at home."

"Good idea. I'll check," I replied feeling that there was finally a glimmer of hope in an otherwise hopeless situation.

"Call us back if you don't find any."

I rushed back to my parents' bathroom and carefully examined every bottle in the medicine cupboard, hoping to find an alpha agonist. I swore in frustration when it became apparent that there were none. I dejectedly made my way towards my room and told the boys the bad news.

"Don't worry, we'll get some alpha agonists and meet you shortly," said Copper hanging up the phone.

I buried my head in my hands as I wondered how such an improbable event could have happened. After some time, as the pain began to worsen, the doorbell rang. Copper and Peter had arrived. In too much agony to put on any clothes or care about maintaining any semblance of modesty, I rushed to the door and opened it. Unfortunately, it was not Copper or Peter at the door – it was our neighbour, Mrs. Miller. There are moments in one's life when time seems to stand still and which one will recall vividly for the rest of one's days. The image of the elderly Mrs.

Miller standing in our doorway, looking at me naked with an erection, will haunt me for the rest of my life. My heart skipped several beats before I recalled that the old lady was legally blind. This explained the playful Labrador at her side. Within seconds, it became apparent that she didn't realize that she had found me in a compromised position. Thank heaven for small mercies!

Mrs. Miller strained to identify me. "Is that Priya?" she asked, referring to my mother.

"No, Mrs Miller. It's Manju here. My mother has gone out. Why don't you come back later this afternoon?" I hurriedly suggested, simply wanting to close the door as soon as possible and return to my shame in private.

"Oh, I see. Okay then, I'll come back this afternoon."

I breathed a sigh of relief. But then, Mrs. Miller leaned forward, straining with her eyes and to my horror, stared straight at my priapism.

"Sorry dear, I forgot my manners. How are you?"

It took a moment to realize that her diminished vision had mistaken the priapism for an attempt on my part to shake hands with her. Whether I was frozen with shock or that she moved with the speed of a younger woman, I shall never know. But before I knew it, she was shaking hands with my penis saying "So nice to see you. It's been such a long time". In absolute agony, I bit my lip and yelled an inward scream. I hoped that Mrs. Miller would continue to be in the dark, complete the handshake and walk away. But it was not to be. I clearly recall the moment when she realized that she was not shaking my hand, but rather, half a foot. Her benign smile slowly transformed into an open-mouthed expression of disbelief before climaxing in a horror-filled scream of 'Pervert'. And then she died. That is to say that she grabbed her chest, went very pale and collapsed, pulseless and not breathing. I always assumed that I would first perform CPR on a real person somewhere in hospital, something that I could always tell my children about. I never imagined that I would be standing at the entrance to my house, naked and sporting a painful erection when the opportunity finally presented itself. *Mais, c'est la vie.* So I got down on my knees and started CPR. Her guide dog seemed to think that it was all some wonderful game and was running around the two of us, yelping with delight.

About five minutes into CPR, Mrs. Miller was still pulseless and not breathing. I had never realized how exhausting CPR was and wondered how much longer I could continue unassisted.

"God help us all," a voice cried out followed by another astonished voice in a foreign language.

I couldn't really blame Peter and Copper for their reaction. They arrived to find me erect and naked, giving mouth-to-mouth to an unconscious elderly woman while her dog was sniffing my bum. I quickly told them the story and, to their credit, they jumped to action. Peter took over from me while Copper called an ambulance from his mobile phone. I quickly rushed upstairs to throw some clothes on. As I began to change, it hit me – the priapism had gone! Whether it was due to the shock of Mrs. Miller's cardiac arrest or simply that the drug effect had worn off, I wasn't sure. In truth, I didn't care. I was simply relieved that the wretched thing had gone away. Within ten minutes, the ambulance arrived. Copper had taken over from Peter but Mrs. Miller was still unresponsive. Then, just as the paramedics arrived, she coughed and groaned. We had revived her! The paramedics transferred her to the ambulance and rushed her to St. Ivanhoe. Hopefully, the CPR had been effective and there wouldn't be any permanent damage. Copper jumped in the ambulance and accompanied Mrs. Miller to hospital.

I invited Peter in and thanked him profusely for their help today.

"You guys are amazing. We barely know each other, yet you both went out of the way to get me out of this fix."

"It is nothing," said Peter.

"Are you crazy? Of course, it's not 'nothing'. I just hope that no one ever hears about this," I said to Peter, staring at him in a suggestive manner.

Peter put his arm around me. "Do not worry – the events of today will remain secret. I will speak to Copper and ensure that it is so. I consider you my droog. This is Russian word for friend. And let me tell you that friendship in Russia means so much more than it does in the West. In times past, it often meant the difference between life and death. We do not betray the confidence of our droogs. Your secret is safe with me, Manju."

I'm not ashamed to say that tears came to my eyes at my 'droog's' words. I had never considered that one reward of internship would be such a sense of camaraderie. We had a beer together before calling Copper on his mobile. The news was reasonable. Mrs. Miller had not arrested again but it was clear that she was in the midst of a heart attack. At the time we spoke to Copper, she was being rushed for an emergency angioplasty to try and unblock the culprit arteries.

I showed Peter out and thanked him once again. As I closed the door, a wave of exhaustion hit me. I really needed to get some sleep. However, I had to do two things first. I called my father on his mobile to let him know that Mrs. Miller had suffered a heart attack. Then I stopped in the shrine room and prayed for Mrs. Miller, sending rays of loving kindness in her erection *(We presume that Dr. Mendis meant 'direction' rather than 'erection'. This Freudian slip probably reflects his exhaustion at the time of making this entry – Editors)*. Then I stumbled into bed and fell asleep – no prescription drugs required.

February 11

I slept like a baby and woke up at 9pm. I rushed downstairs and asked my parents about Mrs. Miller's progress. Thaththa had spoken to the hospital only an hour earlier – the news was good. The angioplasty was successful and Mrs. Miller was out of immediate danger. She had been admitted to the Coronary Care Unit under a good cardiologist. I was so relieved. My parents asked what happened and I told them how she had collapsed at the front door. Of course, there was no mention of the state in which Mrs. Miller had found me. My parents praised me no end about how wonderful I had been in saving her life. Despite their praise, a worrying thought relentlessly gnawed at me, namely that I was responsible for Mrs. Miller's heart attack. Jabs of guilt repeatedly stabbed me like a dagger as I concluded that she wouldn't have collapsed in shock if she hadn't found me naked.

After dinner, I headed off to St. Ivanhoe earlier than usual. I planned on visiting Mrs. Miller in CCU before starting my shift in ED. From the moment I left home however, a thought entered my head and grew with intensity as I approached the hospital. It was a thought that filled me with dread; the thought that Mrs. Miller would confront me about the state in which she had found me, and even worse, accuse me of causing her heart attack. I steeled myself as I recalled the old adage 'Act like a man!' Well, I could act like a man. I could make love to a beautiful woman, drink beer with my friends and pee standing up. Men did all those things. But could I do this? Could I really face Mrs. Miller? I felt nauseous by the time I arrived at the hospital. I was so nervous that I didn't even Elevator Groove on the way to CCU.

I made my way to the Nurses' Station and introduced myself. One of the nurses, a young brunette, smiled at me. "Oh, so *you're* Dr Mendis."

What did her smile and words mean? Was it an accusation? Had Mrs. Miller told everyone? Suddenly, every word and every expression fuelled my simmering suspicions.

"You'd better come with me," she said beckoning with her index finger and leading me through the unit.

She stopped at the door to a single room. "Go in – she's expecting you."

Tears welling up in my eyes, a sickly feeling in my stomach, I took a deep breath and stepped in. There lay Mrs. Miller with a multitude of tubes and wires emanating from her wrinkled old body. But she was awake and looked alert. Next to her in a chair was a middle-aged woman whom I'd met only once before – Mrs. Miller's daughter. The daughter caught sight of me and anxiously stood up.

"Is everything alright, Doctor?" she asked.

"Oh, no, I'm not one of the cardiology doctors. I'm Mrs. Miller's neighbour. She collapsed at my place."

"Is that young Manju? I want to know!" Mrs. Miller shouted out.

This didn't sound good. I barely squeaked out a timid "Yes," before she ordered me to her bedside. I stood next to her, dreading the furious reprimand. Out of the blue, she put her arms around my waist and hugged me.

"Thank you so much," she said. "Jill, this is the young man who saved my life along with his doctor friends. If it hadn't been for him, I'd be with your father in heaven right now."

The daughter came around and hugged me too. "Thank you so much, Manju. We met when you were just a teenager. How things have changed. Such a handsome young man and a wonderful doctor. Thank you for saving Mum's life."

I was speechless. This was not how I had expected things to turn out, although I was certainly not complaining! But I had to ask...

"Mrs. Miller, what do you remember about the collapse?"

"You know it's very strange. I remember coming to your house to look for your mother. I had a slight pain in the chest and my left arm as I walked up the driveway. Then the door opened. But after that, the next thing I recall is being in this hospital bed. The intervening period is a blank."

She couldn't recall meeting me! Thank goodness for that. Then another thing struck me from what she had just said.

"Mrs. Miller, did you say that you already had some chest and left arm pain coming up the driveway?"

"Yes. In fact, I'd been having the pain on and off since breakfast. I'd put it down to indigestion. But the doctors here say that it was an early sign of the heart attack."

I breathed a sigh of relief. Mrs. Miller had already been having her heart attack when I encountered her. It wasn't my fault at all. In fact, Peter was right. I had probably saved her life. I chatted with Mrs. Miller and her daughter for a few minutes more before excusing myself. As I left the ward, the brunette nurse and many of her colleagues congratulated me and shot looks of admiration in my direction. This couldn't have turned out better if I'd scripted it myself. This time, on the way down in the elevator, I did not forget to do some serious Elevator Grooving to celebrate. I danced to Ricky Martin's 'La Vida Loca' on the ride down to ED.

Despite being my fifth nightshift in a row, I was energized, seemingly rejuvenated by the events surrounding Mrs. Miller. Chris Clayton, the senior doctor for the shift, noticed my upbeat mood and asked me what I was so cheery about. I briefly told him.

"Gee, that's great. That's why I became a doctor in the first place. We make a difference. Admittedly, it's not always as dramatic as what you've just described, but it still happens all the time."

Chris Clayton is an interesting character. He is a 'Career Medical Officer' or CMO, which means that he isn't a specialist or in training to be a specialist; however, due to some formal training in Emergency Medicine, he was able to be the senior doctor for night shifts. But that's not what makes him interesting. He is the only child of extremely wealthy parents, who passed away some years ago, leaving him with an enormous fortune. This left him in the rare position of not having to work for the rest of his life if he so chose. However, due to a love of Emergency Medicine, he chose to work five nights every month. The remainder of the month was spent relaxing at home or travelling around the world. Sometimes he would work with a non-governmental organisation in a developing nation, but, more commonly, he'd spend a couple of weeks in a sunny resort in the Caribbean or the Maldives. It was a life that most of us can only dream about.

The shift proceeded smoothly and before long, it was 7:30am. I presented the patient that I had just seen to Eduardo, the night medical registrar. It was a 45 year-old man with poorly controlled diabetes who needed to be admitted under the Endocrinology team. Chris was sitting next to us. He smiled and said to Eduardo, "I believe Sir Ninian is on for Endocrinology..."

Eduardo's face took on a puzzled look before suddenly breaking out into a large grin. This brief exchange between Chris and Eduardo made no sense to me but I felt that it had been at my expense. Then Eduardo said something that totally caught me unawares. "Manju, you've clearly got a good handle on this patient. I've got to speak to a number of specialists about all the admissions from overnight. So why don't you call Sir Ninian to tell him about this diabetic man?"

"But...but...but Eduardo, interns don't call specialists directly. It's just not done," I said nervously. "It has to be a senior doctor like you."

Eduardo's normally friendly demeanour suddenly turned grim. "Manju, I gave you an instruction. Please follow it. Sir Ninian would rather hear about this patient before he leaves for work than not hear about him at all. And as I said before, I will be busy on the phone for a long time. Please call him."

I looked at Chris who nodded in agreement with Eduardo. "You'll be fine, Manju."

"I'm going to get a quick coffee before calling everyone. Do you want to join me?" Eduardo asked Chris. He nodded and they both left the room.

Reluctantly, I picked up the phone and asked the switchboard to connect me to Sir Ninian's home. He answered almost immediately.

"Yes, who is it?" he asked.

"It's Dr. Mendis calling, Sir. I'm one of the new interns. The medical registrar is otherwise detained and asked me to call you about this patient. I hope you don't mind, Sir Ninian."

"No problem at all, my boy. Okay then, I'll just turn the stereo on. Do you want to sing the verses or just the chorus?"

Had I misheard him? "I beg your pardon, Sir?"

"Do you want to sing the verses or just the chorus?"

"Sing... sing what, Sir Ninian?"

"Sing what? Don't Look Back in Anger, of course! What else would I be talking about?"

I stuttered and stammered incoherently.

"Didn't Susan Stoker tell you to learn the lyrics to the song during your Orientation Week?"

"She did but she didn't say why."

"Oh, I must talk to her again," he said, sounding slightly annoyed. "She keeps forgetting to tell the new interns. Well boy, I always like to start the day with a motivational song. For me, that song is Don't Look Back in Anger by Oasis. Whenever I am on-call, I always get the first doctor to call me in the morning to sing it with me. It's good for your health, you know."

"Is it?" I asked with increasing dismay.

"Yes, it is," he said matter-of-factly. "Now, do you want to sing the whole song with me or just the chorus?"

I looked around the doctor's room in which I was sitting. It was thankfully deserted. Closing my eyes and wondering whether I was in a hospital or a lunatic asylum, I whispered, "I'll just sing the chorus, Sir Ninian."

"What did you say? Speak up, boy!"

"The chorus only."

And so it began. At the other end of the phone, the melody to Don't Look Back in Anger began, presumably from a karaoke machine. To my intense embarrassment, Sir Ninian began singing. I had never anticipated being on such intimate terms with a specialist. Nor did I welcome it one bit. It was even worse than seeing him naked. Then as the chorus approached, he yelled, "It's your turn, boy. Go!"

And so it was that I, a fully qualified medical doctor, began singing over the phone to a consultant physician. I looked around quickly, relieved to find the room was still empty.

> And so, Sally can wait
> She knows it's too late as we're walking on by
> Her soul slides away
> But don't look back in anger
> I heard you say

The song lasted about five minutes. As I sang the chorus for the last time, I looked over my shoulder to find Chris, Eduardo and about ten others pissing themselves with laughter. I'd been set up.

As it ended, Sir Ninian pronounced his judgement, "Not bad, but I want more enthusiasm next time. Now tell me about the patient."

After discussing the diabetic patient with him, I put the phone down. Eduardo and Chris sat next to me, tears of laughter streaming down their faces.

"What on earth was all that about?" I asked, completely bemused.

"It's been like that for about twenty-five years with Sir Ninian. Every medical registrar who calls him in the morning has to sing a song with him. It used to be Rocket Man by Elton John but he switched to Oasis about ten years ago. Then about five years ago, we devised an unofficial policy. We decided to make a first-term intern working in ED call Sir Ninian in the morning. Then that intern would have to sing the song. This year, you were the first intern to do a nightshift so you drew the short straw."

"I wouldn't give up your medical career for Broadway though," suggested Eduardo unhelpfully.

"It's just so weird though. It's like something out of the 'Twilight Zone'. How can he get away with such behaviour? Isn't the Medical Council concerned?" I asked.

Chris said, "He might be a little crazy but don't forget two things. First of all, he is *Professor Colonel Sir* Ninian Tietas. He is one of the most distinguished and well-connected doctors in this country. The Medical Council would be wary to take him on for that reason alone. And, at the end of the day, once you forget the eccentricities, he is still a very competent endocrinologist."

"Has anyone ever refused to sing the song?" I asked.

"A few years ago, a medical registrar called Carla refused to do it."

"What happened to her?"

"She got transferred out of the city completely and now works in a peripheral hospital in the country."

"Just for refusing to sing?" I asked in shock.

"Yep. Remember I said he's well connected."

"He seems as bad as Servilia Gorgas," I said.

Chris shook his head in disagreement. "No, you're wrong. You're comparing apples and oranges. At the end of the day, Sir Ninian is a nice man who has dedicated his life to this hospital. As long as you sing his song, he'll look after you. Even Servilia Gorgas isn't evil. Her problem is that she is really intelligent and doesn't suffer fools. Furthermore, she doesn't have good 'people skills' despite being a great diagnostician. I would regard her as difficult rather than vindictive."

As an intern, I could do without consultants who were difficult or vindictive. I wasn't particularly interested in the subtle differences in their personality flaws.

It's now 10:30 am and I am off to bed. I can jubilantly declare that I have survived my first lot of nightshifts. Now I can look forward to four days off.

February 15

It's been a blissfully unproductive three days. I've been catching up with a lot of sleep. Other than that, I took my nephew Kumar to see 'Horton Hears a Who' which he really enjoyed.

All the interns met for dinner tonight at 'The Nuclear Café', so called because it is known for its fusion cooking. I ordered the Moon Rock (crescentic potato wedges) and had Mushroom Cloud (a tasty combination of stir fried shitake mushrooms with a steaming satay lamb base) for my main.

"How's the Nuclear Fallout Soup?" I asked Alternaria.

"It is quite good," she replied, "but I don't know why it is glowing."

It was good to catch up with the gang. The burning issue on everyone's lips was the Academy Award's scandal. It involved the Oscar for Actress in a Leading Role. The presenters of the award were Jessica Lange and Lupie Karmeleon. Salma Cruze was favoured to win for her brilliant performance as the high-paced Manhattan lawyer who reluctantly moves to a country farm in 'My Life as a Goat'. However, when it came to the announcement, Lupie Karmeleon opened the envelope and declared another nominee, Faye Scarlet, as winner of the Oscar. This was for her highly acclaimed performance as a sadistic vet in 'Three Blind Mice'. It had all seemed quite normal. Faye Scarlet came up on stage and delivered the standard 'Thank you' speech before being ushered off to rapturous applause. The following day, rumours filtered through that there was something dreadfully wrong. Later that afternoon, the Academy announced that Salma Cruze had in fact won the Oscar. Lupie Karmeleon had 'supposedly' made a terrible mistake. By the following morning, the gossip mongers had the true story. Apparently, Lupie had had a recent spat with Salma about something or the other. The bottom line, however, was that Lupie detested Salma to such an extent that she would never announce her winning an Oscar; therefore, when she saw Salma's name on the paper, she simply announced a different actress. Just like that. And in doing so, created a living hell for the Academy. Salma demanded her Oscar and threatened to sue the Academy if she didn't get it. Faye Scarlet said she had been awarded the Oscar in front of the whole world and would sue the Academy if they tried to take it from her. Lupie Karmeleon, who was being threatened with legal action from all three parties, pleaded insanity through her Hollywood lawyer. The unfolding drama was so intriguing it deserved its own nomination for an Oscar!

I hadn't told my fellow interns about having to sing Don't Look Back in Anger for Sir Ninian. To say that they were shocked by my announcement is a real understatement.

Copper said, "The old guy's clearly gone insane. Lost the plot completely. Why does the hospital put up with it?"

I told them Chris' explanation that Sir Ninian was too influential to cross and was such a good endocrinologist that the hospital put up with his eccentricities.

Delilah tried to vouch for him. "I have been covering the Endocrine team because the Resident has been sick. I've done two ward rounds with Sir Ninian and he really seems on the ball when it comes to his patients. He also teaches quite a bit and I picked up a lot about diabetes in those few hours with him. It is the small talk not related to medicine that gives you the impression that he is unhinged. For example, in the elevator today, he said that he puts urine on his citrus trees."

"Actually, there's nothing wrong with that," Alternaria said. "My aunt's an avid gardener and she keeps telling us that urine is wonderful for lemon trees. In fact every month, she gets her husband to collect his urine in a jug and she pours it all over the trees."

"That may be okay, Alternaria," said Delilah. "But does your uncle stand in the middle of his garden, pants down, dick in hand, 'watering' the lemon trees?"

"Of course not," Alternaria replied, looking appalled at the thought.

"Well, Sir Ninian does," said Delilah. "And even worse, he told us so!"

We stared at Delilah in silence before unanimously agreeing that Sir Ninian was completely off his rocker.

Smegman had been relatively quiet and looked rather sullen. He and Lucky were sitting at opposite ends of the table. I sensed that their relationship had deteriorated even further since starting surgery.

"What's up, Smegman?" I asked. "You've been very quiet all evening."

"Ask her," he said gesturing in Lucky's direction.

"Oh, for God's sake, stop moping in self-pity. I've already apologized," retorted Lucky.

"What did you do that pissed him off so much?" asked Alternaria.

"It was just a joke," said Lucky. "Smegman has been so obsessed with ophthalmology that he has been dumping all the ward work on me and spending the whole day in Eye Clinic. I was happy to do it for one week. But when I finished at 9pm for the twelfth day running, I asked Smegman to reciprocate. He refused. Made some pathetic excuse. He has been using me to further his career in ophthalmology without giving a damn about how overworked I have been. So I decided to get even."

"Pathetic, Smegman," Delilah said. "We're meant to support each other – not stab one another in the back."

Smegman remained sullen and silent.

"Professor Croaker and her League of Women were going to Sutton Reserve to protest the logging of trees. The League fears that the logging would lead to the extinction of a rare species of owl, which is found nowhere else in the country. When Professor Croaker mentioned it to us on a ward round, Smegman brown-nosed like a professional, saying how concerned he was about the owls and how he would love to protest. Naturally, Professor Croaker was delighted and invited him along last week."

"Do you know anything about owls?" I asked Smegman sceptically.

He grunted in a non-committal fashion.

"Of course he doesn't know anything about owls," said Lucky. "Anyway, I told Smegman that I admired him for his interest in wildlife conservation and I offered to help him."

"He believed you?"

"I can be very convincing," said Lucky assuredly. "Anyway, I told him that I had the perfect t-shirt to wear for the protest and that Professor Croaker and the League of Women would be envious of him when he wore it. I brought the t-shirt to work the next day. Smegman looked at it, loved it and wore it to the protest."

Alternaria had a puzzled look on her face. "What kind of t-shirt would give a positive message about protecting owls?"

"It was a t-shirt my brother bought in the USA.

It said I ♥ HOOTERS."

Delilah asked in astonishment, "Smegman, do you mean to say that you attended a protest organized by a feminist group wearing a t-shirt saying I ♥ HOOTERS?"

Smegman broke down holding his head in his hands. "I thought 'hooters' were about owls. Owls go 'hoot', don't they?"

"So what happened?"

"The women saw my t-shirt and started yelling abuse at me. I've never seen Professor Croaker so upset. She said that I was mocking the very foundations of her belief system and ordered me to go home. It was humiliating. My career is over."

Copper said to Lucky, "Harsh. Very harsh – but brilliant."

"Oh, for the last time Smegman! I met Professor Croaker the next day and told her that you were clueless about the meaning of the t-shirt. She understands that your intentions had been good and she forgave you immediately. Stop stressing about it."

"So you say..." said Smegman suspiciously.

"Smegman, I wanted to teach you a lesson – not ruin your life. Just please don't use me like that again."

"Okay," Smegman conceded. "I'm sorry. I just got so caught up in ophthalmology that I didn't think about how much I was burdening you. I promise that I'll be more considerate from now on. In fact, why don't you finish at 2:30 everyday this week? I'll cover for you."

"Good for you, Smegman," said Peter, slapping him on the back. "There's hope for you yet."

"Smegman, but how on earth could someone as intelligent as you not know what hooters means?"

Smegman said, "I led a very sheltered childhood. I had..." he hesitated, staring into the distance for a few moments before abruptly changing his mind. "No, don't worry. It's not worth talking about."

There was an uncomfortable pause and I suspect that for a brief moment the unthinkable happened, namely that we all felt sorry for Smegman. Then Delilah said, "For what it's worth, Smegman, we're still your colleagues whether you like it or not. We'll look after you. As for learning about hooters and other vulgar things, look no further than the other men at this table."

"I take great offence at that," said Copper. "I am not vulgar."

"I didn't say you were vulgar. I said that you know about 'vulgar things'."

"Well, I guess that's okay then."

Smegman pepped up somewhat after that and the rest of the meal passed uneventfully.

February 28

I was in Clinics today. This is the part of ED where people with less acute problems are seen. All the really sick cases e.g. heart attacks, bleeding ulcers etc., go to the Acute section. I quite enjoy Clinics.

There's usually an opportunity to perform some minor procedures like suturing and plaster casts. My last patient of the day was a lady in her forties named Mary. I called Mary in. She was slightly overweight with an anxious demeanour.

I greeted her warmly, introduced myself and asked her what was wrong.

She looked at me and pointed at her pelvic region, before saying, "I've got a bush down there."

I didn't know what to say. How do you respond to a statement like that?

"I beg your pardon, Ma'am?"

"You heard me. I've got a bush down there and I'm worried like crazy."

I looked at Mary's triage card. It wasn't very helpful. It simply said, "Gynaecological problem, won't disclose details to me." In particular, I looked for an underlying psychiatric illness but there was none to be found.

So I soldiered on and explored the problem further.

"Mary, it is quite normal to have a 'bush' down there. We all have one, men and women. If you are worried about it, have you considered ummm, ahhh, well, a Brazilian wax or some other cosmetic procedure?"

She looked at me, puzzled. "What do you mean it's normal? I've never had a bush down there before."

I was quite confused by this stage.

"Can I just show you?" Mary asked.

I pondered whether I should have a nurse in there to chaperone me with this clearly mentally ill woman, but Mary had pulled up her dress and removed her panties before I had a chance to act.

I stared and stared and stared. When I eventually did speak again, it was nothing especially original ..."You have a bush down there," I said.

"That's what I've been telling you, Doctor!"

Cross my heart... amidst the pubic hair, a bunch of green shoots was emerging! I had seen many unusual sights in my brief time as a medical student and doctor, but nothing as strange as this!

I quickly called the Gynaecology Registrar. She said that she was busy. "Could it wait?" she asked wearily. I said that it could, but after I explained the situation, *she* couldn't wait. I have never seen anyone appear so puffed in rushing to see a patient.

To cut a long story short, the Gynaecology registrar, Vicki, used a speculum to provide a better view and access for an internal examination. She slowly pulled out the green shoots, centimetre by centimetre, until it all came out. We stared, utterly mystified at the sight before us. At the end of the shoots was the unmistakable top of a very large carrot!

"Mary, can you explain this?"

Mary could and did explain. It turns out that a few weeks ago, she and her lover (Big Al) decided to have a late-night lovemaking session; however neither of them had protection and all the pharmacies were closed. Unable to quell their amorous urges, Mary had devised a cunning plan. She had heard of the contraceptive effects of natural products such as pomegranate. So, she looked through Al's kitchen for suitable produce. Searching around, she came up with two candidates – a carrot that had won first prize at a recent agricultural show and a slice of bacon. Being vegetarian, the bacon was immediately discarded. The prize-winning carrot became the victor in a contest where losing may well have been preferable. While the creator of this mammoth carrot would have expected its fate to be culinary, he would have been no less proud to see his prize-winning legume come to the aid of this voracious vegetarian and her corpulent Casanova as they fuelled the fires of passion. Mary sliced off the top of the carrot which she assigned to her nether regions. Afterwards, she forgot about it completely…until now. We can only presume that the damp, warm, protein-rich environment in which the carrot top had sat acted as a natural greenhouse, allowing it to flourish. The whole episode seemed like a bizarre scene from a television show – but I wasn't sure if I was on *ER* or *Better Homes & Gardens*. Mary didn't need a doctor – she needed a farmer.

The best part of the tale is that Vicki had the sense of mind to take a photo of the carrot with her phone camera, both before and after its extraction. Mary kindly consented for us to use the photos for a photo quiz in a medical journal. I'm so excited! If this gets published, I'll be in the running to win the Steelbone Trophy! I left Mary in Vicki's capable hands, pondering what a priceless episode this had been. As far as amazing anecdotes went, this was pure gold, twenty-four carrot.

March 14

I caught up with Peter. We haven't worked together in ED for a while now since our rosters have diverged somewhat. Even today, I worked in the morning and he started in the afternoon. But our shifts overlapped for a couple of hours which allowed us to meet, albeit briefly. I told him the carrot story and he was really pleased that I might get a publication out of it. He wasn't as surprised as I had expected.

"You know, Manju, with all this global warming and environmental conservation, I am not surprised. Condoms and contraceptives are non-recyclable – carrots are. Sex needs to go organic too you know. Keep up with the times. Sex can't get left behind in the 20th century."

"Ummm... I've never really thought about it like that."

"Anyway, who will be first author of your publication – you or the vaginacologist?"

"Vaginacologist? Don't you mean gynaecologist?" I asked.

"No. This is Western misconception. The term should be vaginacologist."

I was surprised. "Peter, I thought that 'gyna' means woman in Ancient Greek, hence the term gynaecology."

"No, that is nonsense. This is all Western propaganda. Do women have a gyna? No, of course not. Women have a vagina. Therefore, it is vaginacologist. You are very stupid. But you are my friend, so I won't tell anyone how stupid you are."

Honestly, sometimes conversations with Peter leave me utterly bemused. I am sure that the correct term is gynaecologist but I was equally certain that I wasn't going to convince him, so I left it at that.

Turning to matters romantic, I am not looking forward to tomorrow. My mother and aunt have arranged a meeting between this 'astrologically-compatible' girl and me. It's going to be lunch at the girl's house. My mother has been very excited, saying what an auspicious day March 15th will be for 'meeting young lovers'. I looked up the internet. I couldn't find anything good about March 15th. Julius Caesar had been stabbed to death, Lenin had suffered a stroke and Elizabeth Taylor had got married for the fifth time. All portents of doom if you ask me, which, of course my mother never does when it comes to such matters. The day that I get to run my own personal life should be declared a public holiday.

March 15

The lunch didn't go as badly as I anticipated. Ammi, Thaththa and I went there around midday and were greeted by the father, a smartly dressed man about the same age as Thaththa. Clearly, they were out to impress us. There were two shiny Mercedes-Benz sedans sitting in the driveway that led to an enormous house. It was typical of the ostentatiousness that possessed Sri Lankans living overseas. The interior was gaudy with large, low-hanging chandeliers and thick green wallpaper bearing an unknown coat-of-arms. There had been no attempt to hide renovations by blending them into the style and structure of the pre-existing building. They had simply been lumped on, following the philosophy of 'bigger is better' irrespective of what the final product looked like. Mrs. Wickramaratne and her daughter were waiting in the living room and stood as we entered. After friendly introductions, we all sat down. The girl, whose name is Priyanthi, seems quite nice. She has a good figure and a fairly attractive face, although she was shorter than I expected. It certainly wasn't lust at first sight but she had potential. While others may be critical of my clinical assessment of her physical appearance, I feel no guilt whatsoever because she would have been dissecting me in exactly the same manner.

The supposed reason that parents accompany us to these 'introductions' is to make us feel more at ease by creating the relaxed atmosphere of a party rather than an intimate meeting for two. However, the real purpose for their presence is to blatantly observe the interaction between the young couple, after which they will decide whether the relationship should be encouraged or discouraged.

After her mother served a tasty variety of Sri Lankan savouries and sweets, I managed to spend some time alone with Priyanthi. She is a really intelligent girl, and in fact, is an aeronautical engineer working on our national space program. If that isn't intimidating enough for a prospective new boyfriend, she is also a talented artist. On the pretext of viewing her paintings, I was able to whisk her away from the probing eyes of our parents. I'm not a connoisseur of art, but as I admired the watercolour paintings adorning the walls of their study, it was obvious to me that she has skill. While you don't have to be a rocket scientist to take up painting, she actually is one. The conversation between us flowed quite comfortably although we discussed mainly trivial matters. After a while, I made the bold decision to pursue things with her. But before that, I had to clarify one issue.

"Priyanthi, I'm sorry for being so up-front with this. Are you seeing anyone at the moment?" I cringed inwardly as I asked the question, a most personal question but nevertheless one that had to be asked. "I'm sorry for asking," I quickly reiterated.

She looked startled for a moment but to her credit, responded quickly. "That's okay. I was dating a guy called Warren but we broke up a couple of months ago. Things were great for a while but he ended up being a real jerk. What about you?"

"No, I'm not seeing anyone," I replied. "And I'm sorry to hear that it didn't work out with your ex-boyfriend. So, would you like to go out sometime? Meet for coffee after work perhaps?" I anxiously waited with bated breath for her response although externally I looked cool, calm and collected.

"Sure, that sounds good," she replied. I breathed a sigh of relief – so far, so good.

In the car on the way home, my mother praised the Wickramaratnes no end. "Oh, what good people. So well-spoken. Did you see how nicely the wife was dressed? Such beautiful jewellery too. What about the house? So tastefully furnished. Such lovely chandeliers. Manju, did you like the daughter? She seemed very sweet."

I told her that we got on quite well and that we would meet next week after work.

"Oh how exciting, Manju! Where are you taking her for dinner?"

"We're not going for dinner. We're meeting for coffee."

This did not please Ammi. "Coffee? Coffee? You're meeting her for coffee? What men! Remember that you are courting this girl! Do you think that your father ever took me out for 'coffee' after we had been introduced?"

"What's wrong with coffee?" I asked.

"This is a good girl from a top class family. You may not get this chance again. For heaven's sake, take her out for dinner."

"No, Ammi," I said firmly. "I am not 'courting her' as you put it. We're just getting to know each other. Coffee is an informal way to meet someone. So coffee it is. And that's final."

"Why coffee? Why not water or a plain biscuit," Ammi mumbled sarcastically to herself, clearly annoyed that I was ruining her plans for the perfect marriage.

For the rest of the car trip, I was preoccupied with the thought of how high maintenance my mother would be if she ever went back to the singles scene. I could picture guys spiking their own drinks to render themselves unconscious, just to escape listening to her constant nagging.

March 22

I finished my final nightshift for the ED term. While this is a cause for celebration, the shift itself was a tough one due to a number of nutty patients. Karen, one of the veteran nurses, said it was probably due to the full moon. In her experience, a full moon always augured a wild night in the ED. I had the pleasure of two 'unusual' patients.

Weirdo number one was a woman brought in by the police. She had been arrested for assault and was possibly high on some stimulant. Within an hour of being placed in a cell, she had made a fuss claiming that police officers had physically assaulted her. The police were therefore legally bound to bring her in to undergo a clinical assessment. Guess who was fortunate enough to pick up her file from the 'To Be Seen' box? Yes, yours truly.

The woman was not in a single room – she should have been, but patients with a greater need already occupied them. She was among a row of ten beds in the Acute Section of the Emergency Department. The beds were separated only by curtains. In other words, the rest of the ED could hear your conversation if you didn't speak quietly. The curtains around her bed were drawn while two grim-faced police officers stood outside. Their expressions clearly betrayed the fact that they didn't want to be here. I introduced myself to them and they told me to be careful because she was an 'abusive felon'. If there was one thing I had learnt over the last couple of months here, it was that I could quickly establish a good rapport with patients. Many of the senior staff in ED had remarked that I possessed a charm and confidence that even the most difficult patients took to instantly. This woman was going to be a breeze...

I drew the curtains across and came face to face with the woman. She took an instant look at me and cried out, "Oh great! I just got mugged by a fucking Curry Man – now I've got a fucking CURRY doctor! Isn't that just fucking great?" And that was the high point of the whole interview. It kind of went downhill from there. She did answer all my questions but the language...oh the language! Like a trained opera singer, she would begin her 'aria' in a low tone before climaxing in a glass-shattering soprano-esque finale. Mirroring the increase in volume and pitch was the stepwise deterioration in her language. More often than not, her scathing solos were directed at our uniformed custodians of the peace, two of whom were standing just outside the curtains.

I asked her, "Where does it hurt?"

She replied, "My tummy hurts. It is really sore. I want to puke. And you know why? Because *THOSE PIGS, THOSE COCK-SUCKING PIGS BEAT THE CRAP OUT OF ME.*"

The worst part of it all was that there was a sweet eighty-year-old nun, Sister Maria, in the next bed, admitted with a tachycardia. She was on a heart monitor and every time this woman began one of her loud tirades, the heart monitor would beep more rapidly as the poor nun's heart rate climbed precipitously. You could hear Sister Maria fumbling with her rosary beads asking for protection from the devilish foul-mouthed apparition lying next to her. I'm sure that Sister Maria would have agreed that the hills were alive with the sound of something, but it certainly wasn't music.

Eventually after dissecting through the verbal abuse, I had almost completed a satisfactory history and examination. I finally said, "I have examined you so far and there's nothing to find. But since you are claiming that you have an injury to your breasts, I need you to remove your bra so I can examine them. Will you allow me to do it?"

She paused for a moment (an amazing feat for her) and looked squarely at me. Then in a voice unbelievably louder than before, she shouted, *"YOU MEAN YOU WANT TO KNOW WHETHER YOU CAN STICK YOUR BLACK HANDS ON MY WHITE TITS? WELL, I DON'T FUCKING THINK SO."*

Like the quiet after a storm, an eerie silence followed this particularly vehement outburst, which is quite an achievement for a busy ED. Unfortunately, it was all too much for Sister Maria whose heart flipped into ventricular tachycardia, precipitating a cardiac arrest and setting off the alarm on her monitor. I quickly informed the two policemen that I had completed my assessment to the best of my ability and had found no evidence of assault. I sincerely wished them a good night and rushed to treat Sister Maria. The good Sister was pulseless for five minutes. However, we pulled her back from the brink.

The next challenge was writing in the clinical notes: should I paraphrase everything that she had said or should I quote her word for word ie. instead of writing, "The lesbian pig dyke beat the fucking crap out of me," should I paraphrase with "she claimed that a female police officer assaulted her?" And if I quoted her verbatim, should I write all the swear words in full or use keyboard symbols such as * or # to disguise them? In the end, I figured that this would be the only time in my career that I would have legitimate grounds to write swear words in an official document. So unfortunately, some poor female officer was forever more labelled as "the lesbian pig dyke" in the hospital notes.

Weirdo number two came soon afterwards. This man had been admitted for investigation with chest pain. His name was Patrick. He also had OCD (*Obsessive Compulsive Disorder – Editors*). In his case, he was obsessed with cleanliness and cleaning rituals. So the ED was privy to the extraordinary sight of a middle-aged balding man removing the hospital linen from the bed, spraying and wiping down the mattress with some sort of detergent before replacing the hospital sheets with his own. This exercise was performed with gloves (his own, of course) which were duly discarded in the bin when he finished. Don't get me wrong – I would never call someone weird because of a mental illness. I felt nothing but sympathy for the inconvenience the OCD was causing him; however, as I walked past him, he accidentally dropped a pen on the floor. I picked it up and handed it to him. He hurled the pen back down on the floor with a look of revulsion as if I had presented him with a poisonous snake.

"What's wrong?" I asked.

"Don't give me that pen. You've touched it."

"Sir, don't worry. I do wash my hands between patients," I assured him.

"No, it's not germs I'm worried about. It's your filthy black skin. All that dirt and stink – you've transferred it to me. I don't know if I can get it out."

He took a bottle of antiseptic from his bag, and liberally poured it over the pen on the floor before spraying the detergent all over his hands and vigorously rubbing them.

I stared at him in incredulity.

He saw me staring at him and had the nerve to wave me away. "Go away, gollywog."

He quickly grabbed a passing nurse (naturally a white one) and said, "I only want a white doctor. I've got private insurance you know. None of this black, immigrant filth."

I was about to confront him and possibly hit him when Pantene appeared out of nowhere. He forcefully grabbed my arm. "Don't do anything stupid. If you touch him, you're screwed, no matter how bad he is. He's not worth it. Just go to the tearoom and I'll join you."

In somewhat of a daze, I followed Pantene's instructions and had a coffee to calm my nerves. I'd never seen or experienced such blatant racism before. As a medical student, I had witnessed elderly white men complementing oriental medical students on how good their English was, not realizing that these medical students had lived here all their lives. But this was the first time it had happened to me. And there was no misunderstanding here – Patrick knew exactly what he was saying. The smug, self-satisfied, racist git. For the first time as a doctor, I really wanted to hurt a patient, make him pay for making me feel so low and so worthless. Pantene soon joined me and said that he had threatened Patrick with expulsion from the ED if he ever made further racist remarks.

"Are you really allowed to do that?" I asked.

"I don't know, nor do I care. But I won't tolerate racism while I'm in charge."

I thanked Pantene for his support and carried on seeing patients.

However, the enthusiasm and optimism with which I'd begun the shift had been well and truly extinguished. I felt quite low.

A few hours later, in the middle of the night, I saw Mr. Patel getting out of his bed. I rushed over to help him. Mr. Patel is an elderly man, whom I had admitted with twenty-four hours of worsening confusion. The preliminary results suggested that a urinary tract infection was to blame. Anyway, the poor chap was completely disoriented and living in the distant past. He had no idea that he was in hospital and thought that he was in his former house in Mumbai from twenty years ago.

"Mr. Patel, where are you going?" I asked gently.

He looked at me. "Are you the gardener?"

"No, Sir. But why don't we go back to bed? You'll feel a lot better."

"Well, first I want to pee. I really need to pee. I'm just going to the toilet."

"And where's the toilet, Sir?"

"Where it's always been, young man. Just there across from the bedroom." He pointed towards the imagined toilet. And would you believe it? He was pointing right at the bed of my favourite bigot, Patrick. Mr. Patel's acute confusional state had recreated the floor plans of his old house within this very ED – and Patrick's bed stood exactly where the toilet should have been. I looked around to make sure no one was looking in our direction. Then I said to Mr. Patel, "Of course, Sir. You should go to the toilet. You'll definitely feel much better."

I stood behind a curtain and watched as Mr. Patel approached Patrick's bed. The racist git was snoring away, probably dreaming of a cleaner and whiter world. He therefore didn't see the old man come up to him. Mr. Patel proceeded to pull out his willy, aimed it in the general direction of Patrick's face, and started to urinate. It took Patrick about five seconds to awaken from his slumber. This provided ample time for Mr. Patel to urinate over a good portion of Patrick's abdomen and face. As the horrific realization of what had just happened overtook him, Patrick reacted in a rather unusual way. He started screeching like a girl and tore his urine-soaked clothes off before jumping out of his bed.

"*HE PISSED ON ME. THIS BLACK BASTARD PISSED ON ME. UNCLEAN. UNCLEAN. UNCLEAAAANN. AHHHHHHHHHHHHHHHHHHHHHHHH.*"

Being urinated on by Mr. Patel's bacteria-laden and smelly urine was too much for Patrick's defence mechanisms to cope with. The psychological wall protecting any semblance of sanity crumbled. It wasn't long before the man obsessed with cleanliness started running around the ED naked, yelling incoherently and rolling episodically on the dirty floor. By the time Security arrived, he was curled on the floor in foetal position, whimpering like a dog. He was quickly held down and injected with large amounts of sedatives.

Mr. Patel, who had now made his way back to his bed, looked at me. "Was that the gardener?" he asked, pointing at Patrick.

"Yes," I replied, barely suppressing a grin.

He looked on disapprovingly. "Well, he makes too much bloody noise. Tell him that he's fired."

A glow of satisfaction slowly enveloped me. I believe that doctors can't take the law into their own hands but we can give it a prod in the right direction.

However, I decided to make a note: no more full-moon shifts for a while!

March 25

Priyanthi and I went on our first date.

It all started well enough. After being particularly hygienic (cutting toenails, shaving and spraying generous amounts of aftershave all over my face), I put on some cool threads and headed out to the café. My car was being serviced so Akki dropped me. Priyanthi arrived just after me and we chatted. It all seemed to go well. Again, the conversation was limited to small talk: the barrier to the deep and meaningful issues had not yet been breached. I counted only three uncomfortable pauses, which I thought was more than acceptable for a first date. Although no sparks had been flying, I really felt that 'we' were a possibility.

When we left the café, it all fell apart. I was going to do some shopping in the city and Priyanthi kindly offered to drive me. She apparently had to meet a friend for dinner in town so my destination would be on the way for her. She stopped to fill the car with petrol. In order to pass time, I went through the glove box, which in hindsight I shouldn't have done. The only object of interest there was a GPS navigator system. Just for kicks, I entered the address of the shopping mall to which I needed to go. Priyanthi got into the car, saw me with the GPS navigator system and to my complete surprise, snapped my head off.

"Who the hell told you to poke around in my glove box?" she asked, angry for the first time since I'd met her.

"I'm sorry. I was just passing time. All I did was set the shop's address on the GPS. I didn't mean anything." Her anger at such a trivial incident confused me.

She then sighed a deep sigh. To my alarm, I noticed that tears were pouring down her face.

Alarmed at her extreme response to such a seemingly trivial incident, I quickly apologised. "I'm sorry, Priyanthi. I didn't mean to touch your stuff. Please don't cry."

"No, I'm glad you did. Let's drive for a bit and you'll understand. Keep the GPS on," she said cryptically.

I wondered what she meant but within minutes it became apparent. It was all to do with the GPS. As the car started moving, a young male voice from the navigator greeted us with "Hey Priya Baby. I hope that you're driving to me." Then followed instructions such as, "In one hundred metres, take the first turn right, you sexy thing," and "At the roundabout, take the second exit or I'll eat your hot lips for dinner." Priya pulled over after a couple of minutes.

"Interesting GPS," I remarked quietly as the dreadful realization dawned upon me.

She nodded, looking straight ahead, not meeting my eyes.

"The guy, I mean the voice on the GPS, that's your ex-boyfriend Warren, isn't it?"

"Yes."

"How did he program his voice on a GPS like that? I've never heard of anyone doing that before." Despite the fury that was developing in me, I was nevertheless curious about this extraordinary feat of electronic wizardry.

"He's a brilliant electronics engineer. He's impressive – very impressive," she said softly.

As the pieces of the puzzle fell into place, I looked down at the floor and said, "So I'm guessing that he isn't really an 'ex'-boyfriend. You're still seeing him, aren't you?"

"Yes," she said, her voice barely perceptible.

"So," I asked, "how long were you going to string me along before you told me?"

"You don't understand," she said desperately. "My parents won't accept anyone other than a Sri Lankan boy from a good family. I can't disappoint them but I can't leave Warren either."

"Does that make it okay to deceive me and our parents into believing that we have a future together?" I shouted as my simmering anger erupted. "What if I had fallen in love with you? What if we had gotten engaged? When would you have told me – on our frigging wedding day perhaps?"

I tried to open the door. The central locking was on.

"Please unlock the door," I coldly demanded.

"Please, Manju. We need to talk."

"Unlock the damn door! We do not need to talk. That bloody GPS has done enough talking for the two of us!"

She unlocked the door, tears pouring down her face.

As I got out of the vehicle, I had the final word. "Don't worry Priyanthi. Your parents won't find out about your boyfriend from me. Just do me a favour and leave me the hell alone!"

With this parting shot, I slammed the door and walked off, consumed by hurt and humiliation. I didn't go shopping in the end. Instead, I caught a taxi and went to see Akki and Ravi. I related my tale of woe to them. They were both very sympathetic to my plight.

"The fucking little bitch," said my enraged sister. "You're too good for the slut."

Although my sister clearly had my interests at heart, somehow swearing at Priyanthi didn't make me feel better. So, after drowning my sorrows with a couple of beers, I headed home and had an early night. My mother was devastated when I told her that I wouldn't be seeing Priyanthi again. But I refused to discuss it further and Thaththa wisely advised her to leave me alone. Just before retiring, I looked at today's horoscope in the paper: "An important person will give you a message that will bring you closer together." What a load of rubbish!

April 4

Today was my last shift in ED. I can't believe that the time has passed so quickly. I left a chocolate mud cake in the tearoom as the traditional gesture of thanks to the staff in ED. During my shift, I met privately with Dr. Tiberius for my evaluation. Thankfully, he said that I had done well, especially for my first term. Apparently, the senior doctors and nursing staff had all enjoyed working with me and had faith in my clinical judgement.

"One of the most critical parts of being a doctor is being able to recognize a really sick patient. You don't have to know what is wrong with them but you need to know that they need immediate attention. I've met some really clever doctors over the years who couldn't do that. But you seem to have the knack. Keep it up."

It was a nice thing to say. He asked me about my long-term plans in medicine. I replied honestly that it was too early to tell. I didn't tell him though that I wouldn't pursue a career in Emergency Medicine. The pace here was too frenetic and you never saw a patient once they'd been transferred to the ward. For me, not knowing the patient's outcome once they'd left the ED was very unfulfilling. I finished my shift and thanked a whole bunch of people there before heading home.

Ammi is still sulking about how things didn't work out with Priyanthi. I didn't dare tell her about Warren and gave the vague excuse of incompatibility for not pursuing things. On a personal level, I've put the whole incident with Priyanthi behind me. After reassessing the situation with a cooler head, she went from being an object of hatred to one of sympathy. I've concluded that it's the expectation of parents in general that is the real problem. It's easy enough to marry a Sri Lankan when you are brought up in Sri Lanka. After all, the only people in the dating pool are Sri Lankans! When you move overseas, however, the majority of people with whom you grow up, school and socialize with are Westerners. It's only natural then that these 'cross-cultural' relationships develop. While I can't blame our parents for wanting us to marry Sri Lankans, I am critical of their lack of insight into how difficult it is. Although I'm still not thrilled at how she used me, I sent Priyanthi a cryptic text message: "Sorry things didn't turn out well.

Good luck with the GPS."

Surprisingly, later that day, I received a reply from her. "Thanks. I'm sorry too. Have decided to tell parents about GPS. Not fair to others."

You have to admire her. It was a brave thing she was about to do – the correct thing certainly – but nevertheless a brave thing. I silently wished her luck. I too have worries but of a different kind. On Monday, I begin my surgical rotation with Professor Bonkzalot. Judging by how unhappy Lucky and Smegman have been in surgery, it is not something I am looking forward to. I went to the shrine room and prayed for a good term. Only time will tell if my prayers will be answered.

PART TWO

Surgery

April 8

Yesterday was my first day as a surgical intern. The good news is that I will be able to park right next to hospital every day. The bad news is that this is because I have to be at work by 6:45am. I have never been an early riser so this term is really going to be a challenge.

My fellow intern is Alternaria. She turned up to the ward looking as sleepy as I felt.

"Getting up this early just can't be good for you," she said, yawning.

"I hear you, girlfriend," I replied.

In complete contrast to the two of us, a man with wavy dark hair wearing operating theatre blues marched into the room looking remarkably fresh.

"Ah, good morning," he exclaimed cheerfully, shaking hands with us enthusiastically. "I'm Dr. Rodrigo Papas, the Surgical Registrar. You must be the new interns."

We nodded and introduced ourselves.

"Sorry if I seem a bit dopey. I'm twenty-four hours into a thirty-six hour shift. Didn't get to sleep last night due to a lot of operating. Had a few coffees to keep going." Presumably due to the 'few' coffees that he had consumed, he was hopping about like a rabbit. All he needed were the floppy ears, cottontail and buckteeth to complete the transformation.

"I hope that you both enjoy this term. You're going to learn a lot of things over the next few months, but here's your first lesson."

We took out our notepads in anticipation of his words of wisdom.

"Remember that there are three types of people in this world: there are surgeons, those who want to be surgeons and the mentally ill."

"The mentally ill?" asked Alternaria.

"Yes, the mentally ill," said Rodrigo. "Those people who don't want to be surgeons."

"So you class physicians as mentally ill?" I asked dumbfounded.

"Mad. Absolutely mad," said Rodrigo. He placed his face centimetres from mine, paused and yelled, "MAD!" causing me to jump in fright.

Rodrigo went on to tell us about the term.

"Professor Bonkzalot is a general surgeon with an interest in colorectal and breast surgery. He is a hard master but you will find the term rewarding if you put in the hours. Dr. Hart is a cardiothoracic surgeon and Dr. Chow does ENT but they only operate once a fortnight so you'll see much more of Professor Bonkzalot. Dr. Burkina is a vascular surgeon and Dr. Faso is a plastic surgeon, but you will not be working for them. The Ophthalmology unit is separate."

Alternaria giggled.

"What's so funny?" asked Rodrigo.

"It's just their names... Dr. Burkina and Dr. Faso. Burkina Faso – like the African nation."

Rodrigo clearly wasn't amused. "Lesson number two: don't make fun of surgeons' names."

Rodrigo continued. "I have my Fellowship exams in two months. Therefore, I will be busy operating to fill up my logbook. When I am not operating, I will be studying for my written exams. I expect you to look after the ward patients and only call me in the direst emergency. Any questions?"

I wasn't sure whether I was in a hospital or a military boot camp. I half expected to be ordered to do a hundred push-ups followed by target practice.

We did the ward round with Rodrigo. There were about twenty-five patients. He spent about two minutes with each one. Alternaria frantically scribbled in the patient's notes while I filled in blood and radiology forms as quickly as possible, trying to keep up with Rodrigo's numerous requests. We finished at 8am.

"I've got an all-day theatre list now with Professor Bonkzalot. We will need one of you to assist while the other does the ward work. Alternaria, you can come with me. Give Manju your pager."

And off they went, leaving me with twenty-five patients in varying degrees of ill health. Despite Smegman and Lucky giving us a handover of the patients last Friday, I really didn't feel like I knew any of them at all. I stared at the list of tests and consultations that I still had to arrange, thinking how long that was going to take me. Then the pagers started going off with nurses wanting IV fluids for this person, analgesia for that person, reviews of infected surgical sites, low blood pressures and high blood pressures. It was horrible! I went non-stop till 5pm tying up every loose end. I didn't have anything to drink; in fact, I didn't even pee. Then, when I thought I could finally go home, the pagers went off again. The seven patients for tomorrow's operating list had arrived and needed to be admitted. An exhausting three hours later, I headed to the lift, eager to go home.

As the lift doors opened, I saw Professor Bonkzalot, Rodrigo and Alternaria emerge, still wearing their operating theatre blues.

"Is that the other intern?" asked Bonkzalot to Rodrigo.

"Yes, Professor," he replied. "This is Dr. Mendis."

"Hello Sir. Pleased to meet you," I said, extending my hand.

He stared at my hand as if I had leprosy before ignoring it completely.

"Did you ask the Registrar if you could go home?"

"No, Professor. It's 8 o'clock and I have finished all..."

"Never ever leave this place without telling the Registrar. Do you understand me, boy?"

"Yes, Sir."

"Now, come on. I want to see Mr. Sanderson."

I wistfully watched the elevator doors close as the four of us trudged back to the ward. Alternaria and I kept a respectful two paces behind Bonkzalot and Rodrigo. I quickly looked at Lucky and Smegman's handover notes: Mr. Sanderson was day seven post colectomy for a localized colorectal cancer.

Bonkzalot greeted him and examined his abdominal wound. "It's healing nicely, Mr. Sanderson."

The patient said, "That's good to hear. So can I go home tomorrow Professor?"

"Well, have you passed wind yet?"

"Not yet, Professor."

"As I explained before, I have to hear you pass wind before I can let you go. You know the rule: 'Fart, then Depart'."

Looking dreadfully disappointed, Mr. Sanderson nodded in acquiescence.

As we left the room, I needed to clarify something. "Excuse me, Professor. Did you say that you *personally* need to hear the patient pass wind before they can go home?"

"Yes, boy. Patients who undergo bowel surgery develop an ileus postoperatively. Didn't they teach you anything at medical school? Their bowels don't work immediately after surgery. I need to know that they are working again before they can go home," he said impatiently.

"Professor, I know that. But isn't it enough if the patient reports to us that he passed wind or if I hear him pass wind and report it to you?"

"No, it's not. Patients will say anything to leave hospital, including lie to us. Secondly, if all the junior staff are as stupid as you and your colleague here, I certainly won't take your word for it either."

Then, without so much as a 'thank you' or 'goodbye' to the two of us, Bonkzalot and Rodrigo left the ward.

Alternaria looked absolutely stuffed.

"How was surgery?" I asked.

"Horrible," she said. "I spent about nine hours holding a retractor so Bonkzalot and Rodrigo could see what they were doing. My muscles are so sore. Lucky was right – Bonkzalot is a horrible man. He made sexist remarks to the nurses on a number of occasions. They seemed to be used to it but I wasn't. And a couple of times, he leant on my breasts during surgery. I'm sure that it was deliberate, not accidental. Oh well, he won't be the first male sexist pig that I have had to deal with. How were the wards?"

"Horrible," I echoed with feeling as I explained the ghastly day to her.

"Hopefully, it'll get easier with time," said Alternaria.

"Hopefully," I said without much optimism.

Exhausted, I headed back to the elevators. On this occasion, my escape was not thwarted. I drove home and Thaththa opened the door for me close to 9pm. He seemed very upbeat.

"Ah, the young doctor comes home very late! So son, what great things did you learn on your first day of surgery?"

In a daze, I looked at him as I climbed the stairs. "Lesson 1: There are three types of people in the world – surgeons, those who want to be surgeons and the mentally ill. Lesson 2: Don't make fun of a surgeon's name. Lesson 3: Fart, then depart."

Leaving my father completely baffled, I went to my room, removed my clothes and climbed into bed. Despite not eating lunch or dinner, I fell asleep in an instant.

April 14

I have survived my first week of surgery. It is still dreadfully busy but Alternaria and I have become more efficient with time. We are generally able to leave by 6:30 in the evening. Finding time for lunch is a big problem so I make sure that I have a good breakfast. Today, I met the other surgeons for whom we work, Dr. Hart and Dr. Chow. They are both quite pleasant. There are still a number of downsides. Firstly, Rodrigo is so busy preparing for his Fellowship exams that he is fairly inaccessible. Then there's the issue of Bonkzalot. He really is an unpleasant fellow. He barely acknowledges the existence of the interns. When he does so, it is usually to humiliate us in front of a patient because we couldn't remember some obscure blood result or other fact.

Today, Alternaria arrived in the doctors' room carrying a ukulele. She told me that this rotation was really starting to get her down. So she was going to use her panacea, music, to brighten up the term. I'm glad that I'm working with Alternaria. She really is a breath of fresh air. I only hope that Bonkzalot doesn't break her spirit.

Finishing my ward work, I remained at hospital to meet up with Vicki, the gynaecology registrar, to discuss the photo quiz. After an extensive internet search, we concluded that there had been no published reports in medical literature about carrots being used as contraceptives. So we decided to submit to one of the more prestigious medical journals, *The Lancet*. I told Vicki that I was more than happy to have a go at the first draft. She thanked me since she, like Rodrigo, had exams coming up.

"So once you've specialized, Vicki, do you think you'll do obstetrics or just stick to gynaecology?"

"A lot of O+G specialists stick solely to gynaecology to avoid the hectic lifestyle associated with obstetrics. I don't want to be one of those obstetricians delivering babies in the middle of the night. So it's vaginacology for me."

"What did you say?" I asked startled.

"It's vaginacology for me," she repeated.

"Oh, not you too! Isn't the term gynaecology?" I asked.

"It is," she conceded. "But I've heard people using the term vaginacology recently. It makes more sense – women have a vagina after all."

Vicki, do you know an intern called Peter Ivanov?" I asked suspiciously.

"No. Why do you ask?"

"Oh, don't worry. It's nothing."

Was the whole world going insane? Vaginacologists today – who knows what tomorrow? I shuddered at the thought.

April 17

As medical students, we watched doctors answering their pagers and yearned for the day when we too could carry our own pager. It was a status symbol of a medical degree. I was therefore mystified in my final year of medical school when a young unmarried intern held up his pager in front of me and said, "This is a mortgage and three kids."

I didn't understand this remark at the time and thought him quite unsound. As a surgical intern, I am paged between fifty and a hundred times per day. I calculated that I spend about one and a half hours on the telephone answering these pagers, many of which concern tasks of which I was already aware. Whether you use the metaphor of the 'mortgage and three kids' or a millstone, there is little doubt that a pager is a frightful burden, something that denies you even a moment of privacy. I can't even go to the toilet without the wretched thing going off.

Over the last two days, Alternaria and I have become so fed up with our pagers that we decided to destroy them. She dumped hers in the toilet. I, on the other hand, am more adventurous and dropped it from the ninth floor balcony. To our dismay, neither pager was even scratched. Spike, a surgical resident, walked into the doctors' room as we were discussing this remarkable phenomenon.

"Ah yes, let me guess... surgical interns trying to destroy their pagers?"

I nodded in the affirmative.

"This happens every year without fail," he said.

I explained what we had done to them. "They seem indestructible."

"They are. If you had done this to pagers from other hospitals in the city, they would have broken. St. Ivanhoe, though, has privately contracted their pagers from the company that makes black boxes for aeroplanes."

"You mean the black box recording that survives every crash?" asked Alternaria.

"That's the one. You haven't got a hope in hell of destroying them," concluded Spike.

Alternaria and I accepted our lot with fairly good grace and carried on working and answering our pagers. After all, what else could we do?

April 18

Bonkzalot did another late ward round after his operating list today. He was keen to see Ms. Pringle. She had undergone a sigmoid colectomy five days ago because of troublesome diverticular disease. And I finally witnessed it...

"Mrs. Pringle, your wound looks good."

"So can I go home, Professor?"

"You know what I need to hear before you can go home," said Bonkzalot.

She smiled excitedly. "I do, Professor, and I've been practising all day."

Ms. Pringle's face took on an expression of intense concentration. She pursed her lips, closed her eyes and clenched her fists in one mighty effort. Then it happened... a short high-pitched squeak that was unmistakably the passage of wind.

She squealed excitedly. "Did you hear it Professor? Did you hear it?"

"Yes, yes woman. Very good. You may go home," said Professor Bonkzalot waving his hands at her dismissively.

I had never seen a surgeon demand this before of a patient. Alternaria and I thought the whole concept rather odd. Anyway, I didn't mind finishing late tonight since I was rostered as the after-hours doctor for the surgical wards. I was due to finish only at 11pm. Poor Alternaria though, looked like she really needed a good night's sleep.

April 30

Today was the first operating list of Dr. Hart, the cardiothoracic surgeon. It was Alternaria's turn to stay on the wards so I accompanied Dr. Hart and Rodrigo to the operating theatre. So far, I had hated operating. Or rather, I hated *assisting* the people operating. Basically, Bonkzalot and Rodrigo did all the surgery. All I got to do was hold a retractor so they could visualize the surgical field. The only occasions on which I did anything other than retract was when I had to cut a suture for them. Even this was a drama because I am left-handed and the scissors are only for right-handed people. So there would often be multiple attempts at cutting before I was successful, resulting in a mouthful of abuse from Bonkzalot. His favourite insults were "You cut like a girl", "My demented grandmother could have made a better surgeon" and "That dyke intern (referring to Alternaria) is twice the doctor you are." Mind you, I don't have a problem with being told that Alternaria is a better doctor than me, because it's probably true!

Dr. Hart's operating session was thankfully a different kettle of fish. Being a cardiothoracic surgeon, he was particularly paranoid about surgical infections. Rodrigo was the only doctor allowed to scrub in with him. Yet Dr. Hart felt a sense of duty to teach the interns something about operating. Today he had brought three pigs' hearts from his lab at the university along with some vein grafts. He briefly instructed me on how a coronary artery bypass graft is performed. Then I remained in a corner of the operating theatre performing a CABG on the pig's heart while he and Rodrigo operated on the real patient. It was great fun! I don't think the pig would have survived had its life been in my hands, but that wasn't the point. For the first time in my life, I enjoyed my time in the operating theatre.

In the afternoon, I had to attend a consulting session in Professor Bonkzalot's rooms. Susan Stoker had told us that we had to do this once a term to fulfil the postgraduate council requirements for internship. His private rooms were just opposite the hospital so it was a quick jaunt across the road. On entering the waiting room, I was met by an extraordinary sight. A middle-aged man lay on the floor, writhing in agony, while a red-faced Bonkzalot stood above him yelling, "*YOU DO NOT HAVE ABDOMINAL PAIN. GET OUT OF MY ROOMS, YOU BLOODY MALINGERER.*"

The man, refusing to admit to any subterfuge, crawled on his hands and knees out the door, which I held open for him.

With some trepidation, I approached the Professor and explained why I was here.

"What utter bullshit! You should be in the hospital looking after my patients, not sitting here with me. The Postgraduate Council has a lot to answer for – bunch of bloody communists!"

Despite this outburst, he led me into his office, gave me a chair in the corner, told me to keep quiet and shut up. For the next three hours, I watched him assess fifteen patients, most of them privately insured. They had a variety of bowel and breast complaints. Alternaria and I had always assumed that he was much nicer to his clinic patients, especially to the privately insured ones. But we were wrong – he treated everyone like dirt. Ironically, this insight into him made me feel much better. The problem wasn't with me – it was with him. I made it a point to tell this to Alternaria whose self-esteem had plummeted during this term.

When the last patient left, Bonkzalot dropped a coin on the floor which rolled under the examination bed. I bent down to pick it up. Not only did I find the coin under the bed but also a bright red bra.

"Sir, this was under the bed," I said, holding up the bra.

He looked at it briefly and called his secretary through the intercom. "Linda, it's happened again. Call all the women from this afternoon and ask them if they've forgotten anything. Thank God I'm not a gynaecologist – they'd probably all leave their panties behind."

"You mean vaginacologist," I murmured without thinking.

Bonkzalot turned to me, looking clearly annoyed. "Vaginacologist? What sort of idiotic word is that? Get out of here. The show's over. Back to work, you lazy bum!"

I left his rooms thankful that I'd never have to visit there again.

May 12

I had another overtime shift on the surgical wards. At about 7pm, my pager went off. It was a number that I didn't recognize. This surprised me as I thought I knew all the ward extension numbers by now. I dialled the number.

"Hello. This is Nurse Watson."

"Hello. It's the overtime intern. I was paged."

"Thank you. I've got a patient to be admitted on the tenth floor when you get a chance."

The tenth floor – it was an admission to Spyder Croquet's Celebrity Ward. How exciting! I caught the lift and Elevator Grooved all the way to the top to the tune of Who Let the Dogs Out? by the Baha Men.

I went to the nurses' station and introduced myself to Nurse Watson, a plump red-faced lady in her early sixties.

"Nice to meet you," Nurse Watson said. "I suspect you might recognize our latest patient."

I thanked her and walked to the patient's room at the other end of the ward. After taking a deep breath, I knocked on the oak door and entered the room. And there, sitting in bed was Salma Cruze, Hollywood star and, in my opinion, one of the most beautiful women in the world.

"Hello," she said with the famous smile that made me weak at the knees.

"Naaa. Naaa," I couldn't speak! Panic overtook me as I tried again, to no avail. "Naaaa."

"Naa?" she asked looking perplexed.

I was so intimidated by the presence of this screen diva that I lost the ability to form words. But thankfully, after an almighty effort, the power of speech returned to me. "I mean, nice to meet you, Ms. Cruze. I'm Dr. Manju Mendis, the overtime intern and I'm here to admit you to the ward. I'm also a big fan."

She held out her hand, which I eagerly shook. I had just shaken hands with Salma Cruze! I'd have to pinch myself to make sure this wasn't a dream.

"Why did you just pinch yourself?" she asked me with a puzzled look.

Oh my God! I had just pinched myself right in front of her. I made a desperate and silent plea to Mr. Brain to start working again. "Oh, it's this involuntary tic that I have. I just start pinching things sometimes. But I only pinch myself and not other people," I hurriedly clarified as a look of alarm appeared on her face.

To overcome my nerves, I took refuge in our respective roles as doctor and patient. It turned out that Salma was here filming her latest movie. She had developed some chest pain on the set, which had taken an inordinately long time to settle down. I quizzed her about the nature of the pain: its site, its quality, whether it radiated anywhere, what exacerbated it, what made it better and whether she had experienced it before. I examined her and looked at her chest x-ray and a series of ECGs performed through the day when she had the pain.

"It sounds like reflux oesophagitis, Ms. Cruze," I said.

"Dr. Croquet was worried about Prinzmetal's angina," she said to me.

"Oh, of course, Prinzmetal's angina is a possibility," I diplomatically said, although in truth I was surprised at Croquet's diagnosis.

"Anyway, I'm having a whole battery of tests tomorrow: an echocardiogram, a gastroscopy and a sestamibi scan. So we'll know if you are right or not."

A smartly-dressed woman in her forties walked into the room. Salma introduced her. "Dr. Mendis, this is my PA, Karol Keyes. Karol, this is the intern who's admitting me. He doesn't agree with Dr. Croquet's diagnosis. Dr. Mendis thinks that I have reflux."

"An intern disagreeing with the brilliant Dr. Croquet? How very brave indeed. I wonder how Dr. Croquet will react when we tell him," said Karol Keyes.

"No. I didn't say that I disagreed with Dr. Croquet at all," I hurriedly clarified, thinking how angry Croquet would be if he ever learnt that I questioned his diagnosis in front of his patient.

Both Salma and Karol laughed.

Salma said, "You must forgive Karol's sense of humour. She's only teasing you – we won't breathe a word to Dr. Croquet. Mind you, Dr. Mendis, I think that you are right. My initial thought was that I had reflux. I don't know where Dr. Croquet picked Prinzmetal's angina from. I just wanted to start some proton pump inhibitors and begin filming again, but Dr. Croquet insisted on all these other tests."

I was surprised by the perceptiveness of her remarks. "If you don't think it presumptuous of me, Ms. Cruze, you seem to know more than the average layperson about this."

She smiled that famous smile, making me weak at the knees once more. "Would it surprise you to learn that I graduated from medical school six years ago with Second Class Honours? I am a qualified doctor. Medicine runs in the family – my father is an immunologist and my mother a haematologist."

I was stunned. "I never knew that."

"Most people don't. It's not that I purposely hide it but I don't make a big fuss about it either. A lot of powerful male Hollywood executives don't feel comfortable dealing with an intelligent woman, especially one from an ethnic minority. So I just play the 'dumb blonde' and don't flash my medical degree about. One day, when I'm a bit more established, I'll throw my weight around more."

"Will you ever go back to medicine?"

"I don't think so. As soon as I finished my final exams, I made the decision to enter the film industry. So I've never worked as a doctor. I've forgotten so much medicine since then that it would take me years to get up to scratch again. Anyway, life isn't exactly bad at the moment."

Given that she had been paid twenty million dollars for 'My Life as a Goat,' I had to agree with her.

"By the way, congratulations on the Oscar," I said.

The most famous scandal in Oscar history had concluded. The Academy had spent twenty-four hours behind closed doors to resolve who the true winner of 'Actress in a Leading Role' was. They eventually ruled that Salma should be the sole recipient of the Oscar since the Academy had originally and officially declared her the winner. After all, it was her name inside the envelope.

"Thanks," said Salma. "They should make a movie about the whole drama. I still can't believe it. Faye Scarlet is barely on speaking terms with me even though none of this was my fault. All because of that Lupie Karmeleon. Well, she's a *persona non grata* in Hollywood at the moment."

"Why did Lupie do it?" I automatically asked, immediately regretting my question. "Sorry, Ms. Cruze, that's none of my business. I shouldn't have asked."

"Everything we say is confidential because of the doctor-patient privilege, isn't it?"

"Yes, it is," I said, even though I wasn't that sure.

"Okay then," said Salma. "It's all to do with Zebus."

"Zebers," I asked mystified.

"No. Z-E-B-U-S – zebus."

"I don't understand," I said, still perplexed.

"You may not believe this but Lupie and I used to get on quite well. In January, we were both flying from New York to London. We decided to pass the time playing Scrabble. With my final letters, I made the word zebus. It's a type of ox. I got a triple-word score, giving me a grand total of forty-eight points, enough to win the game. From there, it was simply a case of sour grapes. Lupie declared that there was no such word as zebus and that I was a cheating Hispanic who couldn't speak English properly. She was really quite nasty about the whole thing. I wish that I'd had a dictionary that I could have shoved in her face to prove her wrong. But there wasn't one. Anyway, to cut a long story short, she never forgave me."

I was incredulous. "All this over a game of Scrabble?"

Salma said, "Most Hollywood celebrities are fairly level-headed. But some of them lose touch with reality and take caprice and petulance to another level entirely. Lupie definitely falls into the latter category."

I shook my head in bewilderment and bid goodbye to Salma and

Karol, expressing what a pleasure it had been to meet them. Although meeting Salma Cruze had been one of the greatest moments of my life, I left the room pondering one thing: how on earth could Spyder Croquet think that Salma had Prinzmetal's angina when she so obviously had reflux?

May 14

I met everyone for dinner yesterday. Smegman and Delilah were working together in Emergency. Copper, Lucky and Peter were the medical interns. They all seemed to be happy in their new roles, particularly Smegman and Lucky, who were glad to be rid of Bonkzalot.

"I love surgery," said Smegman. "But I can't handle Professor Bonkzalot."

After the small talk had finished, I dropped the bombshell of how I met Salma Cruze the night before. You should have seen their reaction. Stunned silence gave way to an outpouring of questions. I had no ethical dilemma about discussing her case with my fellow doctors but I made a point not to mention Lupie Karmeleon and the Scrabble game.

"Is she really as beautiful in real life?" Lucky asked.

I told them that even without an ounce of make-up, she was the most beautiful woman that I'd ever met.

"She seems like a bimbo on screen. What's she really like?" asked Alternaria.

"Well, she only got 2nd Class Honours at medical school so she's not as bright as Delilah or Smegman," I said in a deliberately blasé manner.

There was an even longer stunned pause this time. Then the outpouring of questions began.

"You mean she's a doctor?" "She's like us?" "She got Honours?"

I patiently addressed each question. We all concluded that Salma Cruze possessed a combination of brains and beauty that would be rarely encountered in this world – or the next, for that matter.

I described her symptoms and asked each of them what they thought. The opinion was unanimous – they all agreed that Salma Cruze had reflux oesophagitis.

"That's what I thought too. But Spyder Croquet told her that he was worried about Prinzmetal's angina."

My colleagues looked shocked. Copper said, "But she never had nocturnal symptoms. None of her ECGs showed ST-segment elevation. And the pain is typical of reflux oesophagitis."

"I know," I said.

"How could such a brilliant physician as Spyder Croquet make such a dumb diagnosis?" Delilah asked. "Even a medical student would know better."

"Maybe he is so brilliant that he's picked up some obscure feature that we missed?"

"Maybe that's it," said Delilah unconvincingly.

I returned to hospital after dinner to finish off a couple of discharge summaries for tomorrow. I had forgotten to turn my pager off and it started buzzing when I reached the hospital. Irritated that someone had the temerity to page me at such a late hour, I was about to turn it off when I looked at the extension – it was from the Celebrity Ward. I called immediately.

"Dr. Mendis, it's Nurse Watson. We weren't sure if you would still be here at this late hour. Ms. Cruze is about to go home. She just wanted to say goodbye. Are you able to come or shall I say that you are too busy?"

"Oh, I think I should be able to squeeze her in for a few minutes," I said. I put the phone down and sprinted to the elevator. When I reached Salma's room somewhat out of breath, I found her and Karol Keyes all packed and ready to leave.

She smiled when she saw me. "Oh, Dr. Mendis. I'm so glad you're working late. I just wanted to say goodbye and tell you that you were right."

"I was right?" I asked.

"Yes, the gastroscopy showed reflux oesophagitis. Dr. Croquet put me on omeprazole so I'll be fine. Your diagnosis was correct. I'm very impressed that you went with your instinct on this one despite Dr. Croquet's alternative diagnosis."

I was quite humbled. "Thank you, Ms. Cruze. And while I wish you all the best in the movie industry, I suspect that my profession has lost a good doctor."

"He's sweet, isn't he," said Salma to Karol. "Good luck, Dr. Mendis," she said as she got into the elevator.

As the doors closed, I quietly said, "Of all the hospitals in all the towns in all the world, she walks into mine."

I went home feeling pretty special. It only got better this morning when I found an envelope in my locker. It contained a black and white photo of Salma. On it, she had written a message: "Dr. Manju Mendis, thanks again for looking after me. I think that you will be a really great doctor one day. Love and kisses. Salma Cruze."

For the rest of the day, Rodrigo and Bonkzlaot were in foul moods and the wards were ridiculously busy. But, as I kept recalling those beautifully written words, I didn't care one iota. It was great to be alive and wonderful to be a doctor.

May 20

I came desperately close to losing my job today on account of Mr. Clause. He is a lovely, old, World War II veteran who underwent bowel surgery a week ago. He was desperately keen to go home by today at the latest on account of a special function. Tomorrow will mark sixty-five years since he and his battalion pulled off an amazing victory in Europe. Their efforts were never acknowledged up till now for security reasons. Only five others from the battalion are still alive. The six of them are meeting the Prime Minister tomorrow who will honour them and their fallen comrades in a special ceremony. In Mr. Clause's words, "This is the most important thing left for me to do. Once I've done it, I can die happy. If I can't go, then I'd rather be dead."

The problem was Bonkzalot's policy of wanting to hear the patient pass wind before sending him home. I had been encouraging Mr. Clause to do so for the last few days. Yesterday, he finally passed wind in front of me, but was unable to repeat the performance in front of the Professor. This afternoon's ward round with Bonkzalot was his last chance. I guess that he could have discharged himself against medical advice but Mr. Clause wasn't that kind of man – he respected the medical profession far too much to do so.

Anyway, Professor Bonkzalot arrived on the ward around 6pm. Mr. Clause was unable to pass wind for the Professor despite his best efforts. The poor man pleaded with him. "Please Professor, let me go home. I need to attend the ceremony tomorrow. It means everything to me. Dr. Mendis heard me pass wind yesterday," he said, pointing at me.

Without so much as batting an eyelid, Bonkzalot heartlessly replied, "No. I personally need to hear you pass wind. If you can't do that, then that's the end of the matter."

Bonkzalot and Rodrigo turned away from Mr. Clause, leaving him devastated. I couldn't stand to see this old man's spirit broken, so in a moment of desperation, I made a decision. Straining my abdominal muscles in one mighty effort, I ripped a fart. Loud, long and low-pitched, it was truly magnificent.

The Professor turned around immediately.

"Congratulations, Mr. Clause," I cried in delight. "What a beauty!"

Bonkzalot looked suspiciously at me and went straight back to Mr. Clause. "Mr. Clause, was it you who passed wind just now?"

I prayed and prayed that Mr. Clause would take the lifeline that I had thrown his way; otherwise, I was in serious trouble.

He paused for a moment. Then he smiled, seemingly delighted, and said, "Yes Professor. Who else could it have been? Can I go home now?"

The Professor gave him a curt nod and grunted something that sounded like "yes."

For the remainder of the round, I would glance up every now and then to find Bonkzalot staring at me thoughtfully. I could tell that he was suspicious about the events surrounding Mr. Clause but thankfully, he didn't voice his concerns.

After Rodrigo and Bonkzalot left, I told Alternaria the truth. Delighted, she high-fived me.

"That's brilliant, Manju! Had you been planning it for a while?"

"Nope. Very much a spontaneous act," I modestly replied.

"So you can fart at will?" she asked, sounding amazed.

"It's a guy thing," I said.

"Thank goodness I'm a lesbian," she replied, laughing.

We both went back to see Mr. Clause. He shook my hand with tears in his eyes. "Dr. Mendis, I'm a lucky man. In the war, my colleagues gave their lives for me. Later on, my brother gave his kidney for me. And now, you have farted for me. Few men have been so blessed. Thank you so much."

"It's nothing," I said. "I just want you to go and enjoy that ceremony tomorrow."

Then suddenly I heard music. I turned around to see Alternaria strumming her ukulele before bursting into song.

> Oh Mr Clause isn't Santa Claus
> But I bet he thinks it's Christmas
> He played his part
> Lied 'bout a fart
> He took the truth and twist it
>
> Now that he's passed some wind
> There's no need for stressing
> Cause when old Monty heard him fart
> He gave his immediate blessing
>
> To Go Home! Go Home!
> Get out of here Man
> If you farted in this hospital
> You better leave as fast as you can

We all clapped in delight as Alternaria sang it again. Old Mr. Clause even did a little sailor's jig around his bed as the nurses and other patients in the room looked on laughing.

When she finished, I gave Alternaria a hug. "I might be able to fart spontaneously, but I could never do that. How did you come up with that song so quickly?"

She smiled. "There aren't any professional musicians in our family but music was an intimate part of our life when growing up. It's a second language to me I guess. So it doesn't take me long to put a song together."

I puffed up with feigned self-importance. "There aren't any professional farters in our family either but farting was an intimate part of our life when growing up. It's a second language to me too."

We both laughed.

Then her beaming face transformed into one of great sadness. "You know, Manju, over the past few weeks there's been so much lifesaving surgery happening around us. Yet it is only now, after deceiving Bonkzalot into sending Mr. Clause home, that I actually feel that I have achieved something here. Is there something wrong with me to feel that way?"

"If there is something wrong with you, Alternaria, then there's something wrong with me too – because I feel exactly the same way. And I think Lucky and Smegman felt the same when they were in this job. I don't know why Bonkzalot chose surgery all those years ago, whether he was ever a kind or compassionate man. All I know is that his soul has turned into some kind of vacuum that sucks the joy and hope from all those around him. It's almost like a malignancy that relentlessly invades and destroys everything within its reach. I fear that we'll have few moments to celebrate this term, Alternaria. We'll just have to put up with it."

Tears came to her eyes. "I don't know if I can, Manju. I don't know if I can."

I put my arm around her and reassured her as best as I could. We could survive this term – we had to.

June 1

I was sitting in front of the TV around 10am, preparing for a rare, relaxing Sunday. Then suddenly, like a juggernaut, Ammi raced through the room, shouting, "Get ready, Manju, we've got a morning tea to attend. We're leaving in twenty minutes."

"I don't want to come, Ammi. I just want a lazy day at home."

"Oh, I see. I have vertigo and your poor father is still getting over the flu. We can't drive. But if you have better things to do, then I'll call and cancel. It's hard for us old people to get around but what to do if you young people have TV to watch? Your aunt is always saying how happy Lal is to drive her around. But I guess that not all children are the same..."

Cursing my mother's shameless use of emotional blackmail, I got off the comfortable leather sofa and changed. In twenty minutes on the dot, all three of us were sitting in the car.

"Where to?" I asked.

"Use the computer thing," Ammi said pointing to the GPS. "Here's the address," she added, handing me a piece of paper.

"I've never been here before," I said to Ammi, puzzled as we began the journey.

"Yes, we're meeting new people."

A dreadful suspicion overcame me. "Thaththa, where are we going? Tell me the truth please."

My worst fears were confirmed. Thaththa reluctantly conceded, "It's to meet a new girl. Your mother is very keen on this introduction."

"Ammi, how could you arrange this without telling me?" I demanded angrily. "This is MY life, you know. I would like a say in it."

Although largely gone, some of the unpleasant memories of my time with Priyanthi still lingered. I didn't want things to end up like that again.

Ammi gave my father an earful. "Mahela, don't put this whole thing on me! I may have organized this meeting but you supported it wholeheartedly."

"Is that true, Thaththa?" I asked.

"Well, Manju. The girl sounds like she's a good catch," conceded my father.

"Don't they all?" I replied sarcastically. "What about the horoscopes?"

"We haven't matched them, Manju. But with such good people, I am sure that the horoscopes won't be a problem anyway."

That certainly took me by surprise. Ammi would normally never introduce me to anyone without first matching the horoscopes.

"Okay then, Ammi, I'll bite. What is so wonderful about these people that you don't need to match the horoscopes? Are they filthy rich or descended from royalty?"

"They are related to the Samaranayakes of Morton Close!" Ammi jubilantly declared, assuming that this piece of information would be sufficient to satisfy my curiosity. It wasn't.

"Ammi, who the hell are the 'Samaranayakes of Morton Close'? Are they related to the Windsors of Buckingham Palace by any chance?"

"They are the best people, I tell you. Old FD Samaranayake was Defence Minister and his sister married Perry Koch, the famous businessman and father of the Koch Cookie Empire. This girl's family must be wealthy beyond our wildest dreams, Manju. If they were wine, they'd be nothing less than that Chinese champagne."

"Chinese champagne?" I asked, perplexed.

"Yes, you know the one – Don Perry Wong."

"Ammi, perhaps you mean Dom Perignon?"

She shook her head and waved her hands dismissively. "Some bloody Chinese name – it doesn't matter. All you need to know is that they are the cream of the cream. Stop looking so morose and consider how lucky you are," Ammi continued with a sparkling whine.

I refused to take things lying down though. "Enough about the family. What about the girl?"

"Oh, she's twenty-two and quite pretty I believe. She's done some communications degree at university."

At least that was something! We drove on for a bit in silence.

"Not that the money's important, but if this family is so rich, why are they living in this part of the city?" I asked.

"What do you mean? Broadley Bay is a very upmarket neighbourhood, Manju."

"Yes, Ammi. *Broadley Bay* is a wealthy area. But they live in *Broadleigh* which is far from the lap of luxury."

Ammi pondered this for a moment. "How strange. Perhaps they bought there a long time ago and haven't been inclined to move. Yes, I am sure that they must have a mansion, the best house in the street."

Eventually, the GPS machine announced, "You have reached your destination." I parked the car in the driveway and we all got down. It certainly wasn't a mansion or the best house in the neighbourhood. There were many signs of neglect. The stone slabs of the driveway had been pushed up by protruding weeds. The front yard was overgrown with more weeds interspersed with barren areas of brown earth. Even the door of the wooden letterbox hung tenuously on one hinge. It looked like a war zone. I half expected to be overtaken by a jeep carrying a UN Peacekeeping Force.

"How very odd," remarked my mother. "Maybe they spent money on lots of investment properties."

"Perhaps people stopped buying Koch Cookies," my father remarked.

Thaththa knocked on the door. We heard hurried footsteps before the door was opened by a lady, presumably the mother, who greeted us warmly. She was dressed decently in a turtleneck sweater and a pair of jeans. Her hair was streaked with grey while her face was wrinkled and lined. It would have been a beautiful face once, but, at some point, life had been hard on Mrs. Samaranayake, and now it showed. As we walked through the small house that was modestly furnished, I got the impression that my aunt's reconnaissance mission had missed something: this was not a family who lived comfortably. I could tell by my parents' glances at each other that they were thinking the same thing.

Mrs. Samaranayake took us through to a lounge room. A sweet young girl in braces, who couldn't have been more than twelve, was smiling at us. My gaze moved to her left and my heart stopped beating. There stood the most beautiful woman that I have ever seen in all my life. Tall, with long silky black hair past her shoulders, an oval face with high cheekbones and a nose that Cleopatra would have been proud of. And the body – oh the body! But it was the eyes that entrapped me. When I met their jet-black gaze, it was as if I was sinking into an ebony whirlpool of ecstasy.

I shook her hand. "Nnaaa. Naaaa. Naa." Oh no, it was happening again!

"I beg your pardon?" she asked puzzled.

I took a deep breath and tried again. "Nice to meet you. My name's Manju."

"I'm Sundari," she said smiling. A friend once said that whenever his girlfriend smiled, all his troubles would melt away. At the time, I attributed his words to the joint he was smoking. But now, as Sundari smiled, I understood exactly what he meant.

The next twenty minutes were the most wonderful of my life. Sundari had finished a degree in Mass Media. I naturally assumed that someone as beautiful as her would want to be in front of a camera as a news anchor or interviewer. But instead her dream was to be behind the scenes directing a news show. She asked me how internship was going and we chatted about a variety of topics: global warming, cricket, oil prices – even The Simpsons. We had so much in common.

I had been so engrossed with chatting to Sundari that I had forgotten about our parents. I had just exchanged phone numbers with Sundari when, all of a sudden, her attention was drawn to the conversation that was taking place next to us. With a sigh of regret I took my eyes away from her beautiful face to find out what had distracted her.

"Oh, so you're not related to the Samaranayakes from Morton Close?" I heard my mother asking with some alarm.

"No. I don't think so," said Mrs. Samaranayake.

"What about the Samaranayakes in Monty Parade in Kandy? There are three doctors in that family and a sister was the Chair of the Monetary Board."

I cringed in horror at my mother's interrogation of this poor woman's background.

"No."

"Where is your good husband?"

A look of intense pain crossed her face and she told us that he had died last year from cancer. To my alarm, I saw Sundari's head bow with sorrow at the mention of this.

"Oh, I'm so sorry to hear that," my mother went on. Then barely missing a beat, she had the temerity to follow-up with, "And what did he do?"

Mrs. Samaranayake seemed taken aback by this. Then Sundari interjected. "My father was a gardener for the council."

My mother looked at Sundari, smiled and said, "Oh, how nice." I groaned inwardly. The tone in which my mother had said "Oh, how nice," would have been better served in response to "My son has his parole hearing next week," or "The diarrhoea's still there but it's getting more solid."

An awkward silence followed. Sundari, who only moments earlier had been chatting to me like an old friend, refused to look in my direction. My mother's lack of tact had, in a few moments, changed the whole dynamic of the conversation.

Mrs. Samaranayake quietly said, "You seem to have been misinformed about us, Mrs. Mendis. I apologize if we haven't met your expectations."

Sundari angrily said, "Ammi, don't..."

Mrs. Samaranayake interrupted her before she could finish, "Sundari, enough."

Sundari reluctantly obeyed her mother but I could tell that she was fuming. Her poor sister felt the tension in the room but was probably too young to understand the reasons behind it.

"What nonsense – no need to apologize," my mother cried with a beaming smile as she and my father stood up. "You have a lovely family and lovely house. It's been a pleasure meeting you all. We must meet again."

Oh, if there were prizes for insincerity...

I shook hands with Sundari's mother and sister and thanked them for their hospitality. Sundari offered a limp hand but refused to look at me, denying me a final gaze into those magnificent eyes.

When we got into the car, I yelled at my parents.

"How the hell can you treat people like that?"

"Don't get so worked up, Manju. They may be nice enough people but they are not suitable for you. It's my bloody sister's fault. She should have thoroughly verified her information before sending us out on this fool's errand."

"You didn't answer my question, Ammi. How could you have treated them so badly?"

"Don't be silly, Manju. You heard the mother apologize – she understands how things work."

"But this isn't Sri Lanka. In this country, everyone is equal."

"You have a lot to learn about life, Manju."

"Thaththa?" I asked my father, looking for some support.

"I'm sorry, Manju. Your mother's right. They are not suitable people."

I couldn't believe I was hearing this.

"Well, I'm going to call Sundari," I defiantly declared. "And we'll meet for coffee. No, perhaps I'll take her out for dinner."

"You'll do no such thing!" yelled my mother. "She is not good enough for you. I'll give you that she is quite pretty. But within five years and a couple of children, her hips will fatten and those boobs will sag. Looks aren't everything."

"Like you can sermonize on the importance of appearances."

"Enough, Manju! We will talk of this no further."

"Don't you have any sense of shame?" I persisted angrily. "Imagine what this would have done to their self-esteem."

Ammi brightened up. "Don't be silly. It is one of the qualities of low-class people – they are used to hard knocks and recover quite well."

The rest of the day was a confusion of emotions as I contemplated how, what should have been a perfect day, had ended in disaster. The only thing I know for certain is that for the first time in my life, I hate my mother.

June 2

"I hate my mother," I declared.

"Oh Manju, I'm so sorry. Remember that old proverb: you can choose your friends but not your relatives," said Delilah. "I don't think that there's anyone on earth who hasn't been embarrassed by a family member at one time or another."

This afternoon, I met Delilah and Lucky for coffee in the cafeteria. I told them about yesterday's encounter with Sundari and her family. They were very sympathetic and unanimously agreed that Ammi's conduct was appalling.

"Do you think that there is any hope for Sundari and me?"

"I really don't know," said Lucky. "But why don't you give her a call and apologize? The worst that can happen is that she'll reject you."

"Oh wonderful," I said without any enthusiasm.

"No, I'm serious. It's not like you've got anything to lose. You're starting from rock bottom anyway. Things can't get any worse – they can only get better."

"Lucky's right," followed Delilah. "You'll probably receive a torrent of abuse over the phone, but on the other hand, she might be impressed that you had the guts to apologize. But don't call her for a few days. Give her time to calm down. If you call her now at the height of her rage, it'll only end in disappointment."

"Okay then. I'll call her early next week."

Lucky asked, "But Manju, if things do work out and she wants to meet, then you'll be defying your parents. Are you ready to have *that* argument? Or will you see her behind their back?"

"Yes. No. I don't know. What a bloody mess!"

Lucky sighed. "I feel for you, Manju. You hear similar stories all the time in the Indian community too."

Despite my misery, Lucky's remark aroused my curiosity about her origins again.

"Lucky, forgive my boldness. But since I've known you, I've got an 'Indian vibe' from you. Do you have some connection with India? I'm sorry for being so intrusive but it's just been bugging me for sometime now."

Lucky actually went pale. "I have an 'Indian vibe'?" she asked, seemingly horrified at the prospect. "After all I've done..." she remarked enigmatically.

"Lucky, what do you mean?" Delilah asked.

Lucky bowed her head seemingly in defeat. "I guess it's okay to tell the two of you. But promise me that you won't tell anyone else about this."

Delilah and I acquiesced to her request.

Lucky took a deep breath and looked around to ensure that no one else was listening. Apparently satisfied that the area was secure, she proceeded to drop the following bombshell: "I wasn't born as 'Lucky King'."

Delilah and I paused as we digested this unanticipated piece of information.

"You mean you were born as a male and had a sex change? Larry King became Lucky King, perhaps?" I asked.

"Are you are in a Witness Protection Program?" asked Delilah.

"For heaven's sake. Both of you have got it completely wrong. I wasn't born as Lucky King or Larry King for that matter. I'm certainly not in Witness Protection. My name used to be Lakshmi Raja."

"So you *are* Indian!" I exclaimed.

"Not so loud," Lucky snapped at me.

"Sorry. It's just that when I first saw you on Orientation Day, I thought that there was something Indian about you. But your name, the blonde hair and blue eyes threw me off the scent."

"It was meant to. My father worked for the Department of Foreign

Affairs. When I was a child, he was posted in Eastern Europe. Usually, children of diplomats attend international schools along with kids from other diplomatic circles. But my father's posting wasn't in the capital – we lived in a small village in a regional province. There were no international schools there. I had to attend the local school. It soon became apparent that the language barrier wasn't the only thing that I faced. The kids there hadn't seen a brown child before. This, along with the fact that our diplomatic presence was resented by the locals, meant that school was a horrible experience for me. Kids can be cruel and for the next three years, I was racially vilified every single day. I had no friends. I never got invited to other children's homes on weekends. I stopped playing team sports because no one ever sent the ball to me –it was truly pathetic. I told my parents repeatedly but my father never took it seriously. Then one day, I got beaten up and urinated upon, after which my father had to take it seriously. The teachers however denied that there was a problem and even pointed the finger at me for not being able to effectively integrate. My father requested a transfer and we went to Madrid. That was much better but the damage had been done."

"Damage?"

"Yes. For the rest of my childhood, I tried to find ways to look like the white kids. I would stay out of the sun so my skin would remain light. I made a conscious effort to speak without an Indian accent and I stopped speaking Hindi. As soon as I was old enough, I dyed my hair blonde and got blue contact lenses."

"But surely the racial abuse stopped after you moved from that village?" I asked.

"It did. But you don't understand, Manju. When this happens to you day after day, when older kids keep telling you that you are inferior and not welcome because you are black, then of course it makes a lasting impression."

"What do your parents think?"

"They don't understand. They think that I'm nuts. There were arguments about seeing a psychiatrist but I never let them take me. Anyway, I haven't seen them since I started university."

"You haven't seen your parents for six years?" I asked incredulously.

"Yep. I went interstate to university. I suspect that my father was glad to see the back of his most peculiar child. As soon as I was accepted to university, I changed my name to Lucky King. I haven't been called Lakshmi Raja for six years now."

"Do you at least speak to your parents over the phone?"

Lucky shrugged. "Perhaps a handful of times a year. Anyway, even they call me Lucky, now."

"Have you ever dated an Indian guy?" Delilah asked.

"No. Just white guys."

"But you must be miserable," I said, trying to comprehend the enormity of this change to her life.

Lucky laughed. "Miserable? Are you crazy? I've never been so happy. I am Lucky King, the blonde, blue-eyed intern. Guys love how I look and I never get racially abused. The world is my oyster."

"Well, I never get racially abused either," I confidently declared. Then I remembered Patrick the bigot that awful nightshift in the ED. "Well – hardly ever, anyway."

"For me it's not hardly-ever. It's never, Manju."

Delilah said, "If you're so happy, Lucky, then why did you just tell us all this? It sounds like you wanted to get this off your chest."

"No, Delilah. You misunderstand. If I hadn't told this to you now, Manju might have voiced his suspicions to the others and many more people would have gotten involved. Now the damage is contained to just the two of you."

"Oh, okay," Delilah replied, sounding baffled.

Just then, my pager went off. It was the ward wanting me to admit tomorrow's surgical cases. "Oh well, back to work, I guess," I said, standing up.

I thanked them for their advice regarding Sundari and left.

If the purpose of meeting with Lucky and Delilah had been to distract my mind from the issue of Sundari, it had been successful beyond my wildest dreams. For the rest of the day, I just couldn't get Lucky out of my mind. How could she be so blasé about what she had done? How could she so casually shrug off her heritage, her identity, the fundamental core of her being? And why did it bother me so much? Late at night, while watching TV alone, it hit me. I was not just bothered by what Lucky had done – I was offended. The South Asian culture and heritage she had rejected did not belong only to her. No, it belonged to me too. In rejecting her background, she was also rejecting mine. In many ways, Lucky is a far worse bigot than Patrick because, despite what she claims, she is still one of us.

June 4

I must be in love. The temporary solace provided by Lucky's revelation has eroded away as thoughts and images of Sundari relentlessly batter my mind. Last night, I slept poorly, twisting and turning as Sundari's bewitching smile invaded my dreams again and again.

Even the hectic pace at work hasn't been free from her. In those brief moments, those few seconds of free time, I find my mobile phone in my hands, looking at her phone number. Like a suicidal man with a gun to his head, I torture myself over whether or not to push the 'Call' button. Then the pager goes off and I return to reality.

I ran into Delilah in ED. She took me aside and asked me what I thought of Lucky's secret. I was honest and said that I found it both disturbing and offensive. I asked Delilah if she thought that Lucky is as genuinely happy as she claims.

"I don't think so, Manju. I don't blame her for her attitude though. It sounds like she was truly traumatized as a child. But this is nothing more than a defence mechanism – a massive case of denial. I'm amazed that she's been able to carry it for so long. But I know one thing for sure: she needs to confront this problem at some stage otherwise it's going to blow up in her face. We should try and help her."

"It sounds like she doesn't want to be helped," I replied.

"Possibly. But she clearly hasn't shunned the whole South Asian culture. She obviously regards you as a friend and has never tried to avoid you. You should use that to your advantage."

"What should I do?"

"If I knew that, Manju, my name would be in big bright lights around the city and I'd have my own talk show. Let me know if you think of anything. By the way, are you still going to call Sundari?"

"I really don't know, Delilah. I yearn to see her so badly that you can't imagine. But I don't know if calling her would be a good thing for either of us."

"Boy, it's tough," she said.

"How is it working out with Smegman in ED? Is he driving you crazy?"

Delilah smiled. "Actually, he's been unexpectedly pleasant. I think that Lucky playing the 'Hooters' t-shirt joke on him was a sobering experience. He has opened up a lot more and I'm really enjoying working with him. He told me his life story. It turns out that he came from a very wealthy family where academic achievement was paramount."

"It sounds a bit like a South Asian family," I said.

"Yes, except that South Asians are very social people with extensive networks of friends and relatives. Smegman's parents were very aloof and mixed with very few people. And while they provided Marcus with a lot of material resources, I suspect that he was starved of affection. The poor boy's been socially isolated for most of his life. That's why he's so awkward and inappropriate around people. But as I said, he seems to be coming out of his shell. I genuinely like him now."

"Wow," I said with surprise.

"Also, Marcus may be the first person I've ever met who is brighter than me. Sorry if that sounds arrogant but I'm saying it to show how intelligent he is."

"Get out of here!" I cried, genuinely shocked. I couldn't imagine anybody being brighter than Delilah Convex.

"No, I'm serious. He has an amazing mind that can grab the most difficult concepts and twist them into something simple. If he lightens up a bit more, he'll be an extraordinary teacher."

First I learn that Lucky is Indian and now that Smegman might actually be nice. Was the whole world turning upside down?

June 9

This evening I called Sundari. Last night, like some inexperienced teenager speaking to a girl for the first time, I wrote down a script of the anticipated conversation. I planned to read off the sheet of paper while on the phone. It would give me a sense of security and confidence that I desperately needed, like the netting below a trapeze artist just in case he fell. I couldn't believe how nervous I was. Throughout the day at work, I had been rehearsing the conversation in my head over and over again. In fact, it almost got me into trouble during the ward round with Bonkzalot.

While on the round, I had submerged myself into the imaginary conversation with Sundari when Bonkzalot's screaming voice burst forth.

"What the hell do you mean, boy?" he shouted, becoming red in the face.

"I beg your pardon, Professor?" I asked startled.

"I asked you what the oncologists were going to do with Mr. Farling and you told me that you love me."

"I didn't, Sir."

"I distinctly heard you. You mumbled 'I love you'. What's the meaning of this insolence? I won't tolerate buggery on the ward."

Oh my God! I had been imagining myself telling Sundari that I loved her. However, I hadn't meant to say it aloud. Oh shit! How was I going to get out of this pickle?

Then Alternaria spoke up. "Sir, Dr. Mendis actually said 'I-L-two' as in 'interleukin-2'. It may have sounded like I love you because he spoke softly but it was definitely I-L-two."

Bonkzalot looked at me suspiciously. "Is that true, boy?"

I took Alternaria's cue. "Yes, Sir. The oncologists talked about a variety of chemotherapy agents for Mr. Farling, including interleukin-2. That's what I said – I-L-two."

I don't know if he was convinced. But I suspect that this explanation was preferable to Bonkzalot than the possibility that his male intern might have carnal yearnings for him. That revelation would have been too much for a homophobe like Monty to bear.

I thanked Alternaria later.

"No problem, Manju. We're mates. But are you okay?" she asked me. "You seem to have been really distracted lately. Now I'm guessing that it has something to do with a girl."

"It does, Alternaria. But right now, it's too messy to talk about. If things work out though, I'll tell you about it."

"No problem, buddy," she burst out laughing.

"What's so funny?"

"You realize that you're probably the only man ever to tell Bonkzalot that you love him and survive the experience. He probably even beat his father up when he said it to him."

I laughed. "That's *if* his father ever said it to him. Knowing Bonkzlat as we do, that's a big 'if'!"

After dinner, I went up to my bedroom and closed the door. I took a deep breath, tightly holding my script for the upcoming conversation and dialled Sundari's number.

One ring, two rings, three rings, four rings- no answer. Perhaps I should hang up. Then on the fifth ring, there was a click and she spoke.

"Hello." It was so good to hear her voice that I forgot to reply.

"Hello?" she said again.

"Oh hello. Is that Sundari?"

"Yes. Who is this?"

"It's Manju here."

"Manju who?"

"Manju Mendis. We met last week at your place."

There was a long pause.

"Can I help you?" The initially neutral voice had turned cold.

I read from the script. "I just called to say hello and see how you are." So far so good.

"I'm wonderful thank you," she replied with biting sarcasm. "Now is there anything else?"

I read the next line. "Look Sundari, I just wanted to apologize. I didn't expect things to turn out the way they did that day." That sounded good.

Her tone became aggressive. "I didn't hear you say anything at the time to help the situation. You kept quiet while your mother insulted us. We may not be 'high-class' people but we welcomed you into our house with open arms. How could you treat us like that? Nobody deserves to be treated like that!"

None of what she had just said was in the script! I was overcome with panic. I had no choice but to press on with what was written before me.

"Please don't apologize, Sundari. And yes, I'd love to meet sometime,"

I read out word for word.

She became furious. "Are you high on drugs? I am not apologizing for anything. Nor do I have the slightest interest in meeting you. Goodbye!"

She hung up leaving me in a flustered state. I pressed 'redial' on my mobile phone, unsure if she would answer. Thankfully, she did.

"What do you want?" she angrily demanded.

"I didn't mean to sound arrogant or crazy just now. It's just that everything I said to you was written on a script. You veered away from the script and it all sort of fell apart from there." I took a breath and paused, awaiting her response.

"Script?" she said. "Oh my God, were you reading from a script?" she laughed contemptuously. "Is that how 'high-class' Sri Lankans prepare for phone calls? Is that the current fashion in Milan or Paris?" she asked in mocking tones.

I cringed with embarrassment. "I'm sorry, Sundari. And yes, I did write a script because I was so damn nervous about calling you. Look, I can't change the awful things that my mother said. But talking to you that day was the most wonderful experience of my life. If you enjoyed talking to me half as much as I enjoyed talking to you, why don't we give things a chance?"

She hesitated. There was a long silence. I was sure that I'd struck a chord with her.

"Okay then, answer this. How did your mother feel when you told her that you were going to call me and ask me out?"

Of all the questions to ask, why did she have to ask that one? It would have been so easy to lie, oh so easy. But I was inexplicably possessed by the Truth Fairy and simply admitted, "I didn't tell her."

There was another brief pause. "Sorry. I'm nobody's dirty little secret. Goodbye."

She hung up and left my life forever. I felt empty then and I feel emptier now. Jean-Paul Sartre was wrong. Hell isn't other people. Hell isn't *having* other people. And right now, I am in Hell.

June 18

It has been two weeks since my last entry. Sundari still invades my thoughts regularly. But now, I am not so much in Hell as in purgatory. Hopefully, heaven will beckon one of these days. I told Delilah about the phone call. She consoled me but all she could offer were platitudes: "there are plenty of fish in the sea", "when the time is right..." Not that I am being critical of her – after all, what else can she say? In fact, I'm grateful for having a shoulder to cry on. I haven't spoken to Lucky on the matter though. After her revelation, I feel odd confiding in someone who is probably more messed up than me.

Peter, Copper, Delilah, Smegman and I had a rare afternoon coffee in the cafeteria. Peter was very excited.

"I was on overtime yesterday. At about 7:00, I got paged from the tenth floor," he said smiling, as if revealing a delicious secret.

"The Celebrity Ward!" Smegman cried. "Don't leave us in suspense. Who is our new celebrity patient?"

Peter did a fake drum-roll with his hands. "And the winner is... Greg Smythe."

"Greg Smythe!" I exclaimed, careful to contain my excitement. "Get out of here, Peter!"

Delilah, however, looked puzzled. "Who on earth is Greg Smythe?"

Smegman answered, "He is one of the highest profile players in English Premier League football."

"Oh, a sportsman," she said, apparently losing interest.

"Not just 'a sportsman'," said Smegman excitedly. "He led Liverpool to three consecutive premierships and two FA Cup championships in the last four years. He's been the leading goal scorer for the past five years in the premiership."

"He's pretty amazing," Copper concurred.

"And pretty rich," I chipped in.

"What's wrong with him, Peter?"

"He has been having fevers on and off for much of this year. It has really limited his football season."

"That's true," I said. "I remember a TV story from earlier this year saying that he was off with a glandular fever-like illness."

Peter continued. "It's not glandular fever though. He was investigated by leading physicians in London but they haven't been able to figure it out. So he travelled all this way to get Dr. Croquet's expert opinion. And guess what?"

"What?"

"He is so desperate to get to the bottom of this that he has offered a hundred thousand pounds to whoever makes the correct diagnosis."

We all gasped. One hundred thousand pounds! In dollar terms, that was almost five times our annual salary.

"What does Dr. Croquet think?" asked Delilah.

"He came in and assessed Smythe while I was there. He is of the opinion that it is due to recurrent sepsis from an occult source of infection. I organized an extensive septic screen for the patient. But you should have seen the way that Dr. Croquet's eyes lit up when he heard about the reward."

"Wow, I guess we'll have to see what happens," I said.

Yet again I marvelled at how lucky we were to be working at St. Ivanhoe. How many doctors around the world could claim that they had met celebrities of the calibre of Salma Cruze and Greg Smythe, especially during their internship? Mind you, we couldn't claim it either, since we would get sued for breaching confidentiality. But you know what I mean.

June 23

Today Vicki, the vaginacology registrar, and I finished the case report on the lady who used the carrot as a contraceptive. Now that the hard work had been done, our final task was to give the article a title. I thought of two: "An apple a day keeps the doctor away – but what about a carrot?" or "What's up (there), Doc?" accompanied by a caricature of Bugs Bunny gnawing on a carrot. We decided that *The Lancet*'s editorial team would die of shock if the latter title was used so it had to be the former.

Vicki was gracious enough to allow me to be first author. Honestly, I am just thrilled to be part of the paper. Being first author is more than I could have hoped for. This evening, after work, I submitted the manuscript through *The Lancet*'s online website. It took ages. I suspect that I wrote more for the submission process than we had written for the actual case report! Anyway, it is now submitted so all we can do is wait.

After work, I dropped in to see Akki. Luckily, I managed to see Kumar before he went to sleep. He is at an age where he loves hearing a story before going to bed. I hadn't read one to him for a while. After reading Snow White and the Seven Dwarves, I gave him a kiss and he fell asleep. It had never occurred to me previously but fairy tales have a lot to answer for. I was particularly thinking of this issue in the context of Lucky's rejection of her Indian culture. When you consider it, nearly all these fairy tales are about white girls. In addition, all the main characters are beautiful. Even the ugly ones become beautiful in the end such as the Beast from Beauty and the Beast and the Ugly Duckling. Heaven forbid they remained plain or ugly! And who do these hot-looking white girls marry? Prince bloody Charming of course. Why couldn't Snow White have married one of the seven dwarves? They are decent and compassionate individuals who earn an honest living by working in the mines. Why couldn't Snow White have gotten hitched to one of them? Oh no – perish the thought of the beautiful upper class white girl marrying a labourer from a minority group. Instead, she marries some handsome git in ridiculously tight tights prancing around on a horse. And how did he meet her? Prince Charming apparently found her dead in a coffin and was so entranced by her corpse that he wanted to take her back to his kingdom. In fairy tales, this is called romance. To me, it sounds like necrophilia. Rich white people with too much time on their hands. I just hope and pray that Kumar doesn't get influenced in the wrong way by these tales, which promote physical beauty and elitism.

When I came out of Kumar's room, my sister and Ravi were having a minor dispute.

"What's up guys?" I asked.

Ravi said, "It's just not fair. I never got to see Iron Man in the cinema. I haven't had a free day for months except last Saturday. But on that day, Saesha decided to go to see another movie with her friends. That was my last opportunity to see Iron Man before it closed."

"Akki, what did you see with your friends?" I asked my sister.

"Sex and the City," she replied.

I shook my head in disgust. "Akki, what a waste of a big movie screen and its surround sound system. Those resources should be used for a movie with awesome special effects like Iron Man, not Sex and the City."

"Exactly what I told her," said Ravi. "Now I have to watch Iron Man on our crappy little TV when it comes out on DVD. It won't be the same."

"Sorry Akki, he's right. You chose poorly."

Saesha exploded with rage. "Fuck you both! I hadn't seen a movie in the cinema for almost a year. I have to work, clean this fucking house and look after an active three-year-old who hates to sleep. I thought I deserved at least this small thing. Ravi, how could you be so fucking insensitive?"

Then she started crying. Women and their emotional blackmail. I've got to hand it to them though – it works every time. We are defenceless in its onslaught. As Akki went running out of the kitchen, I put my arm around my brother-in-law's shoulder. "Ravi, just raise the white flag and apologize like crazy. It's the only way."

"After seven years of marriage, don't I know it, Manju? Don't I just know it?"

As an image of Sundari popped into my head I thought – sometimes I'm glad that I'm still single – but only sometimes.

June 27

During my overtime shift, I got called to the Celebrity Ward to review Greg Smythe. It was a thrill to meet him. Unfortunately, he wasn't particularly well. Although he had been in hospital for the last ten days, it had only been for investigations. He had otherwise been perfectly fine. But tonight, his fevers returned with a vengeance. In addition, he had developed some abdominal pain and generalized muscle aches. When I got to the ward, he was shaking rhythmically, almost as if he were having a seizure. But I knew better – this was a sign of a high fever known as a rigor. In the elderly, a rigor was a very strong indicator of a bloodstream infection or septicaemia. But what it meant in this young athlete with a relapsing-remitting illness, I had no idea.

I examined him carefully. Apart from the high fever, there were a few abnormal findings: he clearly had periorbital swelling and the red eyes typical of conjunctivitis. His abdomen was generally tender with mild peritonism. There was a rash across his trunk. The really unusual thing about the rash was that when I examined him again about fifteen minutes later, it had moved. Despite these findings, I couldn't really put together a unifying diagnosis. I reviewed all his blood tests and radiology results – again there was nothing specific to find. Registrars and other more senior doctors weren't allowed in the Celebrity ward so it was up to me to call Dr. Croquet.

Dr. Croquet sounded flabbergasted.

"I just don't understand it. Every four to six weeks, he develops exactly the same illness. We've done every test known to medicine and there's still no diagnosis. I want you to repeat the septic screen, scan his abdomen again and commence meropenem and vancomycin. Got it?"

"Yes, Sir," I said.

I went back to the room and informed Greg of Dr. Croquet's plan. He shook his head in frustration. "This is exactly what the doctors back home did. I flew all the way here because I heard Spyder Croquet was special, that he could diagnose anything. But he's just the same as the others. If no one can diagnose this, then my football career's over. I'm completely screwed."

I left the room feeling sorry for Greg. Like him, I was somewhat disappointed with Dr. Croquet's response. Admittedly, this was a tough case but I had expected something more from him than ordering another septic screen. Also, his odd diagnosis of Prinzmetal's angina in Salma Cruze still bothered me. Oh well, who was I, a fresh intern, to question the ways of this country's most brilliant diagnostician?

July 4

We now have two celebrity patients in the hospital. However, the latest admission is more of a quasi-celebrity. He is not instantly recognizable but has a tremendous reputation in the business world. Mr. Pik Freiman is a seventy-nine year old, with acute cholecystitis *(an acutely inflamed gallbladder –Editors)*. He owns the massive Serpentine Diamond Company that was founded by his grandfather over a hundred years ago. I was surprised on two counts. Firstly, I would have expected him to be admitted to a fancy private hospital rather than here. Certainly, St. Ivanhoe is the most prestigious public hospital in the country, but at the end of the day, it still is a public hospital. The reason for his presence at St. Ivanhoe soon became apparent. It turned out that as soon as he developed the fevers and upper abdominal pain, he was rushed in to Professor Bonkzalot's room. The Professor diagnosed acute cholecystitis and immediately sent him to St. Ivanhoe on the off chance he might need admission to an Intensive Care Unit. Apparently, the ICU at the private hospital isn't as well staffed as ours. The second surprise for me was Pik Freiman's demeanour and personality. I assumed that an elderly mining magnate would be an arrogant, ruthless brute, throwing orders around in an imperious manner. Yet Pik Freiman is one of the sweetest men I have ever met. He is patient, polite and even interested in my career plans in medicine. His weathered face may once have been handsome but age has taken its toll on Pik Freiman who looks every one of his seventy-nine years. Standing next to him was an anxious woman of similar age, whom I presumed to be his wife. She said little during my interview with Mr. Freiman but smiled benignly. Towards the end of the consultation, another woman burst into the room. She seemed in her late thirties, had long curly blond hair and wore a black suit with a white, wide-brimmed hat. She was easy on the eye, but as it turned out, rather hard on the ear.

"Who the hell are you?" she demanded of me.

"I'm Dr. Mendis, Professor Bonkzalot's intern."

"An intern? Isn't that a first-year doctor?"

"Yes, Ma'am."

"Where the hell is that Professor? I don't want some inexperienced fool involved in Mr. Freiman's care! Do you know who we are? Do you know how powerful we are?"

"Yes, Ma'am," I replied. I almost said that I had naturally heard of her father but for some reason I kept quiet. Her next remark made me grateful that I'd maintained my silence.

"My husband is one of the wealthiest men in the country and I want him to be personally looked after by the Professor and not you!"

Her husband? So this loud blonde was Pik Freiman's wife? Then who on earth was the nice old lady standing next to him? Anyway, I explained the whole situation to Mrs. Freiman, namely that her husband would be Professor Bonkzalot's personal patient and that the Professor would be in charge of all the decisions concerning his care. We junior doctors simply carried out his wishes. The presence of this social hierarchy within the hospital seemed to appease her sense of outrage and she calmed down. However, as I walked out of the room, she said, "Please make sure that nothing happens to my husband otherwise you and this hospital won't know what has hit you."

Judging by her ferocious expression, I didn't doubt her for a moment.

July 6

We had a rare dinner where everyone turned up. The gang looked well. I wasted little time before telling them about my encounters with our two celebrity patients – Pik Freiman and Greg Smythe. When I mentioned Pik Freiman's wife, whom I initially mistook for his daughter, Copper introduced a new word to my vocabulary.

"A classic case of sugardaddiphilia," he pronounced.

"Of what?" I asked him.

"Sugardaddiphilia. It's when young women marry rich old blokes for their money. Mrs. Freiman is your classic sugardaddiphile."

"Is that a real word?" asked Smegman.

"No," Copper conceded. "I made it up because there wasn't a specific term for the phenomenon. 'Money-grabbing harlot' and 'opportunistic bitch' just don't have the same ring to it."

Although my private school English was slowly being eroded away, I had to admit that vaginacologist and now sugardaddiphile were both very catchy terms. I could certainly see their appeal.

It has been just over a week since I reviewed Greg Smythe. I asked if anyone else had seen him since then. Alternaria nodded. She had been called to rewrite his medication chart last night. Now, he was only given paracetamol for the fevers and muscle pains. She had gone through all the results from the tests that I had ordered. Once again, nothing remarkable stood out. Interestingly, the whole episode appeared to be settling without any intervention from us. This seemed to be the whole natural history of his illness: he'd be sick for a week or two, spontaneously get better, then relapse about six weeks later. It was a real mystery.

Smegman said, "Peter, Manju and Alternaria – you three have all seen him. Tell me everything about him. Leave no stone unturned. Let's try and sort him out."

"Smegman, I know that you are bright. But I doubt that even *you* could solve this mystery over dinner."

"Come on, Manju," urged Delilah. "It's a challenge. Let's see if we can fix this poor man."

Little did we realize that we were about to be privileged to the rare sight of not one, but two geniuses, at their brilliant best. The three of us explained everything that we knew about Greg Smythe, from the things that he had told us, to what we'd found on examining him, and finally the results of the battery of tests that he had undergone.

"So it's periodic," said Smegman. "And between illnesses, is he completely well?"

"Yes," I replied. "Completely well, so much so that he starts training for football again. Then suddenly after a few weeks, he gets struck down once more."

"So it's a true periodic fever syndrome," said Delilah thoughtfully. "If he is completely well between episodes, I would have thought that cancer and connective tissue diseases would be pretty unlikely. Given that he has had so many negative blood cultures, a normal transoesophageal echocardiogram and no obvious intra-abdominal collection, a bacterial infection seems pretty unlikely too. Did he have malaria films?"

"Multiple," replied Peter. "Not just here, but back in the UK too. Even though the films were negative, they treated him for malaria anyway. But, as you can see, it hasn't made a difference."

Smegman then asked, "What about thyroid function tests and screening for carcinoid syndrome and phaeochromocytomas?"

"All performed and all normal."

Delilah actually got up from her chair and started pacing up and down. A few other diners looked at her quizzically before returning to their meals. "Dammit," she said, clearly frustrated. "All his symptoms and signs fit with something. I just can't quite pin it down. Help me guys."

We all looked helplessly at her. This case was way out of our league. Apart from Smegman, the rest of us had thrown in the towel.

Smegman spoke. "Let's think... a periodic fever syndrome... completely well between episodes. But when he gets sick, he has high fever, a migratory rash, severe myalgias and peritonism. Manju, you mentioned periorbital swelling and conjunctivitis..."

Then simultaneously, Delilah and Smegman yelled, "I've got it!" They both looked at each other excitedly before turning to us. We were spellbound.

"Guys, what is Greg Smythe's ethnic origin?" Delilah asked. "Come on, quick!" she almost yelled.

"Irish mother and Scottish father," said Peter.

Smegman took over. "So that rules out Familial Mediterranean Fever. What about serum immunoglobulins?"

I answered that. "He had a mild polyclonal hypergammaglobulinaemia."

"But what about the IgD?" Smegman asked.

"I'm pretty sure that everything else was normal."

"Then that must be it!" cried Smegman.

"It just has to be," said Delilah, jumping up and down as if she were riding a pogo stick.

Then they hugged each other in sheer delight, once more earning the puzzled attention of neighbouring diners in the restaurant.

Copper said, "I'm sorry to interrupt the celebrations, but before you start making babies with each other, we'd all be grateful if you tell us *WHAT THE HELL IS WRONG WITH HIM.*"

"Oh, sorry," said Delilah, as she untangled herself from Smegman. I noted that he seemed rather reluctant to release her from the embrace.

"Basically, what you've described to us is a periodic fever. If he had an infection, it should have been discovered by now through all the tests that he has had. As Smegman said, the fact that he is completely well between episodes makes cancer and connective tissue diseases, like lupus, pretty unlikely. Anyway, you'd have expected some of those tests to identify either of those. So that just leaves a group of autoimmune disorders known as the periodic fever syndromes: Familial Mediterranean Fever, Hyper IgD syndrome and Tumour Necrosis Factor Receptor Associated Periodic Syndrome, also known as TRAPS. All the information that you guys have given about him would fit perfectly with TRAPS. It is autosomal dominant but not everyone can give a family history of it."

"TRAPS? I've never heard of it," I admitted as Copper, Peter, Alternaria and Lucky echoed similar sentiments.

"I read about it in a journal a couple of years ago," said Delilah.

"You mean that review article in *Immunology*?" asked Smegman.

"That's the one," said Delilah.

"Me too," exclaimed Smegman. "Wasn't it great?"

Perhaps if I'd spent more time reading reputable journals as a medical student instead of those lingerie catalogues that we received in the mail, I'd probably be a more knowledgeable doctor. Mind you, even if I had done so, I still wouldn't be anywhere near as good as Smegman and Delilah.

"Guys, that was simply amazing! But how do you confirm the diagnosis of TRAPS?"

"There's a genetic test."

"And what about treatment?"

Smegman replied. "Some of the tumour necrosis factor antagonists are pretty useful."

"Well, you'd better tell Dr. Croquet first thing in the morning. And if you're right, there's a hundred thousand pound reward waiting for you."

"I'd forgotten about that," said Smegman, his eyes widening.

"Well, if you resurrect this guy's football career, you'll both deserve every cent," said Lucky.

"Awesome work, guys," we said, as we all congratulated Smegman and Delilah on what had truly been some extraordinary detective work.

July 7

Smegman and Delilah called up Dr. Croquet about the possibility of TRAPS in Mr. Smythe. Apparently, he was sceptical of the diagnosis. Mind you, according to Delilah, it sounded like he had never heard of it before. But in the end, he grudgingly agreed to test Greg Smythe for TRAPS, mainly because he didn't know what else to do. He told Delilah and Smegman that he would discuss the diagnosis with Greg Smythe and asked them to make preliminary enquiries about the genetic test. It turned out that it is only performed in one lab in the country and would therefore take about seven days before a result was available.

On the surgical front, Pik Freiman is slowly recovering from his episode of acute cholecystitis. He still has a lot of abdominal pain and requires intravenous antibiotics. Today I learnt that the elderly woman whom I had initially mistaken for his wife is a servant. She has been with their family for the last fifty years or so. Unlike the wife, Ms. Agatha Highcue is a quietly spoken and cheerful lady. Mr. Freiman seems quite at ease whenever she is in the room. If you ask me, he'd have been better off marrying Agatha Highcue than the sugardaddiphile.

July 14

I got an urgent call to see Mr. Freiman late in the afternoon. I was surprised, as his recovery was quite uneventful so far. It turned out that the problem was with his blood pressure and not his gallbladder. The blood pressure had been gradually rising throughout the day and it was 210/130 when the nurse contacted me. He had a headache associated with it, raising the real possibility of a hypertensive crisis. I examined him thoroughly. Thankfully, he had no papilloedema, focal neurological deficits or cardiac disease due to the elevated blood pressure. Apart from reducing his blood pressure, the priority was to find out what had caused it to become so high. He certainly wasn't in pain (apart from the mild headache) nor was he in urinary retention, both of which are common causes of an acute rise in blood pressure.

I examined the list of medications given by his family doctor, which confirmed that he took 10mg/day of enalapril for blood pressure. I double-checked his medication chart, which showed that the enalapril was charted at the correct dose and had been given everyday since his admission. I went into his room where both he and Ms. Highcue waited. I showed them the list of medications given by their family doctor and expressed my uncertainty as to why his blood pressure had risen so much. When Ms. Highcue looked at the family doctor's medication sheet, she gasped.

"What's wrong?" I asked her.

"Oh, Dr. Mendis, there's been a mistake. Mr. Freiman has given you an old list of medications from his family doctor. I can tell by the date."

"Would you have an updated one?"

"I should," she replied, as she rifled through her handbag, eventually producing another sheet of paper, which she immediately handed to me.

I examined it carefully. It was dated only two months ago and was definitely more recent than the sheet he had given me. On this current list of medications, the enalapril was listed at 35mg/day, not the 10mg/day for which he had been charted. So here was the problem. I explained it to Mr. Freiman.

He apologised. "Sorry, Dr. Mendis. I'm becoming a bit forgetful with age."

Ms. Highcue took me to one side of the room. "Oh, it's my fault, Dr. Mendis. I have known for sometime that Mr. Freiman's memory is not as good as it used to be. I should have double-checked the list of medication that he gave you."

At this point, Mrs. Freiman stormed in and accosted me in the corner of the room. She was wearing tight black leather pants and a bright red leather jacket that accentuated her gorgeous figure. If only she weren't such a bitch...

"What the hell is going on, Dr. Mendis? The nurse said that my husband's blood pressure is dangerously high."

I explained the situation to her and said that no harm had come of it. Unfortunately, Mrs. Freiman did not take this view at all.

"So you're telling me that my husband has been receiving the wrong dose of blood pressure medication since he was admitted here ten days ago? And because of that, he's having some sort of blood pressure crisis?"

"That's right, Mrs. Freiman," I replied.

She continued. "I take a medication called warfarin, Dr. Mendis. Do you know what that's for? It's to thin my blood. You see, I developed a clot in my leg while travelling to Paris last year despite flying first class. Because of that, my doctor put me on warfarin. If I ever take the wrong dose, my blood will become too thick or too thin. If it's too thin, I'll suffer from life-threatening bleeding. If it's too thick, then the clot might go to my lungs and kill me. Taking the wrong dose of warfarin could be fatal. Did you know that, Dr. Mendis?"

"Yes, Mrs. Freiman. I'm quite familiar with warfarin," I patiently replied.

She began to get worked up. "Oh, I don't think that you're familiar with a lot of things. My husband is critically ill because you didn't write up the correct dose of blood pressure medication for him. Whether it's warfarin or a blood pressure medication, giving the wrong dose can be fatal. You have been negligent and I am going to speak to my solicitors to ensure that you and this pathetic excuse for a hospital are sued."

I couldn't believe that I was hearing this. I protested my innocence. "But Mrs. Freiman, I only charted the dose of enalapril from the sheet that Mr. Freiman gave me."

Ms. Highcue sprang to my defence. "Mrs. Freiman, he is telling the truth. I was there when it happened. Mr. Freiman gave him an old medication sheet."

Mrs. Freiman looked at Ms. Highcue as if examining a mangy stray dog. "Agatha, shut up! We don't pay you for advice. You're a fucking servant. And right now, you will serve us by shutting your working-class trap. Got it?"

"Yes, Mrs. Freiman," Ms. Highcue bowed her head in shame.

Although I was worried about my own predicament, I was still appalled by Mrs. Freiman's contemptuous and dismissive words to Ms.

Highcue. Why did Ms. Highcue tolerate such language?

Then Mr. Freiman spoke up. "But darling, Dr. Mendis is right. I did give him the wrong medication sheet. How could he have known that I should have been on a higher dose?"

Mrs. Freiman went up to her husband and hugged him tenderly, shamelessly putting his head between her visible and ample cleavage. "Oh Pik sweetie, you're so kind to these fools. It's not your job to worry about medications. It's their job. After all, they are the doctors. You just let me handle the situation."

It was as if her breasts had sucked all the fight out of him. He just nodded his head in acquiescence as she released him from her double C cup embrace.

"As I was saying, Doctor, you'll be hearing from our lawyers very soon. And just a word of warning: I sued the airline after I got the clot. They settled out of court for ten million dollars. I play hardball, Dr. Mendis... and I never lose. Good day."

And without so much as a 'goodbye' to her husband, she walked out of the room, presumably to call those nasty lawyers of hers.

As soon as it was clear that Mr. Freiman's blood pressure was under control, I left the room to lick my wounds and contemplate my first lawsuit.

July 15

"I am so screwed," I moaned.

Copper, Peter and Delilah joined me for coffee this afternoon and listened in amazement to the antics of Mrs. Freiman.

"A typical sugardaddiphile," said Copper. "Despite being worth hundreds of millions of dollars, she's out for every cent that she can get."

Peter said, "In Moscow, we consider such women better off dead. My uncle knows a good hit-man..."

"Oh, Peter, if only it were that simple here," I said, wondering if I would find anyone listed under 'Hit-man' or 'Assassin' in our local Yellow Pages.

Delilah, practical as ever, said, "Manju, I really wouldn't worry. First of all, you didn't do anything wrong. Mr. Freiman gave you the wrong medication sheet. Secondly, the hospital indemnifies all of us against litigation so you are not in any financial danger."

"Haven't you ever watched Boston Legal or Law and Order *(Popular television dramas of the time about trial lawyers – Editors)*?" I asked Delilah. "Even an open and shut case gets turned on its head when the rich people's lawyers take on the case. They have so many assistants who can research obscure legal loopholes that can turn the case in their client's favour. The only two people who can vouch for me are Mr. Freiman and his servant, Ms. Highcue. Freiman's lawyers will probably argue that Pik Freiman is an old man whose memory is fading, therefore, his testimony is unreliable. As for Ms. Highcue, they'll probably hide her for the duration of the trial so she can't testify either. Then it'll be my word against that of the sugardaddiphile and her lawyers."

Copper said, "Don't worry, Manju. I'm sure that Mrs. Freiman will forget the whole thing when she calms down."

"You're more optimistic than me," I said glumly.

Just then, Smegman arrived in the cafeteria, looking really excited. He rushed towards us, panting heavily.

"Guess what?"

"What?" we all asked him.

"The results of the genetic test are through. Greg Smythe has TRAPS. We were right, Delilah! We were right!"

"Oh Marcus," she cried, "That's wonderful!"

"Fantastic, guys!" I said. "So have you told Dr. Croquet yet?"

Smegman shook his head. "No. I just called the lab a few minutes ago." He looked at Delilah. "We can tell Dr. Croquet now."

Peter said, "So what are you going to do with the fifty thousand pounds you are each going to get?"

Smegman said, "Maybe it's time to look into that new convertible..."

Delilah shook her head with disbelief. "Guys and their cars! What a waste of money. The sensible thing is to buy an investment property. That's what I'm going to do. There's a new block of apartments on Broadley Bay that I've been eyeing for some time now."

As they went off together, Peter, Copper and I marvelled at how privileged we were to be working with such brilliant people.

July 16

Late this afternoon, I got a message on my pager: "Please meet us in cafeteria – Delilah and Smegman. It's urgent." I still had a few odds and ends to do before going home but nothing that couldn't wait. So I rushed to the cafeteria. By the time I arrived, everyone else was already there, including Alternaria who had just finished the operating theatre lists.

I had assumed that this was going to be a big celebration of Delilah and Smegman's brilliant diagnosis. But I was horrified to see Delilah in tears and Smegman looking miserable.

"Guys, what's up? Why aren't we celebrating?"

"Watch the news," said Smegman, pointing to the large TV screen behind us.

The six o'clock news had just begun. A reporter was standing outside the unmistakable entrance to St. Ivanhoe with a media spokesman from the hospital.

The media spokesman read a prepared statement to the reporter. "Mr. Greg Smythe, Premier League and England footballer, has released a statement. Mr. Smythe says that he has now been diagnosed with a condition called 'TRAPS', which is eminently treatable. It is a very rare condition that causes periodic fevers. He expresses his thanks to Dr. Spyder Croquet who came up with the brilliant diagnosis himself. Dr. Croquet, once again, has shown his ability to diagnose difficult conditions that even the best specialists in the UK failed to pick up. His brilliant reputation is well deserved and as promised, Dr. Croquet will receive the hundred thousand pound reward."

The reporter then went on to discuss the backgrounds of both Greg Smythe and Dr. Croquet before throwing back to the studio.

We all sat there stunned.

"What the hell was that?" asked Lucky. Gesturing towards Smegman and Delilah she said "You guys made the diagnosis, not Croquet."

Delilah was too upset to speak so Smegman told the story. "Yesterday, we phoned Dr. Croquet with the news that the genetic test was positive. He was very excited and congratulated us. He told us to meet him this morning in the Celebrity Ward. But when we arrived there, he took us to the Doctors' Room instead of to see Greg Smythe. That was the first sign that something was up. He said that he had just seen Greg Smythe and told him that he had TRAPS. No problem there. But Croquet then went on to say that Greg Smythe was so grateful to *him* for making the diagnosis that he was rewarding *him* with the hundred thousand pound reward. Delilah and I initially thought that we had misheard and asked why Greg Smythe was giving him the reward. It was then that the unscrupulous bastard laid all his cards on the table. He said, 'I'm getting the reward because I made the diagnosis.' When I tactfully put it to him that Delilah and I had made the diagnosis, his response was as follows, 'I don't ever recall either of you interns suggesting the diagnosis of TRAPS. To my knowledge, you have never discussed the issue with Mr. Smythe. In fact, I don't believe that either of you have ever met him. The only mention of TRAPS in his medical records is by me. So I hope that you aren't trying to steal the credit from me. It would be a career-ending move.' And that was that. Without admitting to any wrong-doing, Croquet made it clear that he was taking the credit for Greg Smythe's diagnosis and that he would ruin our careers if we made a fuss about it."

The seven of us sat there like stunned mullets, unable to comprehend what had just happened.

"And the money?" I asked.

"You heard the TV report, Spyder got every cent for 'his brilliant diagnosis'," said Delilah sarcastically.

Copper shook his head. "So why would someone as brilliant as Croquet need to cheat two interns out of the credit and money they deserved for making a superb diagnosis? I just don't get it."

"Perhaps he isn't as good as everyone thinks," I said. "I still can't believe how he thought Salma Cruze had Prinzmetal's angina. So what are you going to do?"

Smegman said, "What can we do? He'll crush us if we try to tell the truth."

"We can all vouch for you," said Alternaria. "After all, we were all at dinner when you and Delilah came up with the diagnosis of TRAPS."

"No, Marcus is right. Even with all your testimonies, it would be the word of seven interns against the 'great and powerful' Spyder Croquet. No one would believe us. Furthermore, he wouldn't just destroy

Marcus' and my career – he'd destroy yours as well. We have to keep our silence."

"Damn it! It's just not fair!" exclaimed Peter.

"No, it's not," Delilah said, "My shift starts in four hours. I better go home." She walked away, a broken woman. Ever since the start of this year, Delilah had been a rock of optimism and wisdom from whom I had drawn so much solace and strength. To see her walk away, head bowed with the spirit sucked out of her, was too much to bear. Smegman too excused himself and walked away dejected.

The five of us sat there and angrily voiced our universal condemnation of Spyder Croquet. Just before we left, we made a vow – somehow, sometime, Spyder Croquet was going to pay for what he had done to Delilah and Smegman. God knows how we would pull it off, but pull it off we would.

July 18

This evening I met Greg Smythe again. He was leaving hospital and needed all his discharge papers completed before he could leave. I handed him his discharge summary and wished him well. He sang the praises of Spyder Croquet. Oh how I wanted to tell him the truth about the double-crossing ignoramus he held in such high esteem! But I held my tongue. As Delilah had said, what was the word of an intern against the great Dr. Croquet?

As I left his room, I heard a kafuffle near the elevators. The nurse was arguing with a woman who was trying to meet Greg Smythe.

"I'm sorry. No reporters are allowed here. Even if Mr. Smythe were here (and I'm not saying that he is), you wouldn't be allowed to see him."

"Do you know who I am?" the reporter asked.

"Yes, Ms. Hipz, I'm quite familiar with your work. But even *you* aren't allowed up here. Please don't make me call Security."

She had called her 'Ms. Hipz'! I looked closely at the reporter and silently gasped. It was indeed Fabulus Hipz, the famous and gorgeous TV presenter from The Morning Show.

"Okay, no need to get all aggressive with me," said Fabulus, "I'll go then."

"I'm terribly sorry, Ms. Hipz," reiterated Nurse Watson. "I really am a big fan but it'll be my head if you don't leave here."

"Very well then," she said, pushing the elevator button.

The elevator door opened immediately and she climbed into the lift. I shouted, "Hold the elevator please," sprinted and jumped in with her.

As the doors closed, I introduced myself to her. "Hi, Ms. Hipz, I'm Dr. Manju Mendis, also a big fan of yours."

She looked at my badge and said, "Ah... an intern. How very interesting." Then completely unexpectedly, she reached out and pushed the 'Stop' button, bringing the elevator to a grinding halt.

"Do you know one of the keys to being a successful investigative journalist, Manju?" she said, drawing closer to me and never letting her beautiful brown eyes leave mine.

"No, Ms. Hipz," I replied slowly inching my way to the corner of the elevator as she continued her relentless approach towards me.

"Please call me Fabulus," she purred alluringly.

"No, Fabulus," I corrected myself.

"It's having a reliable source who has access to the most privileged information."

"But I'm just an intern. I'm bottom of the food chain. Surely you want someone higher up?"

"But that's what makes you perfect. High-ranking officials will happily blab in front of you because they regard you as insignificant. You'd be amazed at how often it happens."

"Well, Fabulus," I said quite firmly, despite my knees feeling like jelly, "I can't breach doctor-patient confidentiality either."

"Oh, I wouldn't dream of asking you to do that. As a journalist with confidential sources, that'd be the greatest hypocrisy on my part. St. Ivanhoe is the most prestigious hospital in the country and many of its scandals will involve its high-profile staff. I'm only interested in those systemic problems, not a one-on-one issue with your patients."

"So you're not going to ask me about Greg Smythe?"

"Perish the thought!" she exclaimed. "Oh, I know that he's up on the tenth floor. An exclusive interview would have been nice but that's okay. And, as I told you, I'm not going to ask you to breach doctor-patient confidentiality." She then ran her index finger around the outline of my badge. Despite the badge being on my chest, I found another part of my body was responding to her touch. Self-control! For heaven's sake, maintain your self-control. This was no easy task as Fabulus Hipz is an extraordinarily attractive woman. I remember reading that her exotic dark looks came from a Portuguese and Brazilian background. She certainly wasn't tall but the designer dress she wore hugged her extraordinary figure and displayed her smooth, tanned legs. From tabloids, she was well into her thirties and had a couple of young children. Despite this, eighteen-year-old women would have died to look half as good as her. There was no doubt about it – Fabulus Hipz is the quintessential 'yummy mummy'.

Thankfully, when I thought that I could stand no more from this television temptress, she stepped back and pushed the 'Start' button, bringing the elevator back to life so it could continue its descent.

She handed me a card. "Manju, my contact details are here if you ever need to contact me. Don't be a stranger," she said.

"Just one question," I said, as the blood moved from my groin back to my brain. "You are a successful TV presenter. Why are you coming out to do investigative stories?"

"That is a good question. As for the answer, we can discuss that whenever you have an interesting story for me."

The elevator doors opened and she walked away without acknowledging me. I was puzzled by her failure to say goodbye but then realized that she was simply protecting the anonymity of her newfound 'source'. I looked at her card. There was a mobile number and email address. I put it in my wallet, regretfully thinking that I'd probably never have the opportunity to contact her. As she walked away, her hips swinging from side to side, I realized how much I was looking forward to being alone in my bedroom tonight.

July 25

Mr. Pik Freiman left hospital today. The reason for his prolonged stay was due to a number of cardiac investigations. Mr. Freiman needed a cholecystectomy *(Removal of gallbladder – Editors)* otherwise he would suffer from further attacks of acute cholecystitis. But before Professor Bonkzalot or his anaesthetist would operate on him, they wanted to make sure that his heart would tolerate the general anaesthetic and the operation itself. It was a sensible decision as it soon turned out that Pik Freiman's coronary arteries were blocked in multiple areas. He would need coronary artery bypass surgery before undergoing removal of his gallbladder. I had booked Pik Freiman for the bypass surgery which would be performed by Dr. Hart.

It has been over a week since Mrs. Freiman threatened to sue the hospital and me. Since then, I haven't seen her on the ward nor heard any more on the matter. Copper's prediction that Mrs. Freiman would forget the whole thing once she calmed down seems to have come to pass. Mr. Freiman thanked me for my care as the orderly wheeled him from the ward. Ms. Highcue shook my hand warmly and expressed her gratitude. Watching her in her maid's costume carrying a little handbag, she reminded me of Mary Poppins. Just after they left, I was surprised to see a courier on the ward with a parcel for me. The sender's information on the package said it was from Mrs. Tabitha Freiman. I impatiently tore open the package. It was a huge box of Godiva chocolates with hundred and forty pieces in all. This must have cost close to $200! I sighed with relief. At least she wasn't suing me. In fact, this was probably an apology for her outrageous behaviour (or misbehaviour as the case may be). There was a card accompanying the chocolates. Smiling, I opened it. As I proceeded to read, my smile disappeared rapidly:

Dear Dr. Mendis,

In the United States, before a prisoner is put to death, it is customary to offer them whatever cuisine they desire for their last meal.

Unfortunately, I am not familiar with your culinary preferences. But I know few people who can go past a box of Godiva chocolates. So I hope you don't think it presumptuous of me to have chosen this for you as your "last meal".

Enjoy the chocolates, Dr Mendis and... see you in court.

Regards,

Mrs. Tabitha Freiman

Attached to the card with a paperclip was another sheet of paper. I unfolded it – it was a letter from a firm of solicitors declaring that Mr. and Mrs. Pik Freiman were suing me for negligent care of Mr. Freiman. I don't know how long I stared at the letter in complete disbelief. The spell was broken when Professor Bonkzalot stormed into the ward, brandishing a letter and yelling, "What the hell is all this about, boy?" He shoved the letter in my face. He was accompanied by Alternaria and Rodrigo, who were carrying similar letters.

I took it from him and read it. My worst fears were confirmed. Mrs. Freiman's lawyers were suing the whole surgical team: Professor Bonkzalot, Rodrigo and both interns in addition to the whole hospital. I'd never seen Bonkzalot so angry. Despite being able to truthfully assert that I hadn't been at fault, I received no respite from Bonkzalot's fury.

"It doesn't matter, boy!" he said, still so angry that he was spitting words. "These rich people and their fancy lawyers will twist the truth around so much, that at the end of the day, we'll be portrayed as fucking monsters! My fucking reputation's on the line here!"

I shivered at his furious onslaught, appalled to hear a specialist using such foul language.

"Let me tell you one more thing. I will not go down for any of you. You're on your own, the lot of you! You can all go to hell." He stormed off angrily.

Rodrigo looked quite disturbed after Bonkzalot's outburst. He said that he was very disappointed in me and walked off.

As Rodrigo walked away, Alternaria shouted at him, "But Manju didn't do anything wrong. It was the patient's fault."

Rodrigo, his back still turned to us, waved his hand dismissively and continued walking. I thought that I could feel no worse than after Sundari dumped me over the phone. But my sense of despondency had never been lower than now.

"I'm sorry, Alternaria," I looked at the letter in her hand. "I've dragged you into this too."

Alternaria raised her hands in exasperation. "For the last time, Manju, you haven't done anything wrong! It's the wife who is being a complete bitch! And as for Bonkzalot and Rodrigo, they're pathetic. It's their job as consultant and registrar to support us, not wash their hands of us at the slightest sign of trouble, especially when the patient was at fault. For this whole term, Rodrigo has been in operating theatre or in the library studying for his bloody exam. He has provided zero support for us on the ward. Don't listen to what they say. The hospital lawyers will vindicate all of us. You wait and see."

I might have believed her at the beginning of the year. But the last six months had taught me, if nothing else, that life wasn't always just.

August 1

It has been a miserable week. Bonkzalot and Rodrigo have continued to be in foul moods because of the negligence case. We've all been to the legal department of the hospital to sign affidavits of our version of events.

After I'd been through mine with the hospital lawyer, an unfriendly white-haired man, I asked him what the outcome was likely to be.

"It's going to be tough," he replied.

"But I've told you a million times that it was Mr. Freiman's fault! He admitted to the fact and his maid can testify too."

"For heaven's sake, don't be so naïve, Dr. Mendis! This has nothing to do with justice. Don't you realize that this is all about money and power? The Freiman's lawyers are Penman, Pullman and Puttman, the most ruthless and resourceful law firm this side of the equator. It may be better to settle out of court – cheaper, as well as giving less adverse publicity to the hospital."

I couldn't believe that I was hearing this. "But what about me and the other intern? If you settle out of court, this will go down on our medical records as an episode of negligence! Apart from the humiliation of that, my medical defence premiums will rise astronomically."

The hospital lawyer looked at me coolly. "My primary job is to protect the hospital and its assets. You and your colleague won't be financially out of pocket."

"But what about our reputations?"

"Unfortunately Dr. Mendis, that is none of my concern."

I called my own medicolegal company for assistance, 'Doctors

Without Lawsuits'. They supposedly would put my interests ahead of those of the hospital. The call was answered by a recording saying, "This call may be recorded for quality assurance. Please inform the operator if you do not want this call recorded." Given that I was going to be discussing confidential matters with their legal team, the thought of a recorded conversation did not sound good at all. So as soon as the operator answered, I made my views clear.

"Hello. I want to discuss a case with your lawyers. But I don't want the call recorded for quality assurance."

"I beg your pardon, Sir?"

"I said that I don't want the call recorded."

"Excuse me, Sir." I had to hold on for another five minutes till he was back. "Sir, are you sure that you don't want the call recorded? It's really just a formality."

"Is there a problem?" I asked.

The operator was slightly hesitant. "Well, Sir. This is the first time that someone has refused to have the call recorded. We're not sure what to do."

I banged my head on the desk in front of me a few times. "Then why does that silly voice message give us the option of not having the call recorded?"

"We're legally obliged to do so, Sir," he replied apologetically.

I took a few deep breaths and conceded that I was quite happy for him to record the call.

He pepped up immediately. "That's wonderful news, Sir! Now, how can I help you?"

I repeated my request to speak to one of their lawyers and he duly transferred me to someone called Ike. Unlike the hospital lawyer, Ike seemed very welcoming and enthusiastic. But once I had disclosed the identity of the high profile plaintiff and the law firm who would be defending them, his manner changed noticeably and he became rather obstructive. Within minutes, he profusely apologized for not being able to defend me, saying that the case should remain with the hospital's legal team. He knew it was a pathetic response on his part and he knew that I knew. But what could I do? I was just an intern with no official clout. They say that every cloud has a silver lining, but currently, I'm struggling to see it.

Today ended on a rather odd note. At about 7:30pm, as I was about to leave hospital, I remembered that I'd left my car keys in the changing rooms of the operating theatre. I went back there to collect the keys. Just as I was leaving the changing room, I heard the voice of Bonkzalot approaching from a distance. Given how unpleasant he had been to me of late, I hid in a shower cubicle to avoid meeting him. I peered through a slit in the cubicle door and saw Bonkzalot doing a cursory sweep of the changing room.

"It's okay, Stewart. We're alone."

Stewart is presumably Stewart Ponsonby, Professor Bonkzalot's anaesthetist.

"Good," said the voice I recognized as Dr. Ponsonby's. "So we're on for Sunday then, Monty?"

"Definitely. I've got ten cases scheduled, including a brain tumour."

"I didn't know that you could do neurosurgery, Monty," said Ponsonby, sounding impressed.

"Oh, yes. When I first started training all those years ago, a surgeon had to do everything, you know. I've drained more subdural haematomas and removed more brain tumours than I'd care to remember. Having said that, I don't like neurosurgery so I told Damien that it'd cost extra."

"Damien? Is it Damien Wyatt's bitch again?"

"Yes."

"So how much are you going to charge?" asked Ponsonby.

"An extra fifty per cent."

Ponsonby whistled. "Fifteen hundred dollars. Well done Monty."

"Did you take the gas without anyone noticing?" asked Monty.

"Of course. Did you manage to get the cutting equipment?"

Monty raised a suitcase and nodded. "Yes, it's all in here and it'll be back before anyone notices its absence."

Ponsonby grinned. "Monty, do you know the only thing that I like more than resting on a Sunday?"

"What's that, Stewart?"

"It's making money on a Sunday."

They both laughed heartily and walked out of the changing rooms together.

Once I was sure that they had gone, I emerged from the shower cubicle and contemplated the conversation that had just taken place. It was clear that Bonkzalot and his anaesthetist were up to no good. Their plan involved 'borrowing' anaesthetic gas and surgical equipment from the hospital. But the details of their misadventure remained a mystery. I will keep my ear to the ground in the hope that it all becomes a bit clearer.

August 11

The wheels of bureaucracy continue to turn slowly. It has been a week since I last spoke to the hospital lawyer about the Pik Freiman case. Despite our lawyer's initial claim that it may be easier to settle out of court, it appears that our legal team has been investigating other strategic avenues. It has been near impossible to garner further details about what they are doing and it is still quite possible that my head has been served on a platter to the nefarious Mrs. Freiman and her legal team – but I am yet to learn about it. So until I hear anything different, I have decided to remain optimistic about our chances of winning the case. Perhaps this is a foolish attitude to take but this faint hope allows me to carry on. The possibility that I may be found negligent for something that I didn't do has really jaded me and ingrained within me a new level of cynicism for this profession that I hadn't thought possible. I haven't told my family about this as it will achieve nothing other than upset them.

On the surgical front, I performed a procedure that I had managed to deliberately avoid through medical school, namely manual disimpaction. *(The term 'manual disimpaction' refers to a method of relieving constipation. It involves manually removing hard faecal matter from the patient's back passage in the hope of stimulating bowel movement – Editors.)*

The patient was one of the hospital's 'frequent flyers'. He used to be a lightweight world champion boxer of much renown. His biography, 'Jabbing for Gold, Hooking for Glory', revealed a sordid aspect of his boxing career. He had systematically abused laxatives and diuretics in order to keep his weight within the requirements for lightweight boxing. Although the International Boxing Federation officially stripped him of all his titles on learning this information, the book became a best seller, earning him more than enough to secure a comfortable retirement. Despite stopping the laxative abuse, the book revealed that it had already taken an irreversible toll on his bowels. Now he suffered from chronic constipation of the most severe kind, requiring a combination of at least five different aperients a day to achieve a single miserly bowel motion per week. But even this was not enough and every three months he would be admitted to our surgical ward for a variety of powerful oral laxatives and enemas to overcome a particularly prolonged period of constipation. If all that failed, he would then undergo manual disimpaction. It had been an extraordinary six months since he had last been to hospital so he was probably overdue for this admission. The boxer's real name is Quentin Wyoming but due to his chronic constipation and well-known love of Mohammed Ali, we had nicknamed him Gaseous Clay.

Alternaria admitted him three days ago to our ward. Yet nothing had budged despite various concoctions of laxative milkshakes, pills and enemas. This morning on the ward round, Rodrigo kindly allocated the task of manual disimpaction to me. He did it with more enthusiasm than was necessary, probably reflecting his ongoing anger at being included in the lawsuit.

I was not looking forward to this and had gagged a number of times at the prospect. In preparation for the procedure, I made my way to Gaseous' room carrying numerous pairs of gloves and a bedpan. He looked me up and down, the veteran boxer seemingly sizing up an opponent.

"You a new intern?" he asked. Even though he'd been in hospital for a few days, I hadn't had the chance to meet him properly.

"Kind of," I said. After all, it was halfway through the year.

"You ever disimpacted someone before?"

"No, Sir."

"Well, let me tell you that it's not going to be as bad as you think," pronounced Gaseous.

I doubted the veracity of his words and wondered how much brain damage he had suffered due to numerous hits to the head during his career.

"Well, it's probably best that we introduce ourselves properly, considering that in a few minutes you're going to have your hand up my arse. The name's Quentin or 'Gaseous Clay'."

"Pleased to meet you, Gaseous. I'm Manju Mendis."

"You Sri Lankan?"

"That's right. How did you know?"

"I knew a Sri Lankan guy called Mendis. Met him on a trip to Southeast Asia. You remind me of him."

"You mean he was a doctor too?"

"No, but after a few drinks, he tried to stick his hand up my arse!" he laughed. "Those were fun times. Well, that's enough foreplay, Manju. Go ahead and do it."

I removed Gaseous' underpants, rolled him onto his side, took a deep breath and began the procedure. Gaseous was right – it wasn't as bad as I had anticipated. This was largely due to the fact that Gaseous was so constipated that the contents of his rectum were like pieces of rock – completely dry, hard and with nil odour. It reminded me of being on an archaeological dig with Indiana Jones in 'Raiders of the Lost Arse'. After finishing the 'excavations', I handed the bedpan to the nurse. I thanked Gaseous for his patience and we both hoped that this would do the trick.

"I hope that you'll have good news for me tomorrow morning," I said to Gaseous.

"You and me both," he replied.

August 12

Today, I had an unexpected call. But before expanding on that, I ought to give an update on Gaseous Clay. My manual disimpaction did not have the desired effect and he remained constipated. Rodrigo asked us to arrange a transfer to Central Point Hospital, the home of the country's leading constipation specialist. He would work Gaseous up for a revolutionary surgery to overcome the constipation. The constipation surgeon Emmanuel Peres had the misfortune to be known throughout his field as 'Emmanuel Disimpaction'. After completing the necessary paperwork for the inter-hospital transfer, I wished Gaseous well and apologized for my unsuccessful attempt. He was most gracious about it. "No problem, Manju. You tried your best. I was hoping that it would never get to surgery but I guess that my time has finally come."

Rodrigo was quite excited about the upcoming operation. "It's revolutionary you know! I have to study the technique for my Fellowship exam. Oh, what I'd give to be there as Professor Peres performs the surgery."

I, however, could not muster similar enthusiasm to Rodrigo. This further confirmed the inevitable fact that had become more and more apparent throughout this rotation, namely that I was no surgeon. Bonkzalot's brutality and Rodrigo's emotional vacuum simply strengthened my resolve to leave the cutting to someone else. On Rodrigo's classification of humanity, I belonged to the 'Mentally Ill' ie. those who don't want to be surgeons. But frankly, if it meant that I wouldn't turn into some heartless monster like Bonkzalot, it was a cross that I was more than willing to bear. As these thoughts swirled around my head, my pager went off. It was an outside call. When I answered it, I was shocked to find that it was Pik Freiman's maid, Agatha Highcue.

"Dr. Mendis, I'm so sorry to call you during work hours as I know how dreadfully busy you are."

"That's okay, Ms. Highcue. But you know that I shouldn't be talking to you," I said guardedly. The St. Ivanhoe lawyer had told me in no uncertain terms to avoid all contact with the plaintiff and those around her.

"I know, Dr. Mendis. But I really need to talk to you – to explain what this is all about. This in no way will hinder your case, I promise you."

Although I knew that the hospital lawyer would have been furious, I was nevertheless intrigued by what Agatha Highcue had to say. I arranged to meet her at 6:30pm in a café near the hospital.

When I arrived at the café, she was already there. Again, she wore the Mary Poppins costume with the dainty handbag. She greeted me warmly saying, "Dr. Mendis, I truly appreciate you meeting me today. It is very kind of you to do so."

I told her not to bother and offered her a drink, which she politely refused.

I was upfront with her. "Ms. Highcue, forgive me for asking, but how do I know that this isn't some ploy by Mrs. Freiman's legal team to gain an advantage before the trial?"

"Of course I forgive you. You'd be a fool for thinking otherwise. But let me state at the outset that both Mr. Freiman and I know that it was his fault and not yours that led him to take the wrong dose of blood pressure medication. I just hope to goodness that I get to testify on your behalf."

"You don't think that you'll get an opportunity to testify?" I asked, quite concerned.

"Not if that 'woman' has anything to do with it," she replied contemptuously.

"I presume you are referring to Mrs. Freiman?" I said.

"Indeed," she replied. "What I am about to tell you is strictly confidential and I will deny telling it if ever asked."

"That's fine," I said.

She nodded, as if satisfied. "My family has been in the service of the Freimans for generations. We had a cottage on the Freiman estate and I grew up alongside Mr. Pik Freiman who is only two years older than me. Modern society has done away with the class system but back then, it was rigidly enforced. However, on that vast estate which was so far from the nearest city, rules were more relaxed. Mr. Freiman and I always understood the difference in status between us, yet we were allowed to spend a lot of time together on the estate. In our pre-school years, we were inseparable. Even when he attended boarding school, he would write letters to me. I suspect that his parents wouldn't have approved of that. However, one advantage my father had as chief butler was being the first to see the mail. He ensured that Pik's parents never saw the letters. That is not to say that the contents were improper. They were simply correspondence between two young friends."

She paused briefly, looking into the flame of the candle at our table, before continuing.

"At the age of twenty-three, Mr. Pik got married to a beautiful heiress, Ms. Helena Bertram. They moved back to the estate to settle down. In due course, they gave birth to two beautiful children. At this time, I had completed a secretarial course. My father was considering sending me to the city to find employment. Yet fortune smiled upon me, not for the first time in my life. The late Mrs. Freiman took a liking to me and asked me to be a nanny to their children. And so it was that I spent the next fifty years with Mr. Pik, Ms. Helena and their wonderful children."

"Fifty years?" I asked quizzically. "Their children wouldn't have needed a nanny after adolescence."

"That is true, Dr. Mendis. But I am blessed enough to say that I had become part of the family. When the children grew up, Mr. Pik promoted me to Head of Household, a position that I still have today- at least, for the moment."

"So when did the current Mrs. Freiman come into the picture?" I asked.

"Four years ago, after fifty-two years of marriage, Ms. Helena died. I have never known such a good woman in my life, nor have I ever seen a man mourn a wife's passing as much as Mr. Pik did. The current Mrs. Freiman was then Ms. Tabitha Spysee. She was a divorced woman in charge of the floral arrangements for Ms. Helena's funeral."

Her tone suddenly became savagely critical, surprising for a woman who had, a moment ago, seemed so composed. "The money-grabbing little vixen had her claws into him before Ms. Helena had even been buried. She visited Mr. Pik daily and wore his defences down. How can you blame him, a seventy-five-year-old man, lonely and empty so soon after losing the love of his life? Many a younger man would also have fallen prey to the clutches of this greedy temptress with her heaving bosom and seductive ways. And so it was, within six months of Ms. Helena's death, Mr. Freiman announced his marriage to Ms. Tabitha Spysee."

"I vaguely remember reading about it in the newspapers," I said.

"I'm not surprised. It was quite a scandal at the time. His children have never forgiven him."

"What about you, Ms. Highcue? Have you forgiven him?"

"I can't forgive him because I never blamed him. That succubus took advantage of him at a time when he was weakened emotionally. He didn't have the strength to fight her or see reason."

"So he's a weak man who got trapped by a good-looking woman less than half his age. Sounds pretty pathetic to me," I said, deliberately baiting her.

She became agitated. "No. *She* took advantage of him. He is a wonderful man. In seventy-seven years, I have met no one better. Despite his power and wealth, he treated everyone, whether servant or equal, with compassion and generosity. I would die for him, I tell you! He has been such a wonderful friend to me…"

She stopped, realizing that she had revealed more than she had wanted.

"So you love him." It was more of a statement than a question.

She closed her eyes, as tears began to stream down the canyons of her face forged by numerous deep wrinkles. "Oh, Dr. Mendis. My feelings for Mr. Pik are irrelevant. I'm a servant and he's my master. I consider myself lucky to have been able to spend all my life around this tremendous individual. I met you today to explain why the current Mrs. Freiman is so angry with you."

"Yes?"

"It concerns his will. Despite falling prey to her charms, Mr. Pik's lawyers managed to force her to sign a prenuptial agreement. It states that if Mr. Pik comes to any serious harm or dies before his eightieth birthday, she will not be entitled to anything. Once he reaches eighty, half the fortune is hers."

"He's seventy-nine now, isn't he? When does he turn eighty?" I asked.

"October 10th."

"How much is the Freiman fortune worth?"

"I believe that the last estimate was twelve billion dollars."

I whistled in amazement.

"So you understand now?" she continued. "If Mr. Freiman had died that day in hospital when his blood pressure was so high, Mrs. Freiman would have been six billion dollars poorer. You gave her the fright of her life and she won't forgive you or the hospital for it."

"But isn't she worried about his upcoming heart surgery this month? That's an operation which has its own risks," I said.

"Of course she is, Dr. Mendis. You have no idea what a fuss she has been causing in the background. She insisted that the heart surgery be postponed till late October – after his eightieth birthday. Her excuse was that she was worried that Mr. Pik hadn't fully recovered from his gallbladder problem. But really..."

"Really, she just wanted the high-risk operation performed in late October because he'd be eighty and she'd get all the money if he dies on the table," I said, completing her sentence.

She nodded. "She even tried to get an injunction on the surgery. But thankfully, she was unsuccessful. It still goes ahead at the end of this month."

"By now, doesn't Mr. Freiman realize what she's really like?" I asked, perplexed.

"I think so. But he's an honourable man, the last of a dying breed. He won't confide in me but I see the pain of her betrayal in his eyes. Yet, for him, she is his wife and he will defend her to the hilt, even if her actions aren't in his interest."

"That's all very noble on his part, but it really doesn't help me and my colleagues out of this predicament. We're being sued for something that we didn't do," I said.

"I wish I could help you more on that front, Dr. Mendis. But I can't. I just want you to understand that Mr. Freiman isn't behind this ridiculous claim. And please believe me when I say that you are a wonderful doctor. Mr. Freiman thinks ever so highly of you."

She stood up and placed some cash on the table. I stood up and immediately returned it to her. "No, Ms. Highcue. It's my shout." While I was grateful to Ms. Highcue for enlightening me on why I was in this situation, I would have much preferred if she could have solved it.

August 18

Over a large plate of potato wedges, sour cream and chilli sauce, I went over yesterday's conversation with Miss Highcue with Alternaria, Delilah and Copper. I was pleased to see that Delilah was back to her perky best. I suspect that she is still devastated at being double-crossed by Dr. Croquet; however, she is so brilliant that some other groundbreaking discovery or brilliant diagnosis is only just around the corner. I have told her that a number of times since the incident and it appears that she has finally taken it to heart.

Copper shook his head in amazement. "That Mrs. Freiman is the mother of all sugardaddiphiles. She's trying to keep him out of any danger whatsoever till he turns eighty. Then..."

"Then she'll murder him with some exotic poison or another," said Alternaria, completing his sentence.

"I disagree, Alternaria," said Delilah. "From what I know of the woman, she'll wait till he turns eighty and then shag him to death."

Although we didn't know how it would happen, we all agreed that Mr. Pik Freiman's chances of living far beyond eighty were infinitesimally small, courtesy of the delectably diabolical Tabitha Freiman.

I asked Delilah how ED was treating her. "Oh it's really good apart from dealing with Dr. Wyatt."

"Who's that?" asked Copper.

"He's one of the ED specialists."

"I rarely worked with him during my ED term," I remarked. "But he seemed fairly nice whenever I did talk to him. What's wrong?"

"You're right, Manju – he normally is lovely to work with. But Dr. Wyatt's one of these unmarried types who is devoted to his pet dog. It recently died of a brain tumour, on the operating table. He's been miserable ever since, snapping at other staff and not being particularly helpful when we've had a problem."

Copper shook his head. "It's amazing what some people will do for their pets. Imagine brain surgery for a dog."

Suddenly something clicked. "Damien Wyatt's bitch," I mumbled to myself.

"What was that?" asked a startled Delilah.

"Was Dr. Wyatt's dog female?" I hurriedly asked.

"Its name was Marta, so I guess so," responded Delilah, who was clearly bemused by my line of questioning.

"So that's what they were up to!" I exclaimed.

"Can someone please tell me what on earth we are talking about?" asked Copper in exasperation.

I told them all about the conversation between Ponsonby and

Bonkzalot that I had overheard in the changing rooms of the operating theatre almost three weeks ago.

"It was clear that they were secretly 'borrowing' anaesthetic and surgical equipment for some dodgy purpose. Now it all makes sense. Bonkzalot has a surgical list for animals and he gets Dr. Ponsonby to anaesthetize for him. They get paid $1,000 per case – Bonkzalot charged Dr. Wyatt fifty per cent extra for his bitch because it involved neurosurgery."

Delilah then said, "Well, that explains something else. Bonkzalot came down to ED to review a patient last week. Dr. Wyatt was working that day. When he saw Bonkzalot, he took him to a corner and they had a heated argument. They kept their voices low but I distinctly heard Dr. Wyatt ask for his money back. Bonkzalot told him to go to hell and that it wasn't his fault that she didn't pull through. I had assumed that Dr. Wyatt was discussing one of his family friends or a relative, but it must have been his dog."

Copper said, "Wow, what a scam! If they do this once a fortnight and have ten cases a list, then that's over $250,000 a year in extra income. Plus there are no overheads for cleaning equipment because they steal everything from St. Ivanhoe's operating theatres."

"And because they are getting paid in cash, they are probably not declaring this income to the tax office," I added.

"Oh my God!" said Delilah, looking horrified.

"What's up?" I asked her.

"What about the Infection Control issues?"

"What do you mean?" asked Alternaria.

"Forget the stealing, forget the undeclared taxable income. Bonkzalot's presumably returning the surgical equipment to operating theatres after operating on all those animals. Then they are being used on humans."

"Wouldn't they get sterilized after he uses them?" asked Alternaria.

Delilah shook her head. "I don't know. Even if they are being sterilized, I know for a fact that standard sterilization techniques won't kill everything, for example, the prions that cause 'Mad Cow Disease'. Bonkzalot and Ponsonby might be putting St. Ivanhoe surgical patients at risk of some ghastly animal disease."

Copper said, "And at the end of the day, it's all about risk perception.

Even if you knew that there was no risk to humans, the fact that the country's premier hospital is using the same surgical equipment on animals and then humans would disgust the public. It certainly disgusts me. There'd be an outcry."

"Exactly," said Delilah. "Can any of you, as doctors, honestly say that you would be happy to undergo surgery with equipment that has just been used on animals, even if it has been sterilized?"

We shook our heads as one, trying to digest the enormity of the abomination that we had just discovered.

"So what should we do now?" asked Copper, echoing what we were all wondering.

"We should tell the Infection Control nurses," I urged.

Delilah shook her head. "Unfortunately without proof, there's nothing that they can do. Imagine if the Infection Control nurses confront Bonkzalot and Ponsonby without any evidence. They would simply deny the 'outrageous' allegations and demand that the poor nurses be disciplined."

"They can't get away with this! Bonkzalot should lose his job," I angrily said.

"I agree," said Alternaria.

"We *all* agree," said Delilah. "But we'll have to bide our time till an opportunity presents itself. Otherwise we'll all get screwed – Bonkzalot will make sure of that. I've already been screwed by one consultant – I'd rather not get screwed by another."

On that grim note, we all got up and returned to work.

August 23

Lucky came around for dinner tonight. I invited her earlier in the week and it took some goading on my part to get her to accept. Despite all the dramas in my life, especially the upcoming court case with Tabitha Freiman, I never forgot Lucky's attempt to disguise, or rather, divest herself completely of her South Asian heritage. It went against everything I believed in. In truth, I regarded her attitude as unnatural, somewhat akin to a talking dog, a green sky or an England football coach who is actually from England. The true purpose of Lucky's presence at the dinner was to gently reintroduce her to her South Asian heritage. Of course, she didn't realize this and may have refused to come if I had stated so up-front. Instead, I played on her longing for genuine Indian food that slipped out unintentionally during casual conversation *(Presumably her longing for Indian food slipped out during conversation rather than the food itself – Editors)*. Sri Lankan food is very similar to Southern Indian food in that it is quite spicy and not particularly oily. North Indian food, on the other hand, tends to be very oily and with little chilli. Anyway, Lucky initially was quite hesitant.

"Your mother sounds like a great cook, Manju. But I haven't been to a South Asian house for such a long time... I just don't know."

"For heaven's sake, Lucky, I'm not asking you to become part of the family. I'm just inviting you to share in a Sri Lankan meal, a really scrumptious rice and curry," I countered.

"Oh Manju..." she said with uncertainty.

"And it's not like you're going to transform back into an Indian just by being in the company of other South Asians. It's not infectious, you know," I said, laughing.

With a sigh, she grudgingly acquiesced to my invitation. "Of course you're right. What harm can there be in going for a meal? I'd love to come. Thanks for the invite. But Manju, please don't tell your family my true background."

"Mum's the word."

It ended up being a pleasant evening. Mallika Punchi, Sarath Mama, Lal and my sister's family all turned up. Mallika Punchi and Ammi had prepared hoppers. It was absolutely superb and I feel no shame in admitting that I stuffed myself like a pig. More importantly though, Lucky seemed to have a good time. Not only did she love the food, but she also got on really well with everyone. She was a 'natural' which isn't surprising since she is one of us anyway. Lal, in particular, was in fine form. My gay yet-to-be-outed cousin has a great sense of humour and does the most amazing impersonations. He could easily succeed as a stand up comic. He and Lucky had some hilarious repartees that we all delighted in. I hadn't realized that Lucky was such a hoot.

Later, a number of family members pressed me about Lucky. She would have been relieved to hear that their enquiries had nothing to do with her heritage. Not surprisingly, everyone wanted to know whether this blonde blue-eyed intern was my girlfriend, particularly my anxious-looking father. I reassured everyone that she was nothing more than a colleague and good friend who enjoyed South Asian food. Interestingly, only my mother had an inkling of what was truly going on. In the kitchen, while I was loading the dishwasher, Ammi said, "Your friend, the albino, is a nice girl."

"The albino?" I asked, puzzled.

"Yes, typical Indian girl with white hair and blue eyes – she's an albino," my mother remarked.

"What makes you think she is Indian?" I asked hesitantly.

"Oh please, Manju. I wasn't born yesterday. I know an Indian when I see one. Haven't you asked her about her background?"

"Ammi, I'm nowhere near as interested in someone's background as you are," I answered evasively but truthfully.

"What, men! You can tell a lot about a person from their background – you young people with all your equality nonsense don't realize this. If a child comes from a good family, it means that they are more likely to be dependable, and fit in. Anyway, I don't give a hoot as long as this albino isn't your girlfriend."

"The 'albino' and I are just friends, Ammi."

My mother brightened up after hearing that. "Mind you, she's a lovely girl, despite her skin condition."

Wondering whether Indian albinos even existed, I saw Lucky to her car at the end of the evening and asked her if she'd had a good time.

"Thanks so much, Manju. It was wonderful. And your cousin, Lal, he's so funny – what a laugh!"

I hugged her and wished her goodnight. All in all, I was happy. Lucky now realized that she could at least mix with South Asian people and enjoy herself. The next step, however, was more difficult: to get her to accept who she really is, namely Lakshmi Raja.

August 26

It is the early hours of Tuesday morning. I fear that I am writing these words as a felon. Perhaps I should be on the run. Two days ago, Pik Freiman was admitted to hospital for his elective coronary artery bypass surgery. He arrived on Sunday so the surgical overtime Resident had been assigned the task of admitting him. It would have been very awkward if I had been the one to admit him, particularly since I was brimming with resentment about the looming litigation case. Despite this, I did have the misfortune to run into his wife in the elevator. This had been especially frustrating as she had entered what would otherwise have remained an empty elevator, thereby denying me the opportunity to Elevator Groove. Not surprisingly, it was a fairly uncomfortable elevator trip. I am ashamed to say my hormones betrayed me. Tabitha Freiman wore a sexy black dress and long black boots that really highlighted her beauty. I couldn't help but notice. Unfortunately, she noticed me noticing.

She laughed a sensual but wicked laugh. "Oh Dr. Mendis! Do you find me attractive? Don't be embarrassed. Most men do, especially the rich, lonely old ones. But just one word of advice – you could never afford this package," she said, gesturing at herself with a flourish and finally revealing her true colours in the solitude of the elevator.

As the elevator doors opened, I fired a quick rejoinder. "That's true. But I never realized it was for sale. I just can't remember what that's called. Perhaps you can remind me."

"You son of a bitch!" she angrily replied.

"No, that's not it," I said, feigning a thoughtful expression.

"Just to let you know, Dr. Mendis, I have been considering dropping the negligence suit. But there's no chance in hell of that happening now. See you in court." And she stormed off angrily.

It was a masterful stroke to end the conversation on her part. I strongly suspect that the heartless harpy never had any intention of dropping the case, but for a few moments at least, she had introduced some doubt into my mind.

I was joining Dr. Hart in operating theatres for his list, on which Mr. Freiman was the second and final case. But about half an hour prior to surgery, an emergency dissecting aneurysm hit the ED. Dr. Hart operated on him immediately. It was a complex operation, requiring a lot of assistance; therefore, I got to scrub in for the first time. Dr. Hart did an extraordinary job and saved the patient's life but it took many hours. The upshot of this emergency case was that Mr. Pik Freiman's coronary artery bypass surgery didn't begin till after 9pm. Unlike the earlier emergency case, this time only Rodrigo scrubbed in for the operation. I was again banished to the corner to practise valve replacement surgery on the pig's heart that Dr. Hart had brought from his laboratory.

After some time, the phone inside the operating theatre rang. The nurse answered it. Amazingly, Mrs. Freiman had somehow got hold of the number and was demanding an update on her husband's case. Presumably the sugardaddiphile wanted to make sure that Pik Freiman and her multibillion dollar inheritance was surviving the surgery.

Dr. Hart shook his head in annoyance. "Honestly, that woman has been so difficult to deal with. Did you know that she almost took out an injunction to prevent the surgery? Now she's bothering me *during* the operation. How the hell did she get this number?"

Dr. Hart looked in my direction. "Dr. Mendis, please go out to the theatre reception area and inform Mrs. Freiman that her husband is doing well."

"Yes, Dr. Hart," I said. Predictably, Tabitha Freiman somehow found ways to inconvenience my life. The valve surgery on the pig's heart had been going well and was now at a critical juncture. The last thing that I wanted to do was interrupt the 'surgery', so I carried it, stitches and all, in my hand and went to the reception area. Being so late at night, the area was deserted apart from Ms. Highcue and Mrs. Freiman who was pacing restlessly. Mrs. Freiman looked at me in horror as I approached her. She pointed at the heart in my hand and said, "What the hell is that?"

"Pig's heart," I replied. It was only later that I realized that, through the muffled effect of my surgical mask, she had mistakenly heard me say, "Pik's heart," rather than "Pig's heart".

She went deathly pale and suddenly hyperventilating, asked, "Dead?"

Still thinking that she was referring to the pig's heart, rather than that of her husband, I irritably replied, "Of course. I'm holding the bloody heart in my hand, aren't I?"

The combination of the sudden loss of her multibillion dollar fortune and the wrinkled heart of her husband in my hand was all too much for Mrs. Freiman. She did what most people in such a situation would have done – she fainted flat on her back. But Mrs. Freiman was a tall woman, rendered even more so by the high heels she wore and suffered a very heavy fall. It was made worse by her hitting her head on the edge of a large cement pot on the way down. Nevertheless, I was shocked to see a large pool of blood gather where her head hit the ground. I bent down to render my assistance but was pulled away by an anxious and pale Ms. Highcue.

"Please Doctor, tell me it's not true. That's not Mr. Pik's heart, is it?" she asked, pointing at the organ in my hand.

"Of course not," I cried. "It's a *pig's* heart – P-I-G. Mr. Freiman is still in surgery and he's doing fine."

"Thank God," she cried, her face lighting up with joy.

I bent down again to minister to Mrs. Freiman. I was shocked to find that her pulse was weak, her breathing slow and irregular and that she had blown a pupil. Why on earth was this happening? Then it clicked. I recalled Mrs. Freiman telling me that she took warfarin for a deep venous thrombosis of the leg. She was anticoagulated and prone to massive bleeding in the event of even minor trauma. The fall had triggered a massive intracerebral haemorrhage. Mrs. Freiman was dying.

Ms. Highcue looked anxiously on. "Doctor Mendis, what's happened to her?"

I quickly replied as time was of the essence. "She takes warfarin which makes her blood very thin. So when she fainted and hit her head, she suffered a massive brain haemorrhage. The skull is a very enclosed space. Too much blood and the brain gets squashed – it'll kill her."

I ran to the other end of the reception area to push the bright red button for medical emergencies. The Cardiac Arrest team would be here within a minute or two.

"Where are you going, Doctor?" asked Ms. Highcue.

"To declare a medical emergency," I yelled over my shoulder as I reached the red button.

"Please don't do that, Doctor. I wouldn't want to hurt you."

Something eerily sinister in her tone made me hesitate. I turned around and saw a sight that I never imagined possible – Mary Poppins pointing a gun at me.

"Ms. Highcue?" I asked, stunned.

"Move away from that red button, Dr. Mendis. I don't want to shoot you, but I will if I have to. Now slowly come and sit down next to Mrs. Freiman."

I complied with her request.

Ms. Highcue looked anxiously at Mrs. Freiman and asked, "How is she?"

I quickly reassessed Tabitha Freiman. I was thoroughly alarmed to find that she had completely stopped breathing and had no pulse. Furthermore, her other pupil was also enlarged. I reported these findings to Ms. Highcue.

"The bleeding has squashed the vital centres of the brain to such an extent that she has no heartbeat and no pulse. The only way to save her is to drill a hole in her skull immediately to relieve the pressure. But if I don't start CPR now, even if she survives, she'll have permanent brain damage. Please let me call the Cardiac Arrest team and start CPR," I pleaded.

"I'm sorry, Dr. Mendis. But I will kill you if you try to do either. That would be a great shame because, though I am willing to go to prison for this, I don't want anyone else to get hurt."

"What's this all about, Ms. Highcue?"

"It's about love, Doctor. I thought you understood that. I have been in love with Mr. Pik for so long that I can't remember a time when I wasn't in love with him. Isn't that extraordinary? I was heartbroken when he married the first Mrs. Freiman, but she was a wonderful woman. In the end, I think she loved him as much as me. She also probably made a better wife than I would ever have. When she died, few people knew that I mourned her loss almost as much as Mr. Pik did. But as for this vulture," she said almost spitting in contempt, "her sole goal is to rob him of his fortune. You do realize that she'll probably kill him as soon as the prenuptial agreement expires on his eightieth birthday?"

"The thought had crossed my mind," I admitted.

"The idea of him falling prey to that banshee was too much for me to bear. So I bought this gun last week."

"And you were going to shoot her? Just like that?" I asked, my curiosity aroused, despite my precarious situation.

She smiled grimly. "Yes – just like that. In fact, I planned to do it once I was certain that Mr. Pik had fully recovered from his heart surgery. But I can't ignore the opportunity presented to me just now."

"But you'll go to prison?" I pressed on.

"I'm fully aware of that. Let me tell you something, Dr. Mendis. Even though he never loved me in the way that I wished, I have spent over sixty years living with the man of my dreams. In all that time, he has never treated me harshly or unfairly, only with kindness and respect. How many women can say that? I could die happily, today, knowing that I've had a blessed life. And I am certainly willing to spend my final years in prison if it means that Mr. Pik won't meet a premature end at the hands of that she-devil."

"Did it occur to you that Pik Freiman may not forgive you for this?" I asked her.

She nodded. "Better him alive hating me than not being alive at all."

"You'd do all that for a man?" I asked, surprised by the intensity of her devotion.

"For *that* man, I'd do anything," she replied simply. She looked at the motionless figure of Mrs. Freiman. "Is she dead yet?"

Tabitha Freiman's pupils were dilated and un-reactive. It was now over three minutes since I last detected a breath or a heartbeat. I looked directly at Ms. Highcue and said, "Yes, she's dead. Even if the Cardiac Arrest team arrives here now, I am fairly sure that she'll be beyond their help."

It was only then that Ms. Highcue's hands began to tremble and her face became grey and anguished, revealing herself as a desperate woman in love rather than a cold-blooded killer.

She put the gun away and said, "It is done. Do whatever you wish."

I ran to the red button and pushed it, declaring a Cardiac Arrest. I then hurried back to Mrs. Freiman and commenced CPR. I realized that these were acts of futility on my part but I had to do something. The Cardiac Arrest team arrived quickly and took over from me. But within minutes, they had ascertained that the resuscitation was a pointless exercise and declared her dead.

The Team Leader of the Cardiac Arrest team asked me what had happened. Ms. Highcue looked at the floor as she prepared to be exposed. Her air of resignation was well founded since this was indeed my intention. I took another look at the corpse of the woman who had been suing me and then at the old woman who had only ever been nice to me (apart from briefly pointing a gun in my direction) and made my decision. I gave the following explanation to the Team Leader:

"I had been explaining to Mrs. Freiman how her husband's surgery was progressing. She asked me details of the operation itself. I suspect that the graphic nature of my answers made her queasy. She fainted, hitting her head very hard on the cement pot over there and then on the floor. She takes warfarin for a DVT according to the lady over there," I said, pointing to Ms. Highcue. "The combination of trauma and anticoagulation probably led to a massive intracerebral bleed. Certainly, she had blown both pupils, was pulseless and apnoeic when I first assessed her. I immediately pushed the Arrest button and commenced CPR. Despite my best efforts, she never responded. And you know the rest..."

The Team Leader seemed satisfied with my response. "It all sounds like a terribly unfortunate accident. You couldn't have done anything else. But since she wasn't a patient of the hospital, the police will have to be called in."

I nodded my head, not daring to look at Ms. Highcue, knowing that a wayward glance or word from her would give me away. As the Cardiac Arrest team slowly moved away, only a hospital security guard remained to await the arrival of the police. I took Ms. Highcue to one side.

She looked both worried and confused. "Dr. Mendis, why didn't you tell your colleague what really happened? You are only putting yourself in unnecessary danger. For heaven's sake, I let an injured woman die. I need to be punished. I am an evil person."

"No, Ms. Highcue, you are not evil. You were simply protecting the man you love and are willing to pay the ultimate sacrifice to do so. Quite noble if you ask me. The only evil woman in this picture is that scheming witch who is lying dead over there who, as you say, was going to kill Mr. Freiman as soon as he turned eighty and was also suing me on false pretences. I don't mourn her passing one iota but I certainly would feel sad if you went to jail. Anyway, now that's she's gone, you and Pik Freiman have a chance together."

Ms. Highcue became visibly surprised at this last remark. "Dr. Mendis, I once told you that we lived in a time when servants didn't marry masters – it was just not done."

"Maybe not then, I grant you," I replied. "But things are different now. The 'class system' is not part of this country anymore (despite what my mother says). And while I'm no expert in matters of love, I did have the opportunity to watch Mr. Freiman during his time in hospital. The way he looks at you, the way he talks to you... I've seen less intimacy between married couples. What I'm trying to say is that you have a chance with this man now that he is widowed."

The beginnings of a smile grew cautiously from her wrinkled lips. "Your optimism is greater than mine. But thank you for even considering it. You have given me hope that I never dared to dream about. I will think on it." Then she suddenly became worried, the wrinkles of her forehead furrowing into waves as she contemplated her current predicament. "But what do we do about Mrs. Freiman's death, Dr. Mendis?" she asked anxiously.

"You just need to tell the police the same story that I told the Team Leader just now. The success of our contrivance lies in the consistency of our stories."

Ms. Highcue grasped my wrists affectionately. "Doctor Mendis, how can I ever repay you?"

"By doing two things," I replied. "Firstly, don't ever tell anyone else what really transpired today. Secondly and most importantly, I want you and Mr. Freiman to lead a happy life – together."

My heart racing, I returned to the operating theatre to explain my long absence. Everyone was shocked to hear about Tabitha Freiman's demise. But thankfully, Mr. Freiman's operation was going like a dream and he would be fine. I excused myself as the police had come to take our statement. Ms. Highcue had just finished giving her statement and she briefly smiled in my direction to indicate that all was well. I was quite nervous when the constable approached me for my version of events. However, he didn't appear at all suspicious and took my statement down, only needing to clarify one or two points.

"Thank you for your time, Dr. Mendis. If we need anything, we'll be in touch," said the constable.

I sincerely hoped that I wouldn't hear from him again.

I went back to the operating theatres but Dr. Hart kindly excused me, given the traumatic experience that I'd just been through. As I drove home in the car, I was on a high: the lawsuit would presumably be dropped since Mrs. Freiman wasn't there to drive it. In addition, by not implicating Ms. Highcue, hopefully she and Mr. Freiman might still have a future together in the final years of their life – all thanks to me.

Having time to cool down and examine events more rationally, my exultation has turned to abject terror. I realize that, at the end of the day, I had covered up a murder. What the hell was I thinking? A 'Law and Order' marathon had just started on one of the cable TV channels. After watching a few episodes, I have come to the conclusion that I am an 'accessory to murder.' If anyone ever discovers that I covered up Ms. Highcue's crime, I might go to prison. I currently have two grave concerns. Firstly, I am worried that the coroner's medical examination of the corpse might show that I did not commence CPR on Mrs. Freiman immediately. If the police discover this delay, they'll have me for breakfast. Secondly, if Ms. Highcue gets overwhelmed by guilt and confesses her crime, I'm completely screwed. I will now try and sleep but am literally shivering with fear. If I were writing this diary instead of typing it, this entry would have been all over the page.

August 28

I've been having diarrhoea for the last forty-eight hours. I have no doubt that it is entirely due to a guilty conscience, which is apparently anatomically located in my rectum. Every time my pager rings with an outside call, I fear that it is the police and my heart rate doubles with anxiety.

I saw Mr. Freiman on our ward round. He is mourning the loss of his wife, much to the annoyance of Dr. Hart who wanted the bad news withheld from him until at least five days after surgery. He was concerned that the emotional shock of his wife's death might be too much for Mr. Freiman soon after surgery, so he demanded silence from everyone. Unfortunately, Mr. and Mrs. Freiman's celebrity status put paid to the best-laid plans of Dr. Hart. Within twelve hours of her demise, at least two major TV networks had picked up the story. And while the nursing staff in the Cardiothoracic Intensive Care Unit did not break the story to him, the TV above his bed did. Despite being very upset at hearing of his wife's death, he did not do Dr. Hart the discourtesy of dying from shock. In fact, today he looked quite well. Ms. Highcue was at his side and afterwards I managed to have a quiet moment with her alone.

"How are you?" I asked her, a simple question yet one full of meaning.

She smiled. "I'm well, considering..." She left the remainder of her reply hanging in the air.

"How is Mr. Freiman taking the death of his wife?" I asked.

"He took it badly when he found out. After all, how would any man feel, hearing about his wife's death from a TV news story just one day after surgery? Dr. Hart should have let me tell him, but he was insistent that Pik be 'kept in the dark'. Oh dear, I am sure that he meant well. But today, Pik seems to be brighter. Perhaps he is starting to see that Tabitha's death was a lucky escape for him."

"I hope so, Ms. Highcue."

"How are you doing, Dr. Mendis? I must say you look rather under the weather. You haven't... changed your mind?" she asked anxiously.

"No," I replied, looking around to make sure no one could hear us before I proceeded further. "There are two things that really worry me. First of all, I hope and pray that the coroner won't find anything on the autopsy that will conflict with our stories."

Ms. Highcue brightened up immediately. "Haven't you heard? The coroner released her report this morning. She concluded that Mrs. Freiman died from a tragic set of circumstances related to her fall and blood-thinning medication – there was no foul play involved."

"But normally, it takes ages for coroners to complete their examination and release their findings. It's only been forty-eight hours," I said, perplexed.

"Normally, the country's second wealthiest man isn't yelling down the phone, telling the Minister of Police to make the enquiry into his wife's death a priority. Pik may be old but he is still extremely influential. In fact, it was the Minister herself who called Pik to tell him the results of the autopsy."

This was tremendous news! "You have no idea how great this is," I said, sighing with relief.

She smiled wryly. "Actually, I do, since I'm the real criminal here and should be more worried than you. What was your second concern?"

I paused, then came out and said it. "I have been worried sick that you'll get cold feet and confess everything, sending both you and me to prison."

She seemed momentarily taken aback before bursting out laughing.

"What's so funny?" I asked, bemused by her response to our precarious situation.

"It's just that I've been wondering the same thing about you. Dr. Mendis, you seem to forget that I am the one who committed the crime. You just covered it up. No, Dr. Mendis, you have given me a chance with Pik that I may never have had. Tabitha was a ghastly woman and I will never reveal the events of that night to anyone. If you've learnt anything about me from our brief time together, it's that I am fiercely loyal. Your actions that night have indebted me to you forever. I will never do anything to endanger you, including confessing my crime."

I felt a wave of relief wash over me. Everything was going to be fine. Then I smiled as I recalled what she had just said. "'Tabitha' and 'Pik' – that's rather informal for you, Ms. Highcue. What ever happened to 'Mr. Pik' and 'Mrs. Freiman'?"

She grinned. "I've taken your advice about living in a classless society. So I asked Pik yesterday if he would mind me calling him by his first name. He smiled and asked me why I had waited so long to do so. It's a start..."

"It's more than a start," I said, feeling glad for them both.

I left the ward, feeling happier than I had in days. And you know what? Ever since that conversation, the diarrhoea has stopped. Go figure.

August 29

Last night, I caught up with the gang. They'd all heard about the death of Mrs. Freiman. No one knew that I was there when it happened, apart from Alternaria. I'd informed her immediately as she had also been part of the upcoming lawsuit. Incidentally, earlier today, Ms. Highcue confirmed what I had been hoping, namely that the lawsuit had been dropped on Mr. Freiman's orders. So it was a night of celebration for me. First of all, everyone was naturally keen to hear what had happened to Mrs. Freiman. Of course, I lied and told them the story that I gave the police. It really was gut-wrenching to deceive these six colleagues, whom I regarded as close and trusted friends. However, the secret of Tabitha Freiman's death had to remain between me and Agatha Highcue.

Today was the last day of the surgical term for Alternaria and me. Like our predecessors (Lucky and Smegman), we were thrilled at the prospect of never having to work with Monty Bonkzalot ever again. It should have been a wonderful day but it ended in disaster and disappointment.

Everything had gone well throughout a typically busy day. At about 6:30pm, Bonkzalot did a ward round following his operating theatre list. The usual torrent of abuse was directed at us but over the past few months, we had become immune to Bonkzalot's ranting and raving. While reviewing the final patient on the round, everything deteriorated. Mrs. Bucket, a woman in her fifties, was being investigated for a kidney mass. The overall picture was consistent with cancer. While this would be a disastrous diagnosis for anyone, it would have been especially so for Mrs. Bucket. She looks after a ten-year-old child with severe autism. Without her, his future would be very uncertain. So Alternaria and I were particularly anxious for the results of her biopsy, which was performed a few days earlier. At her bedside, Bonkzalot pulled out the envelope with her results. He looked at it for a moment and said, "It's benign. You can return to your retarded brat now."

Alternaria and I looked at each other in shock and winced in embarrassment at Bonkzalot's words, which, judging by the outraged expression on Mrs. Bucket's face, had also taken her by surprise. Was

Bonkzalot so clueless of how to act tactfully or did he just not care? Anyway, the most important news was that the mass was not cancer. Mrs. Bucket also seemed to take this attitude and let Bonkzalot's appalling pronouncement pass. Then, just as we started to move away from Mrs. Bucket's bedside, I heard Alternaria strumming her ukulele. She began to sing:

> There was a mass in Mrs. Bucket
> We all thought it was cancer
> If it had been
> She'd have kicked the bucket
> A sad end to this stanza
>
> But happy to say
> That we're feeling gay
> And everything's going to be fine
> Because every single biopsy sample
> Turned out to be benign
>
> Yippee! Hoorah!
> Now it's plain to see
> That Mrs. Bucket and her mass
> Can go back to her family
> Back to her family
> Back to her family

Mrs. Bucket, the nurses and I applauded Alternaria and laughed in delight. As we left the room, however, Bonkzalot was clearly fuming. He dismissed Rodrigo and took us both to the doctors' room and closed the door.

"What the fucking hell was that all about?" he yelled at Alternaria, his face, beetroot red in colour.

"I just thought that it'd brighten things up if I sang a song," said Alternaria, clearly intimidated by Bonkzalot's fury.

"It was really amazing," I added.

"Shut up!" Bonkzalot snapped at me. "I wasn't talking to you, boy."

"Let me say this once and once only – this is not 'Charlie and the Chocolate Factory' and you are not a fucking Oompa-Loompa! How dare you lower the standard of this surgical unit with such nonsense?"

I didn't see it coming. Bonkzalot grabbed Alternaria's ukulele and flung it across the room, against a wall. With a sickening thud and the snapping of strings, it slid down the wall into a mournful heap on the floor.

He continued his verbal onslaught. "I always knew that there'd be problems when we allowed niggers to practise medicine. Niggers make good patients and good menials, but to give them a license to practise medicine... this will be the end of the health system in this country. You are both living proof of that. And by the way, I'll deny that I ever said that. So don't make a complaint –it'll be your word against mine. One final thing, I have completed your term assessments. I passed you – not because I think that you are any good. I just wanted to ensure that you don't repeat this term, because frankly, I can't tolerate the sight of you."

Alternaria ran over to the damaged ukulele and began to weep.

Bonkzlaot looked at the tears streaming down her face and then looked at me. "Boy, it appears that the dyke's leaking. Why don't you put a finger in her hole to try and plug it?"

He opened the door and walked out, laughing.

I had never been so angry and humiliated in all my life. But before I could concern myself with my own feelings, I hurried over to Alternaria. She was almost hysterical.

"My grandmother made this for me," she wept, holding the dented ukulele with a number of broken strings. "She's dead, Manju, and this is all I have left of her. This means so much to me. How could he do that? How could he say that?"

I held her close but she backed away, now furious.

"I became a doctor because I thought that we make a difference. But I don't feel like I've helped anyone this term. And now a surgeon thinks of me as nothing more than a 'nigger' and 'dyke'! What's gone wrong, Manju? It shouldn't be this way. It just shouldn't be."

"Alternaria, I'm as angry as you," I said.

"It doesn't matter! Nothing matters anymore!" she cried as she pushed me aside, and ran out of the room with her damaged ukulele.

"Alternaria! Wait!" I shouted as I ran to catch up with her.

"Leave me alone! I just want to be left alone," she said, as she entered the elevator.

As the elevator doors closed, I hoped and prayed that she wouldn't do anything to hurt herself. I quickly called Lucky and Delilah and told them what had happened. They were shocked. I asked them to somehow or another keep in touch with Alternaria, as she really needed a friend. They both promised to do so.

Although I knew Bonkzalot was nasty, I never thought that he could be so diabolically evil. Within moments, he had reduced us from practising doctors to 'niggers' and a 'dyke'. I thought it ironic that the only racism I had encountered in my life had occurred within the hallowed walls of this hospital, first from a patient and now from a consultant surgeon. This was meant to be a place of intellectual endeavour, heroism and compassion. What had gone wrong? Was it just Bonkzalot or was it the system? Had my childhood and university years shielded me from what the world was really like? Tears started to stream from my eyes. Bonkzalot had wounded us – a deep, penetrating wound into our psyche that would take ages to heal. In Alternaria's case, perhaps never. And his response to this? To walk out of the room, laughing at an utterly despicable joke made at Alternaria's expense. It was at that point that I made up my mind: whether Bonkzalot was only part of a more systemic problem or whether he was the problem itself, he would have to pay for his words and deeds today. I took out my wallet and rummaged through it, looking for the card. I stared at it for a few moments, took a deep breath and dialled the number. After the second ring, there was an answer. I spoke.

"Is that Fabulus Hipz? Hi, I'm Dr. Manju Mendis, the intern you met in the elevator at St. Ivanhoe? Do you remember me?"

She did.

"Good. Is that offer to be your source still available?"

It was.

"Excellent. What would you say if I told you that a distinguished surgeon regularly steals surgical equipment from St. Ivanhoe to operate on animals? He then secretly returns the equipment to the hospital where it is used to operate on human patients. Is that the kind of story that you are looking for?"

Apparently it was, judging by the high-pitched swear word that followed.

"You'd like to meet up with me to discuss this further? Absolutely, Fabulus!"

My hands were trembling as the call ended. I was going to the media behind the hospital's back, presumably putting my job on the line. Yet despite this, only one thought reverberated through my head: "Game on, Monty! You are going down."

August 31

The last twenty-four hours have been amazing. I don't know where to begin. Yesterday morning, Delilah called me. She and Lucky had found Alternaria in her apartment on Friday night, extremely distraught but not suicidal. They managed to calm her down after a few wines and a bonding session. To be on the safe side, Lucky spent the night with Alternaria. By Saturday morning, she was terribly disillusioned with medicine but was otherwise herself. Alternaria's family lives about 1,000km away so a quick drive home was out of the question. But Lucky convinced her to take the one-hour plane trip home. Ironically it was Lucky, the girl who had distanced herself from her family on the basis of ethnicity, who convinced Alternaria that she needed a good dose of family to deal with her encounter of racism. Anyway, I was glad about this outcome and profusely thanked Delilah and Lucky for helping me out. This definitely needed a lady's touch, something that I couldn't provide.

With Alternaria out of immediate danger, I turned my mind to Fabulus Hipz. Despite having a night to sleep on it, I still did not regret calling her about Bonkzalot's animal surgery scam. Revenge was paramount on my mind and she could provide the vehicle for his destruction. The only worry I had was financial. Fabulus suggested that we meet for dinner at 'The Bohemian Turnip', one of the swishest restaurants in the country where ironically they didn't serve any turnip dishes. I went online and was horrified to find that the basic twelve-course degustation menu was $450 per person! And that was *without* wine! Although I was a doctor living at home, I still didn't have that kind of money to throw around. Furthermore, I wasn't sure whether I would have to pay for Fabulus. After all, she was the lady – perhaps she expected me to do the 'decent thing' and cover the whole bill myself. Anyway, I ensured that my credit card still had at least $1200 credit – just in case.

The restaurant, situated in an old estate house on the outskirts of the city, is gorgeous. To find this 'country estate' with extensive lawns and a large fountain in the midst of a multitude of inner city apartments is in itself remarkable. There is even valet parking for guests. I had been puzzled and worried by Fabulus' choice of a meeting place. I am meant to be a covert source whose anonymity is vital. Why would she choose a high-profile restaurant in which to meet? Wouldn't a dark underground car park have been more appropriate? Her reasons became clear on entering the building. Every dining party is given a private room, subtly but securely separated from others by ornate bamboo screens. Apart from a single dedicated waiter, I saw no one else while dining. Despite it presumably being fully occupied, I could not hear any background conversation from other diners in the restaurant.

Fabulus looked stunning. She was wearing a gold strapless gown that somehow seemed to hang off her without completely dropping to the floor. I suspect that it was wasted on someone with as limited fashion sense as me. The food was extraordinary. I resent dining at exclusive restaurants because their portions are too small. But here, at The Bohemian Turnip, they got the portions just right. And as for the quality of the dishes – extraordinary! My taste buds were like inexperienced virgins being tantalized with a flotilla of flavours floating in my mouth. It was literally orgasmic – well not literally perhaps, but there was certainly a lot of moaning and groaning following each delectable mouthful.

In order to enjoy the meal fully, Fabulus suggested leaving the business part of the evening to the end of the banquet. We had a lovely time. Apart from her fascinating media stories, it turns out that Fabulus and I share an obsession with cricket, particularly a love of Brian Lara. While I normally hold fellow fanatics spellbound with my story of shaking Brian Lara's hand, I was clearly out of my league here

– Fabulus casually mentioned that she has interviewed Lara on two occasions and sat next to him at a charity dinner! I cannot convey the simultaneous admiration and envy that such anecdotes evoked. When dinner ended, the conversation became serious as matters moved from cricket to Bonkzalot's foray into veterinary surgery. Clearly, Fabulus was appalled.

"That's disgusting! How can you use an instrument on an animal and then on a human being? And Manju, you believe that there might be a risk of Mad Cow Disease from this?"

"I'm the wrong person to ask. But one of my brilliant colleagues believes that standard sterilization protocols may not kill the prion that causes Mad Cow Disease. So if he has operated on an animal with Mad Cow Disease or something equivalent, who knows?"

"Either way it's despicable. It's not as if this Monty Bonkzalot is struggling to earn a living. I'm sure that he is remunerated more than adequately through the hospital and his private practice," she said.

"Well, he drives the latest BMW and has a six-bedroom house in Broadley Bay," I replied, remembering a piece of gossip from one of the senior operating theatre nurses. "So he can't be that hard up for a crust."

"Presumably not."

"So," I said anxiously, "now you know the story, are you still interested?"

"Oh yes!" she replied excitedly. "As far as media reports go, this is a beauty." Fabulus then looked at me shrewdly. "So, Manju, why are you coming to me with this? You are taking a big risk, you know? The team at St. Ivanhoe wouldn't be exactly thrilled to know that we are having this conversation."

"I know that. Well, I think that it is just unacceptable behaviour for a consultant surgeon at a prestigious hospital."

"Boring," she said, her gorgeous eyes penetrating mine. "What's really going on?"

I hesitated for a while, then said, "Revenge. That bastard humiliated me and my friend and I want the prick to pay."

Fabulus rubbed her hands together, apparently delighted. "Ah – revenge! Well, that I can understand."

I went on to explain how he had treated Alternaria and me, especially his behaviour on that final ward round.

Fabulus whistled in amazement. "After that story, I want to have his balls for breakfast too."

"So you'll run with the story?" I asked hopefully.

"I'd like to, Manju. But so far, all you have offered me is hearsay. We'll need hard evidence before running this story otherwise we'll get our arses sued."

"Oh no," I uttered with dismay.

"Don't worry. It's only a minor obstacle. After all, I'm an investigative journalist. I've got various resources at my disposal to tease the truth out in these situations."

"I'm glad to hear it," I said, genuinely relieved. "You'll keep me updated, won't you?"

"Of course. I promise."

"By the way, you never answered that question I asked when we first met in the elevator."

"Oh?"

"I wondered why an established host of a hugely popular TV show wanted to do investigative stories in the field. I always thought that hosting a show was the pinnacle of TV current affairs. In the medical field, it's like a specialist wanting to be an intern again."

She laughed at the analogy. "It's a good question. You're quite right, you know. I am the envy of every current affairs reporter in the country. Many people in my position would be happy to simply rest on their laurels. I, on the other hand, am always itching for new challenges. Despite the many awards that I have claimed over the years, the one that has evaded me is the National Media Club's Award for Investigative Journalism. So I've returned to the field. Of course, I won't give up hosting The Morning Show – that would be ludicrous. But I am giving up a lot of spare time to work in the field in an investigative role. And tonight, Manju, you may have just given me the ingredients for that prize-winning story."

"Happy to oblige," I said.

She laughed. Then looking at the time, she said, "It's quite late. We'd better be off."

This was the moment that I had been dreading. I rang the bell for our waiter and pulled out my wallet.

Fabulus looked at me quizzically. "What on earth are you doing?"

"I'm going to fix up the bill."

Fabulus smiled and gestured for me to put away my wallet. "How sweet of you. But you're here at my invitation. Tonight's on me."

She then burst out laughing.

"What's so funny?"

"You poor thing! You probably saw the prices on the menu and had a heart attack."

I grinned sheepishly. "Kind of."

"Don't worry. The disgustingly wealthy TV celebrity is going to cover tonight's bill. When you are a distinguished Professor of Medicine, earning big bucks, then you can return the favour."

"Consider it a date!" I said.

After paying the bill, we chatted for a bit longer. Then Fabulus abruptly said, "Sorry Manju, I can't wait any longer. My kids are staying over with my mother only till eleven o'clock so we'd better go home."

I stood up and thanked her again for dinner.

"Where are you going?" she asked me, seemingly puzzled, although in hindsight, I am sure that there was a mischievous twinkle in her eye.

"Home," I replied.

"But I haven't told you where I live," she said.

"Where *you* live?" I said, puzzled.

"Didn't you hear me? I said that my kids won't be home for another two hours. Don't you want to come back to my place?"

I gasped as the realization of what she was suggesting dawned upon me. "You mean that *you* want to sleep with *me*?"

"No, darling. I don't want to sleep with you. I just want to shag you before the kids get home."

"But why me?" I asked, dumbfounded.

"I've been divorced for three months now without any sex whatsoever. It's just driving me up the wall. As for you, well, you're good-looking, charming and judging by that ever enlarging bulge in your pants, more than adequately equipped for the job."

"But I'm your 'source'," I said, covering my groin with both hands in an attempt to maintain some semblance of decency. "Would this be ethical?"

She looked at me with an almost feral look. "Screw ethics! I'm horny."

So it was that I lost my virginity. And while I always suspected that my first lover might share my fanatical love of cricket, I had never imagined she would possess the glamour, celebrity and beauty of Fabulus Hipz. I followed Fabulus home where we hurried to her bedroom in a salacious frenzy. Our carnal contest took place under lights. A skilled tosser, I came up heads and decided to bat, my piece of wood already in hand. Smooth and hard with a sweet spot on the tip, it was a fine piece of willow. She removed the covers, revealing a magnificent pitch that would provide an even contest. It was firm yet grassy with a small inviting crack. I found it to be a pleasant change from the mowed pitches of today. Given that this would be a lively encounter, I ensured that my groin protection was well secured before she bounded in. Being a debutant in this form of the game, I played and missed regularly in the early part of my innings, incurring the wrath of my opponent. However, as I adapted to the conditions, my confidence grew and I dazzled her with a delicate stroke through her fine leg which earned rapturous praise. On reaching 69, there was a fearsome deadlock until she deviously used ball tampering to bring my stump down. After this session, a brief drinks break ensued before the contest resumed with Fabulus on top. With the pressure mounting and balls swinging both ways, the grassy crack began to widen. Finally, I approached her from wide of the crease, catching her off-guard and penetrating her defences. Despite a number of manoeuvres on her part, she was unable to cope with the varying length of my deliveries and the change of pace. Soon victory was mine in a glorious contest where I had come from behind. In this amorous arena, I had truly bowled this maiden over.

Two hours later, I found myself in my own bed reflecting on the most amazing evening of my life. But I was surprised to find that my thoughts were not of Fabulus, but of another woman. I am sure that as I fell asleep, I thought of those glorious ebony eyes that I had seen so many weeks ago and I whispered her name 'Sundari'.

PART THREE

Infectious Diseases

September 1

Today was my first day working in 'Medicine'. As a student, this term confused me as I thought that everything we did was Medicine. However, it's merely a convention to separate surgeons from physicians. Medicine refers to specialities run by physicians – neurology, cardiology, infectious diseases, rheumatology etc., in contrast to 'Surgery' which obviously refers to surgical specialities – general surgery, cardiothoracic, colorectal, urology etc. By the end of medical school, I had determined that I far preferred Medicine to Surgery, a preference that has been reinforced by the hideous experience that I had had under Monty Bonkzalot.

My partner in crime this term is Smegman. I must admit that he really has turned into a decent fellow ever since he started working in ED with Delilah. That girl continues to amaze me with her talents! It would be useful to have a genius like Smegman around this term. Having said that, we will be assigned to different but equally busy teams, so I don't know if we will see each other that often.

I got the shock of my life this morning on arriving in the doctors' room on the medical ward. The Chief Medical Registrar, Precious Thyme, gave me the unexpected news that I would be working for a different team. I had originally been allocated to the Gastroenterology/Endocrinology team, which I'd been quite looking forward to.

"Is it something I've done?" I asked with dismay wondering whether Bonkzalot had put in a bad word about me.

Precious was quick to allay my fears. "No, it's quite the opposite actually. Servilia Gorgas, the Professor of Infectious Diseases, requested you to be assigned to her team."

I was stunned. "You mean that Professor Gorgas wants me to be her intern? What a great honour! I didn't know that she thought so highly of me." My ego swelled with pride.

Precious scrunched up her face. "Well actually, she doesn't know you from a bar of soap. The problem is with the original Resident who was assigned to her. You didn't hear this from me but ... last year, they worked together and Professor Gorgas absolutely detests him. When she found out that he had been allocated to her this term, she went ballistic and demanded that Susan Stoker remove him at once. So now he's with the Gastroenterology/Endocrinology team while you are working for her."

My swollen ego rapidly deflated and I felt quite foolish for having ever thought that Professor Gorgas had specifically picked me. In fact, I became quite unnerved as I recalled her fearsome reputation, particularly towards incompetent junior doctors.

"Oh my God, I'm only an intern! This term is meant to be staffed by a Resident," I moaned. "She's going to have me for breakfast."

Precious put her arm around me. "Don't worry. Her bark's worse than her bite. And I'm going to be your Registrar, so I'll look after you. Just do your work and never ever lie to her. If you don't know something, just say so. Got it?"

"Got it," I said. I felt somewhat less despondent now. When Delilah and Copper were the medical interns, they told me that Precious was the best medical registrar around. I was confident that she would look after me. Furthermore, I had always been intrigued by Infectious Diseases as a speciality. In fact, it is the only area of medicine where I have voluntarily done extra reading. As for movies about infectious diseases, I don't know how many times I have rented 'Outbreak' and 'Twelve Monkeys', although the former may have had something to do with seeing the delectable Renee Russo on screen.

The day went by quickly as I familiarized myself with our patients. True to her word, Precious was wonderful, providing assistance for the smallest thing. Professor Gorgas was meant to round with us but postponed it till tomorrow. Eventually, we managed to finish at 5:30pm, quite a civilized hour in comparison to my surgical term. All in all, it had been a good day.

In the evening, I met some of my fellow interns for dinner at the Burger Bar. While the menu is fairly limited, the burgers are superb, the servings generous and the prices reasonable. True to form, the two new surgical interns, Delilah and Peter, had had horrendous first days and turned up late.

The conversation revolved around Bonkzalot and his treatment of Alternaria and me. The consensus on his behaviour was scathing.

"Damn it! I wish that there was something we could do to get back at him," said Smegman.

"I've already done something," I announced cryptically. Naturally, everyone demanded an explanation. I told them about my meeting with Fabulus Hipz and her plans to break the story in the media.

To say that this caused a sensation at our table is an understatement. A stunned pause transformed into a babble of frenzied questions – just like a press conference. My friends ultimately agreed that my clandestine rendezvous with Fabulus had been daring but brilliant. I must admit that I enjoyed their reaction. I did, however, omit the fact that I had slept with Fabulus. I wasn't quite ready to share that with anyone.

"Be very careful," said Copper. "Speaking to the media without the hospital's approval can get you the sack."

"I know that. Ms. Hipz has promised to be the soul of discretion."

"Fabulus Hipz – what an odd name," said Delilah Convex. "I don't know if I'd like to have the name of a body part."

If other diners had bothered to look in our direction, they'd have been privy to the sight of six intelligent doctors, two of whom are geniuses, engaged in intense and passionate discussion. Were we trying to solve climate change, find a cure for cancer or reduce fuel prices? Many of them would have been disappointed to find we were furiously debating which other celebrities had names of body parts.

"There's Fats Domino," said Copper, "although, I don't know if 'fat' is really a body part."

"And that singer – Pinkie – like your little finger," said Peter.

"No, her name's Pink," I replied.

"And that Bollywood actress – Eye Shwarya," suggested Smegman.

"Nope, it's spelt A-I-S-H-W-A-R-Y-A", said Lucky, once more revealing her Indian background, although nobody noticed.

"Otitis Redding?"

"No, it's 'Otis' Redding. Anyway, otitis is a disease process, not a body part."

"Bones McCoy from Star Trek?"

"That doesn't count because Bones was his character's name, not his real name."

After much heated discussion, we concluded that the only celebrity with the name of a body part, apart from Fabulus Hipz, is MC Hammer, referring to a tiny bone in the middle ear.

September 2

My first ward round with Professor Servilia Gorgas didn't start off particularly well. Akki and Ravi's car unexpectedly broke down this morning so I drove Kumar to day care. The combination of rush hour traffic and the extra distance meant that I arrived forty-five minutes late for work. In the typical manner in which one disaster compounds another, I had left my mobile phone at home so I couldn't call ahead to let Precious know that I would be late.

I reached the ward at 9:20 to find that Precious and Professor Gorgas had already begun the ward round. I apologized profusely explaining why I was late and how I didn't have my mobile phone to call ahead.

Professor Gorgas, who is almost six feet tall and built like a tank with a physical presence that is both formidable and intimidating, looked me up and down. Despite her fearsome appearance and reputation, she seemed quite sympathetic to my plight.

"Oh, I'm sorry to hear that," she said. "Is your sister's car okay?"

"I'm not sure. The mechanic is assessing it now."

"Is your nephew okay, Dr. Mendis?" she asked, in a sugary sweet voice.

"Yes, thank you. He was a bit concerned at why his parents weren't dropping him at day care but he really didn't mind."

"I'm glad to hear it. And how about you, Dr. Mendis? You've had a rough morning. I hope you got to sleep well last night?" she asked, putting her arm around me in a maternal fashion. What a delightful woman! How could everyone have been so wrong about her?

"Thank you, Professor. Well actually, I kept waking up because of a slightly sore shoulder so I had to rub some ointment on..."

And then she exploded. *"MR CASEY HERE, DIDN'T SLEEP WELL LAST NIGHT BECAUSE HE HAS STAPH AUREUS SEPTICAEMIA! I DON'T GIVE A TOSS ABOUT YOUR STUPID SHOULDER, YOUR STUPID SISTER OR HER STUPID CAR. YOU ARE AN INTERN ON THE INFECTIOUS DISEASES TEAM. PATIENTS' CARE IS COMPROMISED WHEN YOU DON'T DO YOUR JOB. DON'T EVER TURN UP LATE AGAIN. IF YOU DO, YOU BETTER LET US KNOW WELL IN ADVANCE. AND GOD HELP YOU, IF YOU DON'T HAVE A GOOD EXPLANATION. DO YOU UNDERSTAND ME, DOCTOR MENDIS? AND LET ME TELL YOU THAT RIGHT NOW, I AM USING THE TERM 'DOCTOR' LOOSELY."*

"Yes, Professor Gorgas. I'm sorry, Professor Gorgas. It won't happen again, Professor Gorgas. I've been really looking forward to working with you – I've heard such great things about you."

"Please stop grovelling – it's pathetic! Just do your damn job," she snapped back. "Now tell me about Mr. Casey's transthoracic echocardiogram results."

"It hasn't been done as yet."

I saw her face begin to turn red and the jugular veins distend, as she was about to erupt once more. I quickly went on.

"It hasn't been done because I convinced the Cardiology Registrar to do a transoesophageal echocardiogram. Mr. Casey has a prosthetic heart valve and I didn't think that the images from the transthoracic echocardiogram would be good enough to exclude endocarditis. It will be performed at two o'clock today."

As quickly as it had appeared, the fury receded. "Fine. Let me know the result before you leave home today."

"Yes, Professor Gorgas," I replied.

The remainder of the ward round went quite smoothly. However, I realized that if I had failed to perform any of the tasks requested by Precious or Professor Gorgas yesterday, I would have been in the line of fire again. Also, there is an expectation of me to not just follow instructions but to use my initiative. Although somewhat liberating, the price of not using my initiative would presumably be getting yelled at again. The final patient of the round was Ms. Preston, a lady with cellulitis of the leg *(Skin infection – Editors)*. She had been admitted overnight and looked quite unwell.

Professor Gorgas quizzed me in front of the patient. "What are the commonest causes of cellulitis?"

I inwardly breathed a sigh of relief. Last night, I had coincidentally read a review article on cellulitis. I hoped that I had retained enough to get me through the next few minutes.

"*Staphylococcus aureus* and *Streptococcus pyogenes*," I replied.

"What antibiotic would you normally give to a patient with cellulitis?"

"Flucloxacillin, as it covers both staph and strep," I said.

"Okay then. Mrs. Preston here was swimming in brackish water when she injured her leg, a few days before the onset of the cellulitis. Does that mean we have to think of other bacteria apart from staph and strep?"

"Yes. I think *Vibrio parahaemolyticus* and *Vibrio vulnificus* are found in brackish water and need to be covered."

"Anything else?"

"I don't know, Professor."

"Although not classically associated with brackish water, *Aeromonas* is another water-borne bacterium that can cause this aggressive blistering cellulitis. This is in addition to the *Vibrio* that you've already mentioned, and why I've added gentamicin and doxycycline to the antibiotic regimen."

Professor Gorgas looked me over once more before turning to Precious. "It appears that Dr. Mendis isn't a complete imbecile," she pronounced before walking off.

Precious smiled and clapped me on the back. "Well done! You nailed those questions on cellulitis. And what a compliment to get!"

"Compliment?" I asked, somewhat bemused. "All she said is that I'm not a complete imbecile."

"Trust me, Manju. Coming from Servilia Gorgas, that's like a declaration of love!"

I went home feeling quite satisfied with the day. My father noticed my upbeat mood.

"Ah son. Did you have a good day at work?"

"Sure did, Thaththa. My professor thinks that I'm not a complete imbecile. It's a great compliment," I proudly announced, as I walked to the kitchen, leaving him utterly perplexed.

September 8

The last few days have been great. Infectious Diseases has been a steep, but very rewarding learning curve. Apart from one or two mild jibes at my expense, Professor Gorgas seems to be largely satisfied with my performance. The fun part of the term is the 'Lab Round' twice a week. We go to the microbiology lab to look at our patient's specimens (blood, urine etc.) and see what bacteria are growing from them. The specimens are smeared onto culture media that are jelly-like substances full of nutrients in which bacteria can grow. The colours of the culture media are great: horse blood agar is a deep red, MacConkey agar is pink and chocolate agar is mahogany brown. On my first lab round, Professor Gorgas showed me horse blood agar on which tiny yellowish dots were visible.

"Do you see those white dots with a tinge of golden yellow, Dr. Mendis? They are colonies of *Staphylococcus aureus*, which we've grown from Mr. Casey's blood. These innocuous white dots are our enemy. Remember them well. They may look harmless enough, but they are alive, multiplying and trying to infiltrate Mr. Casey's bones, brain, heart, in fact, any organ they can. They have a thirty percent chance of succeeding and killing him in the process. Do you know the only thing between his survival and death from this bacterial invasion?"

I shook my head.

"*We are*, Dr. Mendis. Armed with antibiotics and our clinical skills, we can not only wipe out this infection, we can send Mr. Casey home a completely new man. And that's why I love Infectious Diseases. There are very few specialities where you can admit someone to hospital at death's door and send him home without any lingering health problems. Do you understand?"

I nodded– I actually understood. For the first time this year, being a doctor started to make sense.

With regard to my love life, or rather sex life, I've met Fabulus on two subsequent occasions. After making love last night, I asked her how the investigation on Bonkzalot was progressing.

She said, "It's going well. Watch 'Thirty Minutes' on Saturday night. You'll be pleasantly surprised." I eagerly pressed her for more information but she would have none of it. "Just be patient."

I met Delilah and Peter for coffee this evening. We'd all finished late. I asked them how their surgical term was progressing. They shook their heads in disgust.

"Bonkzalot is an animal," complained Peter. "I want to be a surgeon but this treatment of us is unacceptable. He is a durag *(Russian for 'idiot' – Editors)*."

Delilah was no less critical. "Lucky was right. He just stares at my breasts. I can handle that, but what really pisses me off is that he doesn't take me seriously. There was a patient with abdominal pain and a variety of systemic symptoms. I asked him about screening for vipomas, carcinoid tumours and phaeochromocytomas. The condescending brute said I 'shouldn't worry my pretty little head about such things' before laughing raucously with the registrar. The nerve of the man! He really needs a lesson in ...well, everything!"

"If you watch 'Thirty Minutes' on Saturday night, you might find that he gets his comeuppance. But you didn't hear it from me," I said with a knowing smile.

"Did Fabulus Hipz update you?" asked Delilah.

"Yep. She told me last night."

"That's great news," said Peter with passion. "I will watch his downfall with glee."

Delilah had a thoughtful expression on her face. "You said Fabulus told you this last night. Was that in person or over the phone?"

I couldn't lie to Delilah anymore. "In person."

"Manju, are you sleeping with her?" asked Delilah in amazement.

"Yes, actually," I grinned sheepishly, glad that I could finally reveal this tremendous piece of news to someone.

Peter was thrilled for me and gave me a high-five.

"Details, details – I want details," said Delilah excitedly. "How did you end up in bed together? How's the sex?"

"Delilah," I said shyly. "You are my very good friend. But you're a girl.

I feel kinda peculiar talking about this sort of stuff in front of you."

Delilah sighed deeply. "For heaven's sake, Manju. I *am* a doctor and I did get a High Distinction in Sex and Family Planning. Don't be shy!"

I told them how Fabulus had propositioned me and I had gladly accepted. When it came to talking about the sex, however, I had to concede that all was not well.

"There's been a problem," I said, hesitantly.

"What is it?" asked Peter.

"Well, I'm up to scratch with the foreplay. That's thanks to all the years I spent reading my sister's women's magazines. I used to score ten out of ten for those quizzes on being a great lover. It's the actual 'act' where things aren't quite right."

"Tell me more," said Delilah, sounding more and more like Sigmund Freud.

"I can 'do it' a few times, but I can't 'last' more than three minutes and fifty seconds on each occasion."

"Three minutes and fifty seconds? You're timing yourself?" asked Delilah with raised eyebrows.

"So what if I am?" I asked defensively. "But it really bothers me. I'd like to offer her one big 'main course' but all she's getting is a series of entrées."

Peter laughed good-naturedly. "Ah, Manju. Don't worry. With your first lover, it is quite common for things to end prematurely. You'll last longer with practise."

Delilah nodded. "Absolutely, Manju. Practise makes perfect, after all. Has Fabulus said anything about it?"

"Nope."

"There you go. Clearly, she doesn't think it's a problem otherwise she wouldn't have asked you back for more."

"That's true," I said. "But I really want to get over that four-minute barrier."

"You are like Sir Roger Bannister, trying to be the first man to break the four-minute mile."

"The only problem with that analogy is that Roger Bannister was trying to finish *under* four minutes – I'm aiming on doing the opposite," I replied glumly.

Delilah laughed. "Don't worry, Manju. It's a minor matter. And at the end of the day, you've made love to a celebrity. In fact, you've lost your virginity to a celebrity – that's even more amazing."

"I was just in the right place at the right time. She hadn't had a relationship since her divorce three months earlier so she was looking for someone. I suspect that nearly any man who had dinner with her that night would have been the lucky one."

"Perhaps," said Delilah. "But at the end of the day, *you* were the man having dinner with her because you showed the courage to take on Bonkzalot through the media. Not many doctors would have had the guts or vision to secretly meet a reporter and give out a story. Don't ever forget it."

"Delilah, do people ever tell you that you are wonderful?"

"All the time, Manju, all the time."

I daresay they do!

September 15

On Saturday night, I went around to Peter and Copper's place to watch Thirty Minutes. The whole gang was there, eager to see what Fabulus came up with. Popcorn, chocolate cake, chips and drinks were available to maximize the viewing experience. And I'll tell you what – Fabulus didn't disappoint. Using a combination of hidden cameras, access to bank statements and an undercover pet owner whose dog supposedly needed surgery, Fabulus' team completely exposed Bonkzalot's operation. They even managed to show Bonkzalot secretly returning the surgical equipment to hospital where "it will be used on unsuspecting human patients" (Fabulus' words). The icing on the cake was when Fabulus confronted Bonkzalot with the evidence as he was leaving hospital. He became so enraged that he punched the cameraman, who will probably press charges. We all cheered with delight. Even Alternaria, whose normally cheerful demeanour had been rather glum of late, broke out into a big smile. Her expression of happiness, after being put through hell by Bonkzalot during our surgical rotation, was the most satisfying reward of all.

Today at work, the atmosphere was no less charged. The Bonkzalot scandal was on everyone's lips. The print and TV media were all running with it as their headline story. The hospital was clearly worried. This followed an announcement by the Public Prosecutor saying that there was enough material to lay criminal charges against Bonkzalot and his anaesthetist. Further fallout came in the form of angry surgical patients who spent the whole day calling the hospital and the media. They naturally wanted to know whether their own surgery had involved the equipment that Bonkzalot had used on the animals. The words 'litigation' and 'sue' were frequently bandied about. In an attempt to prevent further damage to the hospital, Sir Ninian Tietas held a press conference, during which he announced that Monty Bonkzalot and his anaesthetist, Stewart Ponsonby, would have their employment at the hospital terminated immediately. The State Medical Council quickly followed suit, stating that both doctors would have *all* their clinical privileges suspended, including private hospital work. It had been a triumphant day for me to that point but it only got better. As I was leaving hospital around 7pm, I saw a furious Bonkzalot walking from the hospital, presumably having received a humiliating dressing down from the St. Ivanhoe hospital board. I stepped in front of him and said, "Good riddance to bad rubbish, you ugly old cocksucker." He roared with rage and swung his arm towards me. I stepped aside avoiding his swing, clenched my fist and punched him hard in the abdomen, winding him. He collapsed on the ground. I looked around, ensuring that nobody had seen the altercation. "That's for humiliating me, you old tosser." Then I kicked him hard in the groin. He moaned, starting to dry retch. "And that's for the way you treated my friend." I walked away, leaving him writhing on the ground. Any semblance to the once powerful consultant surgeon was gone, leaving only the pathetic shell of a beaten man. I should have felt sorry for him, but I didn't. Before getting out of earshot, I sang out to him, "I hope you enjoy men's prison, Monty. You'll be pleased to know that there won't be any dykes there, but you might find a nigger or two. Probably best not to call them that though – they might get offended."

As I headed to the car, I reflected on the fact that I'd just physically assaulted a specialist – well, an ex-specialist... It was something I'd never have even contemplated at the start of this year. Had I changed that much or was it the loathsomeness of Bonkzalot that was responsible for my reaction? Either way, it appeared that my internship at St. Ivanhoe had toughened me up no end.

I met Fabulus for dinner at her place. It was a bittersweet meeting. We celebrated the success of her story, which she was certain would put her in the running for the investigative journalism award she so desired. Unfortunately though, with regard to our relationship, she made it clear that it was time to move on. My pride was quite hurt. She did emphasize that she'd loved our time together and wanted me to remain her friend and more importantly, her 'source' at St. Ivanhoe. I sulked openly, as I was not used to being rejected. She offered to make love once more for 'old time's sake'. The dignified thing to do after being dumped would, of course, have been to walk out of there with my self-respect intact. With a stern look on my face, I refused her offer of 'pity sex' and began walking towards the door, determined to maintain my dignity. Just then, she removed her dressing gown, revealing her amazing naked body, and walked into the bedroom, giving me a provocative glance over her shoulder. I hesitated.

Then a record eight minutes and twenty seconds later, I left her bedroom, my dignity in pieces but thrilled at having broken the four-minute barrier. This must have been how Sir Roger Bannister felt when he broke the record, although unlike Sir Roger, I wasn't wearing running shoes nor would I receive a knighthood from the Queen. *(Dr. Mendis eventually did receive a Knighthood; however, it was for 'Services to Medicine' rather than for overcoming premature ejaculation – Editors).*

I left her apartment in a wonderful mood, wondering what dreadful fate awaited Monty Bonkzalot. *(Records show that Monty Bonkzalot was prosecuted and found guilty of a number of misdemeanours. In 2009, he was sentenced to three years in a low-level security prison. During that time, he underwent a transformation, taking up religion and knitting. This was linked to the influence of his cellmate, a 140kg gay African man named Eugene. Despite his improved persona, he never practised medicine again. Instead, on release from prison, he started teaching Tapestry and Cooking at a local polytechnic college – Editors)*

September 17

I took the day off to help my sister with Kumar's school interview. I made sure that Precious and Professor Gorgas knew about the day off well in advance. Although the Professor wasn't thrilled, she was pacified by the fact that Smegman had agreed to cover me. Both his consultants were on leave, so he had hardly any patients. Despite this, it was kind of him to help out. Delilah was right – he had changed.

Getting one's child accepted into a private school in this city is a highly competitive and ruthless affair. This stems from a lack of faith in the government school system, which means that, with regard to private schools, demand for places heavily exceeds supply. This has led to the ludicrous situation of couples enrolling their child in private schools *during* pregnancy. Some private schools, themselves not averse to extra profit, often charge a fee for enrolment. Or they disguise it as a recommendation that 'a donation to the school's new gymnasium fund would be highly desirable'. In other words, pay up or don't bother turning up for the interview. It was never like this when Akki and I were kids.

In Kumar's case, Ravi and Akki had decided to enrol him in my old school – Errol Flynn Grammar. Flynn, as it is popularly known, is regarded as the best private school in the country with regard to academic achievements. It was certainly the case when I was a student there and not much has changed since my departure. I've never quite understood why the academically leading school in the country was named after an actor who was expelled from a number of schools himself. Certainly, anyone hoping to find daring, debonair supermen of the ilk of Errol Flynn at our school would have been dreadfully disappointed. We were a bunch of nerdy, acne-faced pubescents in various degrees of unfitness who ran away whenever a ball rolled in our direction. Apparently, this is just the kind of student the parents of today want their children to be. The competition to get accepted into Flynn is ferocious.

Having been on a waiting list of hundreds for the last two years, Kumar was finally called for an interview. Ravi had to go interstate on an unavoidable meeting, so, Akki asked me to come. This was both for moral support and the fact that I am an old boy of the school. Unfortunately, my connection with the school did not improve my nephew's chances of being accepted. Only the *son* of an old boy would be guaranteed entry into Flynn without an interview. When my sister found this out, it was met by a predictable 'Fuck!', pronounced in front of my mother, which led to another memorable argument about Akki's swearing.

The nature of the interview surprised me. Kumar is only three years old, yet he would be interviewed alone for an hour with two teachers present. Akki heard on the grapevine that the interview process is quite gruelling, and includes assessment of literacy, numeracy, geography and even anatomy. One of Akki's friend's kids was asked to identify the philtrum *(The heaped-up area of skin between the nose and upper lip – Editors)*. The philtrum, for heaven's sake! I'm glad that I didn't have to undergo such a stringent assessment when I was that age as I'm quite certain that I would have failed miserably. Even though my nephew is a bright and interactive toddler, he has never struck me as an intellectual giant. But, at the age of three, which child is?

As we left our house, we all prayed hard to improve Kumar's chances, making vows of religious pilgrimages on our return to Sri Lanka. My sister held her 'O, The Oprah Magazine' close to her, saying aloud, "Please Oprah, oh, divine goddess of the screen, let Kumar get accepted to this school."

I chastised her. "For goodness sake, Oprah might be a wonderful and influential woman, but she doesn't perform miracles."

"You tell that to all the audience members from a year or two ago who received a free car at the end of a show!" she snapped back.

It was hard to argue with that.

With the gods (and hopefully Oprah) on our side, my sister, nephew and I entered the grounds of my old school. You didn't have to be sartorially savvy to appreciate how well dressed we were. Both Kumar and I wore suits and Akki was bedecked in a very expensive Vera Wang dress. An observer may have been forgiven for assuming that we were attending a high society function rather than a school interview for kindergarten. However, anyone who thought that our glamorous clothes would have provided an advantage over the other candidates would have been sadly mistaken. As we walked into the interview area,

I was greeted by the sight of a number of attractive mothers attired in a variety of very expensive-looking dresses. Most of them were accompanied by their male partners who were similarly dressed (*We presume that Dr. Mendis meant that the men were dressed as fashionably as their female partners rather than that the men were wearing dresses – Editors*). Akki and I went to the front desk where the secretary greeted us efficiently but warmly.

"Good Morning. Child's name please?"

"Kumar Bandara."

She looked down a list, identified his name and ticked it. She handed Akki some paperwork. "Please fill this form in and return it to me once completed."

Akki asked her, "How does the whole process work?"

"There are twenty positions available for the kindergarten class. We plan to interview two hundred children over the next ten days. Each day, twenty children will be interviewed and two will be selected."

"Only two out of twenty?" I asked.

"Yes, unfortunately the demand is high and places are limited. But if your child performs well compared to the other children here, you'll have nothing to worry about."

Akki and I sat down, feeling rather despondent.

"Don't worry Akki," I said, trying to brighten our now downcast moods. "Kumar is a bright kid. I'm sure he'll outshine the others."

We looked around the room at the other nineteen children – Kumar's competition. I immediately regretted that decision. In one corner was a Chinese boy saying something monotonous in a foreign language. It took me a moment to realize that he was multiplying numbers in Latin. Next to him another boy was walking up and down the room balancing a book on his head while he sang the national anthem. Another three-year-old child was standing in front of a map of the world while his mother asked him to point to various countries. He performed this task flawlessly, which was all the more remarkable considering the countries that were being asked of him – Chad, Djibouti, Lithuania and Bhutan. Even I didn't have a bloody clue where to find them!

Despite the relentless onslaught of brilliance from Kumar's 'opponents', I kept up a brave face. "Don't worry, Akki. I'm sure that Kumar is as talented and intelligent as those kids."

We both turned to look at young Kumar to see how he would respond to these challenges from his fellow toddlers. He was scratching his bum with one hand and picking his nose with the other.

"Well, I guess that's an example of 'multitasking'," I said, unconvincingly.

Suddenly, there was a kafuffle next to us. I was pleased to see that at least one child other than Kumar was behaving like a normal toddler and having a temper tantrum. His bone of contention appeared to relate to food.

"Mummy, I need pie."

"No darling, you don't."

"I NEED PIE", he yelled again.

His mother shook her head in annoyance. "Darling, for the last time, no."

He started crying. "But Mummy, without pie, I can't work out the area of this circle," he said, holding a piece of paper in his hand.

He hadn't meant 'pie' – he'd meant 'pi'. Another bloody genius! Kumar looked at the piece of paper in the boy's hand and the round shape that he'd drawn, before confidently saying, "Square. Look – square."

"No Kumar, it's a circle," I said, correcting him gently.

The mother of the toddler heard Kumar's incorrect response and stared at him with barely veiled contempt.

Akki and I looked at each other. We didn't have to say anything to know what we were both thinking. Poor Kumar, wonderful as he is, didn't have a chance in hell of beating these kids in an interview.

Akki then said, "Manju, come with me to the front desk. I need to talk to that lady."

I assumed that she was going to let the secretary know that we were withdrawing from the interview process. After all, why put poor Kumar through an hour of humiliation?

The secretary looked at us. "Yes, have you completed the form yet?"

My sister's face took on a confused expression. "I'm a little bit puzzled. I didn't know that there'd be an interview process if a child's father is an old boy of the school. I thought that it was automatic admission."

What was Akki playing at? Ravi hadn't attended Flynn at any stage, so his son, Kumar, couldn't be eligible for automatic admission. She knew that!

The secretary looked surprised. "That's correct. You didn't mention that Kumar's father is an old boy. I'll just look it up on the computer."

Akki should have realized that they'd double-check her claim. And now her lie was about to be exposed – how embarrassing.

"The father's name please?" asked the secretary.

"Manjula Mendis," my sister immediately replied, confidently giving my name.

My name – she had used *my* name! I looked at my sister who refused to meet my eye.

The secretary said, "Ah yes, Manjula Mendis is certainly an old boy here. So you're Manjula Mendis, I presume," she said, looking at me.

"I'm Manjula Mendis – that's correct," I replied truthfully, grinning like an idiot.

"Do you have any ID – a driver's license, for instance?"

I pulled out my wallet and gave her my driver's license. She pulled out another form and took down the details.

The secretary suddenly frowned. "But wait a minute. Kumar's surname is Bandara, not Mendis. How is that possible?"

My sister stepped in immediately. "Oh, that's easy. I've always believed in equal rights for women. So not only did I keep my surname when we got married, I insisted that my child have my surname too. I even tried to get my dear husband here to change his surname when we got married, but he refused."

"I'm a bit of a male chauvinist pig," I said, hoping that I sounded convincing. "Keep the toilet seat up and all that."

The secretary looked me up and down. "I daresay you do. Well, Mrs. Bandara and Mr. Mendis, you will get a letter of offer in the mail in a month or so. Could you please sign the acceptance form that accompanies it and return it to us as soon as possible? We'll also need some photographic evidence of the wedding and a copy of the child's birth certificate, just to confirm the father is an old boy of the school."

"Isn't that a little extreme?" I asked, becoming quite worried.

The secretary apologized. "It's nothing personal, Mr. Mendis. We routinely do this for automatic admissions. As hard as it is to believe, some people are so desperate to have their children attend our school that they lie about the father being an old boy."

"You don't say," I said, looking hard at my sister.

"Well, don't worry. We'll have that documentation to you as soon as possible," my sister said sweetly.

As we left the waiting room, we received a number of venomous glances from parents who'd overheard the conversation and knew that Kumar had leapfrogged their precious darlings in to Flynn.

As we left the school grounds, I stopped my sister and demanded an explanation. "Akki, what was all that about?"

"I just secured the best education for my son and your nephew."

"It's not your motives that I'm questioning. It's your methods. You've deceived the school into thinking that I'm Kumar's father. It's probably a criminal offence!"

"Well, Manju, it was the only way he was going to get accepted. Didn't you see how brilliant those other three-year-olds were? He wouldn't have stood a fucking chance in the interview."

I pressed on. "And what will your husband think about this?"

"You know that Ravi wants Kumar to get into Flynn even more than I do. And you also know that he's not above a little deception every now and then. So I really don't think he'll have a problem with this."

"What about our parents?"

"Well, I won't tell them if you won't. You won't, will you?" she pleaded.

I sighed. "I guess not. But what about all the documentation to prove that I am Kumar's father? There's no way that you can fake those."

"Just leave that to me. Don't worry your pretty little head about it. I love it when you get anxious. It's one of the reasons that I married you," she said, laughing. Then she had the temerity to squeeze my butt!

"Don't squeeze my butt! And don't talk about us being married. You're my bloody sister, after all!"

As Kumar looked at me and said, "Butt, squeeze," I realized that this truly was the only way he would ever get admitted to Flynn. I just hope that Akki and I won't live to regret it.

September 18

We went to ED first thing this morning to catch up with a couple of overnight admissions. Lucky was finishing up her nightshift, while Precious answered a page, I asked Lucky how ED was treating her.

"It was fine up till this morning."

"What happened this morning?" I asked.

"I had to sing 'Don't Look Back in Anger' with Sir Ninian!" she exclaimed miserably.

"Really?"

"Yes. The new Medical Registrar is really slow so he made me call Sir Ninian about a patient because he was too busy. And Sir Ninian made me sing it."

"How was it?"

"Horrible. I sang the verses and he sang the chorus. Even though your experience with the song prepared me, it was still painfully embarrassing. And that wasn't the worst part. A blind patient was admitted last night with his guide dog. The dog had been sitting outside the doctors' room overnight. When I started singing, it began howling as if it was in pain. It was utterly humiliating."

"That can't be good for your confidence."

"Tell me about it. I think I'll need counselling for life." She shook her head in disbelief. "By the way, Manju, I need to ask you something. It's about Lal."

"My cousin? Sure. How can I help you?"

Just then, a buzzer went off signalling the arrival of a trauma case to the department. "Damn it," Lucky said. "I better make sure there's someone to look after this trauma. I'll speak to you later."

I shouted Smegman a coffee later today to thank him for covering me yesterday while I was at Kumar's interview. He'd apparently had no problems with the Infectious Diseases patients and had found them really interesting. In fact, I was more concerned that Smegman's brilliance would have outshone my mediocrity in front of Precious and Professor Gorgas. I told Smegman as much and he laughed.

"Actually, Precious thinks that you are good value. In fact, she felt that as a group, this year's interns are one of the best batches that she has seen for a long time."

It's good to hear that at least one person likes us!

September 23

It is always exciting to get paged from the Celebrity Ward when you are on an overtime shift. The anticipation of that brush with fame is hard to beat. And so, it was with excitement that I rushed up to the tenth floor when I was paged last evening. I even had an empty elevator to the tenth floor, allowing me to Elevator Groove to the imagined tune of Pink's "Get this Party Started".

Nurse Watson was once again rostered to the ward. She told me that the patient wanted extra pain relief. I looked at the patient's name but was disappointed to find that I didn't recognize it. If he wasn't famous, then the only way that he'd get access to the Celebrity Ward is if he is filthy rich. And so he is. Milton Honeypot is a senior bank executive in his late forties with his first attack of gout – supposedly an affliction of the affluent. He has a generally reddish (or perhaps 'radish') complexion. However, the redness in the rest of his body was nothing compared to his right big toe, which was extremely inflamed with gout.

I introduced myself and shook hands with him.

"How much do you earn a year?" he immediately asked me, wincing in pain.

I was so completely taken aback by this question that I actually answered it. "About fifty thousand dollars."

"Pre-tax or post-tax?" he quickly followed up.

"Pre-tax."

He waved a hand at me dismissively as he again winced from the pain in his toe. "I can't allow someone who earns so little to treat me."

I was so stunned by his ridiculous pronouncement that I forgot to get angry. "But I went to medical school for six years. My earning capacity shouldn't dictate whether I'm worthy of treating you or not," I said, exasperated.

"In my world it does! An employee with a small salary has little responsibility because his employers don't have enough faith to give him anything more. That's why the name of Spyder Croquet, who earns millions of dollars a year, is above my bed, and not yours! Who the hell are you?"

"I'm Dr. Manju Mendis, Dr. Croquet's intern and the only person in the near vicinity who can prescribe you morphine. Who the hell are *you*?" I demanded, throwing his question right back at him with interest.

"I'm the Deputy CEO of National Chartered Bank."

"I bank with National Chartered. How much do you earn?" I asked, emboldened by his aggressive questions towards me.

"Fifteen million dollars last year – after bonuses. In fact, I almost earn more in a day than you earn in a year." He laughed. "How interesting."

"Fifteen million dollars a year?" I said incredulously. "Yet you have the temerity to charge all those ridiculous bank fees. If only some of that money went from your executive salaries back into the bank, you could get rid of bank fees altogether."

"Bank fees are necessary. There are complicated fiscal reasons for this that you wouldn't understand. As for our salaries being excessive, let me categorically state that every single executive on that board deserves every cent that they get."

"For doing what?" I challenged him.

"What?"

"What can you possibly do to justify a fifteen million dollar salary?"

Appearing somewhat flustered, he said, "Well, I manage, I supervise, I meet people..."

"What a croc!" I said.

He became very angry at this point. "How dare you address me this way? People have homes, drive cars and send their children to private schools because my bank gives them the damn money! And one more thing, if you don't give me my morphine immediately, I'll have Spyder Croquet on the phone, and demand that you're terminated!"

I held my tongue with great difficulty. Unfortunately, he had a point. I should never have engaged a patient in such a heated argument. It was very unprofessional. In fact, the Manju Mendis from the start of this year would never have dreamed of doing such a thing. There was no doubt about it – I had changed, although I didn't know if it was a change for the better. Mind you, it was hard to pass up this opportunity to argue with Milton Honeypot, given his unapologetic hubris coupled with the greedy bank for which he worked.

I took a deep breath, controlled my temper and said, "Mr. Honeypot, I apologize for what I said. It is just a very emotive topic for me. I'll get your morphine immediately."

Honeypot said, "That's quite alright. In fact, it was rather refreshing. It reminded me of our time in the Bahamas."

"Really?" I said, quite surprised.

"Yes. There was a man named Eduardo in our holiday home who used to have debates of a similar intellectual capacity with me."

"Eduardo?"

"Yes. He was a servant who used to clean the toilets. Mind you, even that was too much for him, so we had to let him go."

"Are you comparing me to a toilet cleaner?" I asked, gritting my teeth and clenching my fists.

"How could I? After all, I think his hourly wage was higher than yours." He burst out laughing. "Now get the damn morphine. My foot's killing me."

He had really overstepped the mark this time. However, I maintained my composure and went with Nurse Watson to draw up 10mg of morphine in the medication room.

"He's a horrible man, isn't he?" she said as she was drawing up the morphine. "And earning fifteen million dollars a year – what on earth can you do with all that money? Well, I'm glad you stood your ground."

I smiled and shrugged my shoulders in resignation.

"Oh by the way, Dr. Mendis, are you interested in buying a second-hand 2006 Mazda sedan for fifteen thousand dollars? It's only done twenty thousand kilometres and is in great condition. My husband's retiring so we don't need two cars anymore."

I said that I wasn't interested but told her I'd mention it to anyone who was looking for a car. She thanked me and handed me the syringe filled with morphine. I waited till she had left the medication room, double-checking that she was well away. Then I removed the cap from the needle of the syringe and proceeded to empty the morphine into the sink. I found a container of sterile water and drew 10ml into the syringe. I returned to Mr. Honeypot.

"Once again, I'm sorry about before, Sir," I apologized. "Here's 10mg of morphine. You've had quite a bit already so I don't want you to have any more for the next six hours. Otherwise you might overdose. Is that okay?"

"Very well. Just give it."

I thanked him and proceeded to inject the 10ml of water into his IV cannula. I repeated my instructions to Nurse Watson, who once again asked me to spread the word about her car. I left the ward feeling quite happy with myself. Mr. Honeypot had a painful six hours ahead of him. If I couldn't screw the banks, then I could at least screw the bankers!

September 24

Amazing news! It is 10pm and I have just checked my e-mail. It took three months but *The Lancet* has finally made a decision on our case report on the lady with the carrot. They will publish it with a few minor modifications! I can't believe it. At the moment, I'm the only intern who'd even be eligible for the Steelbone Trophy and $20,000 prize. Of course, there's still almost four months before the awards ceremony, which is plenty of time for my brilliant colleagues to submit something. But I'm at least in the running, something I would never have thought possible at the start of the year. Furthermore, irrespective of who wins the Steelbone trophy, a publication in *The Lancet* is highly prestigious. It'll look great on my CV.

I have just got home from dinner. We ate at a new restaurant called Moon Landing. It is a theme-based dining experience. You climb down a ladder into a grotto. The roof is filled with hundreds of star-shaped lights, giving the impression that you are on the moon surface, looking up into the galaxy. The waiters are dressed in spacesuits, which look quite genuine. Peter recognized some Russian insignias on a few of them, raising the amazing possibility that they may have been real spacesuits used by Russian cosmonauts. He said that a lot of hi-tech equipment got sold on the black market when the Soviet Union collapsed. Imagine that! The best part is an anti-gravity chamber in the middle of the restaurant. There was quite a queue and only one person is allowed at a time, but we all still managed to have a go. It was great fun. Copper unfortunately developed motion sickness and vomited during his ride. The sight of floating vomit in zero gravity was fairly gross but it all looked much worse when the gravity was turned back on and the vomit fell all over poor Copper. Anyway, he took it in good humour. Well, to be more accurate, we all took it in good humour – Copper wasn't so thrilled about the matter.

I told everyone about my encounter with Milton Honeypot. Surprisingly, no one criticized me for arguing with him. In fact, they all congratulated me. I suspect that the enthusiastic, optimistic and idealistic interns from the start of this year have all but disappeared, leaving cynical and embittered doctors. It's a sad observation but an accurate one.

We eventually did brighten up although the topic of conversation remained on Honeypot and his salary. The verdict was unanimous: fifteen million dollars was an absurd salary for any individual, particularly in a bank which had shareholders and loyal customers. The issue then came up of how much a high-ranking bank executive should be given. We never reached a consensus on an exact figure, but figures as low as two hundred thousand dollars per year were suggested by Peter Ivanov, which I thought was a bit unreasonable.

I drove Lucky and Alternaria home, the former had drunk too much and the latter's car was at the mechanic's for the umpteenth time.

"What's the problem with your car, Alternaria? It seems to be breaking down all the time."

"It's just old. It's been in our family for fifteen years. I've been wanting to upgrade for some time now."

I remembered that there was a car for sale. "Alternaria, go and talk to Nurse Watson from the Celebrity Ward. She's selling a 2006 Mazda with low kilometres for a song. It sounds like a good deal."

"Thanks. That's really helpful. I'll catch up with her before the end of the week."

After dropping the girls off and returning home, I didn't go to bed. Instead, I returned to the problem of how much to pay bank executives like Milton Honeypot. In truth, I personally didn't begrudge them earning a big salary and in fact, thought that Peter's idea of two hundred thousand dollars a year was a bit unrealistic. I have come to the conclusion that five million dollars pre-tax (about three million dollars after tax) would be the perfect compromise. It would satisfy the greedy expectations of the bank executives *(See Dr. Mendis' table below – Editors)*, while the extra money derived from these salary cuts would allow the bank to invest money back into its customers. Perhaps I should send this table around to the Executive Boards of all the banks in the country. It might provide a vehicle for change in the banking sector *(Most unlikely – Editors)*.

ANNUAL EXPENSES USING $3 MILLION AFTER-TAX SALARY ($5 MILLION GROSS)	MONEY
House (annual repayment)	1 million
Private school for three kids	75,000
Three overseas trips – only first-class travel and luxury accommodation	250,000
Lavish gifts for spouse	50,000
Lavish gifts for mistress/lover	400,000
General expenses (food, clothing, bills etc.)	500,000
Weekly one-hour session with high-class call-girl/gigolo	250,000
Charity	12
Leftover change	474,988

September 25

During my overtime shift, I received another page from the Celebrity ward. This time, Nurse Watson sounded frantic.

"Doctor Mendis, I'm in the nurses' station. Please come up *immediately!*"

It certainly didn't sound good. I rushed to the elevator, which rose uninterrupted to the tenth floor. Since I was about to walk into a medical emergency, an adrenaline surge pulsed through me, giving me the impetus to do some Elevator Grooving. I put Bruce Lee to shame as I demonstrated my martial arts moves to the tune of 'Kung Fu Fighting'. As I emerged from the elevator, I saw the door of the adjacent elevator closing. Although I didn't see the face of the occupant, I momentarily glimpsed a distinctly female shoe before the door closed. I ran down to the Nurses' station where I found Nurse Watson in quite a state: she was pale, breathing fast and clearly flustered.

"What's happened?" I asked her.

She composed herself and proceeded to explain. "As Mr. Honeypot's gout is so much better, my shift had been fairly uneventful. Then, I went into his room about five minutes ago to record his ten o'clock observations. Do you know what I found?"

"Absolutely no idea, Nurse Watson," I truthfully admitted.

"I discovered Mr. Honeypot in a 'compromised position' with a woman."

I was intrigued. "When you say 'compromised', Nurse Watson, what do you mean exactly?"

Nurse Watson's face turned a bright shade of red. "I mean completely naked and going at it like a rabbit. Is that clear enough for you, Doctor?"

I laughed to myself. "So why is this a problem, Nurse Watson?"

"Why?" She looked at me as if I had gone insane. "For heaven's sake, a patient is having sexual intercourse in his room! It's disgusting. It might even have put me in danger."

"Put you in danger? How so?"

"Well, thankfully they didn't see me. But if they had, those degenerates might have asked me to join in. Oh, the thought of it!"

I barely suppressed a grin. The chance of the corpulent and matronly Nurse Watson, a woman in her early sixties, being asked to partake in a threesome seemed most unlikely.

"Should I declare a Medical Emergency?" she asked out of nowhere.

I gently said no. Although the thought of the Cardiac Arrest team bursting into Milton Honeypot's room to find they were interrupting a shag session was a tempting one, it would probably annoy more people than it would amuse. Mind you, since the Cardiac Arrest team carries 'recreational' drugs such as insulin and ketamine, not to mention lots of tubing to stick into various orifices, they'd probably be quite popular in such situations. Perhaps they could hire themselves out for bachelor parties etc., in those quiet periods between medical emergencies.

"Why don't we let him and his wife finish what they are doing and just pretend that it didn't happen?" I suggested, taking the holistic approach to the situation.

"It's not his wife," Nurse Watson snapped back indignantly. "I've seen Mrs. Honeypot before. No, *this* woman looks half his age."

"Oh dear," I said, although I wasn't surprised that Honeypot was having 'his bit on the side'. After all, I had included it in my table of annual expenses for bank executives. I then remembered the mysterious woman leaving in the elevator as I had arrived. I wonder if that had been Mrs. Honeypot who had unexpectedly walked in on her husband's infidelity. If so, he had difficult times ahead.

"I still think that we should report the matter, Doctor Mendis. After all, it certainly breaks hospital policy."

Although she was probably right, Nurse Watson had forgotten that the specialist looking after this patient is Spyder Croquet. If it came down to a choice of supporting hospital staff or his powerful patient, I had no doubt that Spyder would choose the latter. I said as much to Nurse Watson who reluctantly agreed that we best do nothing.

As I headed towards the elevator and past Honeypot's room, my voyeuristic tendencies got the better of me. I put my ear to the door, which was slightly ajar and listened to the debaucherous goings-on within. Judging from the frantic rhythms of the heavy breathing and squeaking bed, I had arrived at the climax of the show. Within seconds, Honeypot emotively announced to his coital colleague that he was arriving, and, after a further moment, that he had arrived. After a minute or two to catch his breath, I heard a panting Honeypot compliment the young lady.

"Superb as usual, my dear. I don't know where they found you but you are worth every cent."

"Thanks. And our 'arrangement'?" a sultry female voice asked.

"Oh, of course. The money's on the table – two thousand dollars as usual. In fact, there's another five hundred dollars in my wallet. Take that – you really earned a bonus tonight. I'll see you next week by which time I will hopefully be out of this wretched place."

Two thousand dollars for less than fifteen minutes work – with a five hundred dollar bonus? Not even dermatologists earned that much! This girl must be dynamite. I was so caught up in these thoughts that I hadn't noticed that the escort was leaving the room. She opened the door, knocking me to one side in the process. However, she hadn't seen me and continued walking to the elevator, her back towards me. Even though I couldn't see her face, it was clear that she was a stunning woman. She was tall with long silky smooth legs enhanced by a pair of black leather boots. Her hair was straight, shiny and black and fell well below her shoulders. An expensive, long leather jacket hugged her body tight enough to highlight her extraordinary figure. My thoughts immediately turned to English literature and the phrase 'But me no buts'. I had no idea what it meant but it contained the word 'but' – and her butt was sensational. The elevator door opened and she entered it. With bated breath, I waited for her to turn around so I could take in her face before the doors closed. And turn around she did. For a few brief seconds, our eyes locked. And I had been right. She was beautiful, beautiful beyond imagining. It would have been love at first sight except for one minor point – we had already met. As the elevator doors closed, breaking our gaze, my only thought was "Why, Sundari? Why?"

September 26

It is three o'clock in the morning and I haven't slept a wink. I have been unable to stop replaying in my mind that awful moment in front of the elevator. Could I have been mistaken? Could it simply have been a girl who resembled Sundari? But I knew in my heart of hearts that it had been her. Those twenty minutes spent in her house so many months ago had etched her face in my memory forever – I would never forget it. In addition, I am sure that she had recognized me. It was only a very subtle sign – a widening of the eyes as well as pursing her lips when our gaze locked – but it was enough to convince me. I waited in front of the elevator for what seemed like an eternity, but was probably only five minutes, for Sundari to return and provide a miraculous explanation that would discredit what appeared to be true: namely that she has become a high-class hooker.

This is bloody ridiculous. Why am I losing precious sleep over this girl? Not only did she reject me before, but my parents are right – she isn't good enough for me. What more evidence do I need than this? She's a high-class whore – God knows for how long and with how many men. Perhaps she was doing it when she met me. She can go to hell for all I care. I'm going to bed now.

7pm. Despite the bluster and bravado expressed above so many hours ago, Sundari has remained at the back of my mind throughout the day. The words 'Sundari' and 'high-class whore' have been swirling around in my head like a broken record and even compromised my interaction with patients. The unfortunate episode occurred during a ward round with Professor Gorgas.

My reverie was shattered by an indignant Professor Gorgas announcing, "I beg your pardon, Dr. Mendis?"

I focussed to find that Precious and the patient (an eighty year old nun – Sister Josephine) were staring at me in disbelief while Professor Gorgas was shaking her head with disapproval.

"Professor?" I mumbled, quite confused.

"Dr. Mendis, I asked you what risk factor led to Sister Josephine acquiring leprosy. You said 'high-class whore.' I'm very disappointed in you."

"I'm really sorry but I was..."

She interrupted me. "No one really knows how leprosy is transmitted but it is probably through the respiratory route. So I guess that sexual activity could be a risk factor. But if you had taken the time to get a thorough history from this nun, then her previous work in a leper colony in India is the most obvious risk factor – her whoring days are irrelevant."

I started to explain my terrible miscommunication. "Yes, Professor. I'm sorry. But actually, Sister Josephine was never a pros..."

However, Professor Gorgas again didn't let me finish. "Use your common sense in the future, Dr. Mendis. Mind you, I have to concede that I was unaware of her time as a prostitute. Add a full screen for sexually-transmitted infections on tomorrow's batch of tests." She looked at Sister Josephine. "Did a bit of a Mary Magdalene back in your youth? Oops, should be careful of what I say – *Da Vinci Code* and all that. Ever had the clap? Gonorrhoea? Syphilis?"

"Good heavens, no! I don't know what this is all about," protested Sister Josephine in shock. "I'm still a virgin."

Professor Gorgas patted her forearm condescendingly. "Of course you are, my dear. Just say three Hail Mary's and we won't tell the Vatican."

As we moved to the next patient, leaving poor Sister Josephine apoplectic with indignation, I realized that I'd have to smooth things over with her after the ward round. I had barely survived a lawsuit from Tabitha Freeman – I certainly didn't plan on taking on the Catholic Church as well!

September 30

Just after arriving at work, I received a text message. My heart stopped beating when I saw that the sender was Sundari. It read: "Can we meet tonight at Ranson's café at 7pm – please?"

Given that our last conversation had ended so badly, it must have been humiliating to contact me, even by text message. I can imagine her gritting her teeth as she typed the word 'please' on her mobile phone. Presumably, she wants my assurance that I won't spread the word about her new career. I contemplated refusing her proposal – after all, she snubbed me the last time we spoke. But out of curiosity and a longing to once more gaze into those beautiful ebony eyes, I texted back 'ok'.

I arrived at the café. Irrespective of how things are between us and whether or not she is a prostitute, I have to concede that Sundari remains the most beautiful woman that I have ever seen. The effect of her beauty is such that I found myself trembling as I sat down. But despite all this, I had unfinished business with her...

"So, you'll *never be anyone's dirty little secret*," I said harshly, echoing the words with which she ended our last conversation so many months ago. "Isn't that slightly hypocritical considering what you do?"

Although they were only words, they had the effect of a physical blow, making her slump forward and bow her head in shame. I instantly regretted saying it but stubbornly refused to concede anything to her.

She replied, "I deserved that. It also answers another question. I didn't know if you knew why I was visiting that man at the hospital – obviously you do."

"It was kind of difficult to ignore all the noise. Mind you, it sounded like you earned every cent," I said sarcastically.

She looked even more dismayed. "You even heard *that*?"

"Yep. Two thousand dollars with a five hundred dollar bonus. Great work if you can get it." I realized that she had been counting on the fact that I hadn't been aware of why she was visiting Honeypot. After all, I had only seen her leaving his room. She was probably going to pass it off as visiting a friend, but my words so far dashed any such hopes.

She almost broke down at this point. I saw tears come into her eyes but she blinked them away rapidly. Regaining her composure, she became all business-like.

"Let's make this brief, Manju. Obviously, you understand the situation. I'm an escort. If this news spreads around the Sri Lankan community, my mother and sister would be ostracized permanently, not to mention being utterly humiliated. I need your silence."

I hesitated, appalled by her blasé attitude. She mistook my hesitation for something else.

"I don't have much money left, but I can offer you something to keep quiet."

I went ballistic. "Are you crazy, Sundari? I'm not blackmailing you," I said a little too loudly. A few other diners briefly looked in our direction before returning to their own conversations. I lowered my voice. "I didn't say anything just now because I'm still stunned by the whole situation. Of course, I won't tell anyone else. After all, it's none of my business."

"Thanks," she said sincerely.

"But what do you mean you don't have much money left? That guy gave you over two thousand dollars for your ummm 'services'. How could you have gone through it so quickly? Are you a gambling addict or something like that? There are programs to help those kinds of problems."

She snapped back at me. "No, I'm not a gambling addict. Not that this is any of your business, but I am doing this for my family. When my father died last year, he left us with a $370,000 mortgage and no life insurance. My sister attends Sabatini Grammar, which as you know, is a really expensive school. It has been a struggle to stay afloat ever since he died. Ammi is over sixty and has never been anything other than a housewife. So she was never going to find a good-paying job. All we had was her life savings. But, within six months, they were completely exhausted. We needed lots of money fast otherwise the bank would have foreclosed on our home and Reshmi would have had to leave her school. I wasn't going to let that happen."

"But why did you have to do *this*?" I asked coldly, suppressing the waves of sympathy that arose inside me.

"What else could I have done? With my media qualifications, I couldn't hope to land a job at this stage of my career that would cover the mortgage and school repayments. That was when I heard about this 'position'. It was... the only way."

"It's never 'the only way', Sundari. You could have found something else."

She began to get upset. "Hey, I didn't ask you here to get your blessing. Don't you dare judge me! I did what I had to do."

"Fine," I retorted angrily. "At least tell me one thing – when we came to your house that day, had you started working as a call-girl?"

She looked at me in disbelief and with undisguised contempt. "After everything I've just told you, all you are interested in is whether I was a hooker when we first met? Well, you'll be pleased to know that I *wasn't* a 'working girl' then. Heaven forbid if the wonderful Dr. Manju Mendis had been introduced to a high-class whore as a prospective wife. Imagine the scandal that would follow, not to mention the tarnished reputation of the mighty Mendis family!"

"I didn't mean it like that," I replied bleakly.

"Do you think I enjoy being a hooker?" she asked angrily.

The question was rhetorical but I snapped. I will regret the brain explosion that followed for the rest of my life. "Perhaps you do enjoy it, judging from the moaning in that hospital room," I said. "Maybe you realized that this was the only way that someone from such a humble background could have a brush with fame and fortune. Maybe you thought this would be the way to land the perfect media job."

"You son of a bitch." But even as she said it, her voice cracked. Any semblance of composure evaporated as she burst into tears. She stood up and rushed towards the door.

Having revealed a heartlessness of which I had never thought myself capable, I sat stunned at my harsh words to Sundari. By the time I returned to my senses and got to my feet to find her, she had gone. I called her repeatedly on my mobile phone but there was no response. Could I blame her for refusing to talk to me after I told her that she enjoyed being a whore? Incredulous at my own stupidity, I also stood up and began to make my way out of the café when I heard my name being called.

"Manju!" I looked across and was startled to see Alternaria at the other end of the café. She was sitting at a table by herself. I made my way over there.

"Hi, Alternaria," I said. "What are you doing here?"

"I'm just waiting for some friends." She hesitated as if she had something awkward to say but didn't know how to say it. Her body language suggested some degree of discomfiture, although the reason wasn't clear. She seemed about to say something when her friends turned up. She introduced me to them and I used the opportunity to depart.

The whole encounter with Alternaria was puzzling. Did she know about Sundari? Although Alternaria would have seen us sitting together and possibly seen Sundari storming out of the café, she couldn't have heard anything of our conversation. Perhaps her discomfort related to something else? All in all, it was very strange.

As for the encounter with Sundari, it was once again a complete disaster. I came out of it looking like an insensitive, self-righteous git. But I just can't accept what she has done. There are always better alternatives for earning money than prostituting oneself. No, the more I think on it, it is clear that we have no future together.

October 1

Why, Sundari? Why?

October 2

During the Lab Round, a most unexpected finding emerged. We completed examining the culture plates of the specimens from our own Infectious Diseases patients. Just as we were about to leave, Clive, the Senior Scientist, beckoned to Professor Gorgas.

"Servilia, you will really want to see this." I had tremendous respect for Clive – for his extensive knowledge of Microbiology and because he was the only person who was able to call Professor Gorgas by her first name without having a body part savagely removed.

He led her to a bench with a number of culture plates. She spent a few moments examining them in silence before looking at a slide under the microscope.

"What about the sugar pattern?" she asked.

"Positive for glucose and negative for maltose and other sugars," Clive responded.

Professor Gorgas turned to Precious. "Well, Dr. Thyme, all these specimens consist of Gram-negative diplococci that are positive for glucose. What is the likely organism?"

Without a moment's hesitation, Precious replied, "*Neisseria gonorrhoeae*, also known as gonococcus – the causative agent of gonorrhoea."

"Excellent," replied Professor Gorgas. She turned back to Clive, seemingly irritated. "Why on earth did you drag us all the way to show us gonorrhoea? Big deal! There's a lot of it about. It's not exactly bird flu."

Clive had the smug look of someone who knew a vital piece of information that was being withheld from the rest of us. "What if I told you that all three 'patients' are actually staff members in the ED? Would that make it more interesting?"

Professor Gorgas' expression became almost predatory. It reminded me a lot of the hunger in Fabulus Hipz' face when she asked me to sleep with her. "You mean there's an outbreak of gonorrhoea amongst staff in our ED?" she demanded.

"It appears so," replied Clive. "Fascinating, isn't it? Don't worry, I have already informed the Director of ED and the Health Department."

While everyone else in the lab was 'fascinated' with this piece of news, I must confess that my initial reaction was annoyance. I had spent three months working in ED at the start of the year, hoping everyday that someone would engage me in casual sexual activity. It never happened – not even one little pash. Now, inexplicably, the ED staff were going at it so hard that there was an outbreak of gonorrhoea. Oh, the injustice of it all! Why couldn't I have got gonorrhoea during my time in the ED? However, all was not as it seemed. Clive had deliberately left out another piece of valuable information and he turned to me to help him reveal it.

"Dr. Mendis, from what specimens do you think the gonorrhoea would have grown?"

That was an easy question. "Since it is a sexually transmitted infection, I presume the swabs would have been taken from the vagina, urine, rectum or throat."

Still maintaining the smug grin, he shook his head. "Normally, you'd be right. But would you believe that all three staff members had otitis externa *(External ear infection – Editors)*? The swabs came from pus in their ear canals."

Professor Gorgas grunted with derision. "This can't be right, Clive. In thirty years of Infectious Diseases, I can't recall a single case of ear infection in an adult due to gonococcus, let alone a cluster of three."

"Yet the evidence is irrefutable," replied Clive.

"Indeed," said Professor Gorgas, a thoughtful expression on her face.

"But why couldn't it be possible, Professor?" asked Precious. "For example, someone performs unprotected oral sex on someone with gonorrhoea. By doing that, they develop gonorrhoea in their own throat, so-called 'gono pharyngitis'. What if that person goes on to have sex with these staff members, with foreplay including sucking, kissing or licking of the ear? Couldn't that lead to gonococcal ear infections?"

"Thank you for that very personal insight into foreplay techniques, Dr. Thyme," said Professor Gorgas, which resulted in Precious turning bright red with embarrassment. "Actually, it's not a bad thought. However, if you are right, why haven't we seen this before? Thousands of people over the centuries with gonococcal pharyngitis would have nibbled, blown, kissed or licked a lover's ear. No, something else is going on."

Professor Gorgas called her secretary on the mobile phone. "There is an outbreak in the ED. I want you to arrange a teleconference as soon as possible with the Director of ED, the Health Department and the General Manager's office. Call me back when you have done so."

Clive turned to me. "One of your intern colleagues in the ED has already started collecting data on this cluster of cases. Is the name Copper Tang familiar?"

I nodded my head. I was glad to hear that Copper was involved. This type of investigation would almost certainly lead to a publication. It would pit him against me for the Steelbone Trophy, but I honestly didn't care.

As we prepared to leave the Lab, Professor Gorgas reiterated the need to get to the bottom of this mysterious outbreak.

"Don't worry, Professor. Even if we don't find the source of the outbreak, I'm sure it'll blow over," I said.

"How can you be so sure?" she replied.

"It's like that proverb," I said.

"What proverb?" she asked, baffled.

"Here today, gono tomorrow."

October 3

We managed to catch up for an afternoon snack in the cafeteria. Peter, who was assisting in operating theatre, was the only absentee.

I asked Delilah how the surgical term was going, over two weeks since Bonkzalot's dismissal from the hospital.

"It's absolutely brilliant! The hospital hired a young locum, James Hickory. Not only does he have a wonderful bedside manner but he's even completed a PhD! Today we had the surreal experience of doing a ward round of surgical patients, interspersed with discussion about odds ratios, confidence intervals and the oxidative activity of hepatocytes."

"Sounds wonderful," murmured Lucky, rather unenthusiastically.

"You had to be there," said Delilah as she gave Lucky a light jab in the side. "But he's a really nice, approachable man."

"So it seems that some good has come out of Bonkzalot's departure," I said.

"And that's all thanks to you," said Copper, patting me on the back.

"Not too loud," I quickly said. The hospital board had realized that only a hospital employee could have engineered Bonkzalot's demise. Fabulus Hipz had refused to name her source (ie. me). Sir Ninian had been so incensed that he had threatened the source with extreme disciplinary measures if he or she were ever discovered. I was, therefore, still very wary about openly discussing the incident.

"By the way, Copper, how's the gonorrhoea investigation in ED?" I asked, curious to get the latest update.

"There's a gonorrhoea outbreak in ED? But I'm working there," both Lucky and Alternaria said simultaneously, in horror. Delilah hadn't heard about the outbreak either. So I gave them the facts that I learnt yesterday and opened the floor to Copper.

"It's really weird. There are three staff members affected. Obviously, I can't name them but it appears that sex is unlikely to be the cause of it. All three staff deny any high-risk sexual behaviour."

"But can you really take their word for it?" Smegman asked.

"Normally no. But in this case, they were all really quick to offer urine, rectal and throat specimens for analysis. It's as if they know the specimens will test negative for gonorrhoea. Anyway, the results will be available tomorrow morning."

"So if sex isn't the risk factor for gonorrhoea, what on earth is?" asked Alternaria.

"I have no idea. The Health Department people are drafting a huge survey called a 'hypothesis-generating questionnaire' to try and identify every possible exposure. Hopefully, this will give us some ideas and we'll go on to do a case-control study."

"It's a great outbreak investigation to be involved in," I told Copper. "How did you get to be part of it?"

"I've got a Masters in Epidemiology and Applied Statistics. Dr Tiberius remembered seeing that on my CV so he thought I'd be useful. Also, I'm in the middle of five days off, so I've got the time."

"It's a bit rough to make you work on your days off," said Lucky.

"I don't mind. It's really interesting work and more importantly, I'm getting paid by ED to do it."

"You're the man," I said, high-fiving him. "Keep us updated though. It'll be intriguing to know what lies behind this mystery."

"Shall do."

As everyone stood up, Alternaria asked, "Manju, do you have time to talk for a few minutes – alone? It's quite important." Like that evening in the café, she looked uneasy and uncomfortable.

"Of course," I said, gesturing for her to sit down.

With her head bowed, refusing to make eye contact with me, she began. "About a week ago, I took your advice and went to see Nurse Watson on the Celebrity Ward about the car she's selling. As I reached the ward, I walked towards the Nurses' Station. But as I passed the patient's room, I heard the unmistakable sound of people having sex. Being a bit of a voyeur, I couldn't help but peep around the door to watch the goings-on. I saw a middle-aged man making love to a beautiful young woman." She paused and stared at me hard, as if hoping that I would respond. And then it all made sense. I understood the reason for Alternaria's discomfiture.

"Alternaria, it's okay. I understand. It's Sundari, by the way."

"Sundari?" she asked, baffled.

"Yes. That's the name of the girl you saw having sex in the Celebrity Ward and also the one who met me at the café a few days ago. I take it you were the one I saw leaving the Celebrity Ward in the other elevator just as I arrived?"

She breathed a huge sigh of relief. I was surprised to see tears in her eyes. "Yes, it was me, Manju. I'm so glad that you know about the girl – I mean, Sundari. When I saw her in the café that night, I recognized her instantly as the one having sex in the Celebrity Ward. I didn't know whether you knew or whether it was my business to tell you. But if you didn't know that she was cheating on you, I felt that I had to tell you. The uncertainty's been killing me."

"It's nice to know that I have friends who care enough to get upset about something like this," I sincerely replied. "Actually, she wasn't cheating on me, because we're not in a relationship."

Alternaria looked alarmed. "Oh no, I probably shouldn't have said anything."

"No, I'm glad you did because it's a very complicated situation. In fact, I really could do with a woman's perspective on this one. What I am about to tell you is in strict confidence. Promise me that you won't tell anyone else, otherwise it could ruin her life."

Alternaria gulped at the earnestness of my request. "Manju, the only way I survived that surgical term with Bonkzalot was because of you. You are my friend and can trust me completely."

So I told Alternaria everything about Sundari from start to finish, including her vocation as a high-class prostitute.

Her eyes widened in amazement and she made a comment that caught me completely off guard. "What a courageous woman."

"Courageous?" I questioned irritably. "She's an intelligent girl with university qualifications who has turned to prostitution. I don't see anything courageous about that."

"Really? Remember this then. She has to have sex with strange men for money. And we are not talking about chiselled Greek Gods like Brad Pitt and Will Smith. Most of them are ugly, fat, middle-aged men with body odour and bad breath. Another thing: for most men, sex is about physical pleasure; therefore, there is no need for intimacy, familiarity or love. However, for many women, sex is an emotional experience. So having sex with a strange man with no emotional connection is in itself utterly detestable."

She relentlessly continued, "And irrespective of how much she gets paid, remember that she is naked in a room with a physically stronger stranger. She must be wondering if her next client is going to be the one who beats her, rapes her or forces her to have sex without a condom. Imagine how terrifying it must be. Finally, Manju, remember why she is doing this. This isn't to buy a flash car or some pretty little trinket. It's not even to finance her own career or education. She is doing this to keep a roof over her family's head and give her sister the best education she can. You say that there's always an alternative. But if that alternative means losing their home or having her sister kicked out of school, then is it really an alternative at all? Well, Manju?"

I sat back and took a deep breath. "I guess not," I murmured.

"Face it, Manju. You're just being self-righteous and pissed off because you found out that the girl of your dreams is a prostitute. Also, you subconsciously feel that your mother was right about her 'not being good enough' for you, which is also pissing you off."

As I saw the truth in her words, I angrily banged my fist on the table. "I've been such an arrogant fool."

Alternaria smiled kindly and put her hand on my shoulder. "Don't be too hard on yourself. It's never easy to come to terms with a bombshell like this. All I am saying is that she isn't some wanton slut. She's an intelligent woman who is doing something she finds completely abhorrent for the sake of others. But Manju, tell me one thing – are you in love with her?"

"I really don't know," I said. "It's all very confusing."

"No, it's not. Just answer two simple questions."

"Okay."

"How often do you think about her?"

"At least once a day," I automatically replied, surprised at my own answer. "I didn't even realize that until you asked me."

She smiled. "People often don't. Now this one's a bit harder. Was there ever a time that you thought about her which really surprised you?"

I concentrated hard. After a few moments, I nodded. "Yes, now you mention it. Did I ever tell you that I lost my virginity to Fabulus Hipz?"

Alternaria looked stunned. "You mean that gorgeous TV presenter? When did that happen?"

"Just over a month ago," I said.

How did you manage that, you lucky bastard?"

I smiled. "I'll have to tell you that story another day, Alternaria. But that night, after making love to Fabulus, all I could think about was Sundari."

"For goodness sake, Manju, isn't it obvious? You'd just lost your virginity to a sexy female celebrity, but all you could think about was another woman, someone whom you think about everyday. If that's not proof that you're in love with Sundari, I don't know what is."

It all seemed so clear now that Alternaria explained it. But there was a problem. "I might love her, Alternaria, but a relationship can't be a one-way street. She needs to be interested in me too for this to work, and I know for a fact that she detests me."

Alternaria shook her head. "No, you're wrong. You forget that I was in the café that day to meet my friends. I had got the time wrong so I was there half an hour early. Sundari arrived a good ten minutes before you. I immediately recognized her as the girl from hospital and was naturally intrigued and made a point to secretly watch her from my table. To be honest, even if I hadn't recognized her, I'd have still checked her out – after all, she's one hot babe and I'm a lesbian. Anyway, she was fidgety and looked really anxious."

I shook my head in disappointment. "That's got nothing to do with being in love with me. She was unsure whether she would have to tell me that she was a prostitute. That would make anyone anxious."

"Let me finish. For the next ten minutes, she kept taking out her compact, adjusting her hair, putting on lipstick, removing smudges and making sure her dress fitted just right. I'm a woman, Manju, I know when another woman is trying to impress someone. It wasn't just information that she wanted – she clearly fancies you."

I put my head in my hands and groaned.

"What's wrong," asked Alternaria. "I just said that she's in love with you too. Isn't that a good thing?"

"Of course. It's just the way our conversation ended."

"Oh, that's right. I remember seeing her storm out of the café. What did you say to her?"

I winced. "I sort of told her that she enjoyed being a prostitute."

"Manju, how could you say that?" she asked, completely shocked.

"I didn't mean it of course but the whole conversation had become an emotional rollercoaster. It just slipped out."

"It's all that testosterone, you know. It leads to all this impulsive behaviour. Boy, am I glad that I'm a lesbian. Anyway, why don't you apologize to her?"

"Don't you think that I've tried? The only way I can contact her is through her mobile phone. But she seems to have barred me from calling. Even my text messages bounce back."

"Didn't you say that you've been to her place?"

"Yes, that's right. I went there with my parents some months ago."

"Well, if you remember the address, why don't you drive over there one day and talk to her?"

It was so obvious that I hadn't even considered it. "That's a great idea. Maybe I'll go early next week after she's cooled down a bit and try my luck. After all, what's the worst that can happen?"

"Manju, remember that you don't have to start off as lovers. Take things slowly. Sundari must be the loneliest person in the world right now. All she needs is a friend."

I thanked Alternaria once again for her insightful advice. She had opened my eyes, not just to my own shortcomings, but to something which had hardly seemed possible prior to our conversation – the possibility of a relationship with Sundari.

October 8

It has been a frustrating couple of days. As Alternaria suggested, I plucked up the courage and drove over to Sundari's house on both Monday and Tuesday. I became totally stressed when I found nobody at home on both occasions. My initial fear was that they had defaulted on the mortgage repayments and the bank had taken possession of the home. I peered through a couple of windows and everything seemed normal inside. Certainly, debt collectors hadn't come in and emptied the place. Perhaps they had gone on holiday to escape the financial stress they were undergoing. But that didn't make sense because holidays were expensive and school holidays hadn't started yet for Sundari's sister. I thought it best to leave things for the moment and maybe try again on Sunday. Mind you, this must be the downside of love. I am constantly thinking of Sundari, wondering where she is and if she is okay.

Copper, Smegman, Delilah and I met for lunch in the hospital cafeteria. It was a great opportunity to hear how the gonorrhoea outbreak in ED was progressing. We were surprised to hear that the investigation was already complete.

"That was quick work," said Smegman.

"I know," said Copper. "The outbreak team has been working without a break. Dr. Tiberius even rostered me out of yesterday's shift just so I could finish the statistical analysis."

"So what's the verdict, Copper? How did those three staff members get gono in their ears?"

Copper nodded. "At the end of the day, after trawling through literally a hundred possibilities, only one activity stood out. It appears that all three staff members who got sick didn't have their own stethoscope and had been using stethoscopes belonging to the ED. It was the only common risk factor of any significance."

"Oh my God! So are you suggesting that the earpieces on the ED stethoscope had gonorrhoea on them?"

"We thought that it would explain everything so we sent swabs from the earpieces of all the ED stethoscopes to the Microbiology Lab. And would you believe it – the earpieces from two stethoscopes grew gonorrhoea?"

"Get out of here!" I exclaimed.

Copper continued. "Our theory is that one of the stethoscopes is responsible for starting the outbreak and that the other one was used by one of our three staff members after he or she got sick."

"You don't know that for sure," Delilah said. "Maybe both stethoscopes only got gonorrhoea on them after the three staff members got their ear infections. Maybe they represent a consequence of the sick staff members rather than a cause."

"You're right," said Copper. "We're just guessing but that's our hypothesis."

"I didn't know gonorrhoea could survive on inanimate surfaces," I said.

"Me neither," said Copper. "But Professor Gorgas said it can, although to her knowledge, nobody has ever developed gonorrhoea from an inanimate object before."

"But if you're right, how are you proposing that the gono got on the stethoscope in the first place?"

"Possibly through some bizarre sex game?" said Copper.

"A stethoscope as a sex toy?" I said sceptically. "Sounds pretty unlikely."

"So does a woman using a carrot as a contraceptive – but you still published a paper on it."

"That's true," I conceded. "Talking about publications, you'd better publish this case – it's really interesting."

"And unique," added Smegman.

Copper nodded. "We've just started writing it up. I wouldn't mind your help for a catchy title for the paper."

We brainstormed for a few minutes and came up with "GonorEAR: An Unusual Outbreak of VD in the ED."

October 11

Today Uncle Raj came over for dinner. He is an old family friend, now living in Canada. His brother was my father's Best Man at my parents' wedding. He is here on business and is staying in a hotel in the city. I drove him back to the Pierre Polo, the only six and a half star hotel on this side of the equator. It opened last year and to date, I hadn't had an opportunity to check it out. Although I was keen to survey the hotel, the real objects of interest to me were the elevators. I had seen them on TV. Two of them were made of transparent glass. Located at each end of the opulently furnished and massive lobby, they climbed all the way to the fiftieth floor. Imagine the view from the top. Apart from checking out the view, my intention was to Elevator Groove. I had never Elevator Grooved in a glass elevator, particularly one that reached such a height. It would be an awesome experience. And now, just past midnight, would be one of the few times when I might have the elevator all to myself. I dropped Uncle Raj off in the lobby and pretended to drive off. However, I doubled back, parked the car and entered the lobby. It was more massive than I had imagined, and more opulent. I wouldn't have been surprised if it was a hundred metres from one end to the other – at least. The floor was polished marble, which sparkled like newly cleaned dentures. Jets of water from a large fountain in the middle, danced to the beat of classical music. The circular walls were extraordinary. On one half, the walls consisted of intricately detailed mosaic tiles, which I remember reading were based on the designs of the Taj Mahal. The other half was lined with gold, into which had been placed a variety of precious stones. The thousands of stones on that part of the wall sparkled in a multitude of colours. Gaudy? Perhaps, but, whatever your opinion, you couldn't deny that a lot of money had gone into this. If I recall correctly, the circular wall of the lobby alone had cost twenty million dollars.

I stood in front of the elevator. It was beautiful and big. I conservatively estimate dimensions of 5 x 5 x 6 metres with the back gracefully curved to fit snugly against the circular wall. On entering, the elevator greeted me in five different languages, only three of which I recognized. My hunch had been correct – since it was so late, nobody else was around. I was alone and could do some serious Elevator Grooving. I took a deep breath, pushed the button for the fiftieth floor and waited for the door to close. As soon as it did, I started a medley, beginning with Fatboy Slim's 'Weapon of Choice'. Having valiantly attempted to impersonate the wonderful Christopher Walken who starred in the video clip, I moved to Beyoncé's 'All the Single Ladies' and climaxed with Queen's 'We will Rock You'. As I reached the fiftieth floor, I was exultant and exhausted simultaneously. It had been an awesome experience. But I had never realized how tiring Elevator Grooving could be after climbing fifty stories. If someone had entered the elevator at this point, there would have been no way that I could have hidden my heavy panting. The elevator's computer reminded me that the door wouldn't open until I swiped my electronic room pass, a sensible security measure. Since there was no one below wanting the elevator, it remained at the fiftieth floor, allowing me to gaze at the spectacular view. The hotel lobby with its sparkling gold and gemstone wall and dancing fountain looked amazing from this height. The lobby staff were barely visible. The wall behind the elevator was made of heavily reinforced glass. From the fiftieth floor, I looked out to see the whole city skyline glittering at night. I sighed with contentment as I enjoyed the breathtaking view before reluctantly pushing the button for the lobby. As the elevator began its descent, I got into position for my encore performance. Just as I was about to start Elevator Grooving, I stopped in astonishment. Across the lobby in the other glass elevator, there was someone descending from the same height as me. It was too far to make out whether it was a man or a woman but one thing was clear: he or she was Elevator Grooving. I was not alone! There were others like me, other 'Elevator Groovers'. I started dancing furiously to Footloose and by the time we had reached the thirty-fifth floor, it was apparent that my fellow Elevator Groover had seen me. For the remainder of our long descent, one of us did a quick dance and stopped before gesturing to our counterpart to take up the beat. It was like Tag Team Wrestling in elevators. As the elevator reached the lobby floor and the doors opened, we walked quickly towards one another. As we got closer, the long hair betrayed the fact that my fellow groover was a woman. We waved at each other. Then, when we were about twenty metres apart, we stopped, the smiles leaving our faces, an air of astonishment enveloping us. We continued walking but at a far more measured pace.

"Hi Sundari," I said.

"Hi," she replied.

This was the moment that I had been dreaming of for the last few days but I felt awkward as hell and she looked embarrassed, more so because we never expected to meet each other here of all places. Anyway, I would try my best.

"I didn't know that you Elevator Grooved", I said, opening the conversation as neutrally as possible.

"You mean dancing in the elevator?" she asked.

I nodded.

"I've done it ever since I was a little girl. It's one of my favourite things."

"Me too. I didn't know there was anyone else out there who did it. Well, actually I guess I knew, but I didn't think that I'd ever see them doing it."

She smiled. "I like your name for it – Elevator Grooving. I never gave it a name."

"Thanks," I said. I paused before carrying on. "I went to your house on Monday and Tuesday."

"You went home?" she said, her face mirroring the astonishment in her voice. "But why?"

"I was worried about you. I wanted to see how you were doing. But you were away."

"One of Ammi's cousins has been really sick so we drove interstate and spent most of the week there." She looked down at her feet. "It was nice of you to come by. But you don't need to worry about me. I can look after myself."

"I don't doubt that. But I'm still allowed to worry."

She looked up, then down again and sighed, before looking at me. "Manju, your mother was right that day at our house – about me, at least. I'm a prostitute with no future apart from providing for my mother and sister. You are an amazing doctor from some high-class family. I don't deserve you. In fact, I don't deserve anybody."

I was appalled at how much her self-esteem had plummeted from the fiery girl who had so captivated me and declared that she'd never be anybody's 'dirty little secret'. "No," I hurriedly said. "Don't ever say that! I've sat down and thought about this, agonizing day and night. I now know that I could never do what you are doing to save my own family, even if it meant financial ruin. I'm just too damn selfish and too damn scared. And I'm pretty sure that a hell of a lot of other people would feel the same way as me. Sundari, listen to me." She looked me straight in the eyes. "You are the bravest woman I know. The bravest, the most beautiful and the most wonderful."

She started to cry. "Manju, please don't. I can't offer you anything..."

"I loved you from the first day that we met. I have never stopped thinking about you. I apologize for being such a fool. The things that I said in the café came out of anger and frustration – please forgive me. But I want you to know that I don't expect you to reciprocate anything. Just let me be your friend. Let me be someone you can talk to. That's all I ask."

She completely broke down at this point. I put my arms around her and drew her close. I encountered no resistance as her body folded into mine. She stopped crying after a while, but I still held her, tenderly stroking her hair. After a few minutes, she took her head off my shoulder and looked into my eyes.

"I love you too, Manju. I knew it from the day we first met. That was a real revelation to me because I normally don't believe in love at first sight."

"Me neither," I said, with a sheepish grin.

"Yet there you were. Tall, dark and handsome. And a doctor to boot. But it all went pear-shaped when your mother discovered that we weren't the high-class people she thought we were."

"I'm so sorry about that," I interjected quickly. "My mother is clueless. You'll find her picture in the dictionary under 'tactless'."

Sundari gave a wry smile. "No, don't worry. Unlike us, our parents were brought up in an environment where knowing 'your place' in society was central to their lives. I guess we'd have been the same if we were brought up like that. So I can't blame your mother for her views. I don't have to agree with her, but I don't blame her."

"You're too kind," I said, wondering whether my mother really did deserve such forgiveness.

"I also need to apologize."

"For what?" I asked, somewhat mystified.

"For the way that I treated you when you called me that night."

"You mean when I tried to read the conversation off a script because I was so nervous?" I recalled, smiling.

She laughed. "Oh, you poor thing! I should have been flattered that a guy would go to all that trouble for me. And then I hung up on you, didn't I?" she said, cringing.

"You certainly did. But that is water under the bridge. We've moved on."

She took a step back and suddenly became sad.

Alarmed, I asked her what was wrong.

"I hate what I am doing – what I have become. They are so repulsive – all those men. Most of them are married. Some of them remove their wedding bands before I arrive but I can see the pale outline of it on their ring finger. I know that they are committing adultery, that *we* are committing adultery. Some of them are so old that they must have daughters my age. It is so disgusting – at the start, it used to take all the self-control I could muster not to vomit. Now I just close my eyes and think of something, anything beautiful where my mind can hide till *it* is over."

"I'm so sorry, Sundari," I said, tears coming to my eyes.

Sundari shook her head. "Let me finish. Although it is so, so horrible, Manju, I still need to provide for Ammi and Reshmi. They'll be finished without me. Do you understand what I am saying? I can't stop doing this. It is breaking my spirit, my heart, my very soul, but I just can't stop. And though I love you, I don't want to drag you down with me. Please, forget about me and move on with your life. You deserve better. As for me, to know that you love me is enough."

I took a step toward her and lifted her chin with my hand, allowing me to gaze into those wondrous ebony black eyes that had enchanted me when we had first met. "Give this up – today," I said. "I've been living at home without any expenses so my salary's largely untouched. Take that money. Whatever else you need I'll keep providing through what I earn."

She looked shocked. "No, Manju. I can't let you do that. I won't. You'll need that money. You have a life, a future."

"But I don't have a future without you. It's my money and you can't stop me giving it to you."

"But what if 'we' don't work out? What then? You'll have wasted all this money on a dead-end relationship."

"To see you happy, smiling and away from this living hell that you call a 'job' will never be a waste of money. Please Sundari, walk away from this. And you won't be alone – you'll have me. For better or worse..."

She smiled, giving me hope that my lobbying had been successful. "For richer or poorer..." she said.

"Hopefully richer," I said.

She laughed and suddenly hugged me. "Thank you so much."

I felt weak at the knees. But it was a wonderful feeling. I asked her, "So what are you doing here at this time of night?"

She smiled again. "Well, as you can see," she said, pointing to the t-shirt and jeans she was wearing, "I wasn't 'working'. I wouldn't have been in the mood to Elevator Groove if I had been. A school friend is getting married. She's quite wealthy and her father paid for the penthouse suite for her hen's night. The party's still going on but I left because I have a client early tomorrow."

"Not anymore," I said, giving her a piercing gaze.

She smiled and kissed me on the cheek. "No, not anymore."

"So why don't you go back up and have a good time with your friends?"

She linked her arm with mine and nuzzled her head against me. "Because I'd much rather spend this time with the man I love. Does a late night hot chocolate sound good?"

"Yes," I said, my voice trembling and breaking with an emotion that I hadn't felt for a long time. It took me a few moments to realize that it was joy, pure unbridled joy.

We spent the next three hours in the hotel lobby. I drank so much hot chocolate and ate so many marshmallows that I felt slightly ill. But I didn't care. I was in love! We talked and talked, like we'd known each other for years. Never was there a stage that we weren't in physical contact, whether it was holding hands, rubbing feet or gently touching each other's face. However, the next time that I play 'footsies', I must remember to remove my boots. It turns out that the sensation of the stiletto-like heels rubbing against bare flesh is rather uncomfortable.

"Your parents aren't going to be thrilled about this, Manju. Your mother made her feelings about me pretty clear that day at my place."

"Don't worry about them. They don't run my life. I talk – they listen," I said confidently.

October 12

"Please Ammi. Please Thaththa. Let me date Sundari," I pleaded, my hands clasped together as I begged on my knees.

"What, men! Manju, she's not good enough for you. I forbid it," said Ammi dismissively.

"Chickaaya, Manjula! What's got into you, men?" asked Thaththa, who only used my full name when he was truly annoyed. "You should have forgotten that girl a long time ago."

"Manju, she doesn't have anything," said Ammi. "She's at a loose end – no money, poor background – nothing. Naturally, she wants to get her claws into you – a good boy from a good family. Can you believe that *hora kella*? Bloody cheek, no?"

"But she's beautiful and intelligent," I countered.

"I told you before- those boobs of hers will be sagging in a few years. When that happens, she'll have nothing worth talking about," my mother said, unnecessarily making sagging gestures with her hands.

"Yes, Manju. Ammi is right. Don't lower yourself by seeing this girl," said Thaththa. "Back in Sri Lanka, you'd have had nothing to do with such people."

"In fact, my sister called me today about another girl from a good family who'd love to meet you," Ammi squealed with delight. "What a shame to let such an opportunity pass. Put this Sundari girl behind you. After all, her family is – how do you say it – 'brown trash'."

I am an obedient son. Despite my grumblings and complaints, I always give in to my parents' unreasonable demands, whether they relate to meeting new girls or attending some boring function. Like so many other Asian children, I had been relentlessly indoctrinated with the adage from early childhood that 'Parents are like gods. They must be obeyed without question'. I had become a 'Yes' man whenever it came to them.

But what if your parents aren't perfect? What if they get it wrong sometimes? How does it benefit anyone to blindly follow their instructions? From a kammic point of view, what sort of child are you if, by obeying your parents, you allow them to commit bad kamma? Isn't it better to correct them and turn them into better people? How can someone grow as an individual if his or her faults are never pointed out to them?

My mother's labelling of Sundari as 'brown trash' was deplorable. For the first time in my life, I stood up to my parents. I wish I could say that my motives had been concern about their spiritual welfare married to a need to make them better people. But on this occasion, I was driven by pure unfettered fury. It was the same fury that led to me to work towards Bonkzalot's downfall and subsequently assault him on the street. It was the same single-minded hatred that drove me to replace Milton Honeypot's morphine with water. Even now, as I make this diary entry in the calm after the storm, I can't recall exactly what I said to them. Certainly, there was a lot of yelling – mainly by me, as my parents looked on in horror at this fireball of rage that had only moments earlier been their placid and obedient son. I presumably threatened to move out because the next thing I remember is standing in my room packing a suitcase. This would have been a fairly empty threat on my part as I had never packed my own bag before and had no idea where I'd go. But hopefully, I was convincing when I said it.

Long ago, my sister and I discovered that the air conditioning ducts in her old bedroom clearly carried conversations from the kitchen. I went to her bedroom and listened carefully. As luck would have it, they were still in the kitchen where we had just argued. They were still discussing my outburst. My mother sounded quite distraught, yet, somehow I couldn't feel any sympathy for her.

"How could he say those things to us – his own parents? Even Saesha, who has such a foul mouth, would never speak to us in that manner."

"He is different now, Priya," Thaththa said. "I've noticed it. This year as a doctor has changed him. We've always doted on him, protected him. But his work seems to have thrown challenges at him that have burned and scarred him. Do you remember how much like a zombie he was when he was doing surgery? I was scared that he'd have a breakdown."

(This was news to me. I never realized that my parents knew of the stress I was under during my surgical term.)

"Mahela, are you saying that his personality has changed, that he has become a completely different person?" Ammi asked Thaththa with concern.

"It is more that he has grown up. In the public service, my colleagues would discuss their children's progress. These Westerners really prepare their children for independent living at a young age: they work for pocket money, do chores around the house and many leave home when they start working. On the other hand, we pamper our children and protect them from all this. Though we do it out of love, I wonder if we have got it wrong. Maybe we should have toughened him up at a younger age."

"But what about this girl he likes? I bet you that bloody bitch is behind his character change," my mother said, challenging my Thaththa's theory.

"No, Priya. He had changed even before we met her. It is possible that she has contributed to all this, but she is not the sole cause."

"What should we do then? He is packing his bags to leave us. I don't know, men," said Ammi as her voice broke. "Mahela, do you think that we have failed as parents?"

"This argument aside, remember that we have raised an intelligent, polite, kind son who is practising the noble profession of medicine. We have not failed – he is a fine young man. And because of that, we have to trust him – need to trust him. If he loves this Sundari, then we should give him our blessing."

"But what about her background – such a low-class family?" my mother persisted. "If only she came from good people."

"Perhaps. But think about the last three Sri Lankan weddings that we attended. How many were of a Sri Lankan marrying another Sri Lankan?"

Ammi paused before answering, her voice conveying surprise. "That's true, men. They all married Westerners."

"Exactly. We have fooled ourselves into believing that it is an undeniable certainty that Manju will marry a Sri Lankan girl from a good family. Yet in truth, it would be a miracle. How can we expect these children, who spend their whole life mixing with Westerners, to automatically marry a Sri Lankan? It's luck, I tell you. We should be thanking our lucky stars that our daughter married a Sri Lankan and that our son is interested in a Sri Lankan girl –irrespective of her family background."

"But what will people say?"

"Who the hell cares what those buggers think? As long as our children are happy and not angry with us, I can live with the disapproval of others. I don't run my life to keep those bloody fools happy. And you jolly well know that if I hadn't given the astrologer a fake horoscope all those years ago, there wouldn't have been an introduction, let alone a marriage for us!"

Ammi whistled. "That's true, no? I had almost forgotten that. My God! Do you remember how the first astrologer said that you'd be dead within a year if we ever got married?"

(I was dumbfounded. My father, who was regarded as the bastion of maintaining Sri Lankan traditions in our community, had faked his own horoscope in order to marry my mother. The sly old fox!)

Thaththa continued. "Anyway, by the time Manju has children and grand-children, no one will care where his wife came from. Every noble family in history had a humble start. In fact, sometimes it takes an injection of new blood, that spark of vitality, even from low-class people, to allow a family to evolve. Otherwise things become stale. And Priya, at the end of the day, I don't want our son to think that we let him down. We must support him, otherwise we'll lose him. Don't forget the proverb: 'A daughter is a daughter for life, a son is a son until he finds a wife'."

"I don't want to lose him either. After all, he's our little *puttha*," my mother said quietly. She sighed. "Okay then, let us give him our blessing. In actual fact, that Sundari is one of the most beautiful women I have ever seen. And she did seem like a nice, well-educated girl. And she's Buddhist. He could do a lot worse."

"What, men? I thought that you said that within a few years, her boobs would sag and her hips widen?" Thaththa noted.

"I was just annoyed at the time. In fact, I can't see those boobs going anywhere for a long time."

"They sound like the boobs of another woman I know," he said, his tone changing.

I heard heavy breathing and Ammi giggle. "Let's quickly settle this with Manju. Then why don't we go to bed early? Maybe time for a bit of a poke?" Thaththa suggested.

"That sounds nice," my mother said seductively. "Nobody pokes quite like you. Do you have any condominiums?"

Condominiums?

"Yes, I have a whole packet upstairs – ribbed for your pleasure," he replied.

Is that a condominium in your pocket or are you just pleased to see me?

I ran off shuddering. There are some things that children don't need to hear about their parents. True to their word, they came to my room and gave their blessing for me to start seeing Sundari. I, in turn, said sorry for yelling at them although I remained unapologetic for my motives. As soon as they left, I called Sundari and told her that my parents were cool with us dating. She sounded surprised but ecstatic. We spoke for a wonderful hour before I wished her goodnight.

I can't express how glad I am for my parents' concession tonight. For the last few months, we had been growing more and more apart. Thaththa was right – I grew up in response to the challenges thrown my way at St. Ivanhoe. Yet, even though I had evolved, my relationship with them had not. It led to an immediate strain between us, especially my mother's ridiculous posturing on the subject of arranged marriage. In many Western families, this conflict often occurs in the boy's teens as he rebels against the rules and conventions that have bound his behaviour all his life. In Sri Lankan families, however, sons are doted on and thoroughly spoilt till they get married. This means that they don't mature or rebel till much later, often in their mid to late twenties. I suspect this is what has happened to me. But thankfully, tonight when our relationship reached this critical juncture, my parents demonstrated wisdom and love to concede in this matter. They finally no longer feel like strangers. No, tonight they are my parents once more.

October 22

It has been ten days since my last entry. Work certainly has been busy, but this delay can be attributed to love. I spend any spare time these days with Sundari. She is an amazing woman. More than anything, I can't believe how she has worked her way into the affections of my mother. And not by doing anything special, mind you – just simply by being her wonderful, humourous, compassionate self. Of course, the fact that she can cook rice and curry like a champion has further bolstered her standing in Ammi's esteem. They even went shopping together during the week.

I always hoped that Akki would automatically like her and that certainly has been the case. I introduced Sundari to my fellow interns at the end of last week over dinner. They all took to her instantly and we had a grand time. Alternaria seemed to be the happiest of them all and I quietly thanked her again for helping me in my time of crisis. The next day, both Copper and Peter met me for coffee and repeatedly told me how beautiful she is. I think I can get used to having a hot girlfriend!

October 25

Although our relationship has been progressing like a dream, I keep wondering how her time as a prostitute has affected Sundari. She has not mentioned this awful experience since we started seeing each other and I have been reluctant to bring it up as it might evoke painful memories. But today, while walking under a moonlit sky along the esplanade, I plucked up the courage and asked her if she ever ruminates on those terrible times. I braced myself for the explosion of rage and anguish that would follow my interrogation but there was none. Sundari stopped walking, turned to face me with those glorious ebony eyes, while holding my hands in hers. She smiled softly.

"I think about it often, Manju. It was the worst time of my life. I was a good Sri Lankan girl, raised in a conservative family that prided itself on virtue and decency. And yet I ended up as a prostitute of all things." She shook her head with disbelief as she pondered those dark days. "It is still a nightmare but it becomes a more distant one as every day passes and with every moment that I spend with you," she said, tenderly stroking my cheek.

She then paused before looking at me long and hard with an earnestness that gave me the impression that I was being examined. "I did what I had to in order to protect my family from financial ruin. It has taken a long time but I have finally forgiven myself. Have you forgiven me, Manju?"

So here was the test! "There is nothing to forgive," I answered immediately with a smile. As she responded with a passionate kiss, it appeared that I had passed with flying colours.

October 27

Since it is potentially fatal to think about anything other than Infectious Diseases while working, I have tried my hardest to keep Sundari out of my mind during hospital hours. However, I never realized how observant Professor Gorgas really is. On the ward round, she accosted me.

"Dr. Mendis, you have been performing adequately for the last two weeks but I get the impression that you are distracted. Is something wrong?"

"No, Professor Gorgas."

She opened my hands and felt my palms and wrist. "Sweaty palms, slightly rapid pulse." Suddenly, her hands closed around my throat and I was alarmed that she was going to strangle me. It turned out that she was simply feeling my neck. "No thyroid mass." She turned to Precious who was staring at her in bafflement. "Dr. Thyme, we have a young male who is distracted with sweaty palms and rapid pulse in the absence of a thyroid mass. What do you think?"

"I don't know, Professor," she replied, looking perplexed.

Professor Gorgas took a long, hard look at me before saying, "Diagnosis – Love. Prognosis – terminal. Am I right, Dr. Mendis?"

Rather embarrassed, I admitted that she was.

"Now Dr. Mendis, don't get me wrong. I am happy you have met the woman of your dreams. Or is it a man? Actually, on what side is your bread buttered, Dr. Mendis?"

I wasn't quite sure how to answer that one. "It's buttered on the umm, heterosexual side," I replied.

"I see. Well, I have never been one for these romantic notions of love, but I don't have anything against it *as long as it doesn't interfere with the care of my patients*. Do we have an understanding?"

"Yes, Professor Gorgas."

"You can fantasize about running through the waves, rolling down a hill of daffodils, walking under a moonlit sky or any of those other ridiculous things young lovers do. Just don't think about it while looking after my patients! Got it?"

"Yes, Professor." Sometimes that woman really scares the hell out of me!

I was on overtime today. Finishing at midnight meant that I wouldn't see Sundari which I hated. But I knew that I could put the extra cash towards her mortgage or sister's schooling. My family weren't aware of the financial fix in which Sundari's father had left her and I didn't see the need to tell them. After quitting her job as a prostitute, Sundari found a position as a junior assistant to a producer of one of the news shows. It was the perfect start to a long-term career in the media, but she was right: there was no way that such a salary could have supported her family's massive debts and expenses. Despite her 'humble background', Sundari is a proud woman and I could see how much she hated relying on me to solve her financial difficulties.

At about ten o'clock, I was paged to the Celebrity Ward, by the ever-reliable Nurse Watson. I was excited to see that our latest patient was indeed famous and from the entertainment industry. Claudius Idelic is an executive in the music industry. But he is best known as a judge in 'Music Star' a reality TV show which finds the best singer over a period of weeks from thousands of hopefuls. Claudius was admitted yesterday with cellulitis of the left leg. Nurse Watson called me because he continued to have fever despite twenty-four hours of IV antibiotics. I reviewed his results and was most interested in the cultures of the swab from his leg. Nothing had grown as yet. When I entered the room,

I found that Claudius was very alert but clearly in a lot of discomfort. The skin infection of his leg looked very raw and angry indeed.

I introduced myself. Shaking hands, he informed me of his concerns. "Hello, Dr. Mendis. Dr. Croquet put me on IV antibiotics over twenty-four hours ago but the leg seems to have gotten redder and is more painful. Also, these wretched fevers and shivers are driving me up the wall. Eric, what's the antibiotic he's got me on?" he asked a companion.

"Flucloxacillin," Eric immediately replied.

I examined the leg. He was right. It didn't look good at all. I had seen a lot of cellulitis during my time with Professor Gorgas and this looked different. In particular, there were quite a few blisters. I revisited the history with him. When it came to questions about water exposure, he nodded in the affirmative.

"Yes, I was water-skiing in Grisley Lake about three days before the infection began."

"Did you sustain any cuts or lacerations to your left leg while water-skiing?" I asked.

"As a matter of fact, I did. I had a couple of heavy falls," Claudius replied.

"I know that this might sound ridiculously pedantic but do you know if Lake Grisley's water is brackish or fresh?" I asked.

"It tastes fresh," he replied, referring to a couple of involuntary gulps following the falls while water-skiing. "Why are you asking me all these questions about water? Dr. Croquet didn't even go down that line."

I had not forgotten the lessons on cellulitis that I learnt on my first ward round with Professor Gorgas. The fresh water exposure just before the infection began and the blistering over the infected leg all fitted with an *Aeromonas* infection. Even if I was wrong, he should be on more antibiotics to cover the possibility of *Aeromonas* until the swab results came through. Yet Dr. Croquet had placed him on flucloxacillin, which only covered the strep and staph infections. Once again, I was completely mystified by Dr. Croquet's actions or, to be more correct, inaction.

Given Claudius's concern about his lack of improvement, I told him that I was worried about *Aeromonas* infection and that he'd need broader antibiotic cover. I phoned Dr. Croquet later about the matter.

Unfortunately, Croquet became furious when he learnt that I was questioning his choice of antibiotics and even more so when he realized that I'd made the patient aware of the issue. In fact, he threatened to have me censured by the Hospital Board. As if the pompous git would have grounds for that! But in the end, despite the unnecessary bluster, Dr. Croquet eventually agreed to add gentamicin to cover *Aeromonas*. I informed Claudius who thanked me for my assistance.

When my shift ended, Sundari called. I was surprised as it was well past midnight. "Haven't you got an early start at work tomorrow?" I asked her.

She laughed. "Sure do, Manju. But I've just finished reading 'Gods Behaving Badly'. You know that I haven't been able to put it down these last few days. Anyway, I knew that you'd have just finished work and I thought it would be nice to hear your voice before I went to bed... naked."

"Naked?" I gulped, my eyes widening with excitement.

"Actually, no. But I just thought that I'd wake you up a bit before you drive home. I don't want my poor baby falling asleep at the wheel," she laughed.

"Well, it worked. I'm wide awake now."

"Good. So darling, how was the overtime shift?"

I told Sundari about Spyder Croquet's patient and Croquet's failure to take a good history or put him on the right antibiotic combination.

"I don't get it, Manju," she said, puzzled. "Isn't Spyder Croquet meant to be the best diagnostician in the country?"

"Exactly, Sundari. This sort of case should be bread and butter to him. Yet it required me, a mere intern to show him the correct course of action to take. And this isn't the first time."

I went on to tell Sundari about the other black marks against Spyder Croquet that I had encountered so far this year.

"You don't understand how weird this is, Sundari. Croquet's supposedly a frigging genius."

"Well, maybe you got the right diagnosis because *you* are a better diagnostician than Dr. Croquet," said Sundari, proudly defending her man's medical prowess.

She could be right. And that's what bothers me – because I'm shithouse.

October 28

Lucky met me for lunch at the cafeteria. My strategy to get her to embrace her South Asian heritage seemed to be on track. Since that first time when she came to our house for dinner, we've had her over twice. It is clear that she has become more and more comfortable with us on each successive occasion. She and Lal have become friends. She even went to his house for lunch a couple of weeks ago. Yet, despite this progress, I wasn't prepared for her confession today, a confession that might utterly jeopardize my plans for her reintegration.

"Manju, do you remember about a month ago in ED, I wanted to talk to you about Lal?"

"Sure. But you had to rush off because a trauma arrived or something like that."

"Yes, that's right. Well, your cousin and I have been spending quite a bit of time together. Did you know that?"

"I knew that you went to his place for lunch and that you've met up a couple of times since. He did tell me."

Lucky took a deep breath and continued, "Well, Manju, here's the thing. Despite all my attempts to distance myself from my South Asian culture and South Asians in general, I've gone and done something that I would never have thought possible."

"And that is?" I asked clueless about what was to follow.

"I've fallen in love with Lal. I didn't mean to," she hurriedly clarified, "but it just happened."

"Oh," I said, completely stunned by this admission.

"Anyway, I want to tell him about my feelings soon. I just wanted to know if you had a problem with me seeing your cousin."

What a disaster! But what could I say? "Of course not, Lucky. Why would that be a problem for me?"

She gave me a hug and thanked me before leaving for ED. At that moment the phone rang. It was Sundari.

"How are you, Manju?"

"Terrible," I moaned, as I told her about the conversation that I just had with Lucky.

"So, what's the problem? I've met your cousin and Lucky – they both seem like lovely people. If they want to take their relationship to the next level, isn't that a good thing?"

I shook my head in frustration. "It would be if Lal wasn't gay!" I explained to Sundari my longstanding suspicions about Lal's sexuality. "Imagine what is going to happen when Lucky opens her heart to him and he rejects her. She'll be devastated. Not only that, the whole experience might put her off South Asian men for life. All my good work in bringing her back to the South Asian fold will have been in vain."

"So what are you going to do?"

"I better see Lal this evening and head off this madness before it goes any further."

True to my word, I dropped in to my aunt's place after work. As soon as I got the chance, I took Lal to his bedroom where we could have some privacy.

"What's up, cuz?" he asked.

I told him about Lucky's admission to me earlier today. He looked surprised.

"So what are you going to do about it?" I demanded.

"Not that it is any of your business but when she asks me to become her boyfriend, I'm going to say 'Yes'."

I was stunned. "Why would you do such a cruel thing?"

"Because I love her, you twit. Why else would I do it?"

"But you're gay," I yelled self-righteously.

Lal looked at me in complete surprise before saying, "No, I'm not. What the hell gave you that idea?"

"I know you haven't come out of the closet as yet. But don't deny it. The evidence speaks for itself."

"What evidence?" Lal was starting to get worked up.

"You like Abba and The Village People."

"So do millions of other heterosexuals!" he countered.

"Well, you never wanted to watch X-rated movies with me," I said, accusingly.

"Excuse me if I didn't feel comfortable sitting next to my cousin in front of the TV, sporting a big erection or openly masturbating!" he said, sarcastically.

As the walls of my case appeared to be crumbling around me, I grasped at one last straw. "You always go to the docks when the US navy comes to town. Yet you know nothing about ships. Admit it – you're there to see the sailors."

"Oh my God," said Lal, shaking his head. "And to think that you are supposed to be the brightest person in this family. Listen moron, I go to the docks because I love looking at aircraft carriers. You are right though – I know nothing about the technical aspects of navy ships. But let me ask you this. Don't you like sports cars?"

"Sure," I replied.

"Do you know what a chassis is?"

"Well, no."

"What about a front-wheel drive?"

"Umm, no."

"Come to think of it, cuz, can you even change a tyre?"

"No," I conceded miserably.

"So does that mean *you* are gay?"

"Well, no," I conceded.

"You complete fucking idiot!"

"Point taken, Lal. I'm sorry."

He was still angry. "How many others know about this insane theory of yours?"

"Nobody. You are my cousin, after all. I wouldn't divulge something like that to anyone else – even if it had been true."

He calmed down. "Well, that's something at least."

"But Lal, you and I are so close. I just don't understand why I've never ever seen you show any interest in a girl."

He sighed a deep sigh and sat down at his desk, looking out into the distance. "My mother – *our* mothers – are probably to blame. Ever since we were small, we have had this whole Sri Lankan crap rammed down our throats. And I can't deny that it has affected me – damaged me even. Though I have grown up in this country, I have known in my heart that I could never marry a Westerner. I'm too Sri Lankan to be with anyone other than a Sri Lankan girl. But you know how a baby who is force-fed something day in and day out eventually can't stand the sight of it? The same thing has happened to me. I can't stand the thought of being with a Sri Lankan girl, yet paradoxically I can't marry anyone else."

"I never realized, Lal," I murmured.

He continued, "We both know tons of South Asian guys who sleep around with Western girls. They have no intention whatsoever of taking things seriously – they are just using them for fun until their parents find them a nice Sri Lankan girl to marry. I've also had the opportunity with quite a few Western girls but I could never do that to them. What if they fell in love with me? Imagine how it would hurt them if they learnt that I was only using them for a good time. So for that reason, I'm kind of trapped."

"I'm so sorry to hear that," I said with genuine sadness.

He smiled. "But then Lucky came along. From the moment I met her at your place, I've been captivated. At the start, though, it was the same old problem. She was a Western girl – the cultural divide between us was going to be too great to have a relationship of substance. Despite that, I found that we understood each other perfectly and that she seemed to fit into my life. It was only when she told me that she really is Indian that it all made sense. Manju, for the first time in my life, I can see a future with a woman that I like."

"Do your parents know that she is Indian?"

"Not yet. As you know, she is dead scared about revealing that to anyone."

"But doesn't it bother you that she's too ashamed of her heritage to admit that she is Indian? Do you think that your relationship could overcome such a hurdle, particularly since you are South Asian?" I asked.

Lal seemed confident. "Remember that she is the one who wants to take things to the next level. She hasn't been getting any pressure from me. So at the very least, she is comfortable with going out with me, even if she wants to pretend to be white."

I pressed him again because I wanted him to be sure. "So it doesn't bother you that she pretends to be white, Lal?"

"Not if she loves me for who I am."

"Sorry to keep being the devil's advocate, but what happens when your parents find out? They expect us to marry Sri Lankans, not white girls or even Indians for that matter," I told Lal. "They may not approve."

"They actually are delighted with her – as a friend at any rate. I can probably convince them to accept her as something more. Also, thanks to you, there's a precedent."

"Thanks to me?" I asked, puzzled.

He laughed. "Yes, Manju. We've all heard how you defied your parents and threatened to walk out of the house if they didn't let you date Sundari. My parents naturally think of it as shameful behaviour on your part, but they are dead scared that I'll follow your example. So I think that I've got the upper hand if it ever comes to a confrontation with them."

"Lal, accept my apologies and forget the first part of this conversation. Let me end by saying that Lucky is a lovely girl and I wish you both the best of luck."

He gave me a hug. "That's more like it, cuz."

October 30

It was a torrid day at work. The thought of meeting Sundari for dinner afterwards kept me going. Alternaria was joining us. I would drive as her car was once more incapacitated for one reason or another.

As I finished up my Infectious Diseases work, Alternaria joined me on the ward, ukulele in hand. Despite Bonkzalot's assault on the instrument, Alternaria's brother had been able to return it to a near pristine condition. She continued bringing it to work although she bemoaned the fact that she hadn't had an opportunity to use it in the ED this term.

"Shall we go, Manju?" she asked.

Although I had finished my ward work, I had one more thing to do.

"Alternaria, do you mind if we go up to the Celebrity Ward? I want to see how a patient's cellulitis is progressing."

"Of course not."

When we got to the ward, Alternaria stayed outside the room as I went in. I was thrilled to see that Claudius looked a lot better.

"Ah, Dr. Mendis. So good to see you."

"You look much better than when we last met," I observed with a smile.

"Couldn't have looked any bloody worse. And you were right, by the way."

"About what?"

"The swab from my leg grew that *Aeromonas* bug. It was a good thing that you convinced Dr. Croquet to add that second antibiotic. I told him so this morning."

I visibly cringed. Dr. Croquet's inflated ego wouldn't have taken kindly to being told by a celebrity patient that his intern was more on the ball than him. Claudius recognized my concern. "Yes, he wasn't too thrilled when I said that. Nevertheless, it's the truth."

"So everything's fine now?" I asked.

"From a medical point of view, yes. It's just the usual problems that a man in my position faces."

"I don't follow you," I said.

"Ever since I've been a judge on 'Music Star', people are always trying to impress me with their singing. Take this hospital stay for instance: the cleaner and the woman who brings the meals have already serenaded me. But by far the worst offender has been..."

He was cut off mid-sentence by a booming voice declaring that, "The hills are alive with the sound of music..."

Both Claudius and I jumped as Nurse Watson's head appeared around the doorway. "Is everything all right, gentlemen?"

"It was, till you came along," grumbled Claudius beneath his breath.

As Nurse Watson's head disappeared once more, I expressed my commiserations. "She's not exactly Beyoncé, is she?"

Claudius shuddered. "It's like being ambushed. She'll suddenly sneak up on me and start singing in my face. I've never had so many palpitations in all my life. The only light at the end of the tunnel is that I can go home tomorrow."

I smiled. "Glad to hear it."

Suddenly, Claudius stopped looking at me. I wondered what had so suddenly diverted his attention and then I heard it. Outside the room, Alternaria was singing as she strummed a melody on her ukulele. It only took me a moment to recognize Oasis' blockbuster song Wonderwall. I had heard her sing before, particularly her mini improvisations on the surgical ward, but this was different. It was as if all the heartache and disappointment that she'd had experienced in the last few months was being expressed in her strong unyielding voice. It was one of the most beautiful things that I had ever heard. Without exaggeration, I was not surprised to find I had a tear or two in my eyes.

"Who is that?" he asked excitedly as Alternaria continued singing in the background.

"It's another intern, Alternaria Molde," I replied.

"Call her in. Quick!"

I rushed outside and ushered a confused Alternaria into the room.

Claudius immediately confronted her, "Why were you singing just now?" he asked. "Was it to impress me?"

Alternaria looked even more mystified. "I'm sorry. What do you mean?"

I cut in at this point and spoke to Claudius. "Actually, I didn't tell Alternaria about you, apart from the fact that you had cellulitis. She doesn't know about your job in the music industry. Alternaria is simply someone who loves to sing."

I explained how she always carried her ukulele to work and how she could make up a melody and lyrics on the spot.

"I see," said Claudius, clearly impressed. "I am the CEO of Megamix Records. I'm also a judge on Music Star. Perhaps you have heard of me?"

Alternaria's eyes widened. "Of course, I have."

"When Oasis first released this song, I fell in love with it. Since then, I've heard so many cover bands using it in their repertoire. Not one has come close to inspiring me in the way that Oasis did. If you don't mind, could you please play the whole song for me? Do you know all the lyrics?"

Alternaria laughed. "Like the back of my hand. I lost my virginity to this song – I'll never forget it."

Claudius looked momentarily stunned before bursting out laughing. "You talk like a rock star. Now let's see if you can sing like one." He leaned forward and watched her intently.

I knew that Alternaria *should* have been nervous, but that she wouldn't be. I remember Sundari saying how she'd escape to a beautiful place in her mind while she was with her repulsive clients. For Alternaria, that 'beautiful place' is her music. Within the boundaries of her music, she is secure, sublime and magnificent. Her performance this time wasn't as good as the one in the corridor – it was even better, so much better that Claudius stood to applaud her. Unfortunately, he had forgotten that his left leg hadn't yet healed, forcing him to sit down immediately in agony. We both rushed to his aid. He gestured us away before turning to Alternaria.

"I have been in this industry for thirty-five years. I thought that I had seen it all. But wait till I tell my friends that I saw a girl with a ukulele nail an Oasis song."

Alternaria was genuinely delighted. "Thanks."

"Tell me, Alternaria, do you love medicine?"

"Why do you ask?"

"Because I'd like to offer you a new career – as a singer. You are undoubtedly one of the most talented singers that I have ever seen in the music industry. I don't want anyone else to pinch you so I'm offering you a contract."

"A contract?" Alternaria said, her mouth wide open in astonishment.

"You'll have to give up medicine though. You won't have time, what with all the work on your debut album."

"My debut album?"

"But look, I understand what a big decision this is for you. Here's my card with my number on it. Think about it over the weekend and call me on Monday."

"Monday?" Alternaria repeated seemingly in a zombie-like state. She continued to stare at Claudius open-mouthed.

"You're now meant to say 'Thank you' and leave," he told her, clearly pleased with her stunned response to his offer.

On cue, the befuddled, wide-eyed Alternaria said, "Thank you". I waved goodbye to Claudius and led my fellow intern out of the room. We took the elevator down to the ground floor at which point Alternaria finally snapped out of her trance.

"Oh my God, I've just been offered a recording contract! Manju, it's what I've always dreamed of." She hugged me spontaneously. But then her face became serious. "But how can I give up medicine?"

I took her hands in mine and looked at her. "Alternaria, listen to me. Medicine's a tough master and a rewarding one – but only if you genuinely love it. Otherwise it'll consume you, till you are nothing but a shell of the person that you once were. To be honest, ever since our surgical term together, I've been worried that that's what's been happening to you. The happy, carefree Alternaria from the start of the year isn't there anymore. There have been glimpses, to be sure, but you have really looked miserable for the last few months. There's no doubt that you are a wonderful doctor. But I firmly believe that unless you take a break from medicine, you'll lose your mind. And if you ask me, a generous contract with one of the nation's biggest record labels is a wonderful way out."

Alternaria thought long and hard with a very serious expression before replying. "You're right, Manju. It hasn't been an easy year for me. I've met some wonderful people, especially all of you who have supported me through some pretty tough times. But God, there have been too many tough times. And you're right, Manju – the passion's gone. I need to get out of here otherwise I'll go nuts."

"Then take up his offer," I urged her.

"But the hospital will be one intern short. I can't do that to all of you."

I shook my head. "Don't be daft, Alternaria. St. Ivanhoe is the richest bloody hospital in the country. If Susan Stoker can't temporarily hire a locum doctor to cover your absence for a couple of months, then she doesn't know what she's doing."

"Do you really think so, Manju?" she asked, looking at me for reassurance.

"I don't have a doubt in the world. Take up this recording contract, Alternaria. I bet you'll become as famous as Hans Portello *(Hans Portello was one of the leading celebrities of the early 21st century. He suffered from a growth abnormality and was only four feet tall which made his rise to the top all the more remarkable. He won the first series of Music Star and produced two albums that both went platinum. Apart from his music career, he became an electrician for a blockbuster do-it-yourself show. This prompted the headline 'Mini Hans Makes Lights Work'. He had an untimely death in 2025 during filming of the reality show Celebrity Home Invasion where contestants had to walk through their opponent's house in the dark without getting injured. Unfortunately, after walking into a battle-axe being held by a suit of armour, Hans slipped on a skateboard sending him flying down the stairs before rolling into a TV and ramming his head through the screen.*

The judges unanimously deemed that Hans, had he lived, would have been eliminated from the show – Editors).

"Then I'll accept his offer." It was as if a vast burden had been lifted from her shoulders. Her eyes, her whole body seemed to glow with an all-pervading joy. I knew then that she had made the right decision. The three of us had a wonderful dinner that, in the end, became a celebration of Alternaria's success.

November 5

Yesterday, Alternaria accepted Claudius Idelic's offer of a contract, and handed Susan Stoker her letter of resignation. Since Alternaria is such a considerate person, she had informed Susan Stoker a few days ago of her likely career change. To her credit, Susan didn't storm off angrily or complain about being left short-staffed. Instead, she gave Alternaria a hug and wished her well. I have spoken to a few of my friends working at other hospitals. Their Medical Administration staff aren't nearly as understanding as Susan Stoker – we are very fortunate to have her.

Last night, we had dinner to celebrate Alternaria's success. I'm always in two minds about having parties when someone leaves. It gives the impression that you are happy they are going. There was no ambiguity about last night's occasion. We knew that we would all miss Alternaria but in our hearts realized that this was the right path for her.

I thought nothing could top the excitement of the last few days with Alternaria's dramatic career change. I was wrong. Excitement came in the unlikely form of Dr. Gilbert Probie. Yesterday, he was admitted with a serious bloodstream infection. The admission itself was somewhat of a surprise because Dr. Probie was dying of cancer. He smoked heavily throughout his life, and despite being only forty-five, was riddled with lung malignancy. Further treatment was not an option and his oncologist gave him two months at the most to live. Given that he was in considerable pain and required oxygen via nasal prongs to breathe, we thought it kinder to let him die from his bloodstream infection. However, his daughter is graduating from university in two weeks and he wants everything done to keep him alive till then. So we admitted him and started IV antibiotics.

Having terminal cancer, I imagine he never looks good. Yesterday, he looked absolutely ghastly and I feared the worst. Yet, thanks to being rehydrated and receiving IV antibiotics, today he seems to be over the worst of the infection. I saw him on our morning ward round with Professor Gorgas, and reviewed him in the afternoon because of concerns over his IV cannula. As I entered the room, he greeted me with a paroxysm of coughing and wheezing.

As I fiddled around with his cannula, he watched TV. Suddenly he murmured, "You greasy little bastard."

Alarmed that he was angry with me, I turned to ask what was wrong. I noticed that his attention was not on me but the TV screen. I followed his gaze and saw Dr. Spyder Croquet being interviewed on a lifestyle program. Dr. Probie shook his head, and to my utter surprise, spat at the TV screen, the large glob of green mucus falling well short of its intended target.

"If I were a younger man, I wouldn't have missed," he ruminated looking at the mucus on the floor.

"So you're not a fan of the famous Spyder Croquet?" I asked.

"You wouldn't understand," he said, "Everyone believes all that propaganda about what an amazing doctor he is." He pointed his index finger at himself. "But I know better."

"I'd love to hear more," I said.

He smiled grimly. "A few years ago, I wouldn't have dared tell this story. But it doesn't matter now – now that I've got cancer." He looked at me directly. "Do you know how Spyder Croquet became famous?"

"Who doesn't?" I replied. I repeated the story that we all knew so well. "A Hollywood film executive was lying desperately ill in hospital with a mystery illness that none of the specialists could solve. Then Spyder Croquet saw her for the first time on an overtime shift and made a spot diagnosis of lead poisoning. It was a stroke of pure genius."

Dr. Probie laughed cynically. "What if I told you that it's all bullshit, that he never discovered anything?"

"But how could you know that?" I asked.

"Do you know that I'm a doctor?"

"I do. Are you still practising?"

"No. I gave it up a long time ago. But I know this hospital very well. Back in those days, unlike today, St. Ivanhoe Hospital had its own medical students. Part of the training involved students accompanying interns on their overtime shifts. It gave an opportunity to see acutely sick patients and do some minor procedures."

I put two and two together. "*You* were the medical student with Spyder Croquet on that evening shift, weren't you?"

He nodded. "Croquet had been asked to replace the patient's IV cannula. He missed on his first attempt and left the room to answer a page. I took the opportunity to talk to the patient and examine her. When I looked into her mouth, I saw the Burton's lines and knew that she had lead poisoning."

I was completely stunned. "*You* discovered she had lead poisoning? But I thought that it was Spyder Croquet?"

"That's a lie!" he angrily shouted, before suffering another awful spasm of coughing. His expression darkened visibly. "I was so excited with my diagnosis that I rushed out to tell Croquet. I didn't say anything to the patient at the time. How I wish I had done so – things might have turned out differently. Anyway, I found Croquet and told him everything. He congratulated me and said that such good detective work deserved an early mark. So he sent me home immediately. I thought that I was being rewarded, but in fact, he was simply getting rid of me so he could take all the glory. And that's what he did. The tight-arsed prick waltzed into that room, made some excuse or another to look into her mouth and told her that she had lead poisoning. Croquet then informed the specialist who confirmed the diagnosis a few days later. The rest, as you say, is history."

He saw me shaking my head in shock but mistook it for disbelief of his story.

"Don't worry. I don't blame you. Why would you believe this pathetic dying fool over the high and mighty Dr. Croquet?"

I quickly corrected him. "No, Dr. Probie. I believe you. I was shaking my head because I couldn't believe that Spyder Croquet could stoop so low."

"You believe *me* over *him*?" He seemed surprised.

I told him how I had watched Spyder Croquet make some ridiculous diagnoses throughout the year and even go so far as stealing the credit for Smegman and Delilah's brilliant diagnosis in the case of Greg Smythe.

"That sounds all too familiar," he said grimly.

I continued. "In fact, all of his misdiagnoses and other mistakes only make sense if you think of him as an inept fraud. So have you told anyone else about this?"

"No," he replied sadly. "That's my greatest regret. As soon as he took the credit, I should have said something. But I kept quiet. He threatened me, you know. Said he'd destroy my career if I made a fuss."

"He likes to do that," I said, remembering how he had done the same to Smegman and Delilah.

"Back then, it was an empty threat though. He was only an intern and didn't have the power to destroy anyone's career. But I was still a naïve medical student. How was I to know? So I kept my mouth shut. When I realized my folly a few years later, it was too late. By that time, Croquet had become too powerful to cross. About ten years ago, I approached him and asked him to set the story straight. He said that if I ever made mention of what really happened, he would sue me for libel."

"But you were telling the truth!"

"So what? He had the fancy lawyers, the influential friends and the amazing reputation. I am certain that I would have been crushed if I had taken him on. So for the sake of my young family, I kept my mouth shut."

"But why are you telling me the truth now?" I asked.

He smiled again. "In a few weeks, I'll be dead. Even the powerful Spyder Croquet and his team of high-powered lawyers won't be able to touch me. So I don't really give a damn about keeping quiet anymore."

We both sat in silence for a few moments as I contemplated this terrible and disheartening revelation.

Dr. Probie spoke up again. "Ever since that day, my life has been an unhappy one – apart from my wonderful daughter, that is. I know that I can't blame Croquet for the mess I've made of things. He didn't make me drink, smoke, or be a bad husband and father. But I firmly believe that if that Hollywood executive had taken me under her wing back then instead of Croquet, my life would have been different. He denied me the chance of ever finding out."

Overwhelmed by grief for this poor man, I impulsively gripped his hands and said, "I can't change your life, Dr. Probie, but I'm going to make Spyder Croquet pay for what he did to you and my friends."

Tears came to his eyes. "Thanks for the support but I gave up on miracles a long time ago."

November 6

I arranged to meet Smegman and Delilah in the cafeteria. Given the horrific experience they had suffered at the hands of Spyder Croquet over the mystery illness of Greg Smythe, I felt they deserved to be the first to hear about Dr. Probie's revelations. They were both incredulous and appalled.

"I'm still furious and hurt by what he did," said Delilah. "But I've pretty much moved on. However, it sounds like Dr. Probie's life fell apart when Spyder betrayed him. What a sad story."

"Doesn't Croquet have a conscience?" asked Smegman angrily. "Doesn't he believe that a God or kamma or something is going to punish him for what he's done?"

"Apparently not," I replied. "He does believe in a higher power but their names are 'Fame' and 'Fortune'. He'll do whatever it takes to hang on to them."

We sat silently wondering if the 'Doctor to the Stars' would ever get his comeuppance.

"Manju, talking about Fortune," said Delilah after a while, "I must remember to tell you that your favourite bank executive is back on the Celebrity Ward with an acute flare of gout."

"You mean Milton Honeypot?" I asked.

"Yep. I was on overtime yesterday and had to admit him. He claims to have been compliant with his gout medications, yet it still flared up. It is one of the worst cases I have ever seen. His big toe is swollen like a small fist and really red. All this creamy gouty tophi is just pouring out. It's disgusting."

"Was he rude to you?" I asked, remembering my first encounter with him.

"I got the impression that he would have been if he hadn't been in so much pain. But he was in such agony that he barely said a word to me."

Later that evening, I went over to Sundari's house. Her little sister, Reshmi, had started playing in an indoor cricket competition. She wanted to practise with someone but Sundari had never played. So I volunteered to take them both to the local indoor nets. We had a lot of fun. Reshmi is a delightful child, so much so that I regret never having had a younger sister. Sundari later told me that the feeling is mutual.

"Reshmi adores you, Manju. Ever since Thaththa died, she has really missed having a man around the house. So your arrival in our lives has been like a breath of fresh air."

"I love her too, Sundari. She's a wonderful girl."

November 7

I had just started my overtime shift this evening when my mobile phone rang. My heart stopped – it was Sundari and she sounded hysterical. It took me a minute to calm her down.

"What's wrong, honey?" I asked slowly.

"My mobile phone went off a few minutes ago. It was that banker that you saw me with in hospital."

A chill went through me. "Milton Honeypot? How did he get your mobile number? What did he want?"

"He said that he's been missing his 'Friday night shag'. He wanted me to come next week to see him for a one-hour session. I asked him how he got my number but he evaded the question."

"I hope you told him that you had finished with all that?" I asked her, becoming quite agitated.

"Of course, Manju! I said that I'd left all that behind me and had moved on with my life." Her voice broke at this point. "He then said he knew where I lived and that he would make sure that my mother and sister knew I had been working as a 'high-class whore'. Manju, he knows I have a mother and a sister. He must have had me followed." She started to fall apart. "Manju, I can't go back to that life! I just can't!

But if he tells Ammi about this, it'll kill her. I'm so scared."

She started crying. In between her wails, I could hear her hyperventilating, and her teeth chattering with fear, as if in the throes of a panic attack. My heart broke.

"Don't worry darling. I'll never let you return to that life. Just let me sort it out. I'll call you back soon. For God's sake, don't panic. I'll make everything better again." As soon as I put the phone down, I was overwhelmed by nausea. I ran to the toilet and vomited. Despite my assertion that I'd 'sort it out', in truth I had no idea what I was going to do. The only advantage I had, if it was one at all, was that I knew Milton Honeypot's location – in the Celebrity Ward with his gouty toe. Furthermore, I had a legitimate reason to see him because Nurse Watson had paged me fifteen minutes earlier to review his pain relief. I caught the elevator to the tenth floor and made my way to his room. I looked down the corridor to the Nurses' Station where I saw Nurse Watson making an entry in the notes, too busy to notice me. I took a deep breath and entered the room.

Milton Honeypot was alone. He lay in bed grimacing in pain. Delilah was right. His big toe looked absolutely horrible, far worse than during his previous episode. He recognized me immediately. "Ah, it's 'Doctor $50,000 before tax'. Have they given you a raise yet?"

I stared at him silently. He grunted in disappointment at my failure to take the bait.

"Well, are you here to give me pain relief?"

"Yes," I said. "But first, I want to talk to you about Sundari."

"Who the hell is that?" he snapped angrily.

"It's the ex-prostitute that you've been blackmailing."

"How do you know about that?" he asked suspiciously.

"She's my fiancée."

He looked at me for a moment with a blank expression before bursting out laughing. "Oh, that's just too perfect! My private investigator said that she was seeing a young doctor but I never imagined that it would be you!"

"Why are you doing this?" I asked.

"It's not rocket science. She is the best whore that I've ever paid for. Frankly, I didn't want that to stop. That's why I hired a very effective investigator to track her down."

"Well, *she* wants it to stop. *We* want it to stop," I declared defiantly.

"Do you think that I give a damn about what you want? Here's a bit of free advice, *Doctor*. You mocked me when I dared suggest that money was everything. You whined about your precious medical school and your ability to cure people. Well, here's the thing, sunshine: my money bought me information, and that information gives me the power over you and your fiancée. If she doesn't screw me next Friday, her darling mother and sister will learn everything. I wonder how they'll take the news? Gee, what a shame," he said in mocking tones.

He then looked at me with interest. "In fact, does *your* family know about your lovely fiancée's chequered past?"

I maintained a stony silence, which he correctly interpreted.

"Oh dear, I'm sure your parents would kick up a real fuss if they knew that their prospective daughter-in-law spread her legs for cash. That sort of revelation wouldn't go down well in the old Indian community."

"We're Sri Lankan, not Indian," I corrected him coldly.

"Like I really give a damn," he contemptuously replied.

"You son of a bitch!" I shouted at him.

He became enraged. "Don't you swear at me, you pathetic little moron! I hold the future of your relationship in my hands. Do you hear me? In *my* bloody hands! If you piss me off again, your slut fiancée's secret is out for the whole world to see! So you better show me the respect that I deserve or else…."

I was running out of ideas, running out of hope. "Can I offer you money?" I asked out of desperation.

He laughed so much that he kicked out his leg, lightly hitting his gouty toe against the bedpost. Such was the severity of his gout that even though he had only brushed his toe, he still yelled in agony bringing tears to his eyes. But within a few moments he recovered sufficiently to continue mocking me "Let me get this straight? 'Doctor $50,000 before tax' is offering *me* cash? I earn fifteen million dollars a year. I don't need your pocket money. Is that all you've got to negotiate with? If so, give me my pain relief and piss off."

I became desperate. "But I want to marry her."

"I really don't care what you do with her as long as she turns up for her Friday night appointment with me every week."

Despite my outrage and dismay, I was genuinely surprised at this response. "You mean you don't care if we get married and have a family?"

His face took on a sneer. It was an expression of ridicule, of hatred and of contempt. "Oh, I'm sorry. You can get married but I won't allow you to have kids."

"Why not?"

"I wouldn't want childbirth ruining that tight pussy of hers."

He began to laugh – a horrible sound born out of arrogance and fuelled by contempt. The combination of the diabolical laugh, the heartlessness that he exuded and his reddish complexion gave the impression of Lucifer himself. Yet even as terror and despair began to envelop me, they were shoved aside as a juggernaut of pure rage consumed my very soul. All that negativity and the enormous energy it generated were directed at one spot. Before I even knew what I was doing, I took both my hands, wrapped them around Honeypot's gouty toe and squeezed with all my might, as if my very life depended on it. The pain must have been incredible. A blood-curdling scream rent the air. He instinctively sat halfway up reaching out his arms towards me. But like a lion with his teeth locked onto the neck of its prey, I refused to let go and squeezed even harder. I felt copious amounts of warm liquid gouty tophi pass between my fingers. Honeypot started moaning and grunting like an animal being slaughtered in an abattoir. Then the banker with a beetroot-red complexion became even redder before gasping for breath, making a horrible gurgling sound, grabbing his chest and losing consciousness. Breathing heavily, I let go of his toe and checked for a carotid pulse and signs of breathing. There were none. Oh no, not again? Not another bloody heart attack! I quickly opened the door and looked down the corridor. I could see Nurse Watson in the distance still writing in the notes. She clearly hadn't heard any of the commotion. I always suspected that having the Nurses' Station so far away from the patient's bed was a bad idea. Tonight, I proved my theory correct. I felt a salty taste in my mouth. It was blood. It took me a moment to realize that I had been squeezing his toe so hard that I'd bitten my lower lip.

It was so tempting to just sit quietly in his room for the next few minutes until he was dead. Only then would I call for a Medical

Emergency and say that I had done my best to revive him. No one would know any better. Sundari and I could live in peace, the threat of blackmail lifted from us forever. Even as this plan formulated, the images of Monty Bonkzalot and Spyder Croquet appeared in my mind. If I let Honeypot die, in spite of how evil he truly was, I would be no better than them. Their very souls are devoid of all compassion and they are consumed by greed for power and money. Was I willing to travel down that path too? This sobering thought blanketed the fires of rage within me. With a deep sigh, I realized that I am a doctor armed with a degree to cure. I had little choice but to run back into the room and push the red button behind the bed. Within seconds, Nurse Watson burst into the room.

"Get an arrest trolley quickly! I think he's having a massive myocardial infarction."

In alarm, she rushed off to get the trolley. The Cardiac Arrest team burst onto the scene and took over. After about ten minutes of CPR and three electric shocks for ventricular tachycardia, they finally got his heart to beat spontaneously. A twelve-lead ECG confirmed a massive anterolateral myocardial infarction and he was rushed off to the Cardiac Catheter Laboratory. I later learnt that he died on the table just after his angiogram had identified a severe blockage of his left main coronary artery.

As in the case of Tabitha Freiman, I once more lied to the Team Leader of the Cardiac Arrest team. I told him that I was simply discussing analgesia with Mr. Honeypot when he suddenly had a cardiac arrest. Later that night, I would tell the same story to Sundari. I trusted her with the truth but she didn't need to hear the hurtful things that Honeypot said about her.

As I write this entry in the solitude of my room, I am glad that Milton Honeypot is dead. He was an evil man and I will not mourn his passing. I have no doubt that his bank will have little trouble in finding some unscrupulous, greedy bastard to fill the vacancy that he left behind. But I am most glad that I didn't let him die, that I at least tried to save him. The compassion for life, irrespective of how worthless or cruel that life is, is one of the fundamental tenets that makes medicine a noble profession *(It is interesting to note that Dr. Mendis seems to have forgotten that he precipitated the heart attack by assaulting the patient and that he lied when questioned about what had happened – Editors).*

November 10

On Sundari's request, I went through my banking today. She still feels terrible about having me pay her family's debts and wants to know if it will be feasible in the long-term. My assessment of things is fairly gloomy. Even though I live at home, Sundari's family expenses are draining my bank account at quite a rate. Even with a rise in salary level next year, this means that soon I will have little or no savings left to secure a future for the two of us. Things have just got a little harder as the Reserve Bank put interest rates up. But, I called Sundari and told her that everything is fine. If I tell her the truth, she will go all noble on me and stop me from giving her any more money. I can't allow that. At the back of my mind, I am still terrified that she'll return to prostitution if the financial situation becomes unmanageable.

I had an unexpected outside call today.

"Hello," I said, as the hospital switchboard put the call through.

"Hello, Dr. Mendis. It's Agatha Highcue here."

"Oh, Ms. Highcue. How lovely to hear your voice! It must be at least two months since Mr. Freiman left hospital. How are you doing?"

She laughed. "Very well, thank you. And please, call me Agatha. How are you doing, Dr. Mendis? Is Medicine treating you well?"

"I'm surviving, Agatha. It's not too bad at all."

"I won't take up too much of your time. I just wanted to get your home address to send you an invitation."

"Sure." I gave her my address. "May I ask what the occasion is?"

"Pik and I are getting married next month."

I was speechless. Within seconds, I congratulated her warmly. "That's wonderful! See, Agatha, I told you he fancied you."

She laughed again. "You were right. We're only having a small ceremony. Pik and I are too old for these massive extravaganzas that some of our friends have. But we desperately want you to come. After all, none of this would have been possible without your help."

I was humbled by her words. "You are far too kind, Agatha. But yes, of course, I would love to come."

"I hope you don't think this impertinent of me, Dr. Mendis, but do you have someone special in your life?"

Without a moment's hesitation, I replied. "Yes. Her name is Sundari and hopefully she'll be my wife sometime soon. She is an amazing woman."

"Oh, I'm so glad to hear that. A man as lovely as you deserves such a woman. Both Pik and I insist you bring her along. We would love to meet her. Anyway, I've taken enough of your valuable time. You should receive the invitation in the mail in the next day or two. Please let me know if it doesn't arrive."

"Thank you, Agatha. Bye and once again, congratulations."

I didn't have time to contemplate the wonderful news of Pik and Agatha's upcoming union because my pager went off. The page was about Dr. Probie. His condition had suddenly deteriorated. I rushed up to the ward. Dr. Probie was in respiratory distress, breathing at a rate of about sixty breaths per minute. Despite being on high-flow oxygen, his oxygen saturations were low. He was listless with a reduced level of consciousness. The Intensive Care registrar was here. She turned to me.

"This guy needs Intensive Care. But he's got terminal cancer. I don't think that he is an appropriate candidate for us. Why don't you just make him comfortable on the ward and let him go peacefully?"

I quickly explained how Dr. Probie wanted full resuscitation measures instituted until his daughter's graduation in a couple of weeks.

The registrar shook her head in frustration. "Okay then, we'll take him. But Manju, judging by how sick he looks now, I'll be surprised if he isn't dead within the hour."

As the Intensive Care team prepared to intubate him, I wandered away, thinking how unfair life is sometimes. All Dr. Probie wanted in the end was to see his daughter graduate, but even that was being denied to him. Despite it not being his fault, I couldn't help but blame Spyder Croquet.

November 12

I got into the elevator at the same time as the detestable Spyder Croquet. This is the time he normally comes in to see his patients on Wednesday, presumably after minting money in his Broadley Bay rooms. Typical of his arrogance, he didn't even acknowledge my presence despite having met me a handful of times. As the elevator started to rise, I pushed the 'Stop' button, bringing it to a sudden halt.

He finally acknowledged me. "What the hell do you think you are doing?"

"I want to talk to you, Dr. Croquet. Yesterday, one of my patients died from disseminated lung cancer. I'm sure that you'll recognize the name – Dr. Gilbert Probie."

"Never heard of him," snapped Croquet irritably. "Now start this elevator! I haven't got all day to yak with you."

I ignored him and continued on. "Dr. Probie told me everything, you see. I know that he diagnosed lead poisoning in that Hollywood executive so many years ago. You stole the credit for *his* brilliant diagnosis. Now, twenty years later, you are still taking the credit for other people's brilliance."

"What the hell are you talking about?" he yelled furiously.

"Delilah Convex and Marcus Smegman are the two interns who worked out the cause of Greg Smythe's illness. They are also my friends. I know how you lied about making the diagnosis yourself and threatened them if they ever said anything."

"I don't know what you are talking about," he stubbornly denied.

"You can lie all you want, you crook. Your whole career is built on nothing more than a lie. And trust me, it shows. I have been reviewing your patients on the Celebrity Ward throughout the year. Even I, a mere intern, could have done a better job looking after them than you. You are pathetic!"

This time Dr. Croquet responded, exploding with rage. "Who the hell do you think you are, little man, to talk to me like that? Sure, I took the credit for Gilbert Probie's diagnosis all those years ago. But I don't regret it. Look at the man. He was an alcoholic and a chain smoker who couldn't even keep his marriage together. Imagine if he had been given the opportunities that that Hollywood executive gave me? He would have wasted them entirely! The greatest success stories in life aren't about the cleverest or the most hard-working people. No, it's those people who see an opportunity and seize it with both hands. That's all I've done. And look at me now. I am like a god in the world of Medicine. Everyone knows my name. As for your intern friends, nobody is interested in seeing them make a brilliant diagnosis. They want to see *me*, the extraordinary Spyder Croquet, strut my stuff on the world stage. So sure, Convex and Smegman diagnosed TRAPS in Greg Smythe – but who gives a fuck? Don't interfere in matters that are far beyond your pathetic little mind!"

He pushed me roughly aside and pressed the button to restart the elevator. Within seconds, we reached the tenth floor. Croquet got out and turned back to me. "Oh, by the way, if you think that this is the end of this matter, then you are sadly mistaken. Nobody accosts Spyder Croquet in an elevator and abuses him, especially some little shit of an intern. You will be hearing from my lawyers and the Hospital Board."

He walked away, leaving me alone in the elevator, thoughtful and silent. I pushed a button and the elevator descended to the third floor. I got out and walked into the Intensive Care Unit and entered Room Six. A man lay there, breathing heavily while another man and a woman sat next to him. I walked up to the man who was attached to a number of tubes and machines. Despite this, he was wide-awake and alert.

"Dr. Probie, I am so glad to see that you are better. I honestly thought that you were going to die two days ago," I said with genuine sincerity.

He coughed and wheezed before speaking. "Me too." He looked at me closely. "Did you get the bastard?"

I turned to the woman sitting next to him. "Did we, Fabulus?"

Fabulus Hipz looked at the man sitting next to her who was wearing headphones and playing about with a complex piece of electronic equipment. "How did we go, Myles?" she asked him. He turned to Fabulus and gave her the thumbs up with a smile.

"It appears that you were successful, Manju," she said, smiling. "You can take off the wire now."

"Thank goodness. I didn't realize how itchy it would be," I said, as

I removed the complex wiring that lay hidden beneath the layers of clothing I was wearing.

"So when are you going to run with the story?" I asked out of interest.

"Tonight or tomorrow at the latest. This is even bigger than the Bonkzalot story." Fabulus gave me a hug. "If that story doesn't win me the Investigative Journalism award, then this almost certainly will."

"Don't get me wrong, Fabulus. I hope that you win your award. But all I want is to see Spyder Croquet exposed."

"Don't worry, Manju. Croquet has lived by the media. Now he will die by the media."

Dr. Probie shook my hand vigorously, weeping openly. "Thank you, Dr. Mendis, for believing me. What with this and my daughter's graduation, I can die a happy man. You have no idea what this means to me."

There are many ways to satisfy the sick – I have learnt that Medicine is only one of them. *(True to her word, Fabulus broadcast the story the following night. The response was sensational. Millions of viewers saw the unmasking of a fraudulent, ruthless and nasty Spyder Croquet. The fact that Gilbert Probie was a dying man, despite it not being directly due to Croquet's efforts, simply added fuel to the fire. The image of the omniscient and glamorous 'Doctor to the Stars' was forever shattered. The St. Ivanhoe Board removed his clinical privileges that same week. Although Croquet hadn't broken the law, the Medical Council was able to deregister him on purely ethical grounds. He ended up moving to California where he started a health spa. In 2011, he died after trying to perform colonic irrigation on himself, perforating his colon in the process. When found by his receptionist, he was still smiling. Only a handful of people attended his funeral. On a side note, it is surprising that the hospital didn't censure Dr. Mendis for working together with the media in this story. It is almost certain that his identity would have been discovered. But it was well known that Sir Ninian loved the hospital and its junior doctors more than anything else; perhaps, in this matter, he chose to turn a blind eye to Dr. Mendis' covert actions. For the record, Fabulus Hipz did win the 2009 National Media Club's Award for Investigative Journalism for uncovering Spyder Croquet's fraudulent activities. The title of the piece was A Spyder's Web of Deceit – Editors)*

November 22

At 7:30 this morning, I was rudely awakened by a phone call from my sister. I had been really looking forward to having an old-fashioned Saturday sleep-in so was quite grumpy when I answered the phone. Naturally, Akki didn't care.

"Stop whingeing, you little shit. I need you to get to the entrance of the Botanical Gardens at 9am sharp."

"What for?"

"Wear your full suit – I'll tell you when you get there."

"My full suit? What's going on?"

"Do you trust me?" my sister asked.

"Well, not really," I replied.

Akki clearly had had enough. "Just fucking do it! And don't tell Ammi or Thaththi that you're meeting me."

And so it was that I sneaked out of the house in my full suit on a Saturday morning, arriving at the Botanical Gardens at nine o'clock as requested. I was mystified to find my sister fully made-up and dressed in what appeared to be her wedding sari. Around her were about twenty others whom I didn't recognize, who were all dressed formally. There was also a cameraman. I took my sister to one side.

"What on earth's going on?" I asked.

"Do you remember how that secretary at Errol Flynn Grammar said we'd have to provide evidence that you are Kumar's father?"

"How can I forget?"

"Well, now's the time to submit the evidence."

"So what's all this about?" I asked again.

"It's our wedding day."

"What?" I shouted in disbelief.

"Well, Manju, they requested photographic evidence of our marriage. So I arranged this fake wedding. It's one of the advantages of working in an advertising agency."

"So who are all these people?" I asked, gesturing to the group around us.

"They are our wedding guests."

"I gathered that," I said impatiently. "But I mean where did you find them? Are they friends of yours?"

"Of course not. These are actors our agency occasionally uses for ads. I just called them up and told them that there'd be a photo shoot this morning where they'd have to play the part of wedding guests."

"I hope that the South Asian actors don't recognize us," I said, imagining what a scandal it would be.

"No chance. I made sure that they were Indian, Bengali or Pakistani – no Sri Lankans."

I just realized something. "How much is this going to cost, Akki? These actors aren't doing this out of charity. I hope that you aren't going to put it on your company's account – you'll get fired if you do."

"Don't be silly. Ravi and I will pay for it ourselves. Each actor will get $100 for their half-hour of work. The cameraman gets $500."

"Two and a half thousand dollars!" I exclaimed.

"That's nothing, Manju. If Kumar hadn't been the 'son of an old boy' and had to go through the interview process to get into the school, then there would have been a three thousand dollar admission fee. So we're actually five hundred dollars up on the deal."

"You've thought of everything," I mumbled. "So what do we have to do?"

"We just have to walk around holding hands and pretending to greet all our 'guests' while the cameraman snaps a few photos. That's it really."

"Does Ravi know about this?"

"It was his idea. I wanted him to be your Best Man but he has to stay at home looking after Kumar."

"Even if the photos are convincing, didn't the school want a copy of a marriage and birth certificate as well?"

"That's all sorted."

"How?" I asked, puzzled.

"Ravi used his IT skills to forge a Sri Lankan marriage and birth certificate, predominantly written in Sinhalese. After all, you and I got married in Sri Lanka – don't you remember?" she asked sweetly.

"But even though it's not in English, they might recognize that it's a forgery," I argued anxiously.

"For fuck's sake, Manju, it's not being examined by the Department of Immigration. It's only being sent to a private school. As if anyone there would know the difference."

I sighed. "Okay then. But what do they," I said, gesturing to the actors, "think this ad is about?"

"Well, when you think of an ad with lots of happy women for no apparent reason, what comes to mind?"

"Tampons?" I guessed.

"Exactly!"

At this point, my mobile phone rang. It was Sundari.

"Hi darling," she said. "What are you up to?"

"Would you believe that I'm just about to marry my sister?" I replied.

There was a long pause before she responded. "And I thought that *my* personal life was screwed up!"

"Tell me about it," I replied glumly.

"But you're not serious, Manju?"

"It's actually a fake wedding. My nephew's school needs evidence of the marriage before he can be accepted there."

"Let me get this straight – the school will only accept your nephew if they have evidence that his mother is married to her brother?"

"That's about right. But don't worry. It's a top school. In fact, I went there."

"Why doesn't that reassure me?" She burst into laughter, a musical sound that sent shivers down my spine. "You'll have to tell me the whole sordid story later. Shall we meet at my place at six? I've made a restaurant booking for eight but I wouldn't mind some 'private' time in my bedroom first. Nothing like a bit of exercise before dinner to whet one's appetite."

"Sounds great!" I replied enthusiastically. "I'll see you later."

As for the fake wedding, in the end the whole occasion went smoothly. Akki and I walked amongst the 'guests', like a new bride and groom, shaking hands and giving kisses while the cameraman clicked away furiously. It all looked so professional that one of the female actors later asked where she could buy the sensational new tampons that were being promoted – I let Akki handle that one. The session ended with formal photos of the 'bridal party'. As I stood next to Akki, I couldn't help but notice the stunning blonde standing next to her.

"Akki, I know it's our wedding day, but would you mind if I shagged your bridesmaid?"

This was answered with a thundering slap to my ear.

"Ouch," I cried, grabbing my smarting ear. "It's like being married to my bloody sister. Oh that's right – you are my sister," I whispered to her.

"That's not the worst part," she said. "Remember who your mother-in-law is going to be."

I shuddered, and not for the first time in my life, felt sorry for my brother-in-law, Ravi.

December 6

Sundari and I went to Pik Freiman and Agatha Highcue's wedding. Sundari was naturally excited at being invited to the wedding of the country's second wealthiest man.

"You must have made a heck of an impression on them while he was in hospital to score an invite for the wedding," said Sundari.

I had a brief flashback of Tabitha Freiman lying in a pool of blood while Agatha Highcue pointed a gun at me. "We bonded," I replied, not trusting myself to say anymore.

Our financial situation has deteriorated further in recent times. Sundari's sister's school, demanded upfront payment of *all* fees for next year's schooling. Apparently, the School Board decided to no longer offer payment on a term-by-term basis. Have you ever heard of such a thing? Anyway, I ended up sending them a cheque for $20,000 last week, further draining my savings. This was a double blow. Apart from the impact on our finances, it meant that I wasn't able to surprise Sundari with a beautiful gown for the wedding. Such things aren't important to her and she was quite prepared to pull out an old formal dress from her closet. Nevertheless, it was something I would have loved to do. Mind you, when a woman is as beautiful as Sundari, she will look good even in a beanie and tracksuit. Completely out of the blue, Ammi saved the day by presenting Sundari with a lovely blue gown from Monsoon. I recall her words to Sundari when she presented it to her: "This is a high society wedding. So here's a high society dress for my younger daughter. Anyway, you are so lovely that you don't need anything fancy to look a cut above the rest. But I think that this might give you the edge." Then she gave Sundari a big hug.

More than the expense involved, Ammi's words and the gesture itself finally represented my family's acceptance of Sundari. Given the prejudices which had been instilled in her from birth, I couldn't help but admire Ammi for being able to change her attitudes so late in life. I was even surprised that she hadn't been critical of the fact that today's wedding represented a master marrying his servant. In fact, Ammi had gone so far as to call it a fairytale romance. Mind you, Ammi's use of the term 'daughter' when talking to Sundari implied that my proposing marriage to her in the near future was a foregone conclusion. Well, she is correct, but she shouldn't have assumed it!

My description of the wedding can't do it justice. I don't think Sundari keeps a diary, but her entry would certainly have been more useful for this purpose than mine. But I'll try my best. Being a fairytale wedding, the weather was, of course, perfect. The location was a restricted area of the Botanical Gardens. This puzzled me as I never realized that anything other than rainforest was found within that zone. However, I was very much mistaken. On showing our invitations to security guards, who incidentally had photos of us on their guest list, we were led down a beautifully paved path surrounded by lush rainforest. We emerged in paradise. There stood the most amazing domed structure I have ever seen. It was made predominantly of crystal, supported by gleaming rods of silver. Each piece of crystal somehow seemed to refract and reflect the light, resulting in the amazing effect of a rainbow aura surrounding the building. Sundari and I were speechless. While I am no connoisseur of art or architecture, I couldn't believe that I hadn't heard of this building. It should have been in every tourist guide selling this country to the rest of the world. I later learnt that it had been built about ten years ago as part of a failed Olympic bid *(Government records show that the Crystal Oracle was secretly built as part of the 2004 Olympic bid, which Athens ultimately won. It was meant to be the site at which the Olympic flame would first be brought when it entered the country. However, the nation never ended up bidding for the Olympics because an official forgot to push 'Enter' when submitting the bid online. In order to forget this shameful event, the Prime Minister of the day declared that the bid would never be mentioned in his presence again. For that reason, the bid and all that went with it, including the Crystal Oracle, were forgotten for some time. But, someone with the power and influence of Pik Freiman would not only have known about the Crystal Oracle but have been able to access it for his wedding. With regard to the official who forgot to push 'Enter', apparently he was severely punished by being made Ambassador... to Afghanistan – Editors).*

The building itself stood on the edge of a lake filled with sparkling blue water. The path we used had somehow circumvented the lake and we ended up approaching the crystal building from behind. The lake was filled with white and pink lotus flowers and at the end opposite to the crystal building was a small boat and pier. It was on this boat that Agatha Highcue, clad in white, sailed across the lake to the crystal building, where Pik Freiman and all of us stood waiting for her. It all had a King Arthur and Camelot atmosphere to it. Even Pik Freiman took on the role of a Knight of the Round Table as he bent on one knee to receive Agatha's hand when she stepped off the boat. At this point, the only hiccough in an otherwise flawless ceremony occurred. Eighty-year-old Pik's back gave out on him while he lay kneeling. Agatha and his personal attendant audibly cracked it back into place before the ceremony could resume. The real highlight occurred inside the domed building. In the program, the exchange of vows was written as occurring at 11:37. I was puzzled by this exercise in pedantry. Wasn't 11:35 or 11:30 adequate? The wedding celebrant began the ceremony at 11:37 on the dot and, as soon as he did, the reason became apparent. I don't know how to explain it but at 11:37 the sunlight hit some areas of crystal on the upper part of the dome. This multicoloured light hit two strangely shaped glass structures against the ceiling of the dome, before coalescing into one bright ray of sunlight that shot down on the wedding couple. And so it was that, bathed in a splendid ray of sunlight in a crystal dome surrounded by rainbows, Pik Freiman and Agatha Highcue finally got the wedding that they'd long deserved. At 11:42 on the dot, the passage of the sun extinguished the brilliant ray of light, but not before the celebrant had announced that he could now present to us 'Mr. and Mrs. Pik Freiman'. Sundari had tears in her eyes as everyone applauded the happy couple.

During the ceremony I appreciated how lucky Sundari and I were to be here. As I looked around at the congregation, I realized that there were no more than forty or fifty people - Sundari and I were privileged indeed. The reception was in a glamorously decorated marquis in another part of the Botanical Gardens. I suspect that it will be the only time in our lives when we'll sit next to a Prime Minister and a Treasurer *(Actually it won't be, although Dr. Mendis will have to wait another twenty years for that to happen again – Editors)*. The PM is a family friend of Pik's and gave a typically witty and insightful talk. Sundari and I were lucky enough to hear the 'Lion's Roar' live in person *(The Prime Minister of the time, Selwyn Hector, had developed an unusual way of ending speeches and press conferences after becoming PM. He would conclude by declaring forcefully, "We are the lions of the land!" before raising his hands in a claw-like fashion and making a roar. When he first started doing this at the beginning of his first term, the public thought he had gone insane; but, as the country began to prosper economically and otherwise under his Government, his eccentricity was accepted by the electorate and became affectionately known as the 'Lion's Roar'. In his third term in office, however, he had to modify it after it caused the Japanese First Lady to have a panic attack and fall face first into a chocolate mud cake – Editors)*.

Needless to say, we had a wonderful time. Agatha and Pik were thrilled to meet Sundari. They had no hesitation in saying that she was one of the most beautiful young women that they had ever seen. Most unexpectedly, Agatha asked Sundari if she could borrow me for a few moments. Sundari naturally said yes. Agatha took me to a less well-lit and unoccupied part of the large marquis.

"Are you having a wonderful wedding, Agatha?" I asked.

She nodded happily. "This is the best day of my life. I am quite nervous though."

"Really?" I asked.

"Unlike many of the brides of today, I really do meet the criterion for wearing white at my wedding. I'm a little anxious about 'afterwards' when Pik and I retire to the bedroom."

That was too much information for me! I was surprised at her admission but could say nothing incisive apart from repeating "Really?"

"I've been married to the job for all my adolescent and adult life. No time for romance or casual dalliances."

"That's impressive," I said.

She laughed. "I don't know about it being impressive. As a young woman, I never imagined that the predominant thought on my wedding night, when I was about to lose my virginity, would be 'Should I wear dentures or not?'"

In spite of that being clearly too much information, I laughed. Agatha is one witty lady. She unexpectedly took my hand in hers, the wrinkled pale skin contrasted against my smooth cinnamon brown.

"I am so glad that you brought Sundari tonight. She is absolutely charming and Pik said she reminds him of those Indian princesses from the time of the Raj. Absolutely divine."

"Thank you."

"Meeting her has made this task even easier," she mysteriously said, more to herself than me. "Manju, I have been an only child for most of my life. I had a brother who died of influenza in infancy. My mother had an elder sister, but like me, she lost her sibling in early childhood. What I am saying is that I have no blood relatives remaining."

"You must have been so lonely," I murmured.

She smiled. "Occasionally, yes. But as you know, I devoted my life to Pik and his family, so I was quite content and often too busy to be lonely." She opened her left hand, revealing a small box. "Manju, this is my grandmother's engagement ring. She and my mother never got along so she didn't pass it on to her. Instead, she wanted me to have it when I got engaged. However, Pik already gave me one."

I looked at the ring finger of her left hand. I had seen the ring sparkling at a distance during the wedding ceremony but now had the opportunity to look at it closely. A solitaire diamond, about 3.5cm wide and slightly amber in colour was surrounded by a coronet of nine pink diamonds, each about 3mm wide. I don't know much about diamonds but it was a breathtakingly beautiful ring and probably worth a lot of money. I told Agatha as much.

Agatha thanked me. "Well, it is called the 'Two Million Dollar Smile'."

Two million dollars for a ring! I was speechless.

"Manju, as I said, my bloodline ends with me. I'm obviously too old to have children. But the ring that my grandmother gave me was a symbol of love from a remarkable individual. She was a maid for Pik's grandfather, the founder of the business empire. She was tough as nails and always thought positively. I truly admired her. I don't want this ring to be lost. I once told you that you are like family to me. We share a terrible secret and it was your actions and words that led to this wedding today. Manju, I want you to have this ring. I don't know what the future holds but I truly hope that Sundari will be the recipient."

She handed the box to me. I was overcome with emotion and thanked her again and again. I naturally told her that I couldn't accept it but she insisted. She then became somewhat apologetic. "Obviously, while it has great sentimental value, it cannot compare in monetary value to the diamond ring that Pik gave me. I hope that that's okay."

I told her not to be silly and that it was such a special and thoughtful gesture on her part. I opened the box and looked at Agatha's grandmother's ring. I examined the ring for some time before turning back to Agatha in wonder.

"Agatha, this is absolutely gorgeous! Sundari will love it. But I need to clarify one thing. I'm no expert on rings, but there seems to be an awful lot of diamonds here which are not exactly small."

"Yes, I know. I recently had it valued. The conservative estimate was one hundred and fifty thousand dollars." With the slightest of smiles, she continued, "As I said, it can't compare to the two million dollar ring that Pik gave me."

I was so staggered, I think I said a swear word but I honestly can't remember. I definitely said, "One hundred and fifty thousand dollars? But Agatha, how?"

She smiled, clearly enjoying my astonishment. "Perhaps I forgot to mention that my grandmother was the mistress of Pik's grandfather. He was very fond of her and gave her this ring as a token of their love. Back then, the discovery of such a relationship would have been scandalous so they were waiting for the right time to announce their relationship. Unfortunately, he died unexpectedly before they had the opportunity to reveal their romance to the world. It appears that cavorting with the men of the Freiman clan runs in my family."

"Agatha, I really can't take this. It's just too valuable."

"Would you really upset a bride on her wedding day? And I thought that you were such a gentleman, Manju."

More of that emotional blackmail! I knew when I was beaten so I accepted the ring. Mind you, the prize for defeat had never been so good. Next week, I'll go to my bank and place this in a safety deposit box. It's too valuable to have at home. I can't wait to see the reactions of the women in my life when I finally propose to Sundari and offer that ring.

(It is at this point that the diary became damaged through the vigorous efforts of crayons and colouring pencils. We can only assume that Dr. Mendis' nephew, Kumar, or possibly his own children in future times were responsible. The only entry beyond this point that we were able to salvage from this particular diary was the final one, dated January 16, 2009 – Editors.)

January 16

Tonight was the formal dinner to introduce the new batch of interns to St. Ivanhoe. I can't believe that a year has passed since we were those terrified spring chickens wondering what awaited us in the months ahead. However, they look like a good bunch and hopefully, the rest of us 'old-timers' were able to instil a sense of confidence and optimism that would override the anxiety that they were clearly experiencing. We, the interns of 2009, had a wonderful time because, unlike last year, we didn't have to perform an act demonstrating a singular talent! Mind you, it was a night of four big surprises for me. I don't think that human beings are meant to deal with four big surprises in one night. I must be particularly thick-skinned. Lal later told me it was because I had a 'fourskin'.

The first surprise came in the form of a beautiful woman who came up to me and said, "Don't I get a hug?" The mysterious lady was a gorgeous Indian girl with shoulder-length black hair, light brown eyes and sharp, although slightly familiar, features. Then it hit me in a whirlwind of realization.

"Lucky? Is that you?"

She laughed and, gesturing at herself, asked, "What do you think?"

"The blond-haired blue-eyed Lucky King was pretty good-looking, but the current version is truly spectacular."

Then Sundari and Lucky went all girly and started jabbering in high-pitched voices before hugging a few times. It was at this point that her date for the evening, my cousin Lal, appeared from behind a pillar. He was smiling. "So Manju, did Lucky surprise you?"

"Yes cuz, as a matter of fact, she did." I looked back at Lucky. "Once again, let me say that you look gorgeous, Lucky."

"Thanks, Manju," she replied, smiling with joy. "The 'current version', as you put it, is the original version too. The more time I spent with your amazing cousin," she said, putting her arm around Lal, "made me realize how foolish I've been. I am Indian and proud of it. No amount of teasing or taunting will ever change that. I've even called my folks. The two of us are going down there next weekend to meet them."

"Glad to hear it, Lucky. Or should I say Lakshmi?"

She shook her head. "No, I've worn 'Lucky' for so long that it's part of me. That's the only part of the old me that's going to stay."

"Lucky it is then," I said with a smile.

I was amazed at her transformation but even happier for her. Hopefully, Lucky could now be at peace with herself.

Surprise Number Two came soon after when Delilah and Smegman walked in together. And when I say together, I mean 'together'. They had their arms wrapped around each other in the unmistakable pose of a couple.

"We've been meaning to tell you guys for a while but Marcus is really shy," said Delilah.

"Smegman?" I said again for the fourth time in a row.

"Manju, if you say Smegman once more, I'm going to give you a wedgie."

"I'm sorry, Delilah. It's just so surprising, that's all. He certainly is a changed guy compared to the arrogant oaf we met a year ago but he never struck me as being that lovable."

Delilah smiled. "Ever since we did Emergency together, he's opened up more and more. You wouldn't believe that such a romantic lurks beneath that shy and brilliant exterior."

"I'll take your word for it," I replied. I looked once more at Delilah, who'd been the emotional rock for so many of us throughout this turbulent year. She deserved to be happy. And if someone as intelligent as her couldn't find the ideal partner, who could?

"I guess we'll call him Marcus from now on then?"

"Thanks, Manju. That'll be nice." She smiled and gave me a hug.

As we sat down at the table together, it was wonderful to see Alternaria there. Susan Stoker had been thoughtful enough to invite her despite her resignation so long ago. In fact, I hadn't seen her since she'd left the hospital, although there had been brief phone calls to all of us at various times. Not surprisingly, it turned out that recording a debut album is no easy task. It had been a steep and quite stressful learning curve but, Alternaria had been so quick to pick things up that her first single had already been released. It only took three weeks for it to climb to Number One on the national charts. Now 'Whining and Dining' was being played on all the big FM stations around the country. Alternaria is a celebrity, all vestiges of mediocrity having been ripped away in a tumult of media reports and music videos. Even Fabulus had interviewed her for The Morning Show where she had performed live on Tuesday. As we talked to her, we were pleased to see that despite the rapid rise to fame, she was still the same old wonderful Alternaria. Although I knew that it was an unrealistic expectation, I hoped that she wouldn't change – at least for now.

Sir Ninian announced the winner for the Sir Nigel Steelbone Memorial Trophy. There were four nominees this year: myself for 'An apple a day keeps the doctor away – but what about a carrot?' Copper for 'GonorEAR: An Unusual Outbreak of VD in the ED' and Delilah and Marcus' joint paper on 'Football fever: a case of Tumour Necrosis Factor Associated Periodic Syndrome'. Despite being competitors for the trophy, both Copper and I were particularly delighted about Delilah's and Marcus' paper on Greg Smythe's illness, because it would never have been written without our help. I can take the credit for removing Spyder Croquet from the picture whilst Copper's audacious plan won the support of Greg Smythe himself. As soon as the media frenzy into the unmasking of the true nature of Spyder Croquet began, Copper took it upon himself to e-mail Greg Smythe. Naturally, he didn't have Greg's personal e-mail address but sent it care of the Liverpool Football Club. In the e-mail, Copper gave a full and frank explanation of how it had been Delilah and Marcus, rather than Spyder Croquet, who brilliantly diagnosed Greg's illness. Furthermore, he provided evidence of Croquet's pattern of fraudulent behaviour by attaching a newspaper article and video clip about his deceitful activities. Copper knew that his attempt to right a wrong was a long shot but it paid off.

Two days later, Marcus received a phone call from Greg Smythe himself expressing his sincere thanks and an apology for not crediting them with the diagnosis. Marcus was initially speechless at the thought of being on the phone with one of his sporting idols but had the presence of mind to ask for his permission to publish the case. Greg Smythe heartily agreed and within a couple of weeks, these two geniuses had their case report accepted by a prominent international journal. But that wasn't the best part. One week after the phone call, Delilah and Marcus each received a cheque in the mail, signed personally by Greg Smythe, for fifty thousand pounds! We had forgotten about the hundred thousand pound reward that Greg had originally offered to the doctor who diagnosed his mystery illness, a reward that the crooked Spyder Croquet had snatched from the deserving recipients – Delilah and Marcus. Yet Greg Smythe had remembered and, while a hundred thousand pounds wasn't a huge sum for this footballing multimillionaire, none of us had ever expected him to cough up. Yet cough up he did without even being prompted – what a guy!

Sir Ninian opened the envelope to declare the winner of the Steelbone Trophy and Surprise Number Three. Sir Ninian announced my name. *My name!* I, the dumbest intern at St. Ivanhoe, had won the frigging Sir Nigel Steelbone Memorial Trophy and the twenty thousand dollar prize! I was in a daze as I went on stage to rapturous applause and received the huge trophy from a beaming Sir Ninian. I can't remember what I said in my acceptance speech but have a ghastly feeling that, in my disoriented euphoria, I had thanked the Academy and said that George Clooney would have been a more deserving winner. One year ago, to have dared to dream of the possibility of winning, would have seemed ridiculous. Yet here I am. The twenty thousand dollars will come in handy. Apart from covering the school fees for Sundari's sister, it'll give my bank account a temporary reprieve from the ever-present threat of bankruptcy.

At the conclusion of the dinner, we all went to a new Karaoke bar not far from the hospital. Only then did I truly appreciate the impact of celebrity. As soon as Alternaria entered the bar, there was a mini-riot as people surrounded her, simply to wish her well or get an autograph. Thankfully, the frenzy settled within a few minutes but Alternaria handled herself like an old pro, never getting upset or angry, as she dealt with her adoring fans. As everyone else finally sat down at a table, Alternaria took me aside to speak privately.

"Wow, do you ever get used to that?" I asked, referring to the throng of fans who accosted her.

"It's kinda weird actually. Three months ago, if I had walked in here, no one would have given me a second look. I could have sung as well as I do now but no one would have cared. But now that I am on TV and have my own single, suddenly I'm different. It hasn't quite got to the stage where I can't walk around on the streets by myself but it probably will. I think that I'm going to miss that sense of anonymity."

I smiled. "That's the price of being a musical genius."

"I wish!" She laughed before her expression turned serious. "Anyway, how are things with you and Sundari?"

I told her how being in love is the most wonderful experience of my life.

"I'm so happy to hear that, Manju. How about financially? Are you still supporting her family?"

I nodded and explained how things were becoming increasingly difficult. I met my accountant yesterday. I didn't tell him what I did with the money but he said that I'd be broke in a few months if I continued to spend at this rate. As for setting aside something for savings, he had laughed. I was in quite a fix. Once I ran out of money, to whom could I turn? My parents didn't have enough savings to support Sundari's family, not that Sundari would even allow me to ask them. My sister's family was just starting life so they weren't an option. Last night, I prayed to all the Gods to somehow provide a miraculous solution to this problem. I was so desperate that I followed Akki's example and even said a silent prayer to Oprah: "Oh, Goddess of Daytime TV, whose face beams into millions of homes everyday, please help me out of this sticky situation. This is a small thing I ask of you. After all, you have given away cars to a whole studio audience and many gifts at your last Christmas Special. If you help me, I swear to read a page of 'O, The Oprah Magazine' every night for the next year." However, I wasn't optimistic of my chances of success.

"I'm so sorry, Manju," Alternaria said with genuine feeling.

I shook my head resolutely. "Don't be sorry, Alternaria. At the end of the day, I can look back on my life and say that I saved the woman I love from a seedy world which would have destroyed her. I've also saved her family from becoming destitute, at least temporarily. I just wish I could support them for longer."

"It seems so unfair, Manju. Here you are struggling to support Sundari's family while I've just been offered a million dollar contract with Megamix Records."

I gasped with excitement before giving her a big hug. "Alternaria, that's just wonderful! What are you going to do with all that money? Bathe twice a day in champagne?"

She laughed. "I hope that I never become that pretentious. In fact, right now, I don't need a million dollars. I already own my own house and car. So like you, I decided to do something worthwhile with my life." She handed me a magazine. "Look inside."

I did as she said. In the middle of the magazine I found a cheque, written by Alternaria and made out to me. I looked at the amount, closed my eyes for a few seconds and looked at it again. It was for four hundred thousand dollars, more than enough to cover all of Sundari's family's debts once and for all.

"Alternaria, I can't..."

She interrupted me. "This is my money and this is what I want to do with it. Please don't make this any less special by arguing with me about it. Anyway, I've still got six hundred thousand dollars left over, so life won't exactly be a struggle."

"But Alternaria, I don't know if I'll ever be able to repay you."

She smiled. "Manju, the only way I want you to repay me is by the two of you being happy together. And wiping out her family's debts is not a bad way to start."

I tried so hard to hold back the tears but the floodgates opened. The combination of Alternaria's extraordinary generosity and the financial stress of the last few months were too much and I was overwhelmed by a multitude of emotions. She held me close till I calmed down.

"Sundari will be so grateful," I began, as I wiped away the tears.

Alternaria shook her head. "Manju, the only way that this will work is if she doesn't know that I gave you the money. Otherwise she'll realize that I know about her time as a prostitute. I'm sure that she wouldn't want that. Just tell her that you won the lottery. It'll be much easier that way."

"Are you sure?" I asked her.

"Definitely."

I folded the cheque and put it in my pocket.

"Do you mind if I have that back?" Alternaria asked, referring to the magazine in which the cheque had been placed. "I only just bought it today and haven't had a chance to read it yet."

As I handed the magazine back to her, I looked at the cover and shook my head with wonder. Staring back at me from this month's issue of 'O, the Oprah Magazine', was the smiling face of the deity of Daytime TV. My sister was right – the tendrils of influence of this TV goddess extended far beyond the screen.

As we returned to the table, I couldn't hide the emotional rollercoaster that I'd just experienced. Sundari immediately looked concerned but I reassured her with a passionate kiss that all was well. It was now our turn to sing Karaoke. The crowd was getting boisterous as everyone wanted to hear Alternaria sing. Delilah picked a song for us. When she made her decision, it seemed like the obvious choice and we were unanimous in our approval. We stepped onto the stage, arms around each other, as the melody to Oasis' Don't Look Back in Anger boomed from the Karaoke machine. As our group burst into song, with Alternaria's powerful voice leading the way, I looked at each of my friends fondly. Over the last year, I'd experienced some of the darkest trials and tribulations that I could have ever imagined. But thanks to their loyalty, friendship and love, I had survived. Not for the first time, I was thankful to be blessed with such wonderful friends, family and of course, a wonderful life. I am Dr. Manjula Mendis and I have graduated as an intern.

EPILOGUE

Dr. Manjula Mendis married Sundari Samaranayake on March 11, 2011. The wedding took place in the Crystal Oracle, where Pik and Agatha Freiman got married. Such a venue would not have been easily accessible to the general public, so presumably Pik Freiman used his enormous influence to secure the location for Dr. Mendis and his bride. They remained together for fifty-two years before his death in 2063, leaving behind two sons, a daughter and seven grandchildren. Dr. Mendis' early interest in Infectious Diseases continued, culminating in his becoming Chief of Microbiology and Infectious Diseases at St. Ivanhoe Hospital. The combination of clinical brilliance and an undeniable charisma did not go unnoticed by the government of the day. In 2025, he became the youngest doctor to be appointed as Supreme Medical Officer, the most senior medical position in the federal government. So well did he perform during the 2026 pandemic of Kangaroo flu that he became a household name throughout the country. The subsequent gratitude of the nation and the government ultimately led to a Knighthood in 2033 before a triumphant elevation to President ten years later. Although purely a ceremonial position, his appointment as Head of State was testament to his political savvy and the country's enduring belief in multiculturalism. Lady Sundari Mendis was voted as one of the 'Ten Most Beautiful Women in the World' in 2026. Her global quest to end sex slavery amongst women was rewarded in 2047 with the Nobel Prize for Peace. The relentless determination and boundless energy that she assigned to this task now makes sense in the context of the revelations of this diary.

Marcus Smegman and Delilah Convex also married in 2011. Professor Smegman followed his dream and became an ophthalmologist while Professor Convex specialized in Immunology before becoming Dean of Medicine at Harvard Medical School in 2027. While both these geniuses enjoyed extraordinary careers, it was their only child, Melon Smegman, who achieved eternal greatness by inventing Melon Spice. When ingested, Melon Spice led to people passing wind with a gaseous composition that would negate greenhouse gases, thereby solving the whole problem of Climate Change.

Alternaria Molde went on to become one of the most illustrious soul singers of the past century. Her distinctive voice and melodies led to thirty Number One hits and twenty platinum albums in a career spanning almost forty years. She maintained a lifelong friendship with Professor Mendis and Sundari and even sang at their wedding. But it is for the revival of Paisley pants in the 2020's that many people will remember or revile her.

Dr. Peter Ivanov completed his surgical training at St. Ivanhoe before returning to Moscow. There he became the Professor of Vaginacology at a leading university hospital. Professor Mendis' claims in his diary that this subspeciality was once known as Gynaecology seem utterly ridiculous on the face of it and without substance; however, the recently recovered 'Google Scrolls' confirm this absurdity.

Dr. Copper Tang became a general practitioner. His good looks and friendly manner came to the attention of CNN, who, in 2018, signed him on as their Medical Editor, a position which he held for twenty five years. In addition to his regular appearances on CNN, he produced a number of award-winning medical documentaries and even had a cameo role in the 2030 James Bond blockbuster, Balls of Steel. His social life was no less exciting with a number of relationships with movie and TV celebrities, including a ten-year marriage to Oscar-winning actress, Salma Cruze.

Dr. Lucky King continued to see Lal Fernando (Professor Mendis' cousin). They married in 2012 and moved to California where Mr. Fernando worked in Information Technology till retirement. Dr. King gave up medicine soon after moving to the USA and completed a law degree at Yale. She went on to specialize in Immigration Law with a special interest in reuniting migrants with their family from overseas.

For any omissions or mistakes that the readers may have discovered in this diary, we sincerely apologize.

Editors, 11 March, 2101